Table of Contents

For Erin, Jazmin, Lavender, Lavelle Jr. and Camille.

Remember, anything is possible.

Chapter 1

"Inmate 847130, you need to wake up," said a correctional officer.

That number was attached to former detective Seven House twenty years ago. Seven House was convicted of a crime that he did not commit. House was at the wrong place, at the wrong time.

House was called to a homicide location that left a police officer dead, and House could not remember what happened. When he spoke his truth to investigators, they couldn't be convinced.

House was a peculiar character. He was quiet and reserved. He kept to himself, even though he had his more prominent presence. This was to him being over 6ft tall and around 250 pounds. However, he would be the loudest in the room when it came to interviewing suspects, collecting evidence, testifying, finding the motive, you name it.

House was exceptional at hand-to-hand combat and marksmanship. Even though he rarely ever used it. Before his incarceration, his verbal communication skills made assailants think twice. However, his verbal skills had deteriorated due to his not using them.

"I told you to get up!" the correctional officer exclaimed.

"Yeah, man, I heard you. I'm going to get up here. Just a second," House responded.

While House was in prison, he spent tons of time in solitary confinement. During his incarceration, there were numerous attempts on his life. This was due to him being a police officer. Oddly, he was either provided cell mates he helped convict or with convicted cop killers. When he appealed to the Warden about this, he was ignored. Sadly, this was expected since he was convicted of killing one himself.

Their attempts were futile. House would injure the attackers, so they wouldn't think twice about trying again.

The last cellmate he had, Peter Walsh, aka Worm, was assigned to House's cell so he could protect him. House didn't have a choice in the matter. The correctional officers weren't interested in doing their job.

Peter was paper thin, with unkempt hair. He rarely said anything and kept to himself. Just as House would have preferred.

Peter was in the middle of doing a prison stint due to multiple financial crimes he committed. He and a few others would access the bank accounts of criminals, political figures, and billionaires and then donate their money to worthy causes. Normally, he would do this if you were found guilty of a crime and got off with a slap on the wrist.

Unfortunately for Peter, one of the rookie members of the crew attempted this on their own and was caught. Unfortunately, they sang like a canary, and the entire team was arrested. All but Walsh were killed before trial.

Peter is a master of anything that required technology. So, unlike other people who were periodically able to use phones, tablets, and laptops in a controlled environment, Walsh was banned for fear he could modify his prison sentence and others if he was pressured.

The correctional officers recently removed Walsh to move him in preparation for his being assigned to a different facility.

House exits the cell and heads to the community area. There was a crowd of prisoners gathered a few feet from his cell. Some of the faces seemed familiar, but others did not. One of them pointed in House's direction.

"Here he is. Boy, don't you hear me talking to you?" House looked over at the guy. He did not believe he had seen him before.

He said," You don't remember me? Do you realize I'm here because of you?"

"I would have gotten away with it if you didn't decide to stick your nose into my business," He rushes House.

House quickly dodges out of the way and throws a right hand straight down the middle, knocking the guy to the ground. The assailant quickly gets to his feet, "Lucky punch, it won't happen again."

The crowd slowly started to circle House and his attacker. House realized most of these men he had previously had altercations with.

"Let's go," The prisoner ran toward House. House ducked under one of the punches and grabbed the aggressor, picking him up and slamming him on the ground. The attacker was bleeding profusely from his head.

Correctional officers rush over, "Not this shit again, "one of them said, " I thought we told you that you got to be nice to people?"

"The guy ran up on me with a shank," House pointed to the ground," What do you expect me to do?"

The guy was taken off to the infirmary, and House was again brought down to solitary confinement. "These guys are getting bolder," House thought, "It will be a matter of time before someone gives them an easier opportunity."

Later in the day, The Warden decided to speak to House. "Hey man, what is going on? Do you like being left alone?"

House responded," I've been alone most of my life, so this is nothing new. I have no problems or qualms with being left to myself. So, the ideas and thoughts I have for myself remain with me. I find it beneficial. I have nothing to lose at this point. I have nobody waiting for me. I have not had a single visitor since I've been here."

"I actually have good news for you."

"What's that?"

"You may be getting out of here sooner than later."

"How!" House stood up and walked towards the cell door. This appeared to be the best news House had received in a long time.

"I'm retiring today, and the new Warden has already been named. I don't know who it is, but I heard rumors he was sent here specifically for you.

It might work out for everybody if you're no longer here. But then, you either hospitalize attackers or end up in solitary confinement for months. "As long as your release is quiet, I think it will be alright."

House barked, "You guys do what you want." As the Warden walked off.

As House looked around the space, he realized this was the same one they always seemed to put him in. He noticed all the etchings he could make from this spoon that they tended to always leave him. Maybe they thought he would kill himself. But typically, everybody else had plastic utensils, and they would always give him metal spoons to eat whatever his food was on.

He looked at the corner and saw where he had headbutted against the wall. He was not angry when he did it, nor did he try to kill himself. Instead, he did it so he could feel something. He hadn't felt for something in so long.

Shortly after he was placed in the room, another correctional officer knocked on the door, "We're going to go ahead and remove you from solitary and put you back into your room."

"Why?" House asked.

"That guy that attacked you admitted that he was the one who went after you first," The correctional officer responded, "Just like all the other times, it never seems to be your fault."

"I would say this candidly, I don't believe that you're the person who murdered that police officer years ago. I've worked in prisons for many years. Murders have a different look about them; you can see it in their eyes. You don't have that same look."

House looked at him with wide eyes. That was the first time anybody told him that they could not believe he was the person who committed the murder.

"Are you sure you should be telling me this," House asked.

"I recently learned the type of police officer you were. Now, let's go."

House walked out of the cell and started to head down the hallway. He didn't know how he should take the correctional officer's comments. But, over time, he took some ownership of what happened. He knew he should have had someone with him when he went to the crime scene. That was standard protocol. If he had done this, he might have avoided this.

Recently, House started volunteering time to teach people who were trying to get high school equivalency degrees when they were in prison. This was considered a safer task than getting a prison job.

The classes were conducted in the library. The library was small and rarely received any new materials. Before and after class, he would browse the collection, looking for anything that seemed interesting. House gained an interest in crossword puzzles and Sudokus. To create new crossword puzzles, House would tear out words from discarded books and create hints for them. This was a painstaking process, but it provided House with the mental stimulation he rarely got.

One day, House was told to assist in the laundry room. House was wise as to what was going on. Whenever someone was asked to help in a different part of the prison, they rarely returned. He knew he was being set up. These antics were getting tiresome.

"Why are you taking me here?" House asked, "I volunteer enough time."

"They are really shorthanded," The correctional officer explained," There is a lot of stuff that needs to be folded."

"This is a prison; there is always shit to fold."

House was struck in the back of his head for the statement. This verified what House thought was about to happen, which he grew accustomed to.

Correctional officers are notoriously underpaid; some would do anything to make extra cash, Including jeopardizing their freedom.

As they approached the laundry room. House noticed there were people in there who typically didn't do laundry. Usually, it was an older Asian man, an older white man, and a middle-aged Black guy. However, this time it was all younger, Hispanic individuals in there. The guard left House handcuffed as he put them into the door.

"Why am I in cuffs? How do I fold clothes?" House asked.

"You could fold clothes in cuffs," the correctional officer replied, closing the door.

The smallest one of the individuals turned around to look at House and said, "Do you remember me?"

House looked him over. The individual had a shaved head, face and neck tattoos, and a scar on his left cheek that appeared new. Then it hit him. House realized the person's name was Javier Sanchez. Javier Sanchez was an affiliate of a gang that ran rampant from Chicago down to Miami with little factions, breaking off in different cities with ways to access waterways to move drugs.

House would admit Javier did have a polarizing personality; Javier could get the attention of those who wanted to be in a gang to follow his lead and dramatics. When it came to people in Javier's community, not so much. Most people would say Javier was putting on a front about his gang affiliation. None of the ones in the community even batted an eye when he would speak of such things. Javier had cars, clothes, and girls. However, whenever he needed backup or assistance with anything, no one was ever around besides the folks who wanted to chase the clout Javier had achieved.

House circled away from the door and said, " Javier, it has been a long time. I'm surprised you are on laundry duty."

"Shut up, *puta,*" Javier responds. "Don't act like you are my friend. You are the reason why I am in this shithole."

"You are here because of something you did. It's not my fault your dumbass got caught. It was one of the easiest cases I had as a young detective," House laughed.

"Listen up, *pendejo*, we have nothing to discuss. I have been waiting for this opportunity for years. I thought I would have to catch you on the outside, but you made it easy for me," Javier boldly stated.

"So, you all are going to jump me with handcuffs on? Does that make you feel brave and tough? I bet your boys back home would be so proud of the bitch you have become," said House.

"I'm tired of this shit!" Javier exclaimed, "Get him."

House readied himself for the attack. He started looking around the room to see if anything seemed unusual. The last thing he wanted to do was to put himself near a weapon they had stashed in preparation for his arrival. He saw someone standing in front of the door from the corner of his eye. It appeared they had the same neck tattoo Javier had but crudely done. "Sanchez must have paid them off," House thought. Sanchez and his goons were getting closer and closer to House. House started to examine their hands, and he didn't see a shank on any of them.

"Do y'all really think they are going to whoop my ass empty-handed," He yelled," Y'all would have a tough time fighting out of a wet paper sack!"

"What are you thinking about House?" Javier asked. "You do realize there is no escape. The person on the door won't open it until I give him a password. That is why we aren't in a rush here. It's at least two hours until dinner, four to lights out, and headcount. We miss dinner, and no one would bat an eye. Think about it, we have more than enough time to end this."

"I'm not missing dinner tonight," House aggressively stated. "They are serving catfish nuggets. It is one of the only edible things in this place, and it's rarely served!"

House wanted to put himself in a position to strike first. However, he thought about the person who was at the door. He needed to find out if it was a correctional officer or not. The window in the door wasn't big enough to get a full view of the person. House figured if he seemed to get the upper hand early, it could be over for him if it was one. House also knew he couldn't let them strike first. He wouldn't get back to his feet if he stumbled or fell. Luckily, House didn't have leg shackles on. He was able to move freely as needed.

"You go high, I'll go low," one of the unknown guys said to the other. While these guys were slightly taller than Javier, they were also skinner than him. "If Javier is the same as he always has been, these guys are probably small-time punks that were promised some bull from him," House thought, " The time is now. I have to strike first".

House moved towards the two guys and pressed one of them against the washing machine. The other one swings, and House dodges the punch. "Damn it!" Javier screams, "Do I have to do everything myself!" Javier rushes towards House, who still has one of the guys pressed against the washer, and strikes him in the ribs. House is forced to release the guy from the washing machine and has to circle away. He receives a swift kick in the ribs from the guy who missed the punch. "That's what I am talking about, Mario! Kick the literal shit out of him!" Javier yells.

House falls back against the dryers and states, "You know I would have already ended this situation if the handcuffs were off. Is this all y'all got?" House found he was filled with excitement. It had been a long time since he had to carefully plan his moves.

Mario ran towards House again, trying to go for a takedown. Instead, House strikes Mario in the back. Javier slaps House in the face repeatedly. Finally, House dodges one of the punches and hits Mario on the back of his head.

"Tony, are you going to help, or are you going to just sit back and watch what we are doing," Javier angrily said. "Get your punk ass up!" Tony clumsy attempts to throw a punch and accidentally strikes Javier and causes him to fall back. "Motherfucker, Tony, what is the fucking problem?! Do you think I look like House," Javier states, pissed off while holding his jaw.

House breaks away from Mario and strikes Tony while he is distracted. Tony falls to the floor. As Mario starts to turn around, House grabs his head and smashes it against the dryer, knocking him out. "Two down, one to go," House states confidently, walking toward Javier.

"Fuck you, House!" Javier states as he throws a looping punch toward House. House quickly ducks under the punch and positions himself to start choking Javier with the handcuffs.

Javier starts gurgling, and House states, "Javier, you are going to tell whoever is ever at the door that they are going to let me out of here. Do you understand?"

"Ffff-you, House," Javier struggles to say while being choked.

"Javie, you know you aren't tough enough to die here; just do what I told you to do." House starts applying the choke even tighter. Javier looks like he is about to pass out. The color on his face is disappearing. His grip around House's wrist is weakening.

"Hey, Sanchez! You aren't dying on me until I get outta here," House screams at Javier.

Javier starts coughing, then tells House, "*Vete a la mierda, chupa mi polla (*fuck you suck my dick)," with an overconfident smile.

"This is the wrong time to have some balls, Sanchez!"

House needed clarification about what to do next. Javier seemed to intend to let whatever happened here happen, but why? "You never had plans on winning this fight, did you?" Javier didn't respond. "You figured we wouldn't make head count and get time added to our sentence? Answer me!" Javier still refused to say anything. "Well, since you don't wanna talk, you might as well go to sleep."

Quickly, House released the choke and uncorked a thunderous right hand, knocking Javier out. "Well, I guess I'm not getting those catfish nuggets, shit," House says out loud while admiring his handy work. The three assailants were sprawled out on the ground, unconscious. House padded each of them down to see if they had any weapons on them. To his surprise, they didn't.

House started hearing the sound of people running down the hallway. "Inmate, back to your cell!" House heard someone scream. Correctional officers began surrounding the door.

"We know you all are in there! Lay on your stomach with your arms out to your side," one of them ordered.

House went ahead to lie down. Since he was handcuffed, he stretched his arms above his head. The correctional officers opened the door.

"Well, I thought we would arrive too late for you, House. However, it seems like we got here too late for the other guys," said another while laughing.

"Who are the guys House did a number to? Oh, it's Sanchez and his makeshift crew. Mr. Big Shot. I guess he received another reminder why he isn't. House, we will take you to the infirmary, and then the new Warden wants to see you."

Chapter 2

House spent the next two weeks in the care of the prison doctor. Once House was cleared, he was escorted straight to the Warden's office, a place he was familiar with.

"House, I want to let you know I have reviewed your records since I was told I would be taking over the prison. I know I have only been here for a few weeks, but from what I have gathered from some of my senior correctional officers, you seem to not cause any issues, and I want to tell you this. But this is off the record due to my standing, of course. I hope you understand," stated the Warden.

House was surprised by the appearance of the new Warden; he appeared much younger and had a deep southern drawl.

House shrugs.

"I don't think you could kill a police officer. Not that you don't know how to crack a few heads. I can see that you have busted plenty in your time here. You have a large target on your back. You should never be sent to this prison in the first place. Regardless of how the conviction came out, it's too close to home. They don't imprison the officers alongside the criminals they helped convict. Leaving you around them is normally a death sentence. None of this makes any sense. Whom did you piss off?"

House responded," Does it matter?"

"Fair enough. I reckon it doesn't. I heard about the fight in the laundry room."

"Obviously"

"No need to be hostile. I want to let you know that the correctional officer has been terminated. We are pursuing criminal charges. The HR department didn't do a good job vetting him. You arrested his sister for aggravated burglary. She was sentenced to five years. While she was locked up, she committed suicide."

"I thought that guy looked familiar. As you were talking, I could vision seeing him in the courtroom. That would have been over 15 years ago at this point. So, you know, not surprising, but at the same time, it is what it is."

" Yes indeed. Well, let me get back to the matter, ok?"

"What is that? "

"Alright, House, I'll put it to you like this. The governor has granted you clemency and lowered your sentence to time served."

"Wait, why? I don't even know how this would happen. So, I never reached out to him," House said.

House couldn't help but think who would have attempted to help him. It didn't make any sense. He wanted to be happy, but he feared there could be an alternative motive.

"You don't watch much TV, do you?"

"I do my best not to try to watch any TV since I'm supposed to be here until I die."

"Well, actually, the funny thing about that, House. You do realize that you were never in here for life. You were only supposed to serve a 25-year term and were eligible for parole once you served 10 of those years. So, he just eliminated the paperwork for you."

"I am aware. However, I figured someone would catch me on an off day before then. No matter, nothing's free," said House," What will this cost me?"

"All right, well, I do understand you're not the one for dramatics. I do not know why this is happening. God's honest truth."

"Sure, you don't," said House.

House was attempting to get a read on the Warden but was failing. The Warden maintained eye contact with House during the entire conversation, attempting to show he was being truthful. At the same time, the Warden was doing the same thing to House to get a better feel for him.

"Believe what you will. You'll be released in a few weeks. When we get something more concrete. I will make sure to pass it along to you."

House sat there and pondered for a minute. Did he really want to be removed from prison? Is it that he enjoyed the prison life or the things that came with it, which would be the shitty food, and it always smells like ass everywhere.

No, it wasn't that. House knew if he was released, it would be easier to have him killed. The attempts on his life were getting more calculated. This could just be another step.

"Well, how about it, House? I think most people would jump at this opportunity."

House looks around again, trying to figure out how to put these words together, and he says, "You might regret this."

The Warden looks at him puzzled, then he realizes the Governor might regret his decision. House, "You aren't telling me what I think you are telling me, are you?"

House said," Now, why would I incriminate myself?

The Warden looks at him and nods," Yes, why would you? Well, we won't get to know each other."

The Warden buzzes for the guards and they escort House back towards the cafeteria. About halfway to getting back to the cell, the correctional officers stopped, "You good from here, House?"

House thought he was once again getting set up. He still hadn't fully recovered from his last interaction in the laundry room, "You are kidding me, right?"

The correctional officers unshackled him, "All right, carry on. We're just trying to go ahead and catch the rest of this football game before it's over." They walked off.

House looked at them, not directly surprised at that type of mannerism. Those guys were younger, too, and probably took his job because it came with a pension. House proceeds to start going back to his room. It was safer than going to the cafeteria. Walking in the hallway, he heard someone screaming in pain.

Chapter 3

House started to head towards the sound. If it was a one-on-one fight, he wouldn't intervene. However, regardless of the reason, he was morally against someone being jumped. As he got closer to the sound, he heard a thunderous crack.

Someone said, "I'm so glad we finally figured out that it was your punk ass who screwed us years ago."

As House was getting closer, he realized the screams were pleas for help.

Three guys were standing over a person who was cowering in fear. Their backs were towards House. He slowly approached them to not alert them of his presence. They were speaking to the person on the ground. However, House couldn't make out what they were saying.

House didn't recognize any of the three men standing there, but he did recognize who was being attacked. It was Peter Walsh!

"Leave him alone," said House.

The men turned around and looked at House. "And who the fuck are you," one of them said.

"I'm the one who is going to make sure you leave him alone."

"Screw that. He cost me hundreds of thousands of dollars with his little stunts. This stupid Robin Hood wannabe motherfucker!" he gives him another quick kick in the ribs.

"I won't tell you again," House readied in a fighting stance.

"We'll be sure to make sure you do not get involved with anyone else's business," one of them said while getting in a fighting stance.

The first one threw a punch, and House dodged out of the way. He grabbed the back of the attacker's head and slammed his face-first into a wall. The attacker fell and lay motionless on the ground.

"Who's next?" House asked.

The second attacker took a measured approach. First, he tried to bait House into showing his hand, but House stayed patient. Finally, the second attacker recklessly threw a looping punch at House. House blocked the punch and open-palmed struck the attacker in the jaw, causing him to fall to the ground. House carefully followed and threw successive strikes at the would-be attacker's face.

The third attacker used this opportunity to jump on House's back and try to choke him. House was able to shrug him off. The attacker tackled House, throwing punches like a wild animal. House was able to trap one of the attacker's arms and reverse position. He then placed his forearm on the attacker's throat and applied pressure. The attacker continued to claw and scratch House's face until he passed out.

House stood up and looked around. He heard rumbling in the distance, but it was rapidly getting closer. He figured someone must have gone for help or seen the fight on camera.

"Well, shit," House said under his breath.

"Get down on the ground now," A correctional officer yelled, "Arms out to your side!"

House complied.

"What do we have here? Jesus Christ, what happened," said another.

"LT, do you believe one person did all this?"

"Cuff him and stand him up," The lieutenant ordered, "Well, if it isn't House. If anyone could have done all this, I am sure it would be him."

"Three of those are me; the real small guy was them," House answered.

"Really, well, I guess lucky for him. You know where you are going, House, until we can get this all sorted out."

The lieutenant radioed for additional medical help and ordered the other correctional officers to bring House to solitary confinement.

Chapter 4

Weeks passed, and House had not spoken to anyone about what happened. He was not surprised by this. His decision to help Peter Walsh could have cost him to lose his early release.

Whatever the decision was, it did not bother House. He never planned on being released early. Many people believed he was guilty of killing the police officer. So why would the governor, of all people, reduce his sentence to time served? This was a question House wanted to be answered before his release.

Honestly, it was surprising House never had his sentence extended. He thought about the times he hospitalized inmates. Even though it was in self-defense, he didn't need to go that far. Did he enjoy punishing people? Was this a better solution to the flaws the criminal justice system had?

These were the thoughts House often had when he was in solitary. However, it recently changed. He thought about what he would do if or when he was released. This included if he had to stay until his sentence was originally over. Suddenly, House felt like he was burning. His vision started to blur. At first, he thought something terrible was happening to him then, he realized what was happening to him. This was anger. This was the rage for those who wronged him; instead, it focused on himself.

The empathy he showed towards Peter could have delayed him in figuring out what happened years ago.

"Well, Seven, I hope you think it was worth it," House said to himself, "Your stupid superhero complex may have cost you. Damn it!" House slammed his fist against the wall.

"Calm down in there!" A correctional officer yelled at House.

This was odd. Typically, no one was around besides meals. So, even though House didn't know what time it was, he figured he had received lunch recently.

He also didn't hear shackles scraping the ground. So, someone wasn't getting removed or added to a nearby cell. For all House knew, he was the only person in this specific section. He was familiar with going solitary, or so he thought. When he was being escorted, the correctional officers took a right when they usually took a left.

"Inmate, go to the back of the cell and put your hands on the wall." the officer ordered.

House followed the order. The cell door opened, and House heard footsteps entering the cell.

"Sorry about this, House; it was just procedure."

House recognized the voice. It was the Warden. "Can I turn around?"

"Why yes, of course," replied the Warden.

"Slowly," the correctional officer ordered.

House turned around, and the Warden looked at House with his arms open. Seeming to show he was not armed. The correctional officer who was giving him orders was standing in the doorway.

The Warden turned to the correctional officer, "Give us some privacy. Leave the door open if you want but get out of the doorway. He is not a threat nor a runner."

"Yes, sir." The correctional officer stepped out of the cell and headed down the hallway.

"House, like I said earlier, sorry for the delay. But unfortunately, we had to let the investigation run its course."

House went away from the Warden and rested his head against the wall.

"What investigation?"

"There were some who believe you attacked all four men. I know that's not your MO, but I couldn't undermine my officers. But, of course, you understand?"

House turned around and faced the Warden again.

"Where is Peter?"

The Warden had a surprised look on his face. "So, you don't want to ask me how the investigation went, was your clemency reversed, or anything about yourself?"

"You have already given me that answer. You are standing here without backup. So, as I said, where is Peter?"

The Warden started to pace in the cell. It seemed like he was gathering his thoughts.

"Peter is in bad shape. They really did a number on him before you intervened. Multiple organs were damaged, and he had broken bones; it was like he was thrown out of the top floor of a five-story building. He is lucky to be alive."

House turned and faced the wall again. He was happy to know his efforts were not in vain. He did not want to have any emotions. His time being incarcerated taught him that seeming happy or sad could be viewed as a weakness. "Have you been able to speak to him? Does he know his attackers?"

"Old police habits die hard, don't they," the Warden responded.

House couldn't agree more. Even though it had been years since he tried to help someone else, he realized he was immediately focused on getting justice for Peter. If House had lost his chance at clemency, he wanted to make sure it was worth it.

"The governor did the right thing, which is why I'm down here. Everything is in place. You are being released today."

House turned around. He had a blank expression on his face.

"I'm not saying I thought you would be jumping for joy, but I figured you would do something," the Warden said with a laugh, "What are you going to do now?"

"What do you think?"

"I won't ask; follow me."

The Warden and House continue to leave the cell. The Warden and his chosen officer proceed to escort House around the prison. Making sure no one bothered him. Different prisoners in solitary were shouting at them on the way out.

"What's going on?"

"Are they letting House go?"

"Let me out! I won't do it again!"

"Quiet! Back to your cells," The correctional officer yelled.

Other correctional officers joined in and started ushering the inmates away from the doors.

The group made it to the front gate. The Warden looked at a camera and signaled them to open the gate.

"This is your last look at the yard House. Once we make it through those final doors, you are a free man," the Warden boastfully.

"Free is a loose term. I'm still a felon," replied House.

The Warden stopped walking. "House, you didn't expect a complete miracle, did you?"

House stopped and turned to the Warden, "I've learned to expect the unexpected. I also know nothing is free; what is this costing me."

"You have more allies than you realize, House. That is all I can tell you. So, let's get through this gate."

The group continued, and House was given the possessions; he entered the prison with a wallet, suit, shoes, and cell phone.

"I had some money in here. Y'all really cleaned my wallet out," House asked.

"It's a lost cause, House; honestly, you shouldn't be surprised," said the Warden.

House knew the Warden was right. However, he could not prove if he had cash or how much was in his wallet.

"This is it, House, make the best of it."

"Are you going to tell me how I was granted clemency?"

The Warden breathed deeply, "I told you; it was for time served."

House looked at the Warden. He didn't seem like he was trying to mislead him. Did he really get lucky? Then he remembered what the old Warden told him.

"What's going on in the world, " House asked, "Specifically, here in Tennessee. The old guy asked me whether I had watched the news. Did I miss something?"

"I wouldn't know why he would tell you to watch the news. I don't watch it myself. Now, be careful out there. This was on the hush-hush for obvious reasons. You were part of a high-profile case. If people get wind of your release. It could be bad for you. I am sure some still want you in prison. You were convicted of killing a cop."

The Warden was lying. All of the recent changes were due to it being an

Election Year. He wanted the choice House made after this to be organic. If he went into too much detail, it could change what the Warden and others would hope to happen.

"You mean bad for them."

House looked at the Warden with this cold stare. In the short time the Warden had worked for this prison, he knew House was not someone to toy with. The Warden knew anyone going after House would not be a good idea.

"House don't do something that will bring you back here. This place isn't for you. You might not get so lucky next time."

House walked through the gates, looked up at the sky, and deeply breathed. Hot summer winds went across his face. Birds were chirping in the distance. He looked and saw it was a Cardinal on a tree branch. House remembered when he was a child, he was told seeing one meant good luck. However, he knew the world was vastly different than when he entered these gates ten years earlier.

"About time. I thought they were never letting you out."

House looked down and a person was walking towards him. The sun was on the back of the person, impairing House's vision. As the person got closer, House said, "It can't be."

Chapter 5

Trek Swift was one of House's best friends when he was in the United States Army. They initially met at basic training for military police officers.

Swift was an average-looking person. He was shorter than average height for a male, with ambiguous facial features, dark hair, olive-colored skin, and a slim build.

While in basic training, one of the drill sergeants nicknamed him Shadow. Swift could appear and disappear without anyone knowing. If you put him in a crowd, he would be harder to find than Waldo. This theory was proven correct when the drill sergeant had him infiltrate another company during a training exercise. Swift completed the mission without being recognized.

Due to the mission's success, Swift was selected to complete training to become an undercover military police officer. Because of this, House hadn't seen or spoken to Swift in nearly twenty years.

"Swift, what are you doing here," House asked, "How did you know I was being released from prison today?"

"House! My friend! It's been so long since I have seen you," Swift said. He walked towards House to give him a hug.

House put his hand out to stop it from happening, "Answer me."

"Hey Swift, it's so nice to see you. What have you been up to lately,"

Swift sarcastically replied.

"I don't have time for this shit," House started to walk down the street.

"Where are you going!?"

House ignored Swift and continued to walk down the street. House had no ill will towards Swift. He would be happy to see him if this was any other day. However, this seemed like other secrets people were keeping from him.

"House! You don't have to be an asshole. Just talk to me."

House continued to ignore Swift.

"You want to eat, right? It's been a long time since you had a good meal. Am I right, House?"

House stopped and turned around. Swift had a mile-wide grin on his face.

"That's what I thought; come on, there is a taco spot a few minutes from here. I heard it is pretty good," Swift said as he got in his car.

House walked back towards Swift and got in his car. Shortly, they arrived at *Hartsville Taco Company.* They walked into the restaurant, and the place was packed.

"After we order, let's get a table outside," said Swift.

"So, what have you been up to? Whoops, I shouldn't have asked."

"Can I eat in peace?"

Swift put his taco down, "Eventually, you will have to talk to me. Where are you going to go? Who is going to help you? I am sure you have lost faith in trusting people. Remember, you were there for me in basic. I'm here for you now."

House put his taco down and remembered the first time they spoke to each other.

Swift was being bullied because of his appearance. He wasn't the proud, charismatic person in front of the House. Instead, he was shy, timid, and afraid to disappoint people.

Swift was recycled from his old company due to failing his final physical fitness test. Pure strength was never one of his attributes. Swift had originally lied for reasoning being recycled. Once the other soldiers found out the truth, he was hazed badly.

One day, Swift was late for formation. House heard other soldiers state Swift was going to get jumped. He returned to the barracks and found Swift assaulted by three other soldiers. House intervened before severe damage was done. House, Swift, and the other soldiers were all late for formation. The group was initially pushed until the circumstances behind the reason were revealed. House ended up receiving a reward for his actions. House looked out for Swift until they went their separate ways.

"You remember right? I am forever thankful for that day, House. I could have died," Swift said.

"Anyway, what do you mean 'here for me now,'" House responded.

"Still want to be an ass, I see. We cannot talk about that here. Too many ears. Where are we headed next?"

"I guess getting rid of you isn't going to be easy. I considered going to Lebanon but was told I needed to lay low for a while. It would be too close to Nashville. So let me think…we will head to Cookeville."

"Cookeville, where the hell is Cookeville?

"It's an hour plus away. We are losing daylight. Time to go." House got up from the table and started walking towards the car."

House and Swift started down the road, heading towards the interstate.

"Are we going to ride in silence or what?" Swift asked.

"There's nothing to talk about unless you want to tell me why you're here," House answered.

"Actually, we have a lot to talk about *before* we get to that. I knew you were getting released. You want to start there?"

"What's going on, man? I ain't got no time for no bullshit. I need you to be straight up with me, man. What's going on?"

"I don't know the reason why you were released. Let me get that out of the way. However, I asked the right question and found out you would be released."

"Don't dance around the answer."

"Patience is everything. I separated from the service about six years ago. Shortly after my separation, I started working for the State Department. Essentially doing the same thing, but now I was keeping the balance of power equal for lesser nations. We were having some of the issues other countries were having on the local lev..."

"Are you ever going to get to it," House interrupted, "I'm not interested in your past work history."

"Prison has made you cold," Swift said, "Not only that, but you have also lost your trust in people."

House looked out the window. He knew Swift was right. The people he believed were his friends, no, more like family, had nothing to do with him for the past ten years.

Swift placed his hand on House's shoulder, "When I separated, I wanted to figure out who was around and what happened to people I was close to. After being selected for the basic training program, I wouldn't worry about having a family. I wouldn't worry about having kids. I just had to exist, and I got tired of that. The State Department wasn't as bad but essentially the same. You were one of the first people I decided to look up to. I figured we were best friends, and I thought I could see how you were living, catch up, shoot the shit, whatever, man. Then, I found out that you were in prison. I was confused. I kept thinking, what did you do to get put in prison? Then, I found out you supposedly shot a cop. I knew that couldn't be right."

"Well, what do you know? It has been twenty years or so since you saw me. I could have changed. Just like you could have changed."

"The saying 'a zebra cannot change its stripes' goes for you too."

"I'm not a zebra."

Swift cracked his window and lit a cigarette, "No, you are not. This is corny, but you are kinda like a superhero; you look out for the defenseless. Like you looked out for me. Like you looked out for Parker, I think that's what his name was."

"Peter. How did you know about that?"

"To keep it simple, I have close to unlimited resources, not in terms of money, but information. Due to my operations in over fifty countries, and hundreds of cities, I have created a network of people who can find out almost everything. What might seem hard to hack, untraceable, etc. I have an eighty percent chance of getting something valuable. It's another reason why I left the State Department. But it's a story for another time."

"You didn't answer the question."

"But I did. I was looking for you and found you and what recent event you were involved in. Look, the internet and technology have vastly changed in the ten years you were in prison. State and local security measures don't stand a chance with my team."

House knew the best hackers didn't work for the government. The perfect example is Peter Walsh and his team. However, it seemed odd that there would be a network of people willing to aid Swift.

"Do you pay these people?"

"No, I don't. That's what makes this so great. Everyone is a volunteer. They are everyday citizens, teachers, janitors, painters, etc. But they have all been wronged in one way or another by the criminal justice system. We have a name in Japanese, but to keep it simple, we are known as Team Shadow."

House was even more confused. This sounded like a group of wannabes. Then he thought about it. It was smart. Often, someone's job doesn't reflect their intellect. They could have been a badass forty years ago and retired to something more manageable. Suppose these people experience wrongdoing in the past. In that case, it will motivate them to learn how to prevent it from happening in the future. He personally knew people where this was the case.

They pulled off the interstate and pulled into the nearby gas station.

"House, you want a cigarette?"

"No, I never picked up on that habit. Just grab me some water while you are in there."

While Swift went into the gas station, House took the opportunity to stretch his legs. They were twenty minutes away from their destination. Somehow, he got his freedom back. However, he didn't actually feel free. Something didn't feel right. He couldn't put his finger on what it was. Now, with Swift being here, another wrinkle was added. Currently, it didn't matter what the reason was. He would still be viewed as a felon and the person who really committed the murder was still walking free.

He did feel slight relief. While in prison, he always had his head on a swivel. Most of the time, he was focused on ensuring he would make it to the next day. House had correctional officers as well as inmates making attempts on his life. In the shower, the cafeteria, and even in his cell. No matter how hard they tried, he survived with minimal injury.

With his secret release, he didn't have to worry about anyone looking for him. This allowed him to look into his case and its circumstances without much issue. This provided some relief. It had been a long time since House didn't have a target on his back.

"House, I grabbed us some snacks," Swift said, smiling.

"I never understood how you could remain skinny with as much as you eat," House said, laughing.

"That's all it took to get your sense of humor back, me stuffing my face?"

"Swift, I do need to apologize. All of this is unexpected. You were right. I lost my faith in people who I believed were my family. You haven't done anything to jeopardize that." House reached for a handshake.

Swift shook House's hand, "Don't worry about it. I figured you would eventually come around. So, how far are we away?"

"Just down the street. After we pass the campus, we will be there."

"Campus? Is this a college town?"

"I wouldn't say that, but Tennessee Tech is here. Since it's the summer, most students will be home. So, it should be an easy place to lie low. This is a nice Lexus. Cars have really improved in the past ten years."

"Look closer. This is a Honda Accord."

"Oh, shit! Yeah, they really have. Let's get going."

They both got back in the car and drove down the road. The last time House was in Cookeville, the majority of the area was farmland. As they rode down the main strip, he noticed shopping centers were now taking their place. New restaurants, and advertisements for new businesses everywhere.

"So, where are we exactly going," Swift asked, "Do you know someone up here? Actually, there is someone you can trust who is up here?"

"Many years ago, I invested in some rental property up here. I say property like they were something special. It's just a few trailers. Just something affordable so college students could afford it. I had a management company do most of the work. Honestly, it cost me more money than I made. Moving forward a lot. I had an informant who was in a bad situation. So, I moved him up here and let him manage them."

"Wait a minute, dude," Swift said, confused, "You had an informant manage the properties while you were locked up in prison? So, you are sure he effectively did what he was supposed to do while you were locked up?"

"I'm sure he did," House answered, "The informants I interacted with were chosen for different reasons. Most cops choose them based on the intel they provide and their fear of them. I picked mine based on your trustworthiness; If you had something to lose by lying."

"Explain."

"He is a family man. He had a wife and two kids, and he knew he'd be fine if he just gave him another opportunity. This informant was arrested on some drug trafficking charges. He was a small-time guy. He worked in a pharmacy and was skimming prescription pills from orders to sale."

"It wouldn't have been noticeable, but the FDA started changing the schedule level of some of the drugs. As a result, the pharmacy started ordering more than authorized. He didn't know this, but the pharmacist and some of his co-workers were doing the same on a larger scale. He was only doing so because one of his children was sick. He was trying to provide a way for his child to be taken care of. The others were just in it for the money. I convinced the DA to charge him with a lesser crime, and I will use him as an informant. The DA agreed. We were able to recognize the changes in ordering patterns for other pharmacies. We got more criminals off the street with his information."

"What's his name?"

"Timothy Shane. Make a left up here and there should be a trailer to the right. I think this is the one. Pull into the driveway." said House.

The trailer was in decent shape. The lawn was maintained, and it appeared the steps had been repaired in recent years. House could tell Timothy was doing a good job taking care of it.

It was close to 8 pm, and the sun was starting to set. House approached the trailer and knocked on the door. No one answered. A few more minutes passed, and House knocked again. Still, nothing.

No lights were on, and House didn't hear anyone walking around.

"I'm sure this is the right one."

"House, you should have called him. Well...actually, he could have skipped town years ago."

As Swift finished his statement, a car was pulling into the driveway.

 The driver rolled down the window and yelled, "Hello, can I help you."

House walked towards the car and leaned into the window, "It's me, Timothy."

"Oh, it's you, Detective House. Hold on a second," Timothy turned off the car and exited, "Where have you been? It's been ten, twelve, years?"

Timothy and House shook hands.

"Long story, we don't need to speak about here. Can we go inside?"

"Of course, no one lives here currently. I moved my family around the corner. More room."

Timothy unlocked the door, and they all went inside the trailer. It was clean and furnished.

"The kids that were staying here moved out a week ago. They did a great job keeping the place respectable. Anyway, glad to see you; you look well."

House was inspecting the trailer. Then, looking behind doors and checking the windows, "Timothy, I was released from prison a few hours ago."

Timothy's eyes were as big as dinner plates. He was at a loss for words. After taking a moment to gather himself he stated, "I haven't heard from you in years. I was wondering why. I didn't question it too much because I could take care of the property or anything. But then, I thought this was a test to see if I would stay straight. You gave me a new start. I didn't want to disappoint you. So, I kept pressing forward. Well, what happened? Why were you locked up?"

House turned to look Timothy directly in his eyes, "If you don't know, we are going to keep it that way."

"House, don't you think it would benefit us to tell him," Swift asked.

"No, I don't. But, Tim, I trust you, and you have maintained my trust by keeping this up. I know it couldn't have been easy. There is a reason I cannot tell you. You understand?"

House felt he could trust Timothy, but he wanted to be sure Timothy was truthful in not knowing House was in prison. If Timothy did know something, he would eventually slip up.

Timothy nodded, "I understand."

"I will need this trailer for a while. Did you have anyone waiting for it?" House asked.

"No," Timothy replied, "the summers are a slow period. Not much going on with the school is out."

"Great. Well, Tim, we are going to get settled. I'll see you later?"

Timothy waved goodbye and walked out of the trailer.

"There are two bedrooms. Let's get some sleep."

"House, you have been way too calm in all this," said Swift.

"How so," asked House.

"The first thing I would have done when I was released would have been looking for answers."

"Well, I am glad I am not you. We will talk about it in the morning. But, first, let's get some sleep."

Chapter 6

House woke up and looked outside the window. With the sun's height, he knew he must have slept until the early afternoon. It had been years since he slept that long or that well. He walked to the living room and saw Swift eating a big bowl of cereal.

"House, you finally woke up. I went to the store this morning. I grabbed a couple of things. You want something?"

"I'm good for right now."

"Fair enough, let's get to it." Swift walked out of the door. House heard him open the trunk of his car. Swift re-enters the trailer with an arm full of files.

"This is everything I have been able to gather about your case. Some of these are copies, and some are originals. Hold on a second," Swift returned to the car and replaced it with a few more files and a laptop.

"House, we first need to start with your final case, and then we will proceed with your trial if needed. This is everything I have gathered so far."

"How did you get all this information?"

Swift lit a cigarette and opened a window, "House, I told you I can get almost anything I need. Also, I have this," Swift pulled out his badge from the State Department.

"They didn't take that away from you?"

"Yes and no. When I retired, there was someone who made replicas as a gift. If you look close enough, you can tell it's a fake."

House walked up to Swift and looked at the badge. Swift was right; if you looked at it, you could tell it was fake.

"I see," House said, "Why don't we go over what you know first? This way, I won't repeat anything."

This made a lot of sense to House. When interviewing suspects, he would only let them know what they needed to know. You want to avoid giving someone an escape route.

"What do I need to start with? The case or my trial."

"Your trial was designed for you to be convicted. We can get into that later. Start with the case." Swift answered.

House started, "There were a series of mysterious deaths around Nashville. Being a decent-sized city, there was nothing to alert the public about."

Swift interrupted House, "Why would that be?"

House continued, "The first few bodies were found near homeless camps and vacant warehouses. From the coroner's report, each of them had fresh injection wounds in their arm. They were written off as heroin overdoses. The toxicology report confirmed it. I was working on another case then and didn't pay much attention other than that. But then, someone made their first mistake."

Swift was writing down everything House was saying. Making sure he got everything.

"Swift, as you know, it's hard to hide the actual cause of death. One of the bodies had ligature marks around its neck. The murderer wouldn't have known this would have shown up after the person passed. The press got wind of this and went on a field day. Naturally, the Chief asked us to find out who was committing these murders quickly and quietly. He asked me to be the lead detective on the case. I attempted to decline his invitation, but the case had too high of a profile. I wouldn't be able to investigate with my usual methods. But as you can imagine, it didn't happen."

"I started to go through the case files to see what I could uncover; what was it that the other guys missed? While I was trying to find something, we didn't have another murder for a few months. This is typical. Something hits the news, and criminals go into hiding. While I was looking for a lead, I noticed we weren't receiving any notices for drug overdoses. So, I started digging around and discovered certain ones were being labeled accidental deaths."

"What is wrong with that?" Swift asked, "I assume most users are just attempting to get as high as possible and this is what could happen."

House replied, "You would be correct with that assumption. Let me clarify. In our department, accidental deaths are also included as the reason. For example, accidental death due to heroin overdose falling on a knife. They were just blank."

Swift took a moment from his note, writing, "You believe they were hiding something? The obvious shows someone was. Continue."

"As I was stating," House continued, "I spoke to the Medical Examiner about this. She said she received instructions to mark them as accidental with no reason for the time being. I continued to prod, and she blurted out, 'It's an election year' while walking out of the room. That made a lot of sense. So often, we were asked to make sure our stats for homicide, drugs, and weapons were in the ideal range for solved crimes during elections."

Swift asked, "Was this universal across the board? Meaning all elections or only local ones."

"City and State," House answered.

"Where did this lead you next? Did you face any roadblocks?"

"Unfortunately, that is correct. When I investigated who was getting murdered, the victims all had prior drug usage. This was uncovered during interviews with their families. There wasn't a specific race, age group, or sex. As the election was getting closer, I started gaining ground."

"What happened," Swift asked.

"Someone got sloppy," House said, "earlier, I stated those being killed were heroin overdose, right? The locations were the same. However, now someone was committing the murders in the same places but attempting to make them look like overdoses. The murderer was escalating."

"Explain," Swift still had his head down, writing notes.

"The victims still had injection site wounds, but the Examiner informed us they were done postmortem. These victims also didn't have any in their system nor a history of drug use."

House continued, "The Mayor started hounding me to see if I had made any progress. He demanded I find out who was responsible before the election. Every debate, interview, etc., was asking him if I had made leeway. I told him no. The truth was I was closer than I thought."

"Stop." As he was heading to the kitchen, Swift said, "You need anything? We have been going at this for a while now."

House stood up and stretched. He looked, and he moved the blinds to look outside. It was dusk. "Damn, we have; sorry again about the late start."

"We have more than time. You have been waiting for ten years," Swift re-entered the living room with two bottles of water and chips, "Here, you need something. You need to stay clear-headed. If you think you get hungry or thirsty, you might say anything to get this over with."

House was surprised at how Swift was managing the interview. His demeanor changed as soon as they started. Swift was serious. No jokes, sly remarks, nothing. Just focusing on every word House said.

"Ok, House, we are going to start again. Are you ready? Actually, let me start."

House said, "Go ahead; what do you get?"

Swift started grabbing some of the files, "I wanted to get some of the backgrounds of the case. You would tell me next that you noticed only certain officers were called to scenes, correct?"

House replied, "Not quite. They were not called to the scenes; they were the first officer on the scene. That is what raised suspicion. No officer is that unlucky. All of the murders coincided with the shift these officers were working. With that, there was only one consistent witness, Adam Quill."

"Who is Adam Quill?"

"Adam Quill is a local vagrant…or was. He had a bad drug problem back then. The problem with him is Adam had a history of being used for witness testimony and statements. He was historically unreliable. However, officers knew if they paid him enough, he would say whatever he wanted them to say. Whoever was doing this had a major problem, and I don't know how they didn't figure it out."

"What was the problem?"

"Easy, he was homeless. There was a million-to-one chance he was at every one of the murders or close enough to supply any truthful information. Lazy police work was happening."

"House, I need you to backtrack for a second. Who were the officers who were normally first on the scene."

"Thank you, I forgot. The officers were David Boston, Mike Guess, and Jessica North."

Swift was thumbing through some files, "Have you ever interacted with any of them?"

"No, I am sure the most I would have ever said to them would have been hello. But unfortunately, they were in different precincts than I was. They were also made unavailable for interviews when I arrived on the scene."

Swift looked up at House, "You didn't find that strange?"

"Of course, I did. However, it provided me with much-needed insight. These police officers were covering for someone. I just couldn't say anything without any substantial proof."

Swift thought of his time as an officer. There were less than a handful of times an officer investigated another one. If House decided to accuse these officers of foul play without any proof, he could have alienated himself from other officers, lawyers, and anyone who he might need in the future. At worst, it could have been a possible death sentence for him.

Swift lit a cigar, "Let's go outside House. Let's get some summer evening air and continue this outside," Swift opened the door and went outside.

House followed suit. He wondered why Swift wanted to finish the conversation outside. When House met Swift, Swift was holding a package in his hand.

"Shit, I wonder how long this has been here."

"I didn't hear a car or anything. Is it for Timothy?

Swift didn't say anything. He had a puzzled look on his face. He grabbed his phone out of his pocket and read a message.

"What's up?"

"The package is for you. I need to make a call. Give me a second," Swift walked down the street.

House looked at the package, and it was indeed mailed to him. Whoever sent it used overnight shipping. There was no return address. The box was relatively heavy. House shook, and it sounded like there were papers in it.

An unsettling feeling came over House. The only people he knew that knew he was out of prison would have been the Warden, the Governor, Swift, and Timothy. "Who the hell would mail me a package? Better yet, how would they know I was here?"

Swift was walking towards the trailer. He was no longer on the phone.

"Everything ok, Swift," House asked.

House looked at Swift to see if he could gain anything from his body language. Swift didn't look worried, excited, nervous, or anything that would give House a reason to pause.

"House, we will open this package when you explain your last case. I won't go into it now, but this package could hold valuable information."

This confused House; if everything they needed was in the package, why wouldn't they open it? Also, who was Swift talking to? House knew if he asked Swift, he would dodge the question.

"Why did you want to come outside," asked House.

"Old habits die hard, House," Swift replied, "When I was an officer, I needed to change the scenery around me. There could be something I see that refreshes my memory. We have almost an hour of daylight left. Let's walk and talk," Swift started walking down the road, and House followed, "As you were saying."

"I was between a rock and a hard place. I couldn't question the officers; I wouldn't trust anything that Adam Quill would tell me, and people were still dying."

"The next logical step would have been to ask your Sergeant or Captain to speak to their supervisor," stated Swift.

"Correct," House answered, "We were in the middle of a leadership change. So, I spoke directly to Captain Ellis. He advised me he would see what was going on. A few more weeks went by, and I never heard anything. Finally, I returned to his office and heard him screaming at someone on the phone. The door was cracked open. I peeked inside, and Ellis was furious. He was throwing objects all around his office. Finally, Ellis noticed me and told me to come in..."

"Do you remember anything from his phone conversation?" Swift interrupted.

"Nothing of importance. Honestly, with the election going on, I thought it was something dealing with road closures, needing an extra security detail, etc. Ellis normally had a calm demeanor. This was out of the ordinary. Besides him saying things like 'you're kidding me' along with some other choice words, nothing comes to mind. I asked him if he had made progress so I could speak to the other officers. He insisted on knowing why I needed to talk to them, and they were suspects. I knew how the conversation would go, so I backed off. As I attempted to leave the office, Ellis apologized for being abrasive. He then told me the phone call was about me getting a partner. I rejected the notion of having one. Ellis felt the same but said he didn't have a choice. This is the first time I was told Maria Silva would be my partner."

The streetlights started to turn on. "Let's head back," Swift, I'm going to run to the store and grab some things. Do you need anything?"

"No, I'm good."

"Alright, see you in a few."

House took the opportunity to review some of the information Swift had gathered. While reviewing it, he could tell Swift had invested more time into the case a lot longer than what he led on. However, he was careful not to stare at any information for too long. House did not want it to impact his memory.

Once House finished looking at the files, he started to look around the trailer. To see if anything seemed out of place. At first, he thought Swift was paranoid. However, he wanted to avoid Swift being wrong.

House sat back down and proceeded to go over the case in his head, where he stopped. He was trying to ensure he didn't forget to tell Swift anything. Nothing of importance came to mind. He needed to know what Swift had figured out himself,

When Swift arrived, he started rummaging through the files, "House, I'll do you this favor." He grabs some of the files and walks to the living room wall.

"David Boston, Jessica North, Charles Young, Mike Guess, and Maria Silva," Swift said as he taped their police department headshots to the wall, "Based on what is in these files, they all could have benefited from framing you.

"I don't know about that," said House.

Swift opened one of the files and sat on the couch, "Maria Silva, born in Brazil, and her family moved to the US while in high school. Nothing of note until she entered the police academy in 2005. Even though she had one of the highest scores in her class, she was primarily used as a parking enforcement officer until being assigned for you to train her. Did you know that?"

House took a moment to think, "I don't remember that. Why would they have me train her if she only checked meters?"

"You are asking the wrong person. I'm surprised they even had a commissioned officer do that. Seems like a waste of money. What was going on? Did you lose a partner or something?"

"No, I never had a partner. I never mentored/trained anyone either."

House started to look around the room. He realized he never questioned why in what seemed to be the biggest case in the department's history, he didn't question the decision.

"So, she was just assigned to you?"

"Yes."

One of the skills that made Swift great at his job was questioning things that seemed routine. So often, people are moved around in law enforcement agencies for need, to move a problem child, or cover something up. House being asked to train someone when he never had before should have been a red flag for him.

"Whoever assigned her to you did so with a purpose. We must find out what that purpose was," stated Swift.

"Ok, makes sense. What about the others," House said, searching for a blank sheet of paper.

"Ok, David Boston. Born in South Carolina and played college football at Austin Peay. Boston is a twenty-year veteran of the Metro Nashville Police Department. The majority of his time he spent in the North Precinct. Nothing in his career is noteworthy from what I was able to get. However, in your last case, he is mentioned as the first officer on the scene."

Swift placed the file at the bottom of the stack and opened the next one.

"Mike Guess, the officer you were found guilty of killing, was a terrible police officer. He was an eight-year veteran of the Metro Nashville Police Department. He is a Nashville native. He was assigned to a flex unit in the Midtown Precinct until his death. He couldn't frame you since he died but…"

"This is a good place to start," interrupted House, "However, is this really worth it?"

"What do you mean?"

"Never mind."

House was starting to doubt himself. He figured once he began to get close to the players involved with framing him, things would be as easy. He would have to take a calculated risk for this to pan out.

Then he thought about the years he spent in prison for a crime he didn't commit. At least if he went to jail this time, it would be worth it.

"Continue, Swift; what else do you have?"

Swift looked at House. House was slumping over and appeared to be hearing the information but not listening to Swift.

Swift placed the files beside him and walked over to House, "You haven't been able to speak to anyone about this in years. I know you have a lot to get off your chest. Trust me, you aren't going back to prison. We will make this count."

Swift started going through his files again, "Jessica North, born in Alabama, was a two-sport athlete at David Lipscomb. Hold on a second...like I thought, she was in the same graduating class as Maria Silva. This might be something to remember." Swift walked over to the photos and noted how they previously could have met.

"Last but not least, Charles Young. Young is the most senior in the group. He is a thirty-five-year veteran of the Metro Police Department. For the past twenty years, he has worked in evidence control."

House stood up and examined the wall. "I just thought about something. Why is Young up there? I haven't mentioned him at all."

"Glad you asked." Swift pulled up some reports on his laptop. "House, here are some of the evidence control logs. Look at the discrepancies. What do you notice?"

Swift turned the laptop towards House. House started scrolling, and he saw what Swift was talking about. When Boston or Guess turned something into evidence, everything ended in zeros, like $5k, or $20k. Neither one had turned in drugs or weapons for almost ten years.

North had never logged anything into evidence.

"You see it, House? What are the odds they never ran across drugs for that long? Not to mention how even the money they turned in was. There is no way it always was perfect each time."

House knew Swift was right. He was onto something big a decade ago. He just couldn't figure out what was truly going on. This information would have been great to have. A smile appeared on House's face. With the evidence Swift had gathered, it seemed like a sure thing he would get the justice he deserved.

"How did you find this," House asked, "I should be saying thank you. This is something I should have looked for."

"Evidence logs are archived on paper and the computer after a while. You would have spent months back then looking through those records. Not to mention running into issues from Young." Swift responded.

"People are products of history, whether you believe it or not. Most ideas are not original. Unfortunately, I ran into corrupt governments encouraging this behavior."

House stood up and looked out the window. It was pitch black outside. Swift and he had been talking for longer than he thought.

"Are you sleepy, House? We can continue when you wake up," Swift asked.

House turned to Swift, "No, let's continue."

"Will continue in the morning," Swift said as he headed to his bedroom.

House knew Swift was right. However, this also gave him time to think about the scenario Swift laid out.

House sat in the bedroom and went over everything Swift and him discussed. Swift was moving him in the right direction.

"There were too many questions I left unanswered. Damn it! I could have prevented this." House slung a pillow towards the wall. "Leaving the obvious unanswered is not a mistake I will make again."

Chapter 7

When House awoke the following day, he looked outside the window. The sun was still rising. He heard Swift moving around the trailer. "Did he even go to sleep?" House thought.

House went into the living room, and Swift was cooking breakfast.

"I'm not Gordon Ramsey or anything, but I have picked up a few things over the years," Swift yelled to House, "Let me know what you think."

House went over to the kitchen and grabbed a plate. Swift had prepared pancakes, omelets, bacon, and fruit salad. It was some of the most delicious food House had ever tasted. He was curious to know if it was all the years in prison or if Swift's cooking was really that good.

"It's good, right? I thought I would use my G.I. Bill to go to culinary school. Oh well. Once you are finished, we will start again. I'm going to step out and smoke one."

House finished his breakfast as Swift stepped outside. He looked around and saw Swift had been busy with his files. They were in separate piles. House assumed they were for each officer who could have been involved. He didn't want to look through them and mess something up. However, he knew this wasn't from a few months of research. This would have taken at least a year if not more.

Swift entered the trailer, "You ready, House?"

House stood up, "There is no way you gathered all this information within a few months. Regardless of your connections. What's really going on?"

Swift took a deep breath, "I haven't lied to you, but I have been avoiding this subject."

Swift starts, " When I separated from the service, I wanted to find something more fulfilling, something more promising for myself, something that I could be directly proud of. So instead, I went right back to the State Department."

"How so?" House asked.

Smith replied, "Because of what I did, I had to disconnect from everyone. Even my family. I wasn't enjoying my work, but I was good at it. But I kept getting this feeling something wasn't right. So, I left the State Department to regain my lost years."

"When I returned home to Oregon, I discovered that my brother and sister had passed away two years after I joined the Army."

"Man, I'm so sorry to hear that."

A tear started to run down Swift's face, "They would have been in their early thirties now."

House's stomach suddenly felt empty. The emptiness turns into an uncomfortable feeling. Even though he was an only child and his parents had passed before he joined the service, he could imagine how heartbreaking it must have been for Swift.

"This brings me to why I am here and why I invested so much time into your case. I know we haven't spoken in years, but you are the only family I have left. They were murdered."

Swift was sniffling, looking down at the ground. House could see the tears falling on the carpet. At that moment, the Earth seemed to stand still. The wind you could hear whipping across the trailer stopped. No cars were driving down the street. No birds were chirping. Just complete and utter silence.

House was standing in disbelief. He had to tell many families their loved ones were murdered, and it never got any easier. House couldn't imagine finding out after years of not speaking to anyone in his family.

Swift wiped off the tears from his face and looked up angrily, "My dad was the reason they were murdered."

A cold chill went down House's back. This could not be real. He realized this was the first time Swift had told someone this. That is why he was getting so worked up. He must have been sitting on this for years.

Swift continued, "I learned my dad was involved with some shady characters. He was working as a paralegal for the city. For a fee, he would leak information to local gang members, drug dealers, you name it. Eventually, he was caught by an internal investigation. As you can guess, he started squealing about the other people involved. It had a domino effect on the Mayor's office."

House could tell where this was heading. When everyone benefits from criminal activity, everything is excellent. However, when someone is caught, some are willing to do anything to get the light off them.

"The word got out that my dad was the piece that made the whole thing crumble. Loyalists in the police department found out where my family was hidden. They conducted a baseless, no-knock warrant raid on the House. Killing my brother, sister, and father."

Swift seemed relieved that he could finally say what happened out loud. House knew there was no telling what he went through to get the truth. Swift lit a cigarette.

"What happened to your mom," House asked.

"Her medical report said she died of natural causes but, I know she died of a broken heart. She worked nights, so she wasn't home during the raid. Her last days had to be painful. My biggest regret is not being there for her."

"That's why I am here, House." Swift pointed to the files spread around the trailer, " Was I trying to find what your lawyer missed, what you forgot during your trial, anything to get you released early? I was going to go to great lengths to free my brother. That's what you are to me. The only family I have left," Swift went to hug House.

"Ok, enough with this emotional shit. Let's get back to it."

Chapter 8

"Where were we at, House?" Swift was looking at the notes he made under each officer's photo.

It was mid-morning. A happy medium between House oversleeping the first day and waking up before sunrise. The trailer was filled with the smell of fresh coffee and tea.

"Somedays, I cannot pick between coffee and tea. So, I made both. Feel free to help yourself. Cream and sugar are on the counter."

House grabbed a cup of coffee and sat at the table, "Let's open the package and continue from there."

Swift turned around and looked at House. The look in Swift's eyes let House know there was some hesitancy about opening the package. However, he couldn't figure out why.

"Before we do that, we must review how and why you were arrested. This could help us narrow down a suspect."

This confirmed what House thought. It was odd Swift wanted to continue talking when it could be pointless. House figured he could continue to press the issue, but appeasing Swift could lead to revealing other things he missed.

"I see your point," House said, "I could just summarize it but knowing you, you want the entire story. So, I will attempt to make this as quick as possible."

House started, "These murders continued at random. Different days, times, and locations. Just like they had been before. Silva and I left a different murder scene and returned to the office. Dispatch requested we call them. Nothing unusual about that. I was driving, so Silva made the call. She had the phone on speaker, so I could hear everything. There was a domestic incident they needed her to be a translator for. As fate would have it, Dispatch sent me another scene to our patrol computer."

"We met up with the other patrol officer, and she left with them. I started to..."

"Quickly," Swift interrupted, "What was your relationship with Silva? Did you all talk about hobbies, relationships, etc.?"

"No," House answered, "Most of our conversations were focused on work. From what I could tell, she wanted to be a great detective. She was like you, Swift, detail-oriented, and a people person. Everything she asked me was directly focused on solving the case. I prefer not too small talk when I can."

Swift was pacing back and forth. Absorbing the information provided to him.

"Moving on," House said, "I pulled over to see where I needed to head next. The problem with some of the murders I was sent to had nothing to do with my case. I know what you are thinking. How could I be so sure if there wasn't a certain pattern? It was just a feeling I had. And each time I passed it to someone else, I was right. The other murders were solved in weeks if not days."

"I called Dispatch to confirm what the address was. I am unfamiliar with the area. It was at the edge of Davidson and Rutherford County. It was an abandoned warehouse, slightly off the main road, when I arrived. I drove around the warehouse and didn't see any vehicles around. The windows in my patrol car were slightly down, and I couldn't hear anything either. I called Dispatch to ensure this was the right place and to see if I was supposed to meet someone. Dispatch advised the officer I was waiting for recently left due to a 9-1-1 call. I was able to verify that it was correct."

"I got out of the car and headed in. It was quiet, and the building was a lot smaller inside than it appeared on the outside. Doing my due diligence was my undoing. First, my victims were in or around cars, not in buildings. Second, there was no one else there to confirm anything. Even though I worked by myself, I never spoke to anyone or examined crime scenes without someone to verify I did everything by the book."

"Then, I stepped into an opening, and there she was. A poor woman tied to a chair in lingerie. The color had started to fade from her face, feet, and hands. She couldn't have been dead for more than a few hours. I heard footsteps walking towards me. I drew my weapon, advised them who I was, and told them to move to where I could see them."

House stood up and looked out the window. He wanted to explain what happened without getting overly emotional. He took a few deep breaths and continued, "It was Mike Guess. I asked him what he was doing. Guess stated he was there to replace the other officer who called away. Dispatch didn't tell me they were sending a replacement officer. I assume it was an oversight on their part."

"I lowered my gun, and Guess started walking towards her. He was mumbling under his breath."

***

September 15, 2011.

"Officer Guess, correct? Did you know her?"

Mike Guess was six feet tall, 200 lbs. He had black, short-cut hair and a thin mustache.

"No, but it's a shame, isn't it?"

Guess looked the woman up and down with a slight smile.

"Detective House, one of Metro's finest investigators. I know you have wanted to talk to me. So, what do you have on your mind?"

House wasn't surprised. Guess knew he was attempting to speak to him and some other police officers. He was most surprised that this was the time Guess would bring it up.

"I'm all ears House; what is it that you need to know?"

"Guess, this isn't the time or place. Do you know if the Forensics Team has been here?"

It was apparent they had not been there. House was attempting to get a better read on Guess. Was he followed? Or had to Guess been there the entire time?

"Don't know, don't care," replied Guess

"Guess, are you feeling, ok?"

Guess started pacing back and forth, then suddenly drew his gun, "No, I'm not all right."

"The fuck are you doing, man?"

"House, normally, when people are good at their job, they get rewarded. I'm a shitty cop if I am being honest with myself. Hell, I have been trying to find a way to medically retire. Ain't shit wrong with me, but the twelve years I have left is way too long."

"You, House, are a good cop. Some would even say great. But the thing is, you stick your nose into places it doesn't belong, which is what brings us here today. See, I.., well, we aren't here to talk about me. But, back to you. You wanted to figure out who was killing all these 'innocent' people. These people are far from that."

"How do you know? Mike, that is your first name, right? So, it is not too late. Let me help you fix this. Tell me who is involved so I can help you," House took a step towards Guess.

From what House gathered so far, there was no way Guess could have been acting alone. This was the chance for House to convince Guess to flip.

Guess shoots at House's feet, "I don't need your fucking help. So what? You thought you could win me over by showing sympathy; I don't need anyone's help. I knew exactly what I was getting involved in. We all get caught eventually. The problem is you never know when. We could have all run as soon as we received word you were looking for us. I'm glad we didn't; it let us see how loyal some of us are to each other.

House knew there was no getting to Guess; he was content with how today would end. House didn't know if there were other police officers around waiting to assist Guess if needed. He didn't want to make any sudden movements either.

House looked around and didn't see anything. It may have been just these two. There was limited lighting in the warehouse. However, he could tell people have been in here recently. The chair the woman was sitting on didn't have any dust. House looked at the floor. Some spots were different colors. They were also different sizes. Whatever was there was moved. But by who?

"Ok. Let's cut the bullshit, Guess. Who is the girl?"

"Who," Guess looks at the unknown woman in the chair, "She is a victim of circumstance. Other than that, it doesn't concern you."

House quickly looked her over again. She didn't have any self-defense marks. Meaning she was either taken by surprise or knew her attacker. Based on what she was wearing, she was in a comfortable environment, either her home or her partner's.

"See, this is why you are a great cop. I know what you are doing. You don't know what will happen to you, but you are trying to learn as much as you about the victim. Bravo," Guess started clapping.

"You knew her? She expected you, and you betrayed her."

"What is your point? Morals are what got you into the situation you are in now. Let me break it down for you. I am going to radio in. I caught you tampering with the crime scene. Once you noticed me, you drew your gun on me and didn't announce who you were. So, I opened fire. Simple right? Wait a minut...."

A gunshot went off, and Guess went straight down. House attempted to turn around and was knocked unconscious before he could identify who shot Guess.

Chapter 9

Present Day

"When I came to, there were three or four police officers with guns drawn on me," House said.

"A story so true, it sounds made up," Swift replied while lighting a cigarette, "I'm sure you told Internal Affairs about this."

"I did. It seemed pretty cut and dry. Guess was killed and I was knocked out, but they didn't believe me. I was a dues-paying member of the F.O.P., and they washed their hands of me. I couldn't get a decent lawyer to take the case. So, I was stuck with a Public Defender. Then I learned why people hate them. The one I had just kept telling me to take the plea deal. Sorry bastard. I refused and was found guilty. My lawyer didn't even try."

"You skipped something," Swift said, "How did the evidence play out in court? If you were hit in the head, I am assuming the back or side, how could you have been the one to shoot Guess?

"The prosecution proved I was hit by something that fell in the warehouse. It just so happened after the shot was fired. I know someone else had to be there. Who? I have no idea. I plan on finding that out. Whether they are dead or alive. They swapped the slide of my service weapon with theirs. So, when the lab checked the rifling on the bullet with my gun, it matched. Even though I had no GSR on my hand or clothing, the jury still believed I was the one who pulled the trigger."

"Also, I don't know who was charged with killing the woman. It was never brought up during my trial, oddly enough. Hopefully, they figured that out."

Swift opened his laptop, "I don't see anything here. I'm looking up dockets around the same time you were arrested. She might have been filed under Jane Doe if she was just a pawn."

House replied, "For all I know, Guess was the one who killed her? It could have been someone else; it doesn't matter. I have zero leads, and it has been over ten years."

Swift looked at House. House had a dark, cold look in his eyes. What happened to the woman bothered him. He wanted to get her justice, but it would be nearly impossible at this point.

"I was avoided like the plague. There was no one in my corner. It would have been nice to have someone I had helped over the years to say, 'No, Seven isn't like this. Seven wouldn't have killed a fellow police officer.' It's whatever. Swift, I'll be back. I need to take a walk."

House headed out of the trailer and started to walk down the street.

It was early afternoon. Summer was in full swing in Tennessee. Even the wind didn't provide House much comfort. He was glad to finally get all of that off his chest. For years, he wanted to. From House's small conversations with people in prison, most people felt they didn't deserve to be there. He didn't want to sound like one of the people complaining because the justice system failed him. So, he just kept all the anger and hate inside of him. Some officers used to joke about how doing their job too well would alienate them from those who weren't. There was some truth in that joke.

House headed back to the trailer. The walk helped him clear his head and get back focused on the task at hand.

Swift was outside, sitting on the steps.

"I decided to get some fresh air myself, House. Even though I had read over your case a few dozen times, I never pictured the scenario you gave me. To think you went to a building, found a dead woman and a cop seemed to want to kill you. Just for the cop to end up dead and you in prison."

"Most people wouldn't have either. I need to get some water," House said while squeezing past Swift.

Swift followed House inside, "House, there should be some Gatorade if you want that."

"Water is just fine; it's time to open that package, don't you think?"

"There is no time like the present," Swift walked over to the door and grabbed the package. Then, he pulled out a pocket knife and carefully opened the box.

There were a bunch of separate folders. On top of the folders was a note that said, "Thank You."

House and Swift started going through the files, amazed at what they saw.

"House, do you see this? Look," Swift grabbed a few papers and handed them to House.

They were bank statements for David Boston, Jessica North, and Maria Silva. The ledger went as far back as 2007. Every cash deposit over a thousand dollars was highlighted. Some of the highlighted dates had notes beside them.

"Swift, have you found the file corresponding to these notes?"

"Yeah, right here. The notes are the date of police raids, and I see what the issue is."

"What's that?"

"It's a lot to unpack," Swift went to a blank space on the wall with tape, "There were no weapons, drugs, or money found at any of the raids. The probable cause mentioned for the warrants, including the exhaustion state:

Information from a trusted, confidential informant has provided the whereabouts of a known stash house. Subsequent surveillance on the property confirmed that suspects involved in multiple investigations were going in and out of the home at all-night hours. Traffic stops of different suspects' vehicles were clean. Furthering the belief the house is a central point for storing products and/or money.

It goes on, but you get the point. From what I see here, Boston led these raids."

House stood up and walked over to the wall. He wanted to see if anything else jumped out at him. While he did that, Swift started going through some of the other files.

House turned to Swift, "So, Boston conducted the raids and had officers not report what they found? No. We are missing something. What you are suggesting would involve more people than whom we suspect...I got it; Young never properly logged what was found. By doing this, he and the others would be able to keep anything not recorded. The officers would 'turn' evidence in just to retrieve it at a later date." House walked over to the files and started searching for anything that would prove his theory.

"Oh shit, House, look at this," Swift showed House some photos.

The photos were pictures of Jessica North, David Boston, and Maria Silva with prominent drug dealers and gang members in the Nashville area. In each of the images, the officers were wearing civilian clothing.

"House, I don't think these are photoshopped either."

"What's photoshopped?"

"Man, you did miss a lot. Photoshopping is altering a real image. You could add people to it, take them away, add elements, etc. These photos are old and have noticeably faded. I have seen enough of these to be pretty good at identifying the real ones from the fake ones."

"I don't know. How would someone get these photos?" House said.

"More important is who took the photos. Whoever it was knew how important it was to see their faces. Whoever took the photos did so a small distance away. Maybe another cop was investigating them."

"Whoever it was, it seems they got further than I did. I still cannot shake this weird feeling. How did whoever sent this know we were here?"

House was looking at Swift directly to see if he could see something from him. He still remembered the look Swift had on his face when he first saw the package. However, Swift didn't provide anything. Instead, he seemed to think about it just as much as House.

"House, have you seen anything with Guess's name on it? I haven't so far."

"I haven't either. Maybe Guess wasn't involved."

"Guess didn't plan your set up by himself. He isn't smart enough to be the brains of the operation. He got his cue from someone. Police officers are peculiar people. Some live and die to protect the community, and some believe civilians should worship the ground they walk on. Rest believe they are entitled to make more money by whatever means."

There was truth in Swift's statement. House knew the political landscape between the police and the public possibly worsened when he was incarcerated. When he started as a rookie, he was told the public was out to get him, just for doing his job. He couldn't imagine what it was like to be a police officer now.

There was a knock at the door, "Hey guys, it's me, Timothy."

House opened the door, "What's up?"

Timothy could see all of the papers spread throughout the trailer. "I was just wondering how long you all plan on staying here. No rush or anything. Students tend to want to look at possible rentals a month before school starts. I can just block this one out. Y'all seem busy."

"Let's talk out here. Swift, I will just be right outside the door."

Swift waved his hand to acknowledge House.

House walked down the steps and closed the door behind him.

"Did I do something wrong," Timothy asked.

"I just have a few questions for you," House answered.

"Ok. Shoot."

"You stated you were unaware that I was in prison, correct? I know you are telling the truth about that. My question is: Has anyone come here looking for me? I mean ever."

"Ever? My family and I have been up here for the last fifteen years or so. I'm sure there has been someone who has but no one comes to mind."

"Have I received mail here in the past year? Junk mail counts."

"Yes, you have. When you attempted to transfer some of the utility bills to me, someone screwed up. So, they are still in your name. Don't worry, I paid for everything on time. Sometimes extra. Is there something specific you want to know? The life I have left I owe it to you. Let me know how I can help."

"You are helping me by answering these questions."

Timothy was answering honestly, and House could tell. Timothy maintained eye contact throughout the conversation. He was also answering the questions without having to think about what he should say. However, House did not want to get Timothy involved more than what he already had. Once Swift and he figured out who to go after, there could be an unintentional target placed on Timothy's family.

"Everything ok, House?" Swift yelled through the door.

"Yeah, everything is fine!" House responded.

"Timothy, just a few more moments of your time."

"Yeah, what you got?"

"Politically, what's going on in Tennessee? Could you think of a reason that I would have been released?"

"No, never paid attention to that stuff. Two wings on the same bird. Right?"

"Last thing. How is your family doing?"

"Whoa. The way your questions were going I wasn't expecting that. Well, my wife and I are empty nesters now. All of our kids have moved on with their lives. I thought I would be sad, but it's great," Timothy said laughing, "I have a grandchild on the way. I thought fifty was too young to be a grandfather, but I sprung it on my parents just the same. How about you? I know they have to be excited." asked Timothy.

"My parents had me when they were older in life. My mom was in her forties when she had me. They both passed shortly after I joined the Army. I wasn't close to any of my relatives." House answered.

"Oh…sorry to hear that."

"I made my peace with it a long time ago. Sorry to keep you so long. We'll catch up later."

House headed back into the trailer. He was hoping there would be a small chance Timothy would give him something to assist with figuring out who left the package or why he was released.

Swift had all of the files opened and spread out. "House, I have sent some of this information to Team Shadow. Mainly, I am trying to get the locations of those officers. It's time to get some answers from them."

"There is something else I found interesting. Who is Stephen Knight?"

"Stephen Knight was this young accounting prodigy. He could look at a company's financials and could tell them where they were spending too much money, who was stealing, and projected growth in thirty minutes. He probably had some other skills people were unaware of." House responded.

"His story is what made him popular. He grew up in the system until he was eighteen and then lived on the street. He never completed his formal education. He was self-taught, using libraries and YouTube videos. One day, he overheard some accountants talking and injected himself into the conversation. At first, they thought they would just entertain him. Then, they realized he was right about a lot of things. Stephen was brought to this investment firm, and the rest is history. Why do you ask?"

"You know he was killed," said Swift.

"Yeah, they never found his killer," said House.

"Well, I think I found out who did it. Read this."

Swift handed House a witness statement and a police report. It read:

At approximately 5:40 PM. Dispatch received a 9-1-1 call for shots fired near a homeless encampment. Upon arrival, I was notified the victim was in a nearby vehicle. The victim had multiple gunshot wounds in their face and chest. Homicide was notified. The license plate came back registered to Stephen Knight. Brief canvassing of the area did not uncover any immediate information that would lead to the shooter.

The witness statement read:

I, Johnny Michael, heard at least four gunshots near the homeless camp where I live. This wasn't unusual. I think it was around 5:00 PM. I heard a person yelling on the phone "I fucked up." It was a voice I heard before, so I went to see who it was. It was a police officer named Guess. When I turned around, he had a gun in his hand. I was in the bushes. So, he didn't see me. Another police officer showed up and he was yelling at him. I had never seen the other one before, but he was older than Guess. The other officer said, "Get in the goddamn car!" He took the gun Guess had and they drove off.

House looked at the bottom of the witness statement. It was submitted five days after the police report and taken to the police station.

"There isn't a name of who took this statement," said House.

"I noticed that as well. I think it is a legitimate statement. I just think the officer who took the statement didn't want to believe a police officer was the one who shot Stephen. While you were reading, I tried to see what I could find about the case. No one was ever charged with his murder," said Swift.

"It's starting to make sense," Swift walked over to the wall with a marker, "Stay with me, House."

"From what we know so far, Silva, Boston, and North were receiving large amounts of money from the raids Boston was conducting," Swift had circled the officers and drew an arrow under them. "If I am to believe what Johnny saw is the truth. Guess killed Stephen and a senior officer covered for him," Swift circled Guess and drew an arrow under him. "Stephen was killed before your arrest. This gives me a reason to believe the unknown officer told Guess he needed to throw you off the trail of the other officers. However, the officer didn't plan on Guess killing Stephen. It was insane to target someone that high profile. This is why he killed that lady. You were supposed to be drawn in and boom, you're taken off the board. Someone assumed Guess was going to screw up again. That's who shot him. Why they didn't shoot you is the real question. To summarize, the same officer who let the first group do what they want is the same person who had Guess set you up," Swift drew a large circle under both arrows, "What do you think."

House stood up to look at everything on the wall. In a little over a week, together they had come up with something plausible that they each couldn't do separately. House couldn't find a better way to connect the dots than what Swift had laid out in front of him. Who was the person pulling the strings? He hoped he would find out soon enough.

House looked out the window, "I think it's time for dinner, we already missed lunch." [OBJ]

Chapter 10

A few weeks went by. House and Swift took the time to go through all of the remaining files to see if they had missed anything. The remaining items solidified their belief in Swift's hypothesis. Swift used this time to have Team Shadow pinpoint the locations of the officers involved. He had hoped to convince them to turn on the officer who was responsible for all this. Swift made sure to send copies of the evidence to trusted sources in case something was to happen to him or House.

"House, while I am waiting to get an approximate location for the officers, we need to take care of a few things."

"Like what?"

"Come outside," Swift said as he exited the trailer.

House followed Swift outside. Swift was looking into the trunk of his car.

"Back here House, I got something for you."

"What is it?"

Swift gave House a cell phone, "This a Blackberry. Hard to trace, hard to hack. My number is programmed into the phone. Team Shadow's number is under 'Information', and I just added a number for 'Last Resort'. If something doesn't go right when we start to make our move, call this number."

"Who's under Last Resort."

"That is not important. They will provide you with a sequence you must match if you want to gain access to it. It's something I picked up years ago."

House looked at the phone, "These are a lot different than what I remember. Is it simple to use?"

Swift grabbed the phone and showed House how to access the contacts, make a phone call, read a text message, and lock the phone.

"See, it's simple enough. Moving on," Swift moved the cover off of where a spare tire would have been normally located. Under the cover were weapons and tactical gear.

"I'm always prepared. I don't have anything for you. Did you have anything stashed around here," said Swift.

"No," answered House, "I never thought it would come to something like this. I have an idea of where we could go."

"Is there someone you can trust? No cameras and pay with cash?"

"Even better, an old State Trooper training site is nearby. I was sent for training there a few times. They were given an excessive amount of equipment. I should be able to find something there. It didn't even cross my mind that we would need this stuff."

"House, they already attempted to take you out once. What do you think will happen when they know you are gunning for them?"

"You're right." House thought about the attempts on his life while in prison. Some of them were people he had locked up before. Some were people who hated cops. Now, he couldn't but believe a few of them could have been targeted attempts.

"We also need to get you a car."

"Why?" "I just received the information we were waiting on," said Swift as he turned his phone toward House.

David Boston was injured in the line of duty in 2012. He was paralyzed from the waist down. House saw the headline for a newspaper article. It read *Metro Nashville Police Officer David Boston Injured During*

Shootout in East Nashville.

"Damn, that's unfortunate," said House.

"Keep reading," Swift replied.

House looked again. David Boston had died earlier in the year in an assisted living facility. Boston was placed in his bed incorrectly and choked to death. His remaining family members were in the process of suing the facility.

"That's a rough way to go," said House as he returned the phone to Swift.

"The information about the others is included as well. There is no line on Silva, but Young and North are in two separate states. I sent them to my laptop, so it's easier to view. You think Timothy has an old car or something you use."

"I don't want to involve him more than necessary. Let me think...I'm sure my bank accounts were closed."

"Hold on a second, House," Swift proceeds to step away and make a phone call.

There were students playing flag football across the street from them. House hadn't noticed the number of people who were moving back for school. He knew their time in Cookeville was drawing to a close.

House knew this might be the last case he would ever investigate. However, he was fine with it. It was time to figure out what was going on.

"House, good news," Swift stated as he returned, "I'll grab the laptop. Hop in."

"Where are we going?"

"There is someone who owes a favor to Team Shadow. Luckily for us. They live here as well."

Swift headed to retrieve the laptop while House got into Swift's car.

"Here you go. The information sent to it should be able to be read now."

As they rode down the road, House opened up the laptop and clicked on the first file. It was for Jessica North.

"The only thing in North's files are pictures. None of them are her. They are the type of pictures you would see on a postcard," said House.

"Keep looking. There has to be a description somewhere," replied Swift.

House scrolled further down, "Your right. Here it is at the bottom. Your guys said they believe these photos were taken along the Alabama coastline. How were they able to figure that out?"

"Searching for the origin of an image isn't hard if you know what you are doing. Some image searches are simple, some take a little more work. What I imagine is they found these photos on one of her social media sites; They had to be the only things she was posting since that's the only things they sent, then enhanced the image enough to give them an idea of where the photo was taken."

House looked at Swift with his eyes wide, "What is social media?"

Chapter 11

House and Swift arrived at a used car dealership. Swift advised House to stay in the car while he went to talk to the guy. House used the opportunity to look at the other information Team Shadow had gathered.

House learned Charles Young was medically retired. The notes included Young had liver cancer and had few months left to live. Young was living somewhere in the Middle TN area and efforts were ongoing to figure out exactly where.

The file on Maria Silva was useless. There was no information about her besides when she separated from the police department. What House found interesting is it was a few days after he was found guilty.

"House! Come pick your car," yelled Swift.

House exited Swift's car, "What do you mean pick?"

"The owner owed us a favor. Pick something basic. You don't want to stick out."

House looked at the selection of cars on the lot, "All of these cars look like shit."

"I hope you didn't think you were going to get something fancy. You just need something to get you around. Whatever you pick, the owner is going to make sure it's right." said Swift

House continuing to walk around the lot, "So I got to pick the best of the worst? Great. Well, this doesn't seem that bad."

House walked up to a Chevy Impala, "Swift, I guess this will work."

"It seems you're still a cop at heart," said Swift laughing.

"What do you mean?"

"Impalas were and still are police cars."

House further examined the car and realized his police department was in the process of changing to them. "I thought this looked familiar."

"I let the owner know and we can roll out to that training area you were talking about." said Swift

Swift went back into the office. House continued to walk around the Impala, checking for imperfections.

"House, he's going to have the mechanic check it out. We'll come to get it in a few days. Let's roll out. How far is it again?"

"Livingston is about an hour away." answered House.

House and Swift started to head towards Livingston. It was a cooler summer evening and there were no clouds in the sky.

"I don't think I've seen one streetlight. I'm glad there are a lot of stars out tonight," said Swift.

House was looking out the window and didn't respond to Swift. He had flashbacks of driving down this road to training. With everything he had recently learned, he wondered how many officers were using what they were learning to benefit themselves, rather than the public.

"Earth to House. Are we almost there? We have been driving for a while."

"My bad. If I remember correctly, you need to turn right up here. There should be a sign."

Swift continued to drive until he saw a sign, "This is taking me down a dirt road."

"Yeah, a mile or so down the road and we are going to be there."

House and Swift pulled up to what appeared to be abandoned buildings.

"You sure we are in the right place," said Swift.

"Yep, this is it," House said as he stepped out of the car.

The training site appeared like someone had not been there for a few years. House started to walk towards some of the buildings in the back, "This way Swift. Something should be back here."

"There better be. I didn't want to drive out here for nothing."

"Swift, to clear things up for you. This entire training site was built by militia extremists in the 90s I believe. Periodically, some locals come out here and shoot. The State Troopers and other local law enforcement know this area isn't checked as it should be. So, this is the perfect place to store weapons, ammo, and tactical gear without getting unwanted attention."

House walked into one of the buildings and started feeling on the wall, knocking randomly.

"Got it," House found a false board and removed it, "Well shit."

The items House found had been left there for a while but some of them appeared to be in decent shape. There was a small dual-threat vest, a 9mm handgun, and some ammo.

"I hope you didn't think you were going to find an armory," said Swift.

House walked around the building to see if he could find anything else. He found a few more items but nothing of significant value.

Swift was looking around as well, "House, I got a bigger vest for you. You need to fire that gun. You don't want to figure out it doesn't work at the wrong time."

House knew Swift was right. He looked for some potential targets and set them up. He loaded the gun and started shooting.

"It's just like riding a bike, House. Good shit."

House was easily able to reload and fire successive shots without issue.

"I don't think we are going to find anything else. Time to head back."

A couple of days went by, and Swift received a phone call from the used car dealership advising him it was ready for pickup. House and Swift headed to the dealership and found everything was in working order.

"Swift, are we good now? This wasn't cheap," said the owner.

Swift looked around the car and everything appeared good as new. He popped the hood and could tell their mechanic went the extra mile to make sure there wouldn't be any issues.

"Yeah, we're good," said Swift as he stuck out his hand.

The owner and Swift shook hands. Swift turned to House, "I'll follow you back to the trailer. You haven't driven in a while."

House got in the car and headed back to the trailer. As he was driving down the road, he felt as if he had made the right choice. The car accelerated and braked with ease, it was roomier than he expected, and he noticed plenty of other ones on the road, making blending in easy.

As they arrived. Timothy was walking down the steps. He waved at House and Swift trying to get their attention.

"Everything ok, Timothy," asked House as he was exiting the car.

"I made a mistake and rented this trailer early by accident. I can put the kids up in a hotel for a few days unless I need to tell them something different," said Timothy.

"No, we will be leaving soon. Within the next 48hrs."

"Oh ok. Well, thank you for making this easy."

"Timothy, let's walk and talk."

House and Timothy started to walk down the street. "Timothy, I'm going after those who put me behind bars. From what I was able to figure out, it has something to do with some crooked cops in my old police department."

Timothy stopped walking. He was shocked House told him this. There was a slight feeling of joy that House trusted him with this information. However, he wondered why now?

"Are you sure it's safe," said Timothy.

"Of course, it's not safe. That doesn't matter. I just want to thank you once again. Never did I picture myself being in the situation I found myself in years ago. Looking out for you and your family seemed to be one of the smartest decisions I ever made."

"No, House, I need to thank you. There is no telling what would have happened to me if you didn't see the reason why I was doing what I was doing."

"The reasoning you provided wasn't the first time I had heard that. A lot of men are willing to go to great lengths to provide for their families. It was just a hunch, or some would say, divine intervention that told me if I gave you a way out, you would do the right thing. Anyway, I am letting you know what my intentions are. If anyone comes to speak to you, you will tell them you haven't seen me in years. Swift is currently removing everything we brought into the trailer. Have a cleaning crew thoroughly clean it. As a matter of fact, have two different companies clean it."

"Do you really think that is necessary?"

"We are dealing with what I believe we are, yes. We cannot afford to make a mistake."

Timothy remembered how thorough the police were when they came to the pharmacy. They went through everything. Even the things he swore they would miss. If the police thought there was something involving one of their own, Timothy knew they would be more determined to find something.

"I will make sure it's dirty between both cleanings. If it appears clean, one of the companies might not do anything," said Timothy.

"Sounds like a plan," said House, "Continue to do great things and make your family proud."

"Why does it seem like you are saying goodbye?"

House turned towards Timothy and stuck out his hand, "It's because I am. Regardless if things go right or wrong, I will not be returning here. I don't want to risk anything happening to your family. You take care of yourself."

Timothy shook House's hand. In the handshake, he felt how sincere House was about protecting his family. There was an intensity in House's eyes. Timothy had never seen House like this before. However, that look let him know House was on a mission. A mission he would complete regardless of the risk involved.

They headed back to the trailer and Swift was still loading items into both cars.

"House, you square everything away," said Swift.

"Yeah. Everything's good," replied House while acknowledging Timothy's departure.

"Well, this is where we part ways. I will head to Alabama for North; you head to Nashville to see what you can find out about Silva."

"What about Young?"

"My abuela told me a long time ago it's hard to leave this world and have peace in the next if something is weighing heavy on your mind. There is a reason he has lived this long having cancer at his age." said Swift.

House figured Swift was right in his assessment of the situation. The reason is Charles Young wouldn't be much help either way. A deathbed confession could seem forced. Also, if everything went as planned and this case was brought to trial, there was little chance he would be asked to testify.

"I have one more thing to give you," Swift opened up his car door and reached under the passenger seat.

Swift handed House a shoebox, "I do my best to keep some cash on hand. From here on out. Only pay with cash. This goes for food, gas, hotels, everything"

"This isn't my first rodeo."

"Well, they do say cops make the best criminals. We know what to do and not to do. I am going to head out. I prefer to do most of my driving at night. One more thing. Limit the calls to me. We should only be speaking to each other if we have new information to share. If one of us doesn't respond to a phone call within 48hrs. We are to assume the worst and continue the mission."

House was impressed by how serious Swift was taking the investigation. Swift was treating this like one of his operations overseas or when he was with the State Department. This also reminded House how serious this was. House knew all the preparation was well worth it. It was time to right the wrong.

"House, it's time to clear your name," Swift got in his car and drove off.

Chapter 12

Swift was riding down the interstate headed towards Alabama. He had already called his connections for a place to stay near Gulf Shores. It was one of the cooler evenings in the summer. Swift had the windows down, breathing in the air.

Most of the travel he did was during the evening or at night. He hated waiting in traffic or having someone ride his bumper. Swift also felt the more cars on the road, the more likely someone would have the ability to recognize his vehicle. Even though it was an everyday car and color, everything would be more accessible if they couldn't identify the make and model.

"This is as good a spot as any," Swift said as he pulled over to the shoulder of the road and reached into his glove box.

When Swift went undercover in a new city for years, he did two things. The first was to smoke a Cuban cigar to signify victory before it happened and write a haiku. He never allowed anyone to see his ritual. Swift was always the gun-ho person ready to do what needed to be done. He believed someone saw him do these things; it would be a kink in his armor. He would become "normal" by showing he was actually nervous.

"Shit, I must have smoked that last cigar when leaving Cali," Swift said to himself.

He looked at the clock. It was 8 pm. He proceeds to get out of the car and say, "Where the fuck am I?" He sighed, "Well, I am sure if there was a cigar shop near, it's closed now. I'll get the cigar in the morning."

He went to the car trunk and got a small mat with writing material. He was running short on daylight and had to at least get his haiku done. He laid the carpet on the ground and kneeled down. "Ok, let's get this done."

Summers glowing sun

Winds of change occurring soon

Waters bringing life

He stood back up and placed the items back with the other few dozen haikus he had written. He never re-read what he previously wrote nor cared if they were viewed as good. He was content with them as long as they met the five-seven-five syllable rule.

He added this to his ritual during one of Swift's operations in Japan. In Swift's little spare time during his career, he loved studying warriors from different eras. Samurai was his favorite; he learned about the death poems written before missions or battles considered suicidal. Traditional death poems are focused on reflection. Swift rarely took the time to reflect on his life. He instead continues to look forward to his next adventure. So, his poems reflected what was currently happening around him.

Understanding what could happen in an unknown situation is why he did this after smoking the "victory" cigar.

Swift understood this would be considered contradictory to most people. Claiming victory in one instance and preparing for death in another. However, like the Kamikaze, Swift believed there was a victory to be had even with death. Achieving success is absolute for Swift, even if it costs him his life.

Swift's phone started ringing. It was House calling.

"Yes, the phone works," Swift answered.

"Someone sent me an encrypted message. Did they send it to you?"

House responded.

Swift also looked at his phone and saw he had received the message. He recognized the number. It was from Team Shadow. He opened the text. "Shit."

"What's going on," House asked. "Obviously, it cannot be good."

"The message states Maria Silva traveled back to Brazil in 2018 and has not returned to the United States. I have limited connections in other countries. So, I must believe this is correct.

"It's a good thing I planned on leaving in the morning," House replied. "Time to speak to Young."

"Let me once again verify Young's location. I'm about an hour away from the Alabama border. I'll reach out and let you know when I have something." House agreed and ended the phone call.

Swift took a deep breath and lit a cigarette. House wouldn't have had the ability to access the encrypted file. There was a specific code that changed weekly. Files that were not opened deleted themselves in 48 hours. Incorrect codes prompt the device for a factory reset. Swift figured House knew this or figured it out, and that's why he called him.

Swift had lied to House. The message had revealed Maria Silva's last known location. She was also in Alabama.

Chapter 13

The next day, Swift informed House he confirmed Charles Young's location. He recently switched to in-home hospice care. Signifying his passing was happening sooner than expected. Swift wanted to wrap up his investigation with North quickly. From what they were able to figure out, Young appeared to be a key player. Swift wanted to be there to ask questions House may not.

"House, Young lives in Goodlettsville, TN, near Moss Wright Park. Do you know where that is?"

"Yes," House replied. "I used to work out and run around the two-mile trail there. There is a big subdivision over there. It will be hard to pinpoint a home."

"Research hospice companies in the area and compare costs," Swift stated," I assume Young would be using a more expensive company."

"How are things on your end?" House asked, "You have an idea of where North is?"

"Lucky for me, it is the end of summer, and I'll I would need to do is go to where the locals hang out. Plan on hearing back in a few days, House."

Swift ended the phone call, and House started to head toward Nashville.

Swift had asked some locals about the picture he acquired from Jessica's Facebook; from what he was told, it was taken around Fort Morgan. Unfortunately, this didn't help Swift because no houses or apartments were nearby.

While driving back into the city, Swift went to *Sassy Bass Amazin' Grill* from the local's recommendations. He hadn't taken the time to eat since starting his road trip. This was normal for Swift. When the mission begins, he focuses on getting the job done as quickly and efficiently as possible.

"What can I get you, sir," said the waitress.

"I'll just take a water for now," said Swift, without looking away from the menu.

"Ok, my name is Jess; let me know when you are ready to order."

Swift quickly up. Jess looked at him with a big, beautiful smile and walked away.

"Did I really get this lucky?" Swift said to himself. "No, it cannot be her."

Jess returned with the water. "Have you decided on anything yet?" She asked.

"How long have you been working here?"

Swift didn't have much to go on. However, he figured this would give him some insight.

"Umm, well, just a few months. Why do you ask?"

There was a quiver when she answered. Jess was hiding something, but what was it?

"I just wanted your recommendation on something. I'm not picky. I assume you have tried a few things by now."

"Our lunch menu is limited, but we have a large dinner menu. So, please be sure to come back for that one day, but The Bird is a popular choice for lunch."

"Ok, I will take that. I don't need fries or anything."

"I'll get it started for you."

Swift stepped outside to smoke a cigarette and to quickly look up information on Jessica North after she left the MNPD. Swift's only photos of North were from when she arrived at the academy and at her first precinct. They were pretty much identical since they were only a few months apart. However, those photos were twenty years old.

Jessica separated from the MNPD shortly after House was incarcerated. There were no public records of her that were of interest. However, there was an interesting news article he found.

The article's title was *"Former Metro Nashville police officer involved in a hit and run incident."*

It continued' *"Jessica North was a former Metro Nashville police officer. She was struck by a vehicle while crossing Jackson Hill Road in Montgomery Bell Park. Witnesses nearby said they heard a vehicle suddenly accelerate and then a loud bang. North was life-flighted to Vanderbilt Hospital and underwent emergency surgery."*

"If you have any information to help the investigation, please contact the local Sheriff's department."

"If this is her, she may have visible scars from the accident or surgery."

Swift returned to the restaurant, and Jess brought the order to the table.

"Oh, there you are. I thought you left."

"No, I just stepped outside to smoke a cigarette. Thank you."

As Jess started to walk away, he noticed some surgical scars on her face and hands. Swift tipped over his cup.

"Sorry about that, do you have any more napkins?" Swift asked.

"Don't worry. I'll get it." said Jess.

When she leaned over to clean the spill, Swift noticed her hair was a different color at the root, which meant she could have dyed her hair.

She walked away as Swift was preparing to take a bite of his sandwich. Then, however, she turned back around and headed toward the table.

"If you don't mind me asking, what is your name?" Jess asked.

"It's Trek"

"Trek? Like *Star Trek?*"

"Yes."

"Oh, cool! You seem familiar, so I thought I would ask…. I'll take a break in a few minutes. Is it ok if I sit with you?"

"Why would I turn down the chance to sit with a pretty lady?" Swift said with a smile on his face.

Blood rushed to Jess's face, "I will be back in five minutes."

This was just the opportunity Swift needed to gain valuable information to see if this was whom he thought.

Jess and Swift talked for thirty minutes. Jess talked about living in Gulf Shores and working at the restaurant. Swift spoke about his time in the military.

"So, before you moved here, where did you live?" asked Swift.

"Well…I."

"Ms. Patrick, someone is on the phone for you," Someone yelled from the front of the store.

Jess looked at her phone first. "Shoot, I forgot they were going to call me today," Jess said. "My break is almost over anyway; it was nice talking to you, Trek."

"Same," Swift responded. He left cash for his bill and walked out of the restaurant.

By hearing Jess's last name, there was a chance he could learn something. He sent her name to members of Team Shadow.

Swift decided to stay near the restaurant to see when Jess got off. Unfortunately, a few hours went by, and Swift was losing sunlight. Tracking her in the dark would be easy if he had a better idea of her mannerism.

Swift also considered going back into the restaurant. It was dinner time, and he could state that he was interested in the menu to not raise additional suspicion. However, more and more people were showing up, decreasing his field of vision. "Shit," Swift thought, "This may take longer than expected."

Swift observed the restaurant outside the building for the next couple of days. It wasn't the easiest thing to do because of the restaurant's location: There was only one way in and one way out for vehicles; all of the nearby homes seemed occupied, so Swift couldn't be near them for long. In addition, the restaurant was on the beach, so the terrain was flat.

Swift found it odd that he did not see Jess any of these days. Even though it was the end of summer, they were still busy. So, he went in for dinner one day to see if she switched shifts.

He went in and sat at the bar. "Is Jess working today?" He asked the bartender.

"Is she a friend of yours?" he replied

"Sorta, I came in a few days ago, and we had a good conversation."

"Hm," He replied, "Well, she hasn't been her…."

"Bill, stop lying! Hi, Trek!" Jess said with a smile. "Did you come back to try some stuff on the dinner menu? It's really good."

Jess explained to Swift herself and Bill went on a few dates when she first started working at the restaurant. Bill was still upset it didn't work out.

"Yes, I did. Actually, what time do you get off tonight? Maybe we can go to another local spot?"

"Sure, I'm game. I actually just got cut, so let me grab my things. Meet me out front?"

Jess proceeded to walk to the back of the store. Swift looked at Bill with a smirk, and Bill threw the towel he was holding.

Swift went to the parking lot and waited for Jess. "Trek, do you just want to follow me"

"Sounds good to me," Swift replied. "You have an idea of where you are taking me?"

"It's a surprise. You just have to keep up."

Swift walked Jess to her vehicle, and he proceeded to walk to his. Swift had purchased a small pickup from a local when he arrived in Gulf Shores. He put his car in storage. This was a common practice to avoid being identified in smaller towns.

Once Swift got into the truck, Jess pulled in front of him, and they headed into town. After close to thirty minutes, they pulled into *Tacky Jacks*. Swift and Jessica exited their vehicles.

"I hope you like local music!" Jess screamed, "I love this place. The only downfall is they close in an hour. I am glad I was able to get off early."

Swift and Jess went inside the restaurant and ordered a few drinks. Neither Jess nor Swift was hungry, so they ordered some appetizers.

The local band was covering some 2000s country.

Jess was singing along with the band. "I'm sorry, Trek," Jess started laughing. "I think I might have had one too many. Carrie Underwood is one of my favorites."

"I don't think I know that many of her songs. The country isn't my thing."

"I went to college in Nashville. My roommates played country all the time."

"Bingo," Swift thought. He placed Jess in Nashville. While he was still waiting to hear back from Team Shadow, he already established Jessica North was a college athlete in that city. Swift decided to ask follow-up questions that would provide him with a better timeline.

"When did you move down here? Do you have family here?"

"I engaged in a bad situation and needed a change. We all need that sometimes, right?"

"Bad situation." Swift thought. "Is it her involvement with the police department or the accident she is referring to?"

"Trek, what's going on? You have this distant look in your eye."

"Huh? Sorry, I'm just tired."

"You can crash at my place tonight. It's walking distance from here. My girlfriend wouldn't mind."

"Girlfriend," Swift asked, puzzled. "You never mentioned her."

"Well, I am now. She is like the sister I never had. Plus, she isn't in town until the morning."

Jess started rubbing Swift's leg and started kissing him on the neck.

Swift was still waiting to hear back from Team Shadow, but he wasn't going to let this opportunity slip away. Swift couldn't risk finding concrete evidence of who she was, "I'm ready when you are," Swift stated, throwing cash down on the bar top.

Swift and Jess walked about two blocks down the street, hugging and kissing each other the entire time. Once they arrived at Jess's home, she advised Swift to wait in the living room while she took a shower. Swift used this opportunity to look around the house.

The home was relatively small, and there weren't any pictures of Jess or her roommate anywhere. It appeared they could have only been in it for a couple of months. Beside one couch and a breakfast table, there was no other furniture. Boxes were pushed into a corner. From what Swift could see, they were unopened. The tape on them looked new.

On the table was a laptop. Swift heard Jess singing in the shower, so he figured he still had some time. Swift's phone contained spyware for situations like this. He connected this phone to the laptop and started running the software.

"Hey, Trek, why don't you join me? I'm sure you could also use a shower!" shouted Jess.

"On my way," Swift responded. The spyware was close to being downloaded. It only needed about a minute or so left. He lit a cigarette and opened a window.

"Trek, you don't want to shower with me?" Jess said sadly. Swift turned around and saw Jess standing in the hallway naked. Swift smiled. "I knew what I was getting into, so I grabbed a cig first."

"It's impolite to keep a lady waiting; come on." Jess turned around and started walking back towards the bathroom.

Swift looked at the laptop and saw the spyware had completed downloading. He unplugged his phone and headed into the bathroom.

Chapter 14

Jess woke Swift up around six in the morning.

"Trek, I have to get ready for work. What are your plans for the day?" asked Jess.

Swift didn't attend to spend the night. He realized he had gotten too comfortable and knew he could let this happen again. Swift quickly gathered his things and started to exit the bedroom.

"I don't mean to sound like I am kicking you out. Last night was fun, Trek. How long are you going to be in town?" Jess inquired.

Swift turned around, "A Day or so. I'm retired, so I am in no rush."

"You're a little young to be retired."

"Yeah, I get that a lot."

A car was pulling into the driveway. "Is this your girlfriend…I'm sorry roommate. Should I be nervous?" Swift said jokingly.

Jess walked out of the bedroom and looked out the kitchen window, "No, why would you need to be?" Jess started to wave at the person in the vehicle. "Do you want to meet her?"

"Maybe at a different time. How do I get back to my truck?"

Jess and Swift walked out of the house and onto the patio.

"Just make a right and keep straight for a few blocks. You will see the sign. Here's my number if you want to meet me before heading out of town. Goodbye, Trek" Jess kissed Swift on the cheek and moved to the driveway.

Swift started walking towards the road. "Once I get back to my laptop, I'll see what I can get from the spyware. As a matter of fact." Swift a message to Team Shadow advising them of what he had done. Since everything ties back to their secure network, they would be able to access it and provide Swift with some answers quicker.

The person in the vehicle got out and said, "Jess, it seems like you had fun last night." with a laugh. This individual had an accent Swift couldn't place at the moment. He was experiencing the side effects of his drinking last night. He looked back to see what the person looked like. He only saw a side profile of her face. She was around Swift's height, 5'8-5'9, with brown skin, an average build, and long dark hair. He couldn't see any visible tattoos.

Jess waved at Swift while the roommate was gathering her items from the car. Swift waved and started walking back to *Tacky Jacks*.

Swift's phone started ringing. It was a blocked number. A common practice Team Shadow used when they had information. Swift answered, *"Anata wa kage ni sunde imasu ka?"* This is Japanese, meaning "Do you live in the shadows?" The person responded, *"Ōku no uchi no 1tsu,"* meaning "One of many." Because of this, Swift knew he was speaking to someone from Team Shadow.

"Make this quick," Swift said.

"From the spyware you installed last night, we figured out Jess Patrick *is* Jessica North. After her accident, she has moved from state to state and has changed her name many times."

"Currently, we are not able to get any financial information. She has no property in her name. No known children, never married, her parents are deceased, and no contact with her siblings after she was discharged from the hospital."

"Anything else?"

"We have reason to believe you have been compromised. The laptop attempted to locate a source of the spyware. We were able to prevent it from recognizing the Blackberry. However, the laptop could recover the day, time, and approximate hack location within a klick. We have already attempted to access data from other data points in the area, so it doesn't look like this is an isolated attempt."

Swift stopped and surveyed the area around him. It didn't appear that he was being followed. "How is this possible? I took every precaution as usual. Fuck!" Swift ended the call and proceeded to call another number in his phone, "Stay within 30 meters and maintain visual," and hung up.

He continued to *Tacky Jacks* to pick up his truck.

****

House had arrived in Nashville and attempted to familiarize himself with the city. A lot had changed during his incarnation. He still needed to find Charles Young. He took Swift's advice and looked for an upscale, in-home hospice company. Some of the companies were more helpful than the others, however, none of them provided enough information to let them know if Young was one of their patients.

House then went to Goodlettsville and started knocking on doors in the subdivision near Moss Wright Park. He pretended to be a new neighbor. A few of the residents talked to him. The ones that did confirm there were a few retired police officers that lived there. In the evenings, House would rotate the homes he was watching to see if he could see if any of them were Young. There was one address that seemed promising but when House knocked on the door, no one answered, no matter the time of day. The SUV in the driveway had a bumper sticker stating, "Lead from the Front," a motto from the precinct. There was another MNPD decal on the rear windshield. House took a photo of the car with the license plate and sent it to the Information number programmed into the phone.

Since House had been in Goodlettsville, he would spend the mornings at Moss Wright Park and would workout. This was a method he used as an officer to help him think about a case without being interrupted.

After his morning jog, he took a cooldown walk. First, he listened to the distant laughter of children playing at the jungle gym. Then, he heard the perfect connection between a bat hitting a baseball and the parents screaming for their child's team.

As House finished his cooldown lap, he headed towards *Mansker's Station, a* replica plantation house and fort. As he approached the fort, he heard some yelling. A voice yelled, "Charles, this is the third time we have taken this tour; there isn't anything new we are going to learn!"

"Quit complaining," he responded. "I'm just wanting to get out of the house!"

It had been days and House still hadn't heard back from Team Shadow. This could have been the break House desperately needed. The person assisting them with the tour calmed them down and continued showing them around.

After seeing the people in question, he returned to his nearby car. This was the best way for him to track them once they started to leave the park.

There were two males. The first one was older, had to be in the mid to late 60s, and the younger one had to be in his early twenties. He wasn't wearing scrubs, so House figured it was possibly the older male's grandson. The older male also was wearing a facemask and looked fragile.

House didn't know how long the tour would take, but it was nearly noon, and the fall sun could be unforgiving in Tennessee even though it was a week passed Labor Day. So, they would want to get the older male out of the sun soon.

Thirty minutes passed, and House saw them heading his way. The younger one helped the older one get into the SUV, and he soon followed suit. Once they started to leave, House followed them, giving them enough distance to not seem obvious.

It was the same vehicle House was waiting to receive information on. The SUV pulled into Hendersonville Hospital. When they arrived, a nurse was outside of the hospital with a wheelchair. "They must have alerted them of their upcoming arrival," House thought, "This isn't standard practice for any hospital I know of."

The younger one exited the car, assisted the older one into the chair, and drove off.

House parked his vehicle and headed inside. There was a sign on the door saying, "Mask required upon entry." House complied and grabbed one from a nearby table.

The hospital looked generic, nothing different from what House had seen before. There were signs in the hospital advising visitors to stay six feet apart and to stay home if they exhibited cold symptoms.

"Hi, can I help you?" said the receptionist.

"I'm looking for the guy just brought in here in a wheelchair."

"Are you family? I don't think I have seen you before."

The receptionist was a short, heavy-set woman that appeared to be in her fifties. She had short hair and wore glasses. The hospital ID she was wearing said "caring for patients since 1996." In the past, House had dealt with tenured hospital staff before. They were the most difficult to get information from.

"You are right; you haven't. My aunt said he didn't have long. We haven't talked in years, but I feel like we should clear the air. I pulled up as soon as he was being dropped off. I was told he undergoes some treatment here."

The receptionist's eyes narrowed, and she looked at House over her glasses. House realized what he said didn't make sense. Why would his aunt have him meet here instead of at her home or somewhere more intimate?

House thought about abandoning the conversation and going to look for Young himself. However, he felt as if he did that; she would have security search for him in the hospital.

House looked behind him. There was a small line forming. He turned back around and saw a sign that said "Out-patient surgery check-in here." House knew the best course of action was to disengage and walk out of the hospital. He thanked the receptionist for her time and stepped aside.

"What to do now," House said to himself. He knew there was little possibility he could wait for Young to leave the hospital, but he didn't know what kind of care he was receiving.

House used this time to call the Information number to see if they had anything to tell him. No one answered.

He received a callback and was informed the car was registered to Brian Young, his grandson, and the address provided for the SUV was Brian's home.

House decided to wait for Young to be picked up from the hospital and follow him to his home. Another hour or so went by and House saw a nurse pushing someone in a wheelchair back out front. A car was pulling up at the same time. However, this was a different one that House had seen before. He still couldn't get a good look at the person in the wheelchair because he had a mask on his face.

House got out of his vehicle to take a picture of the license plate and text to the information number programmed in his phone. He quickly received a callback and was told the car belonged to Chelsea Williams. Chelsea was a registered nurse in Tennessee and has worked for a private company specializing in at-home hospice care. She had a home in Hendersonville.

This provided House with much-needed information. He was able to gain two possible addresses for Young. "Let's see where you are going."

Chelsea and the other nurse assisted Charles into the car, then drove off.

House followed them at a safe distance. Chelsea had made one stop for gas and another stop at a restaurant. House waited in his car for them to return to theirs.

It was close to 7 pm, and House would soon lose daylight. He was unfamiliar with the area of Hendersonville he was in and knew he had to get closer to them as they were headed into a neighborhood.

"Indian Lake Road," House said to help familiarize himself with where he was at. It was a cooler night, so he had the windows down and heard jet skis and boats. He looked to his right and saw a marina close by.

Chelsea was taking a series of rights and lefts. He felt he did a great job of not giving; he was tailing them. The neighborhood was densely populated, so he periodically let a vehicle or two get in front of him to hide his attention.

Chelsea had appeared to turn on a dead-end street, and *smash* House was rear-ended and knocked off the road.

Chapter 15

"He is finally waking up," a voice said.

House was stirring. His head felt like someone had smacked him with a sledgehammer, and his body was no better. He was tied to a chair and couldn't tell if he had broken bones. His nose was running, he wondered if it was blood or snot. His mouth was taped shut, and he was blindfolded.

"Why were you following me, House?" said another in a dry, raspy voice.

The voice sounded familiar. However, House couldn't place it. Nothing was identifiable on him, and the phone would have been erased if the wrong password had been entered too many times. Even the car he was currently driving was registered to Timothy Shane for this situation. To say his name, the person had to be familiar with what he looked like, even after ten years.

Someone started to take the blindfold off. It was an older Black man who was frail, shaky, and looked like someone had drained the majority of water out of his body. If it wasn't for his walker, he would surely fall over.

"You don't recognize me, do you? Well, I remember when you were a rookie officer. This is Sergeant Charles Young." Young stated as he was walking toward a chair.

A college-aged adult was walking towards House. He must have been the first voice he heard. He looked like he could be a relative of Young.

They proceeded to take the tape off of House's mouth.

"You have gotten rusty due to your time in prison. You wouldn't have made such rookie mistakes."

"How so?" asked House.

"For starters, you would have been so anxious to see if it was me in the hospital. You also wouldn't have made up that terrible lie about why you needed to see me."

Deep down, House knew Young was correct. He played his hand too early instead of walking around the hospital and possibly running into Young. He also knew it was highly likely that the receptionist would have told Young a relative was looking for him.

"I see it in your eyes, House. You want to know how long I knew you were following me. Well, my grandson first mentioned watching us at the park. He's always paranoid, so I ignored him." said Young.

"*cough cough* Excuse me. Son, can you bring me some water."

The grandson grabbed a bottle of water, opened it, and gave it to Young.

"Sorry about that House. I am sure you know I don't have much time left."

"You seem to have plenty since you decided to kidnap me." House replied.

"Fair enough. So, what do you know so far? Let's not waste the little time I have."

House could sense Young was being serious. House started to look around and couldn't figure out where he was. They were not at a house, and it didn't seem like they were in a warehouse. From what he could see, everything seemed clean. Plastic covered the walls and drop cloths were on the floor. "This must be a newer building." House thought, "Or one in the middle of a remodel."

"You won't figure out where we are, so you might as well tell me what it is. Fate didn't bring us together. Someone told you something." said Young.

Young's demeanor was that of someone thirty years his junior. He did his best to hide how his illness was affecting him.

However, Young didn't realize his grandson did a terrible job tying him up. When House looked into his grandson's eyes, he could sense his fear. House looked down at his hands, they were trembling. It appeared he was following orders more than wanting to do this.

"What is your name," House said to the grandson.

"Brian," He responded.

Brian was a short, average-built, bi-racial young adult.

"You don't want to be in—" "Stop talking to him!" Young interrupted. He started coughing again due to his yelling.

"Grandad, you have to calm down," Brian said to calm his grandfather.

"Shut up, boy!" Young responded. "You don't need to speak to House. I knew one day you would come looking for answers. You must have had help to get this far. You should have let an older man die in peace. I will give you one more chance to tell me who is helping you."

Young walked over to a table and removed a towel covering a gun. "Here, Brian. Are you ready to earn your keep?"

Brian's eyes widened and his heart appeared to be beating a thousand beats per minute. He struggled to push the words that were on the edge of his lips. He couldn't have been a day over twenty-five, and he was being tasked to take the life of someone he didn't know. He didn't even know why his grandfather wanted to kill this man.

Brian took a deep breath and grabbed the gun. His hand was shaking. House had already freed one of his hands from the terrible knot job that Brian had done.

"As soon as the moment presents itself, I have to go for the gun." House thought, "I don't want to hurt the kid, let me see if I can convince him to toss it."

"Brian, you aren't built for this. I can tell." House stated, " Just put the gun down and walk away. You have nothing to do with this."

"Son, this is the price we must sometimes pay to protect our family," Young said. "Do this, and we can go home."

"Both of y'all can go to hell!" Brian shouted, pointing the gun toward House. "I don't need anyone to tell me what to do!"

Brian had once wanted to be a police officer, staying with family tradition. When he was a child, his father was killed in the line of duty. The murderers were never brought to justice. In his teenage years, he heard rumors his father didn't believe in covering for his fellow officers; and this is what led to his death. His father called for backup, but it came late, very late. When he asked his grandfather to tell him the truth as an adult, he was dismissive; claiming he didn't know what happened.

Now, being in this situation, Brian felt this must have been what his dad felt. Do the wrong thing and gain the approval of other officers or do the right thing and risk your life.

"Do it," said Young.

"Shut up," Brian responded.

"This doesn't concern you," said House.

"I said, SHUT UP!" Brian closed his eyes and started to raise his gun toward House.

Brian had mistakenly walked too close to House, and House suddenly lunged at Brian with his free hand. The gun went off, and a round went into the wall.

House struck Brian in his ribs and wrestled the gun away.

"Brian, you are a worthless muthafucka, you know that?" Young said with a disgusted look on his face.

"Answer me, Brian!" screamed Young.

"That is no way to talk to a member of your family. Let alone your grandchild, Young." House said as he was walking to Brian.

Brian was sitting on the ground with a defeated look in his eyes.

"Get outta here, Brian. As I said, this has nothing to do with you. I promise you I won't kill him."

House stuck his hand out towards Brian. Attempting to show he had no ill intentions toward him. Brian looked at House's hand and then at House in his eyes.

"There is still time, Brian. You can still kill House."

"No, grandad. It's over." Brian took House's hand and stood up.

"You're as good as dead to me."

"Good thing you don't have long to live...House, we are in one of my newer office spaces in Gallatin off of Airport Road. Handle what you need with my grandfather, but I will not provide you with a ride back once we are done here, regardless of what happens. Consider me telling you where we are as my sign of good faith. No cameras and limited electricity in this building." said Brian.

House nodded and turned towards Young. Young was visibly upset. He snarled and was breathing rapidly. House knew even at his age if he wasn't dealing with cancer, he would have been a tough person to deal with.

"Balls in my court," House said with a laugh.

"Get to it, House," Young angrily replied.

"As you stated, let's not waste each other's time."

Young slammed his fist on the table. "Thinking you were so cunning was your downfall, House. No one likes you. That's why you didn't have assistance during your trial. No one cares. However, receiving your release was the biggest mistake that Warden ever made!"

"I understand how you feel about me, and we aren't here to talk about that. I have a friend that told me you cannot pass into the afterlife unless you try to make amends in this life. If you want to suffer for five or ten more years, no problem. I will get my answers eventually. You just gave me one of them. Good to know y'all were keeping tabs on me."

"You are one of the smuggest bastards I have ever met in my life. I don't have shit to tell you. I thought I'd be dead and gone before you ever saw daylight."

House started walking towards Young, and Brian stepped in, shaking his head no.

"Move, Brian"

"I cannot let you harm him. He is a sick old man."

"I understand." House swiftly punched Brian in the stomach. Knocking all the wind out of him. Then, threw him to the side.

While Brian was gasping for air, Young attempted to get up and confront House. "I'll kill you if you touch him again!" Young exclaimed.

"You didn't seem worried about him a few moments ago. Interesting."

Brian was writhing on the ground in pain, and House picked him up and cocked his fist back.

"Stop! He is my only grandson. You want to know what went down, right? I'll take it to my grave if you hit him again."

Young had shown he was human. This could have been an old, dying man's attempt to make things right in the world; realizing he was trying to make his grandson something he is not.

House let Brian go, and Brian slumped over, reaching for a chair.

Young's phone started ringing. "I have to answer this. It is Chelsea, my nurse. If I don't, she will call the police.

House couldn't risk the chance Young wasn't bluffing. The best course of action was to let him answer the phone, "Choose your words wisely," House responded.

"This is Charles…. yes, Brian and I are still out looking at some properties…..I know it's late; we'll be back soon enough." Young hung up the phone.

"We better make this quick, House."

House looked around for something to take notes with since he noticed the phone was nowhere in sight and all his other possessions were with him. "Where is my phone?" House asked.

Brian pointed to a Faraday Bag on a table between coughs. House took his phone out and realized they had never tried to unlock or destroy it. House opened the voice memo and pressed the record button.

"Sargent Charles Young, what was your involvement in my arrest and/or prosecution?"

"Zero. And that's God's honest truth."

"Why should I believe you?"

"Somehow, I knew you would end up asking me some questions. Earlier, I said I thought I would be dead before this would happen but honestly, the universe has a funny way of doing things. I'd be lying if I said you lacked natural investigative talent. So let me tell you what you may already know."

Young began, "I worked in the evidence control room for the last twenty years of my career. I wasn't one of the cops the department or neighborhood would remember forever. I had a nagging injury from some scrap with a wannabe thug and needed to be off the streets. Pushing paper was something I never wanted to do. "

"Moving into evidence was the end of my career, House. There was no way that I could make rank and make my retirement the size I figured I could. But, on the other hand, I thought I could be a halfway decent lieutenant. So anyway, I was approached with an offer most people wouldn't refuse."

"What was that?" House asked. He leaned forward to make sure he would hear what Young had to say clearly.

Young got up and started to shuffle around the room. He appeared to be gathering his thoughts.

"What do we do with items that are in evidence? The obvious doesn't always happen. Simply put, many things that go into evidence aren't used for their intended purpose. Rape kits aren't checked, and weapons aren't returned to owners. Hell, even some departments use them to supplement their own armory. Drugs aren't destroyed. Drug money funds departmental needs while telling citizens we need more of their tax money. The system is shit when it comes to this."

"Did I help them with this?" House thought. "How many officers thought they were doing the right thing just for other officers to put it back on the street? How many innocent people were harmed? How many cases were thrown out?" House's head was swirling with the endless possibilities. However, he knew he needed to keep focus on what Young was saying.

"I was asked to use some of this to our...my advantage."

"You said it right the first time. We are doing good, Charles. Don't screw it up."

"Yes, ours. However, I don't know who the "our" actually was."

Young's eyes were getting heavy, and his breathing was getting shallow. House knew it would be a matter of time before passing out. However, he didn't know precisely what he could ask to get the next piece of the puzzle.

"I need something, Young; come on."

Young had sat back down and was taking deep breaths. Brian had finally regained his breath and went over to his grandfather.

"I need to take him home now. I can tell you what I know." Brian said.

House perked up. Brian would have been too young to know anything unless Charles had confessed something to him.

Young looked up at Brian with a look that said, "Don't say anything." However, he was too weak to verbally communicate it. Which could have been a good thing.

"What do you know, Brian?"

"When my grandfather was diagnosed with cancer, he started writing down what he did as a police officer. He did this for two reasons. First, some of my young cousins would never hear him speak about his past. Second, the doctors said it would keep his cognitive functions from rapidly declining. From chemo and the medications, he was on, sometimes he wrote about the things he was not proud of. When he was out of his lucid state, he would ball them up and throw them away. I collected all of those and read them."

Young had a shocked expression in his eyes. This let House know Brian was telling the truth and might have some information to help him.

"Did you ever read anything pertaining to me?" House inquired.

"A lot of it doesn't make sense to me, and I didn't keep them after I read it. My grandfather seemed to be involved in making items from evidence disappear. He would put something fake in the place of the actual items and would give them to a few police officers."

"Is that right?"

Young weakly looked at House and nodded his head; yes, then said, "The officers reintroduced these weapons, drugs, etc., back to the street. If the weapons were returned to me, I would ship them out of state. There were a few exceptions."

"What did you get out of it?" asked House.

"A percentage of the sales of everything. It seemed like a foolproof plan.

I carefully selected what was released and paid attention to the court cases for certain things. I made sure to pay attention to who was charged and who the lawyers were. If they were someone small time and used a public defender, the evidence was good to go." answered Young.

"We need to go now. I promise you what was discussed today will leave this room," Brian pleaded to House.

"Final question. Who was the one that approached you about this?"

"A female, easy on the eyes. She told me someone with some rank wanted to see this done. Don't remember her name. Some conditions need to be met to ensure I wasn't being set up. After that, we started until I had to retire…. which was shortly after your arrest."

"We are leaving now," Brian said firmly. He helped Young down a hallway, then stopped halfway and turned around. "I don't want to get involved with this more than I already have. Please leave us alone and don't follow us." He continued back down the hallway.

Chapter 16

After House heard Brian and Young leave, he went to a nearby gas station. It was the middle of the night, and no cars were in the parking lot. House went inside and an attendant was watching old cartoons.

"Hello, are there any cheap hotels nearby?" House asked.

The attendant looked up, "When did you get here? I didn't see a car pull up."

"I walked here. Listen, I'm in-between living situations and I'm not familiar with this city. I completed a job a few hours ago for cash. I'm just looking for a place to lay my head.

The attendant looked at House. He could see the dirt on his shirt, pants, and shoes.

"It must have been a big job. There is a place, but it is a few miles from here. I'd give you a ride if I wasn't the only person here. Just follow the road to the next red light then make a right. You will walk straight to it."

"Thanks."

House started to walk towards the hotel. "Young was receiving his queues from a woman. Was it North or Silva? Even if it was one of them, I doubt they were the ringleader. There is no way Young would ever listen to someone whom he outranked. I'm missing something but what is it?"

When House woke up, he noticed an alert on his phone. Charles Young had passed away in his sleep in the early morning hours. House figured this confirmed what he initially thought and that everything he did with the phone was routed back to Team Shadow.

It had nearly been two months since House had made contact with Swift. Even though it was now in the middle of October, the weather in Tennessee wouldn't have let you know it was indeed the fall.

Upon their last conversation, either of them could reach out once they gained some valuable information.

House called Swift, but there was no answer. House wasn't worried about Swift not answering. He also wasn't going to call directly back due to worrying about how it could impact Swift's investigation.

As House was preparing to leave, he decided to turn on the tv, and an interesting commercial came across the screen.

For the better part of my life, I have dedicated myself to protecting the great citizens of Nashville. As a result, I reduced crime, created after-school programs, and have the highest approval rate of any acting Chief ever. Now, I am ready to protect the great state of Tennessee.

This ad was paid for by Chief Wilson Ellis for Governor.

"Who would have thought he would have run for governor? Wait a minute. This is it! This is why I was released. Ellis must have campaigned for my release. Hold on. If it was him, then why would it be a secret?"

****

Swift went into hiding after the revelation that he might have been compromised. He bounced from nearby cities, only paying in cash. This made it nearly impossible to know when he ever left or entered a city.

Swift stayed in constant contact with Team Shadow to see if they had any new development on him being tracked. Every time he reached out to them, they confirmed that accessing the other data points nearby seemed to be through whomever it was off the trail.

Swift couldn't bring himself to tell House what could have happened. He didn't want House to end his investigation to assist him in his mistake.

He looked at his phone and saw he had missed a call from House a few hours prior. "Of course, he would find Young before I'd finish up here." Swift said disappointingly, "I should have been done a month ago." There was also a notification on his phone stating Charles Young had passed away in his sleep at a hospital.

"I guess my Abuela *was* right. He had something that needed to be said to House."

Even though Swift was able to find out Jessica North was indeed whom he thought she was. He felt there was something off about her roommate. Why would she need to tell Swift she had one and why would he need to leave before her arrival? When he looked back on the morning after, it seemed she was rushing to get him out of the home more than she was focused on getting ready for work.

Which was the main reason he hadn't left the Gulf Shores area. Tourism season was over, and he believed he was running out of practical places to stay.

Whenever he was able, Swift slept outside under his truck to reduce his spending. Not to mention lowering the possibility of being spotted on camera somewhere. Usually, Swift isn't the type of person to be rattled about, almost blowing his cover. He would have preferred it, actually.

In the past, when Swift's cover was blown, he was able to wrap up cases quickly. He no longer had to put on an act. He could get straight to the facts. In this situation, he *might* have been. He couldn't risk showing his hand too early.

Swift was getting antsy with all of the hiding. "It's time to shit or get off the pot," Swift said to himself. It was time to see if he had the correct suspicions about North's roommate.

Later that evening. Swift drove and parked his car near *Tacky Jacks* so he could walk back to Jessica's home. Swift was adept at remembering routes he had previously taken. It was a gift he had ever since he was a child. He could remember by pace, landmarks, the direction the shade from the trees was facing, or a combination of them all.

As Swift was preparing to infiltrate Jessica and her roommate's home, he received an alert that a hurricane was 100 miles away and was rapidly approaching. The alert said to expect a severe thunderstorm around 7 pm. The rain would help Swift in two ways: mask his arrival and increase the likelihood they both were home. In addition, he wanted to see how they conversed with each other.

As he approached the home, he noticed all the lights were off. Clouds were rolling in, providing Swift additional cover as he approached the home.

Swift looked in a couple of the windows and noticed the furniture was missing. So, he went to the back of the home and gained access from the back door. The house was empty. Everything was gone.

The move did not seem like a hasty one. However, it did raise some red flags. The House was *too* clean. Whoever moved them out didn't want to leave a crumb behind. Swift couldn't get a sense of when the move occurred either. The home smelled of cleaning material. This signified someone came and cleaned the house today.

He sent the address to Team Shadow and quickly received a notification that the home should still be occupied by Jessica.

"What the fuck is going on? This shit ain't right." Swift said to himself.

Swift decided to call House back since it seemed he had officially lost Jessica.

"House, this is Swift."

"Did you find Jessica?"

"I did…. but I lost her."

"What do you mean "lost her"?"

"It's complicated. Charles Young, what information did he have?"

"Complicated, how is it complicated?" House thought. "This should have been easy for him. He has done this recently, I'm out of practice. Well, no matter. I have something that gives us something to go on."

"He pretty much stated he was the cog in the wheel that kept everything going. He got his cues from someone who got their cues from someone else. The person he had contact with was female. However, he said he didn't know her name. Before you lost her, did you learn anything?"

"No, and it appears she has moved. I have two spots to check out if I come up empty, I am heading back to Nashville, and we can figure out our next steps."

Swift hung up the phone and continued looking around the empty House in hopes that he would find something to help him relocate Jessica, but he came up empty.

As he left the House, it started to downpour. Swift quickly made his way back to his truck. While Swift told House, he had two places to check. He really only had one. There was no point in heading out to *Sassy Bass,* where she worked at. Since it was closer to the coast, it more than likely would have been closed due to the weather. His only hope was to learn something from the staff at *Tacky Jacks*. If she was a regular, she may have been close to some of them.

Swift walked into the *Tacky Jacks*. It was a ghost town, which was expected. A few workers were cleaning up in preparation for closing early. Swift made his way over to the bartender to see if he could help.

"Hey, you might not remember me, but I was here with Jess a few weeks ago. She said she was a regular." Swift asked.

"You are vaguely familiar. We haven't seen her in a while. It's kinda unusual." The bartender replied.

"Oh, you didn't hear," said a waitress. "Jess and her roommate were killed during a home invasion. It was all over Facebook. I think there is more to the story than that, though. They were such nice people, and we never have anything like that happen here."

"No, I didn't," said the bartender sadly, "That is unfortunate…but Sarah, why do you think there is more to it? The world continues to be an unsafe place."

"Because someone keeps going to Jess's house like they are looking for something. Every other day I see lights in her House on my way home. I wonder if they are going there tonight…. whomever they are." said Sarah, "I hope this was a one-time event. Unfortunately, I don't think our local police department has what they need to handle this."

"Whoever is going to the home believes I left something there." Swift thought, "That's what they are looking for. The people are cleaning the house each time to remove footprints, fingerprints, and anything else that would prevent me from figuring out who they are. It seems like we are playing a game of cat and mouse."

The drizzle of rain turned into a full-fledged storm. Swift looked outside of the restaurant, and he couldn't see more than ten feet in front of him. The breaks between the thunder and lightning were getting shorter and shorter.

While the bartender and the waitress continued talking about what had occurred, Swift stepped into the restroom and called Team Shadow. Something like this would have made the news if it was as rare as they claimed. Surprisingly, nothing had been run in the local newspapers or was ever broadcasted. However, he did receive some interesting news. Silva was recently in the United States. In fact, she visited David Boston a week prior to his death. There was no indication that she had gone back to Brazil either.

While that was good news, it did not fix his current problem. Because Swift went into hiding, he didn't know when they moved. What was months of work seemed to be gone in an instant. He seemed to make a critical mistake, and instead of continuing with the mission, he went into hiding. This could have made all of their efforts moot. Swift punched the wall and tore the hand dryer off the wall, "Damn it!"

He quickly got over himself and decided to carefully inspect the house. There could have been something he missed. Even with most people home now due to the storm, he could regain access to the house without being seen. At this point, he didn't care if he was. He had already jeopardized the mission.

As Swift made his approach, he noticed there was a car in the driveway. "Sarah might be on to something," Swift said to himself. Swift double-checked himself to make sure he was aware of where all of his weapons were. But, with the rain and the darkness, he refused to take an unneeded chance.

Swift walked under a window and could hear the faint sound of someone talking. He snuck his way back to the rear door where he had made entry earlier in the day. The door was still slightly open. He drew his gun and gently pushed it open.

The voice Swift was hearing was a female on the phone.

"There is nothing here. We even took the furniture out…..Wilson, stop being so paranoid."

Swift, while crouched, made his way down the hallway slowly. The female had an accent. It was a pretty peculiar one, at that. You could tell she had lived in the South for a while, but English was not her first language.

"I thought we were done with this….this isn't my problem….I'm done; we're done." She hung up the phone, "*pedaço de merda!* (piece of shit!)"

Swift recognized the language the female spoke in. "She speaks Portuguese," Swift confirmed to himself. One light was on in the living room, and she was standing near it. She was around Swift's height and weight, 5'7-5'8, and seemed to be 160-170 lbs. She was wearing light tactical gear. Swift did not see any weapons on her person.

She yelled, *"Ainda estou pagando por um erro que tem mais de dez anos! Foda-se aquele velho filho da puta! (I'm still paying for a mistake over ten years old! Fuck that old son of a bitch!")* " She then threw her phone in Swift's direction while pacing back and forth.

The back door suddenly slammed shut, and it gained her attention. "Motherfucker, I thought I closed the door," Swift whispered. He heard the woman getting closer to him. She appeared to be moving with caution.

Swift prepared to grab her once he believed she was close enough. "This could make up for my earlier mistake. She must have valuable information about North." There was a break in the storm, and you could hear a pin drop.

The woman stopped walking, and Swift didn't know why. He made sure he wasn't casting a shadow and hadn't made any sudden movements. At this point, Swift knew he had two options. The first was to be aggressive and look for her. The second was to wait it out. He preferred to make the first move but wanted the storm to help mask his movements. So, Swift decided to do a countdown, hoping the storm would start again.

During Swift's countdown, a flash of lightning went across the sky, and a loud boom happened nearby. "Lighting must have struck something," Swift thought. The rain started again, and Swift made his move. She was gone. "She has to be somewhere in here," Swift whispered.

Suddenly, Swift heard footsteps rapidly approaching him as he was struck from behind. "What the fuck!?"

"I knew someone was in here!" She screamed.

She pushed Swift against the wall, pulled a knife from her thigh holster, and stabbed him in the leg. Swift groaned and threw her to the side. She rushed back at him, forcing Swift onto the ground. Swift successfully blocked the arm with the knife and attempted to reverse their positions but failed. The pain in his leg was tremendous. He couldn't tell where exactly he was stabbed, but wherever it was, it did the job.

Her moves were of someone who had military or police training. She had great control of Swift's movements, and she beat him to the spot every time he tried to make a move.

Swift thought about reaching for his last resort weapon, but he couldn't risk killing or seriously injuring her. "She didn't choose to flee when she had the chance. Why? She is defending the home like it's the last thing on Earth."

Swift struck her with an open palm directly under her chin, rocking her briefly, giving him the window he needed. He used military training to take her back and choked her unconscious.

He applied a tourniquet to his leg and limped over to his gun.

"Man, that was one tough bitch."

Chapter 17

A few minutes went by, and the female started to stir. Swift felt like she was playing possum since she shouldn't have been out for that long. However, he had already patted her down and taken the additional weapons she had on her off.

"Glad you are still with us," said Swift.

The woman was looking through Swift, rather than at him. She was mumbling something under her breath Swift couldn't make out. Then she started laughing, "Did I just get my ass-whooped by a homeless person?" she said.

"You are not far off. So why did you attack me?" said Swift.

"Why were you in this house?"

Swift pointed his gun toward her. "You aren't in the position to be asking questions."

Swift didn't have anything to tie her up with and hoped brandishing the gun would be good enough to keep her at bay. But unfortunately, he didn't have any energy due to the amount of blood he lost from his leg.

The rain continued, but the thunder and lightning were getting further away. Swift felt he was no longer in the position to take her in anymore.

He didn't know how badly his leg was damaged. However, they both had seen each other's faces. Swift couldn't risk her alerting anyone. He would shoot first to keep control of the situation and only shoot to kill if he believed it was necessary.

The woman was still gasping for breath. He hoped this was a good sign that she would be disinterested in fighting again.

"Let's start with something simple. What happened to Jess and her roommate?" Swift inquired.

"Fuck you!" She responded.

They were sitting on the floor, looking at each other. Neither seemed interested in laying their card out on the table. Swift was oddly proud of the resilience she was showing. He felt as if either she believed he wouldn't shoot her, or he *couldn't* shoot her. Swift knew this was a challenge he was going to have to overcome and was willing to accept it. Not many people would show tenacity in the face of death.

"Look, I know her real name was Jessica North. Let's trade information."

"Of course, he was right; he always is."

"Who is always right?"

"Wilson"

"Who is Wilson"

She started to mutter something under her breath.

"Who is Wilson, "Swift asked again. "If you don't want to tell me who he is, why don't you tell me who you are? My name is Trek."

"We both could be after the same thing." Swift thought, "Maybe she will respond to this better. I'd rather not have to figure out how I would hide her body."

"If you knew who she really was, you should know who I am." She responded.

"Sorry, I can't say I do."

She started to reach up and touch her face.

"I apologize, Trek; I see why."

She reached up to her nose and started to scratch and pull at it. She was wearing a fake nose and mouth. She then started to wipe away some of her makeup. She had slightly darker skin than Swift initially thought.

"Do you know who I am now?" she asked.

"Maria Silva. I wish we could have met under better circumstances."

"Was Silva the roommate?" Swift thought," Why would North keep her a secret? It appeared they were living secret lives. We might *actually* be in this together."

"So, you do know? Where is Seven? I assume you are helping him." said Silva.

"He isn't here. He isn't even in this state." replied Swift.

"What do you want to know? I have grown tired of hiding who I am and what I have done for years." asked Silva

"Did you really kill Jessica?" Swift questioned.

"I was supposed to, but I did not. I refused to be used anymore. She moved somewhere. She didn't know Wilson kept tabs on her this entire time." answered Silva, "I found her as soon as I got her and told her she needed to leave, and I would make sure she was never bothered again."

"How did you do that?"

"I found another couple to rent out her place for several days. I told Wilson Jessica had moved, and we couldn't find her. He felt like I was lying to him…. of course, I was. Jessica was like a sister to me. I couldn't let him kill her."

"So, what happened?"

"Wilson was worried something in the house could connect him to

Jessica. He had me look for it for weeks."

Swift was relieved to learn that Jessica was not killed. However, this did let him know he was too attached. Then it finally hit him. "Wilson, Wilson Ellis, the former police captain," Swift stated.

"The one and only, don't forget he is now a candidate for governor," Maria said with a laugh. "I hope my pretty face didn't distract you this long. I'm often told it does."

"I'd be lying if I said it didn't cause me any issues." Swift replied, "He is running for Governor? That's news to me."

"Are you going to kill me, Trek? If so, please get on with it."

"Kill her? Why would she ask me to do that?" Swift thought.

"If I need to."

Silva started to stand up, and Swift shot her in the leg.

"Shit!" Silva screamed out in pain.

"It didn't hurt that bad. It was just a .22," Swift said with a smirk. "Now, since you know I will shoot you. I am sure we can answer my questions faster."

Silva slid back down to the floor, "If you know who Wilson, Jessica, and I are. I assume you know about the others as well?"

"I might, how about you clear it up for me."

Silva took a deep breath. While gathering her thoughts, Swift wanted to make sure his phone was still recording, which it was.

"I have been protecting a man using me for over fifteen years. I have been discredited for most of my life because of my looks. I look more like a model than a police officer. I had a top 5 GPA in my graduating college class and was the top cadet in my police academy class. Regardless, I was offered positions because of my appearance rather than my accomplishments."

Swift could understand the frustration Silva had. Even if she was selected due to her natural talent. Many would assume it was due to how she looked.

Silva continued," Wilson approached me one day before I went to issue parking tickets. He told me he noticed how excellent my report-writing and note-taking skills were. He told me, 'I could see the unforeseen.' I was only doing parking duty because I refused to sleep with any of the guys in my unit. They thought that this would break me and make me quit. Little did they know I would take a lot more than this."

"Back on Wilson, he told me there was a way I could make more money and help the citizens of Nashville. I would do almost anything to stop writing tickets on the same cars for weeks. He was a captain then and told me he created a task force to do controlled stings in specific neighborhoods. And that's what we did. As a result, we got tons of weapons, drugs, and counterfeit cash off the street. I was so happy to actually be doing police work.

Silva had this bright smile on her face.

"Then, something happened; I don't know when, but Wilson started to get really mean. He never got mad at me directly, but David, Jessica, and Mike were consistently yelled at. I thought we were doing good. Wilson told me to speak to the evidence sergeant, whose name was Charles. I told him we would need money and drugs for an undercover investigation. Depending on the success, we would do this often. He would be rewarded OT for helping us. I thought we were given the ok by the current Chief. I never thought to question him."

Swift could tell Silva was making this up as she was going on. A lot of what she was saying contradicted itself. There was also a change in her voice. Swift wanted to usher her on to get her to slip up on something more concrete. "I need you to get to the point, Maria. At this rate, you will be talking until tomorrow night."

Silva rolled her eyes. "I am trying to let you know as much as possible.

I don't want to hide anything. If I rush, I will miss things."

"So, if I may, Wilson and I started to get involved…romantically, even though he was twenty years older than me…. I loved him; he gave me everything I wanted in my career. I finally thought I was receiving validation for everything I worked for…. He played on my emotions."

"One day, he told me what we were actually doing. I threw up after he told me."

Swift was reading her body language; she was having trouble hiding her lies.

"What were you all really doing?" Swift sat up and leaned in. Showing he was really interested in what he was going to hear next.

A tear rolled down their cheek. "He told me we gave the gangs weapons, money, and drugs. I did not know what we were doing when I agreed to the task force. We started with items in evidence. Then, before things were cataloged into evidence, we would sell it to the highest bidder through informants."

"Then he had David, Jessica, and Mike cover up murders. He told us as long as the murders happened in certain areas, they would be listed as a suicide or something."

At this point, Silva was full-fledged, crying with snot running down her nose.

"I know you're thinking, "Why didn't I say something?" I was in love, Trek, foolishly in love. I kept going on and on with whatever Wilson was saying. I was hoping this was just a bad dream. It wasn't."

"The day Seven was arrested was when I decided enough was enough. I knew something was up when Wilson called me back to the station. Seven was so close to freeing me from this nightmare. He was the best investigator in the department. Anyway, I went into the warehouse and heard yelling. I could tell it was Mike and Seven, but I didn't understand what they were discussing. They were shouting at each other at the same time. I thought I had stuck up behind Mike, but it was Seven. He saw me, and I panicked and shot him. When Seven started to turn around, Wilson knocked him out in the head. I didn't know he was in the warehouse!"

"Why should I believe you?"

Silva's story wasn't making sense. She would have been well aware of Ellis' plans if they were involved. She was backing herself into a corner. Swift just had to wait for the right time to show his hand. Silva was getting more animated with her movements and her voice changed throughout her last statement.

"He told me if I had to disappear so I couldn't be used as a witness during the trial. I refused, and he struck me on the top of my head. I was hospitalized for a week because my concussion was so bad. I had to have staples." Silva parted her hair and showed Swift a six-inch scar she had. Swift couldn't tell how old it was, but he knew enough that it was done recently.

"My life has been ruined! Wilson has been keeping tabs on Jessica, David, and myself since we left the police department. I know he had someone hit Jessica, and I know he set up David! I just cannot prove it!"

With Silva bringing up Jessica's hit and run and David being involved in a shootout, Swift felt as if she was grasping at straws. However, no matter what Silva said, Swift kept the same expression on his face.

On the other hand, Swift found it peculiar that she mentioned these things. Silva must be confident Swift knew of David and Jessica's past. Swift did have an ace up his sleeve. Earlier that day, he was notified Silva visited David a week before he died. She wouldn't have known that. If she was sent to kill North, she may have been sent to kill David as well.

Swift knew he needed to take control of the conversation. Silva's ranting may have finally caught up with her.

Swift started laughing.

"What is so funny!?" Silva screamed while wiping her tears away.

"You are a great actress. Maybe you should have been a model." Swift replied while making his way to his feet. "You almost had me. Think before you speak. After about twenty seconds, you started lying." said Swift.

"What are you talking about?! Everything I said was true!" Silva yelled.

Swift limped to a nearby window to see if anyone else had unexpectedly arrived. Unfortunately, the rain had picked back up. It was falling so fast, it looked like an endless ream of white sheets. He could feel the wound in his leg was deeper than he imagined. Swift tried his best to be unbothered by the pain. He didn't want to give Silva any ideas. However, he couldn't help but favor his leg.

"In this type of discourse, which I would look at as a police interview, information is introduced for a few things: You are trying to recycle things the interviewer already knows, you are answering a question truthfully, or in your case, you are trying to see what I already know. And I know you just lied."

One of Swift's greatest traits was recognizing flaws within someone's speech. Swift could realize if someone was lying to him, pretending to be happy, bored, sad, you name it. His natural skill was enhanced when he took classes focusing on body language. All of which he noticed when Silva was talking. It was time to end this.

Silva was still sitting on the floor and had a puzzled look. "I'm not lying."

Swift slowly went to Silva, "To be a great actor or actress, the crowd has to believe in your adaptation of the character. You can get angry, scream, cuss, or cry, but it doesn't mean the crowd truly feels your pain or frustration."

Silva looked toward the ground and started to clench her fist.

"The worst you can do is drag on what you know is a shaky performance. It makes the crowd restless and gives them more time to pick out the flaws....or recognize what is being forced, which is happening in your case."

"Still confused? Let me clear it up for you. You told the truth about Jessica, her being alive, and your past relationship with her. Same with your relationship with Wilson and him surprising you about what he was truly doing with the police department, but then you started thinking."

"There was a subtle change in your body language and the pitch in your voice when you started adding to the story, especially when it came to House."

Silva was looking lost. "Why would I lie to you? You think everything he did to me was ok. I wish I was half the police officer Seven was. Maybe then I wouldn't have gotten into this mess!"

"See, you just told the truth again," Swift replied. He pulled out some zip ties and threw them at Silva's feet. "Put these on. Let's go visit your old pal Seven. I am sure he has some questions to ask you."

As Silva started to comply, the power went out.

"Ain't this bitch," Swift said. He threw a pen in front of him, and it hit the ground. Silva was no longer in front of him. "Maria, where are you?"

Silva started laughing maniacally, " *você vai morrer!* (you're going to die!), I'm right here!"

Lightning flashed, and Swift briefly saw Silva swing a blade toward him. He put his arm up to protect his face and received a gash on his forearm.

Swift fell back towards the wall. Since the room was empty, this was the best way for Swift to ensure Silva couldn't get behind him. Also, the front and the back doors were closed. So, Swift would know if Silva opened one to exit the house.

" I should have known I couldn't get one over on you, " said Silva, "You can't blame a girl for trying, can you? I thought Jessica might have given you a sob story. She told me all about you; I didn't let her know you hacked her computer, isn't that right, Trek? *I* am her roommate. I knew one day Wilson would want us all dead. We know too much about his past. This gives us power over him. Us girls decided to stick together after he tried and failed to kill her years ago. I cannot let you leave. You would go after Wilson, which means he would go after me. I'm tired of running."

Silva's voice was trailing off. With his leg and arm injured, Swift figured it would be better to leave, take care of his wounds and attempt to regroup with House as soon as possible. He had more than enough information to get Silva and Wilson arrested.

"Trek, are you thinking about leaving me? I haven't been able to finish my story yet." Silva said with a sense of bravado. "You were such a gentleman when you searched me. However, you only took my weapons, you could see. If you had thoroughly searched me, maybe tonight could have ended differently for the both of us."

Swift shot in the direction he thought the voice was coming from. Unfortunately, Swift had underestimated how deep the wound to his leg was. He thought it had only gone through the first two layers of skin. Still, when he moved, it felt like it had reached the hypodermis, an injury he had previously experienced.

He knew he would need to kill Silva now. The .22 caliber round she had in her leg was a flesh wound in comparison. He was no longer in a position to take her with him.

"You want to know a secret?' Silva said. "There is a pipe bomb under the floor where you sit on *menino bobo* (silly boy). Nothing huge, just enough to make it look like a gas line exploded. It's the best way to make sure if anything related to us is destroyed."

Then it hit Swift, "That's why she had been coming back and forth to the house." He said to himself. He didn't pay much attention to the construction dumpster down the street. Doing part of the work during the day wouldn't raise suspicion. People would believe whoever was at the House was just remodeling. Same for coming back in the evening.

This would also explain the cleaning smell. Whatever they were using to clean was designed to mask the smell of gas. "She must have hit the line while planting the bomb." Swift thought.

"You know what else, Trek, if that is your real name, we were waiting for tonight. We could say lightning struck the House, a power surge happened, endless possibilities." Silva said sinisterly

Swift knew he wouldn't reach the door; his only option was to jump out the window. He feared he wouldn't be able to crawl away before the explosion once he jumped out of the window. While House will still be able to receive the recordings, it could do him no good if there was a manhunt for him. All it would take is Ellis spinning the entire situation around.

Swift looked and could tell the doors were still closed; he knew Silva was still inside.

It was apparent why Silva hadn't made her way to the door. They were stalemated. He had a gun, and she had a knife. He would shoot if she opened one. If he attempted to escape, she could stab him before he could react.

"*vamos jogar um jogo (*let's play a game*)*, Trek. Who will move first? Will it be you or me? It would be so much easier if it was House *mas filho da puta (*that son of a bitch) had to send you!?" Silva angrily screamed. Then she calmly stated, "How much time do you think we have? I know the answer."

Suddenly, there was a beeping sound. "She must have armed the bomb, but how?" Swift thought.

Swift's eyes had finally adjusted to the dark. He could see what appeared to be a silhouette of Silva to his right, which would be going toward the back door. However, she still had a line of sight for the front door and window he was by. So, he assumes she must also know where he's at this point.

Waiting until the power came back on wasn't an option. Shooting without him confirming where she wasn't a good option either. He had already switched from his Glock G44 to his Glock 45. Firing would alert nearby neighbors, even with the storm suppressing the sound slightly.

"You know, when I was a little girl growing up in the *favelas,* I had to learn how to protect myself. My *mãe e pai (*mom and dad) were always working. We moved to the US when I was in high school. I saw these boys messing with this girl, so I intervened. One of them slapped me, so I broke his arm, and the others ran away. The girl was crying and thanked me. That's when I decided to be a police officer." Silva said, still in a calm tone. "I hope she grew up ok."

"You don't want to talk to me, Trek? I know you are still here."

"Trek?"

The shadowy figure started moving towards him, and suddenly the power returned. They both covered their eyes due to the sudden brightness in the room. Swift lowered his arm and saw Silva approaching him, still holding her knife. Swift readied himself to fire, and Silva knocked his arm out of the way.

They wrestled to the ground, and Swift ended up on top. He punched Silva in the face and attempted to separate. Silva grabbed Swift as he got up and stabbed him in the shoulder. Now on top of Swift, Silva attempted to stab Swift in his face. He was able to move out of the way just in time, and Silva's knife got stuck on the floor.

Swift used this opportunity to push himself away from Silva and fired two shots at her as the power went out again.

Swift was panting," Holy…shit! I've gotta get out of here."

He started crawling his way to the door. Even though his body was in bad shape, Swift knew he needed to escape, recover and plan his next move. With the weather and his injuries, he knew he wouldn't make it back to his car. Instead, he would have to find somewhere safe until the morning.

The beeping was speeding up. It would be a matter of time before the pipe bomb exploded. Minutes had passed, but nothing had happened. Was Silva bluffing? Swift wasn't going to find out.

He made his way to the door. The storm was still going strong. A lightning bolt went across the sky just as the power turned back on. Swift turned around to ensure Silva was dead.

Silva was lying on the floor, motionless. Swift turned around and stepped on the front porch. Silva weakly said under her breath, *"junte-se a mim no inferno! (*Join me in hell!)"* as the home exploded.

Chapter 18

It had been weeks since House had heard from Swift. At first, phone calls were ringing through to voicemail. Then they stopped. Swift had been in many operations in different countries throughout his military career. This gave House confidence Swift wasn't in any trouble he couldn't handle.

During this time, he asked Team Shadow to look into what happened with his old police department. From what he learned from Young, there is no way someone didn't slip up when he was in prison. However, Team Shadow didn't find anything else that they didn't already know. He needed to get answers from Swift.

House pulled out his phone and saw he had a text message. The message stated he needed to confirm he had received the text and await a phone call. Shortly after confirming, he received a call.

"Seven House, we have not had contact from Shadow since his contact with Maria Silva."

House was confused, " What do you mean? He was supposed to be looking for Jessica North?"

The Team Shadow representative responded, "We received a recording from Shadow the last night the phone was used. From the analysis of the voice recording and the voices on the recording, we can confirm he spoke to Maria Silva. We will be sending you the conversation after this call."

"Seven, I should inform you. We have reason to believe Trek is dead."

A cold chill went down House's spine, "Dead.... what do you mean dead?"

"The phone has been in the location since the night we received the recording. The location is accurate within twenty meters. We also have this."

House's phone vibrated, and he pulled the phone away from his face. He was sent a link to a news article: *"Two Dead After Gas Line Explodes."* House quickly skimmed the article and saw that Maria Silva was identified and efforts were still ongoing to confirm the identity of the second person.

House felt sick. He couldn't help but feel responsible for Swift's death. It was true Swift interjected himself into House's situation. However, that didn't provide any comfort to House

"The local police will not be able to identify Trek. Long ago, Shadow's medical and dental records and fingerprints were only made accessible to specific government agencies. Eventually, we will be able to retrieve his body. Agents are en route."

"After you listen to Trek's conversation with Maria, call the "Last Resort" number and let it ring six times, then hang up. Call it back four times, then hang up. Please make sure you do this correctly. Goodbye."

The Team Shadow representative hung up the phone. House didn't know what to do. "Damn it, Swift! Is this what you meant when you said you were compromised!? Why didn't you tell me!?"

House's phone beeped. It was an encrypted message. "This must be the information Swift gathered," House said, regaining his composure. "I don't want to listen to this here."

House lived in a rundown, extended-stay hotel a few miles outside downtown Nashville. House went to his car and headed to Seven Oaks Park. Since the park was relatively small and off the main road, he didn't have to worry about many people being around.

In the past, House would eat his lunch here. When people saw a cop car at the end of the road, they would leave. However, House was no longer a police officer. So, he wouldn't have that luxury anymore. It was close to 10 am. He didn't know how long the recording was, but he didn't want someone to hear something they didn't need to. He got out of his car and made his way down the hill, into the wood line. He might have been there for a while; he didn't want to raise suspicion if he sat there too long.

When House listened to the recording, he was filled with various emotions. But one was more prominent than any of the other ones. That was anger, specifically on how until this, he would have defended Maria Silva until the end of time. She never gave him a reason to suspect her of anything. On the contrary, she appeared to want to be his student and learn everything he could teach her.

House, like Swift, noticed the change in Silva's voice when she described the events that led him to be set up. He paused the recording and thought about that night. As he was struck, he went out. He had more pain near the bottom of his head and neck area rather than the top of his head. Logically, it would make sense if he was hit by someone smaller than him. Silva and House had worked out together in the past. He knew she was a lot stronger than her physique would suggest. He had no doubt she could generate enough power to knock him out.

Even with this being a possibility, he didn't want to make another mistake by only focusing on her since he had excluded her previously. House finished the recording and sat down in disbelief. He hoped there would be something on the recording to prove Swift was still alive, but there was nothing.

"Swift, your passing won't be in vain. You did all of this for me. Someone you haven't spoken to in years. You called me family. We should have split up!"

He remembered Swift told him to call the "Last Resort" number if something happened to him. At first, he wasn't interested. He wanted revenge for Swift's death, but Silva was dead. Then the question was, *who* sent Silva, or was she acting alone? He decided to listen to the recording again. This time, he would keep his emotions in check. Then he heard the name, Wilson Ellis.

"It was you! It's all starting to make sense!" House screamed.

House realized he was being played for a fool. Ellis was the one who assigned Silva to him. Ellis also attempted to overload House with unrelated cases. Ellis could have made the other officers available to speak to, but he didn't. However, it was becoming clearer this was an attempt to distract him.

House regained his motivation. He was ashamed of his moment of weakness. However, the goal was still the same: Expose those who wronged him and clear his name.

It was getting close to 11 am. House looked up the hill and saw a few more cars had parked. He decided to go deeper in the wood line to call the "Last Resort" number. More cars were appearing at the roundabout. House wanted to ensure he wouldn't be interrupted.

After completing the sequence, House was sent another encrypted message. Once he opened it, he was provided these coordinates 36°05'12.9" N 86°40'27.7" W and advised he had one hour to arrive. House quickly looked it up and found it was on a park trail nearby. House made it back to his car and headed in that direction.

House arrived and exited his car. He heard flowing water in a nearby creek. Most of the leaves had fallen from the trees. If this was another occasion, this would have been a beautiful location for an afternoon walk.

As House headed down the trail, he saw someone standing in the field.

House looked at them and waited for some sort of signal, nothing happened. He decided to ignore him; he figured if this was the person he was supposed to meet if it even was a person, he would let them address him.

When he got to the trail's end, nothing of note stuck out. Even though this was the end of October, it was still in the seventies, and some adults were playing soccer. House looked at his watch and saw he had fifteen minutes to spare. "Well, what to do?" House said to himself. He pulled out his phone and saw no missed calls or messages.

The fifteen minutes had elapsed, and nothing had changed; the adults were still playing soccer, and no person or package had shown up. "This is stupid. What am I waiting for? I hope this isn't a weird game from beyond the grave, Swift."

Then, his phone started vibrating. When House pulled his phone out of his pocket, the screen read "factory reset in progress."

"Well, that's just great. What am I supposed to do now?" He didn't want to leave the area; this was the last information he would get. What was worse is everything he had that would be damaging was in the process of being deleted.

"Mr. House….is that you?" said a skittish voice.

House turned around. It was the guy who was standing in the field. He was a white guy, a little younger than House, but he looked like he had been in a terrible accident. Part of his skull was sunk in. He had multiple surgical scars on his face and neck.

"It's... it's me, Peter Walsh…you...well, not you…people called me Worm.

Chapter 19

House stood there shocked. Why was Peter here? They didn't speak when they were cellmates. How was he involved in all this?

"Peter…what are you doing here?" House asked.

"Well...um, I'm here to help you if you need me to….rather." Peter stood talking and looked House straight into his eyes, "I owe you, my life; you saved me. You didn't have to, but you did."

At first, House was confused. "When did I save him?" He thought to himself. Then, it hit him. He remembers seeing Peter being attacked as he returned to his cell. The only information the Warden told him was he was still alive.

Peter started crying, "I never got to tell you to thank you. Thank you so much!"

"You are welcome," House said. "Not to be rude, but I am waiting for someone…or something."

Peter wiped the tears from his eyes and the snot from his nose, "You were waiting for me. I…I can help you."

"Waiting for you?" House thought, "How would he know that I would be here?"

"I'm sure you don't know what I'm doing, and even if you did, you don't need to get involved," said House.

"Did you get my package?"

"Package…what pa…" House thought, "How did this dude know I got a package?" House started looking around and didn't see anyone else around him. He grabbed Peter.

"Talk. Why are you here, and how did you know where to send that to." House demanded.

"Please…please…I'm sorry, I can explain!" Peter replied.

House released Peter and stood there and stared at him. "Get to it."

Peter replied in a shaky voice, "I…. I was beaten so badly that they sent me to Vanderbilt and put me into a medically induced coma. When…uh…when I was woken up, I was told my sentence had been reduced to time served. I…I don't know why but I am thankful."

"Good for you. None of that helps me." House started to head back down the trail.

"Just…just let me explain. I…I can help you." Peter pleaded to House. "Let...let me explain. I wanted to thank you and…and I found out you were being released soon. So..so I found out everything I could regarding your case. Then…then I found the people mentioned in your police reports and the last cases you were involved in."

House stopped and turned around.

"Once…once I got that, I wanted to hand it to you in person. But…but the day you were released, I saw you talking to someone. I... I was too nervous and didn't want to interrupt. So..so I followed you. When…when we got to Cookeville, I…I wrote the address of your friend down and sent the package. I…I just really wanted to help."

Thinking everything over, House and Swift took precautions to make sure they were followed. Then it hit him. Peter was phenomenal with technology. From what House had learned since being released, Peter could have tracked his movements and been hundreds of miles away with the use of cell phones and cameras. The "we" he felt Peter was referring to was them moving as a unit, not him doing it separately.

He also remembered Swift wasn't interested in opening the package right away. Did he know something? Was he worried Peter was going to outdo him? Maybe if Swift had told House about Peter, Swift could have still been alive.

There were so many questions House wanted to ask Swift about those first few weeks. However, he couldn't ask him now. However, Peter revealing this led to his next question.

"As creepy and weird as that sounds, how did you know I would be here?" House asked.

"Well...well...um, I was able to...please don't be mad...hack your friend's laptop," Peter responded. "It...it wasn't easy. When I attempted to initiate a hack, the firewalls I faced were insane. So, the pre-written code I normally would use didn't work. Lucky for me, I have a different protocol I use in these situations. But when I attempted to reconfigure the network and triangulate the...."

"Stop. I have ZERO ideas of what you are talking about," House stated. "Look, sorry we got off on the wrong foot. Explain how you can help me."

Peter lit up after House's words and confidently stated, "With what I have already gathered and what you can tell me. I can spread the truth about Wilson Ellis all over the internet."

"Really"

"Yes, really. I can take over every campaign ad, every social media site, every news station; nothing is off-limits."

A huge smile went across House's face. Finally, he was blessed with some good news after only getting bad news for a long time. "Peter, come with me. We have much to talk about."

When they were making their way back down the trail. Peter told House he attempted to contact Team Shadow members after successfully accessing Swift's phone and laptop when they were originally in Cookeville. However, it wasn't until one of the members recognized the code Peter had used. This individual wasn't directly affiliated with Peter's previous group but followed all the fan pages about him.

After confirming Peter was who he said he was, it was decided to place the "Last Resort" number on Swift's and House's phones. This was the only way Swift would allow Peter to be a part of the case.

The main idea was if the investigation didn't turn up anything valuable, Peter would just spread what he had gathered to the FBI and local news stations. This would ensure a proper investigation would take place. Peter stated he was never told he would only be contacted if they were in a situation they couldn't get out of. Including death.

"Peter, you are going to have to come with me. I don't have a phone anymore; the one I had was reset," said House.

"They…they told me that would happen if we made contact. So, I…I guess that's a good failsafe in case I was setting you up," Peter replied with a slight chuckle, "Don't worry, I have all the information I need."

House looked at Peter sharply. Peter took a step back, "Sss…Sorry. I won't make a bad joke like that again. "Wher…where are you taking me?"

"This shitty ass hotel I've been staying in. Let's find out what you know, c'mon."

House and Peter started to make their way back to House's hotel room. An ad on the radio stated Wilson Ellis had one final campaign rally before Election Day at the Music City Center.

"I…I think you should go to that." Peter said, "It..it could be beneficial to see face to face."

"Why is that?" House inquired. "At this point, I'm better off not interacting with him. From what I have recently figured out, I don't know if I could control myself."

"Well...um...I"

"Just say it, Peter."

Peter took a deep breath and said, "Wilson needs to lose the election. People are drawn to him for lies. If he is elected, I...I feel he could harm more people. I believe the best way for this to happen is for you to confront him. Tell him the things you know to be true. I predict he will be unable to focus on his campaign and will attempt to silence you. I have already gained access to Wilson's phone. Suppose he makes a call or sends a text directly after speaking to you; I think he would contact someone asking about your release. Maybe...maybe have someone silence you? In..in that case, I'll include the incriminating comments in the media blast we will do."

House looked at Peter and nodded his head, "Seems reasonable."

Peter was filled with joy after receiving House's approval. Peter stood up and held his head up high," For this to work, we must arrive at the perfect moment. Wilson has been doing private meet and greets before his rallies. You must be a donor of a certain level and receive an email notification. I already took the necessary steps to procure one.... I was hoping I'd get the chance to repay you for saving my life. Anyway, we have some more planning to do."

"Indeed."

The final rally would occur in two days, on a Sunday. Road closure around the Music City Center had already started.

"Hou...House, I was able to access the city's cameras around the building," Peter turned his laptop toward House, "There...There are vehicle entrances on Demonbreun, 6th, and Korean Veterans. But...but if you look here, it seems this is where they would let VIPs in." Peter pointed to a set of double doors.

House pulled over to look at the areas Peter highlighted. Those doors being used as an entry/exit point made sense. House saw a couple of cars easily pull up, drop someone off, and leave without an issue.

"If Ellis uses these doors, he will arrive early." said House

"How…how early do you think he will arrive?" Peter asked.

"Honestly, there ain't no telling. He could arrive anywhere from one to four hours early. When I was an officer, Ellis would be one of the first ones to show up for the media. He loved getting camera time. If some arrived before him, he would show up even earlier to the next one."

House resumed driving down the road while Peter continued to examine the Music City Center.

They pulled into the hotel and parked. House got out of the car, and he was suddenly anxious. What he had planned for months looked like it would finally happen. His heart felt like it was beating in his ears. He took a few deep breaths to regain his composure. Peter appeared to be walking on eggshells, and he didn't want to allow him to waver.

"Are you sure you are up to this?" House asked. "This isn't your fight." I can tell you are unsure if you are doing the right thing."

Peter sat in silence for a moment. He had been waiting to assist House for a long time. After all the things he did to help others, Peter would do that and more to help House.

However, fear had been holding him back since he was released from prison. Peter did not speak to anyone from his past after his release. He just went into hiding, waiting for the call to assist House. Peter felt as if he shouldn't have been idly waiting by.

"Peter. Are you good?" House asked.

Peter snapped back to reality. "Yeah...yeah, I am. I... I can't go back to prison. I…I want to help, though."

"I'll do my best to make sure that doesn't happen. I can't make any promises, though," House thought for a second. "You won't have to be nearby, and you can hide your actual location…that is a thing, right?" asked House.

"I... I always do that. But someone, if…if they are good, could…could find me." answered Peter.

House reached out and put his hand on Peter's shoulder, "Give me what you have; explain what I need to do, and I will take care of it. Thank you." replied House.

Tears started flowing down Peter's face. Peter knew he had let House down. He couldn't help it. He would already be dead if anyone other than House walked down that hallway. If he returned to prison, he would die within a few months, if not weeks.

Peter looked at House. House had an understanding look in his eyes. It was warm and comforting. The expression on House's face let Peter know there would be no ill will towards him if he walked out of the car and didn't look back.

This is what bothered Peter the most. He felt House knew sooner or later, he would eventually walk away from this. Suddenly, Peter felt a surge of anger come over him. This was the moment he was going to be able to repay House for saving his life, and he was offered a way out. He struggled to find the words to say he would see it through.

"The last person who decided to help me is dead." said House, "He died a few weeks ago…," House paused. " I don't want someone else dying because they believe their actions are right. So, I'm telling you, show me what I need to do and go live your life."

Peter was disappointed in himself. He hadn't even helped yet and was already being turned away. With the bit of courage he had left, he raised his head and looked towards House. He felt House tighten his grip on his shoulder. Signifying House wasn't going to be convinced of this.

Peter grabbed House's hand, "I am here until the rally starts. After that, we will go our separate ways."

House was impressed Peter refused to accept the easy way out. If things were different, maybe he would have. "Ok then. Let's formulate a game plan on how we should approach this. We get one shot."

"Ab..absolutely."

Peter and House went into the hotel room. Peter was looking at all the photos House had sprawled over the place. To most people, it would look like they were just random things he was interested in. However, they served as reminders of key players and information he received. There was a picture of the Boston skyline with a date on it. The date was the day he found out David Boston was dead. There was a picture of kids playing *Guess Who* for Mike Guess. House also had a photo of a funeral; this was for Charles Young.

"All these people are dead," Peter thought, "Why does he have these photos? Is he going to kill Ellis? Get a hold of yourself, you have to see this through. House is counting on you."

Peter sat in a chair and opened his.

"I…I have another plan," Peter said, "You...you will go in as part of the security detail. Not...Not a part of Wilson's detail but...but one of the ones who work for the Music City Center." Peter turned his laptop towards House, "And..and it's done."

In that short time, Peter had reinstated an employee who quit months ago that vaguely looked like House. He even reinstated House's POST status.

House was amazed at how fast Peter accomplished this. "He must have been working on this in the car." House thought.

"No…no one will recognize this happened. It..it appears like a computer glitch." Peter said, seeming pleased, "The...the dress code requires everyone to wear suits. Do...do you have one?"

House walked to the closet and pulled out a suit. "There is some irony that this was the same suit the day I was arrested might be the same one I get Ellis arrested with."

House walked to a nearby suitcase and opened it. Inside it were concealed carry holsters and some less-than-lethal equipment. "Good thing I grabbed these a few months back…let's see here: OC spray, ASP, handcuffs, and…yes, I did grab it...a slim profiled vest."

"Why...why do you need all that?" Peter inquired, "It..it's a bit much"

"I'm not taking all of this. I need the vest, hostlers, and handcuffs. To play the part, you have to look the part," House responded.

"You...you plan on shooting him," Peter said in a panic, thinking about the photos he recently saw.

"No promises. Can you get access to cameras inside the building?" asked House.

"Yes…yes, I can." said Peter, "Give…give me a few minutes," Peter started the process of accessing the computers and had a startling revelation, "Hou...House, the cameras don't work. It..it seems like they have been out for a while."

"Can you tell if it was something done purposely or what?" House asked.

"I…I couldn't access the necessary information to explain the reason is…. I searched for work orders for this issue, and nothing came up. This…this could work in our favor." replied Peter.

"How so?" House inquired.

"Well…well, for starters, you wouldn't have to worry about facial recognition. Any...anything you need to do won't be on camera."

"How positive are you that they won't get the cameras up before the rally?"

"Ve…very. I…I'm sure they didn't let Wilson's people know. It..it would cause a major problem."

"I'm going to step out for a second," said House.

House walked out of the hotel room. It was 4 pm, but it was already dark outside. Typical for Tennessee in November, but House forgot about it. This was going to play mainly in his favor. Everyone was required to wear suits to blend in with the crowd. So, after House entered the rally, all he needed to do was separate himself from the security detail. Better yet, he didn't need to be a part of the detail. "Act as you belong, and no one will question you" was a motto he remembered his parents telling him.

The cool breeze strangely gave House a feeling of warmth. "Swift, is that you? The winds of change are among us," House said under his breath, "Just two more days."

Chapter 20

The day had finally arrived. Peter and House spent day and night going over the plan. House needed to contact Ellis in public before he started to give his speech. Peter had already gained access to the local network and programmed the cell phone he passed to House to play the audio and the slideshow of Ellis and crew's crimes.

As Peter thought, the cameras did not go back into service. Nor was there any attempt to bring the system back online. So, they both decided it would be best to combine Peter's plans. First, House would use the security credentials to enter a control access point of the building and find the location of the rally. Once Ellis takes the stage, House will let him gain the crowd's full attention, and when the perfect moment strikes, he will play the slideshow to uncover the truth about Ellis.

Peter attempted to track Ellis's movements leading up to the rally but was unsuccessful. Even though Ellis's address was blacklisted, he could easily find it. However, it was a dead end. It was vacant when Peter and House went to scope out the home. I checked the utility bills and showed no one had lived in the home for years.

Ellis was divorced, and there were no records of a new marriage, property purchase, or anything that would lead to where he could be. House and Peter found this odd. Someone was doing their best to hide his information but why?

During Ellis's campaign, the same person introduced him each time. It was an older, light-skinned Black man. Peter advised House he didn't know who he was nor had the time to give it the attention it deserved.

It was a beautiful Sunday afternoon. On the way into town, House looked at all of the posters advocating for Ellis. "I was blinded by my own goals and the answer was right in front of me the whole time." House thought, "You have ruined too many lives."

Peter and House stopped at a warehouse a few blocks before the Music City Center. House exited the car and leaned in to say his goodbyes to Peter.

"This is it. Peter, thank you for your help. This tech shit is confusing; I couldn't have done it without you," House stuck his hand out, "Take care of yourself."

"Are…are you sure you don't need me anymore? What… if the cameras come back on, and the slideshow doesn't work? What if…" asked Peter.

"I'm not worried about 'what ifs'," House stated, cutting Peter off. "If it's not today, there is tomorrow or the next day. My waking moments will be used to clear myself of this crime. If I'm being honest, no one cares besides me. No wife, kids, siblings, or parents, but they really pissed me off." said House.

Peter was worried about House. He thought House was on edge and wondered if this would cause him to make a critical mistake. Sadly, Peter was too scared to comment on his feelings, believing he would worsen matters.

"Ho…House once the slideshow starts, the…the phone has been programmed to reset at its conclusion. I did this so that if something doesn't go right, it would be harder to trace back to me. So, this…this is your only shot." Peter said with worry in his voice.

"This isn't my only shot, just the first one. Shake my hand and get out of here, man," House laughed. He could tell Peter was considering staying to see this through.

Peter shook his hand, "I... I hope I was able to help. Goodbye," Peter drove off in the distance.

House was unsure if he was ever going to see Peter again. "Thank you, Peter." House thought, "Who would know by choice to save your life would have helped me this last week? I hope he takes care of himself."

House made his way to the Music City Center. It was the first time he had ever been in the building. He entered through the parking garage and told the attendants he was looking for Ellis's Campaign Rally. They showed House where it was, he needed to go. Inside the Music City Center was massive. Designers were putting up campaign flyers and posters everywhere. Even though the event was a few hours away, there was already a large crowd gathered outside of the ballroom.

An announcement came over the intercom:

If you do not have an access pass attend the event that starts in the next forty-five minutes. Please start making your way to the exit.

"Time to make my move," House said to himself.

He looked around and saw some individuals who may have been on the security detail for the Music City Center. They were in cheap suits. They only purchased them because they were required to work today.

"Hey guys, I worked here long ago and returned for today's job." House said walking towards the guards, "Heard they paying well? Where do we need to go?" House asked.

"We are just supposed to be here and kick people out. Our supervisor and manager didn't show up...which was expected. That Wilson guy has his own people following him. Our break room is down that hallway to the left. Here is a badge or whatever. There are a few of yall starting today."

House was handed a badge and a key.

"This can get you anywhere you need to go in the back hallway. Nice meeting you. I'm Bob, by the way." Bob stuck out his hand towards House.

"Likewise, I'm Seven," House replied.

"I would hate to have your name; I bet you couldn't get away with anything when you were a child," Bob said jokingly as he walked off, "How many people do you know are named after a number?"

House looked around, and a crowd was gathering. It seemed to be celebratory shouting.

"That has to be Ellis, time to introduce myself." House started to make his way to the crowd.

As House got closer to the crowd, different Ellis fans were yelling, "You got this!", "Ellis for President!" and so on.

"Thank you, thank you! I will be Governor of this great State in a few days!"

He wasn't sure, but that had to be Ellis. House made his way into the crowd, and there he was. Wilson Ellis was now in his late sixties but aged better than House expected. Back when he was Captain Ellis, he was obese and had a drinking problem... Now, he was in surprising shape. Well-groomed salt and pepper hair, clean shaven. He looked the part of a rising political figure.

"We are almost to the finish line," Ellis said commandingly, "But there is work to be done. So, make sure you get out there and let the great citizens of Tennessee know I got your back!"

The crowd erupted with cheers. Ellis was moving his arm in a motion to quiet down. As the group was calming, House yelled. "Captain Ellis, it's been a long time."

"Captain, I haven't been that in a long time. Is this one of my opponents' party members trying to upset me?" Ellis said with a smile on his face, trying to figure out where the voice was coming from.

"No, just an old friend," House pushed through the crowd to face Ellis. "Long time no see." He opened his arm to embrace Ellis.

All of the color left Ellis's face and his mouth hung open. He didn't mimic the motion House did.

"Come on, man. So, you aren't going to give me a hug?" House said to entice Ellis.

Ellis begrudgingly hugged House and whispered, "What the fuck are you doing?!"

"I'm here for you." House turned and faced the crowd, "When I was a young officer, Captain...I'm sorry, Chief Ellis; as you all know, he believed in me and assigned me to a fantastic career-defining opportunity. However, I couldn't finish it due to circumstances out of my control. I just want to thank him for the opportunity. It's been what…ten years since I last saw his face. Give him a round of applause," House started clapping, and the crowd followed with cheers and chants.

Ellis leaned over to House," How are you here? You should have at least fifteen more years!"

House ignored Ellis and silenced the crowd. "Everyone let's get inside the ballroom to properly give Chief Ellis his welcome. I know there are more coming. Let's make sure the entire state of Tennessee hears us tonight!"

The crowd once again erupted in cheers. You could hear murmurs in the crowd, trying to figure out who this mystery man was. The detail around Ellis was confused as well. Was the stranger a threat? Or was he a friend?

"Good, I've flustered him. He will be worried about my next move and cannot remove me from the building after my public affirmations." House made his way toward the back hallway.

The event was set to start at any moment. House checked the badge and key he was given to verify they worked. They did. House started to make his way to the ballroom and heard screaming.

"Why didn't anyone tell me they released his ass?! No one thought it would be nice for me to fucking know?!" yelled Ellis.

"Sir, we attempted..." replied someone.

"Shut the hell up. I don't have time for your bullshit! Ok. Let me think for a moment. I'm far removed from that. Nothing can come back on me. So, let's calm down for a second." said Ellis.

House got as close as he could to see who was talking. It was Ellis, but the other person had their back facing House, and their voice was unrecognizable. They didn't seem to be a part of his security detail. House thought it was probably his campaign manager.

"We are awaiting your orders, sir," said the unknown person. "Do you want us to locate and remove him?"

"We can't do that now. After House's grand gesture, which I'm sure he planned.... goddamn it! Too many people would be asking why. I bet you all don't have eyes on him now either!" Ellis said furiously. He kicked over a water cooler and unknowingly threw a chair toward House.

"Sir, I do not understand the problem. Why are you so upset?" said the unknown person.

Ellis was pacing back and forth, mumbling to himself.

"Look.... just...," Ellis whispers in the unknown person's ear.

"Sir, we ca.." "Just do it!" Ellis interrupted.

"Right away, sir," the unknown person walked off.

Ellis started walking down the hallway and kicked over a trash can, still visibly upset.

House made his way to where the unknown man was heading. He was able to hear his footsteps in the distance. House was quickly closing the distance to ensure he regained sight of him. House saw the unknown person enter a room and close the door behind him.

The door had a narrow window. House peered inside what seemed like a control room. The unknown person was talking to a group of individuals, but House couldn't hear them. He opened the door slightly.

"...it will be announced soon," stated the unknown person.

One of the people replied, "So, let me get this straight, Wilson wants to cancel an event due to a guy he hasn't seen in ten years showing up? That guy seemed to like him. What's the real problem, Lance?"

"He won't talk about it. "No point in speculating either, "Lance replied. "He will address the crowd to tell them he will host the event on Election Day at a different location. Prepare to leave."

"Yes, sir," they responded in unison.

"Uh, Lance, you should see this," one of the guys showed Lance his cell phone, "This can't be true, right?"

"Henry, who sent you this?" Lance asked.

"There was a breaking news alert on my phone. Check yours." Henry responded.

All the remaining people in the room checked their phones and had the same alert.

"Hurry up and find Wilson. We need to go now!" Lance ordered.

House quickly opened the door to an adjacent room and closed the door behind him. Then, he pulled out his phone to see if he had the alert. He did. The alert read:

Numerous law enforcement agencies received an anonymous video highlighting possible crimes orchestrated by gubernatorial candidate Wilson Ellis.

House opened the alert.

Early reporting believes an investigation has been opened, and officials are attempting to locate Wilson.

House punched the wall, "Fuck! You didn't believe I could do it, Peter. Damn it!"

House heard people running down the hallway. Once they passed, he opened the door. Someone yelled, "This event required attendees to put their cell phones in Faraday Bags! So, none of them should know about this!"

House hurried in the direction of the ballroom. "I have to make sure he doesn't get away."

House pulled out this cell phone and prepared it to play," This is probably pointless now."

As he approached the ballroom, he heard cheers and praises shouted. "I guess whatever those bags are worked... of these folks don't care." House opened the door and saw a raucous crowd. Ellis was on the stage, soaking the cheers in.

"This Tuesday, I need your votes! A better Tennessee starts with y'all electing me as governor!" Ellis said, "Believe in me as I believe in you!"

The crowd erupted. House pushed his way through toward the front of the group. There was a screen behind Ellis rotating between showing his lead in the polls, policy changes he promised, and prominent individuals that endorsed him.

"Calm down, please calm down," Ellis requested. The crowd complied, "Due to an unforeseen circumstance, I have to leave earlier than planned. Do not worry. All of you who have come today will be allowed to attend my election night celebration at a different location. Be sure to..."

"What is that on the screen?" someone yelled.

"Some fake news, one last pathetic attempt." said another.

The cheers turned into mixed boos. Ellis turned around to see what upset everyone, his heart dropped. Across the screen were intricate details of his dealings, distribution of weapons and drugs from evidence, falsifying documents, illicit payments, and more.

Members of the crowd were shouting at Ellis:

"We don't believe one word of this!"

"Tell 'em this isn't true!"

"I can't be. I was going to vote for you!"

"So much about backing the blue! You back gang bangers!"

People in the crowd started pushing and shoving while still yelling obscenities. Ellis was still on the stage, staring in disbelief at what he saw in front of him. Lance approached him, "We have to get you out of here! Sir...sir, do you hear me? We need to go. Now!"

Ellis snapped out of it and turned to face him. "Ok... let's go."

House attempted to get on the stage but was grabbed by crowd members. He quickly wrestled away from them and climbed up. "Shit, where did they go?" House ran to the nearest exit and saw them running down the crowded hallway. He proceeded to give chase.

Ellis turned around and saw House in pursuit. "I knew it!" Ellis yelled, "I fucking knew it! Get the hell outta my way!" Ellis started knocking down people, chairs, trash cans, and anything to slow House down.

Ellis entered the parking garage and started running down the ramp, barely dodging cars attempting to leave it. As they got to the bottom floor, Ellis noticed House was still on his trail. He yelled, "Lance, shoot his ass!"

Lance turned around and House was still giving chase.

"Sir, with what is going ...," Lance replied while trying to open the car door.

"I said shoot!"

"It wouldn't be..." Ellis struck Lance in the jaw. Knocking him to the ground. He retrieved Lance's gun and started to open fire.

House hid behind a nearby car and drew his gun. "It's over, Ellis; give up." House projected.

"You should have stayed your ass in prison." Ellis responded.

House peered over the hood of the car and Ellis started shooting again. "Stay away from me!" Ellis yelled.

House went back into cover. He heard someone enter a car and the sound of tires screeching. He looked up, and Lance was still lying on the ground. He ran over and lifted him.

"Where did he go?" House demanded, "Tell me now!"

"Nnnn…no," Lance replied.

House punched Lance, "Now!"

"I…I don't know. I swear."

"Worthless piece of shit," House tossed him back on the ground.

He looked around and saw someone entering their car. He rushed over there. "Sorry, I need this." and pushed them out of the way.

House took off after Ellis. He was still determining the direction Ellis went. Then someone screamed. "That guy is driving like a bat outta hell! What is so important?"

House heard tires squeal, and he headed in that direction, driving at a high rate of speed. He looked to his left and saw a car driving erratically. "That has to be him."

Ellis appeared to head towards Broadway and quickly left, barely avoiding a collision. However, House was on his tail as they raced down Broadway, headed toward Midtown.

Due to it being a Sunday evening, there was barely any traffic on the roadway. However, House could hear the sirens fading behind him. "They must be heading to the Music City Center," House thought, "Where is he going?"

Ellis was swerving in and out of lanes and crashed into a sign near the entrance to a park. He quickly got out of the vehicle and ran into the park. House hopped out of his car and chased him. "Ellis, stop! It's over."

Ellis started shooting at House blindly, scaring the people who were nearby.

House didn't return fire. "You're not getting the easy way out! I've been waiting years for this!"

They ran across the lawn and up the stairs of a white concrete building. He tried to open a set of bronze doors but failed. Ellis was visibly winded. He knew he was cornered. Ellis turned around to face House.

House drew down on Ellis, "It's…over…turn yourself in," House said while catching his breath, "This has been a long time coming."

" Is this what you wanted?!" Ellis screamed, "Everything I have worked on for years is about to be flushed down the goddamn toilet!"

It started to rain. This was a perfect way to symbolize how House was feeling. For years and even the months leading up to this point. He felt everything was raining down on him. From losing his best friend, uncovering what his police department was doing, and the betrayal, all of it led to this moment.

As they stood in the park with the rain coming down, Ellis started barking, "Everything I did was for the good of the city! Whether it was me or someone else, the dope fiends would get their drugs, criminals would launder money, and guns would still be on the city streets! At least with me orchestrating the whole thing, we already knew who was doing what. How does it make you feel, House? How does it make you feel that your accomplishment will be the boulder down the mountain? Do you think the buck stops with me? No sir! I was just a little fish in a big pond."

"Ten years, I did ten years because of you," House stated, "Ten long-ass years. now, it's your turn."

"Just who in the hell do you think you are talking to, House? Do you believe anyone is going to believe you? You are a convicted criminal. One that was found guilty of killing a fellow police officer. Guess deserved better than that." Ellis stated.

Ellis started pacing back and forth. He still had the gun he shot at House with in his hand.

"Drop the gun, get on your knees, and put your hands behind your head." House ordered, "Slowly."

Ellis looked at the gun, "Oh this, here you go, it's empty anyway," Ellis tossed the gun into a nearby pond, "Go get it."

Ellis throwing the gun in the pond didn't bother House. Nothing was pointing to it being used in a crime until today.

"Get down on your knees," House again ordered.

"Go fuck yourself. You're not in the position to tell me to do anything." Ellis replied.

Ellis was acting just like House expected, smug and arrogant. Relinquishing control of a situation was something Ellis rarely ever did.

House knew time was running short. He needed answers quickly.

Ellis started to walk towards House, "For over sixty years, I have walked this earth. For more than forty of them, I have served the people of this city. Do you understand what I saw long before you were born? The things I saw before your time at the department? Nothing ever changes, House, nothing! You remove the drugs from the streets one day, and they are brought back the next. You get the weapons off the street, and two days later, an innocent child is killed by one straight off the boat. Who is accountable for these crimes? Who will hold that mother, father, brother, or sister who just lost that loved one? No one. That's why I did what I did, House. I had a system designed to keep those accountable in check, and it would limit new people from flooding the ecosystem I created."

House knew Ellis was right. This happened more often than not. "Regardless of that, Ellis, we swore an oath to protect people. Not help facilitate the activities."

Ellis was still approaching House, "Get off your moral high horse and understand the bigger picture here."

House fired at Ellis's feet, "Stop right there."

"I'll be damned, you're serious about this?" asked Ellis, "What do you think is going to happen? Do you think I'm going to jail? Ha! Stop kidding yourself."

House heard police sirens in the distance, and they were getting closer.

"You hear them too, House?" Ellis asked. "What are you going to do? Hope that they arrest me?"

House needed something concrete. He thought back to his conversations with Young and the recording between Silva and Swift, "I know you were there that night. It was you, Silva, and Guess, right?"

Ellis took a step back, "No, I don't know what you are talking about. Guess was a shitty cop. Did you read any of his reports? They seldom went with the witness statement of accounts. His paperwork could have been ripped to shreds by a day one attorney."

"He is being careful with his words." House thought. "I need to find the opportunity to trip him up."

Ellis continued, "Don't get me started on his file. He had a laundry list of complaints. Ninety-eight percent of them were warranted. Abuse of power accusations, people calling him racist, illegal searches, etc., it went on and on. It's not surprising he finally went bat shit and killed someone."

"Like when he killed Stephen Knight?" answered House. Originally, House had planned on revealing this later. However, this was the perfect time to see what kind of reaction Ellis would give him.

The color from Ellis' face started to fade.

"Bingo." House thought.

"You don't have an answer for that?" asked House.

"How did he know about that!" Ellis thought. "I thought we got rid of everything!"

Ellis started pacing back and forth. He figured if House knew that there were other things House hadn't shared yet.

"Also, I have a recording where Silva states you were the one who knocked me out," said House.

"She's a lying bitch. She did that," answered Ellis.

"So..you were there."

Ellis took another step back. "I… I didn't say that. I said she did."

"You don't seem sure in your response." replied House.

"I..."

Police swarmed the field in front of the building.

"Seven House and Wilson Ellis come out with your hands up." an officer stated from a loudspeaker.

"Damn it, I ran out of time," House thought.

House looked at Ellis.

Ellis took a big breath. He seemed relieved at their arrival.

"I had the son of a bitch on the ropes." House thought.

"Wilson Ellis and Seven House come out with your hands up." repeated the officer.

House holstered his weapon and started to walk towards the steps.

"I'm not going to lie, you almost made me slip up there, House. How does it feel to get this far to come up short?" asked Ellis.

House stopped, "You lost. Do you think you're going to be elected after all this? You stole a car and shot at innocent civilians. Your voter base, the news, and other law enforcement agencies all know what you allowed to happen. There will be an investigation. They have no choice. Things didn't go according to plan, but they seldom do."

"I survived for ten years, but I don't think you will be so lucky."

Ellis knew House was right. It was less than twelve hours until the polls opened. Not enough time to spin the story or damage control.

Ellis leaned down and started pulling his pant leg up. He had a concealed pistol in an ankle holster.

House turned around since Ellis didn't respond.

Ellis pointed the gun towards House, "You're not going back to prison, I'm sending you straight to hell!"

Two gunshots went off within seconds of each other. Ellis and House both went down.

They were shot by sharpshooters with rubber bullets. The acting Chief of Police wanted to make sure they were brought in for questioning. Aside from being sore, no permanent damage was done. 🜨

Epilogue

"I know these last nine-ten months have been troublesome, but I want to thank those who stood by me. Since we now understand the claims against me were baseless and an attempt to ruin my good name, we can look forward to what God has planned for me."

Wilson Ellis spoke on the courthouse front steps directly after a grand jury unanimously agreed they did not have enough evidence to bring him to trial for the crimes House had accused him of.

Prior to the grand jury, Ellis spoke to investigators with the promise nothing he said could be used in the proceedings to follow. The local news stations reported any leaks they received.

Ellis told them the corrupt acts of the police department were led by Charles Young, David Boston, Mike Guess, and Maria Silva. He presented evidence to prove Young was lying on the evidence sheet, Silva was facilitating payments to the colluding members, and Boston was having judges sign off on warrants without proper probable cause.

Ellis also had a voicemail of Guess admitting to killing Stephen Knight and the other's House was investigating.

A cold case detective was able to prove Guess killed the woman in the warehouse the day House was arrested.

Each officer was charged and convicted posthumously.

For Jessica North, Ellis stated he had never heard of her involvement with any of this. House believed this was a tactic to keep her in hiding. If she was to reveal herself, Ellis surely had dirt on her as well.

His lawyer, family, and friends were both sides of him. His speech and the decision were being broadcasted to all local news stations.

"Mr. Ellis, with these allegations behind you, do you plan on running for office again?" a news reporter asked.

"Well, it is unfortunate that these allegations against me cost me my governorship in the first place. However, I do believe it was God's plan so I could do something better for the community or perhaps the entire nation. What do y'all think? Should I give it another shot?"

"We believe in you!" said someone in the crowd. "You already have my vote!" said another.

The crowd erupted into cheers. Then, chants of 'Ellis 2024' started.

House was standing nearby, leaning on a tree.

The Innocence Project provided lawyers for House to get his conviction reversed based on how the trial was conducted and how House being in prison would have and continued to benefit Ellis until his release. The judge who heard the original hearing was brought up on bribery charges during House's incarceration. Further strengthening the Innocence Project claims. House's conviction was reversed quickly. He was now a legitimate free man with the abilities of an everyday American citizen.

House flicked his cigarette away, a habit he picked up after the death of his friend Trek Swift.

Chants were still singing, and Ellis was soaking it all in. Then, as House began to leave, a voice said, "You thought they got me, didn't you."

A shiver went down House's spine. He recognized the voice, but it couldn't be who he believed it was. So, he turned around, and there he was. Trek Swift in the flesh.

"You look like you've seen a ghost House," Swift said, extending his hand.

House slowly grabbed it, still shocked at the man standing before him, shook it, then pulled him in for a hug. "Where the hell have you been!?" House said as a tear was running down his face.

"After I was assumed dead, I went into hiding," said Swift. "I wanted to see if I could uncover more players involved with this. I had faith that you and Peter could finish the job."

"I had staked out Silva's home days before we spoke there. I figured I wouldn't leave her home unscathed, so I had one of my young guys trail me in case things got squirrely, which they did."

"Never would have imagined she would blow up the House. When I came to, he and Silva were dead. I removed anything identifying him from his person. His face was smashed, and his real fingerprints required special clearance for years. They only assumed it was me due to something they found in a safe. She must have been tipped off of my arrival."

"So, what have you been doing this entire time?" House asked, "Just waiting for the right time to show up?"

"You see the guy to the left of Ellis," Swift asked, "That's the State's Comptroller. His name is Quincy Quentin or Double Q to his friends. To make a long story short, Ellis and Quincy went to college together and remained friends. Ellis was playing with house money, no pun intended, while Quincy was playing with the state's money. Frankly, Ellis was doing child's play compared to Quincy."

Swift lights a cigarette. "We aren't done, House; our work is just starting."

Printed in the USA
CPSIA information can be obtained
at www.ICGtesting.com
LVHW020913161024
793703LV00005B/64

9 798218 146559

Creating Democratic Citizenship
Through Drama Education:
the writings of Jonothan Neelands

Edited by Peter O'Connor

 is an imprint of

UCL Institute of Education Press
20 Bedford Way
London
WC1H 0AL

First published 2010

British Library Cataloguing-in-Publication Data
A catalogue record for this book is available from the British
Library

ISBN: 978 1 85856 456 2

Cover photograph: Andy Bradshaw

Printed by CPI Group (UK) Ltd, Croydon, CR0 4YY

Contents

Acknowledgements

I first met Jonothan Neelands at the International Drama In Education Congress in Brisbane in 1995. I remember Kate Donelan introducing us to each other at the Iguana bar. Of course, I had known Jonothan's work for much longer, having read *Making Sense of Drama* when I was a student on the RSA course at the London Drama and Tape Centre in the early 1980s.

We seem to have run into each other often at conferences all over the world ever since. I remember us going to a great tailor in Hong Kong for jackets to wear when I gave my first international keynote at a conference in Hong Kong, then trying out reflexology together. In 2004 we both gave keynotes at the IDEA Congress in Ottawa. At the time there was significant turmoil in my personal life and I will be forever grateful for Jonothan and Rachel's friendship.

At a party at Joe Winston's place a year later, Judith Ackroyd and I decided to edit this book. After three years lying fallow, Judith was happy for me to start it on my own. When I first suggested it to Jonothan he was genuinely surprised and humbled that someone would be interested in doing it.

I am indebted to Jonothan for his generosity in sharing his work and agreeing to share some of his personal story in this volume. It has been an honour to be the *kaitiaki* of his words. *Nga mihi nui a koe te rangatira.*

I'd like to thank and acknowledge Andy Bradshaw for the magnificent cover photo which epitomises Jonothan's work and the potential of drama education. Thank you to the following for permission to reprint material from the following publications: *Structuring Drama Work, 2nd edition* (2000) Jonothan Neelands and Tony Goode (editors) © Cambridge University Press. *Learning Through Imagined Experience* (1992) Jonothan Neelands. Reproduced by Permission of Hodder and Stoughton Ltd. *Beginning Drama 11-14*, Jonothan Neelands © Taylor and Francis. Reproduced by permission of Taylor and Francis Books, UK. To Chris Lawrence and the team at National Drama UK for their generosity in granting permission to reprint several articles from their back catalogue, to Chris Sinclair, and Drama Australia for their generosity in permission to use an article due for publication this year in the *Drama Australia Journal*. I am grateful for their support and desire to see these important articles in this book.

I'd like to thank Gillian Klein for so quickly and readily seeing the value in this book and her ongoing commitment to publishing drama education texts.

The cover photo represents the hope of a theatre without boundaries, distinctions or exclusions. Jonothan and I love the energy, confidence and purpose of these children bursting out onto the Globe stage and making it their own. They joyfully reclaim the playhouse and their right to use theatre in all of its rich diversity to make sense of their worlds. The stage provides the space for them to join in the social conversation about who we are and who we are becoming. It is a picture of hope based in action and a powerful reminder of how far we have travelled towards making theatre accessible and relevant to children and young people's lives. The picture is also an important reminder of how cultural organisations like the Globe, the RSC and others are socially committed to tearing down the walls and encouraging direct participation in all forms of theatre making. It heralds a new golden age for theatre and drama as acts of community and togetherness.

Foreword

David Booth

Reading this manuscript, I was swept in time over the last forty years of drama education, from my perspective of living in Canada. Throughout this period, I was certainly deeply affected by the British impact on the nature and form of this art form called, at various times, speech arts or creative drama or theatre arts or dramatic arts or drama in education or drama education or applied theatre. Fortunately, Peter O'Connor has set about creating a multimodal book based on the articles, book excerpts, transcripts and speeches of Jonothan Neelands, who entered the drama farrago about twenty-five years ago, in the middle of the often rancorous changes and challenges that teachers of drama were undergoing in their schooling, their professional texts and journals, and their conferences.

Since 1967, my Faculty of Education had run summer certification programmes in dramatic arts, and over the years had brought over many British drama educators – Dorothy Heathcote, Gavin Bolton, David Davis, Geoff Gilham, Tony Goode, Warwick Dobson and others, to lead our teacher courses for intensive six-week sessions. Those were heady times, and the political and philosophical attributes of the instructors, along with their practical and theoretical knowledge base, offered our teachers complicated yet enriched opportunities for growth as drama educators. The learning was never easy and never dull, and the tension-filled energy of the class experiences often spilled over into ideological debates about conflicting cultural references, differing curriculum outcomes, socio-political challenges, and variations in educational outcomes and how to go about achieving them.

In his introduction to this book, Peter O'Connor chronicles this time period so succinctly and with such insight in so few pages; he brings a clear understanding of the historical frame of drama's journey from England to other countries, including Canada, Australia, New Zealand, and even to parts of the

United States. Of course, in retrospect, drama, for us, serves as a backdrop for understanding the social movements in England and Europe, the debates and upheavals of the activists and academics in the struggle for dreamed of change. During my study years in Durham, England, I found myself inside the controversies, wondering about my own teaching goals, and nervous about everything.

The arrival of Jonothan Neelands on the educational drama scene coincided with a more organised and structured approach to developing a drama curriculum in many countries, now controlled by government policies and documents. This young man, with his softly spoken ways and his inclusive teaching style, perfectly fitted our teaching needs. I had met him at conferences in England, and was anxious for our teachers to work with him. And so began our years of his visits to Canada, especially Toronto. His teaching style embodied our newly acquired methodologies and strategies, yet the contexts for the work drew upon significant and troubling social issues, often thematically linked to the community where he was a visiting drama specialist. He was able to continue the artistic struggle of helping youngsters, and their teachers, in working towards building, or a least envisioning, a better world through the medium of drama, while offering and articulating teaching methods that appeared possible in an ordinary classroom, and that celebrated the art form.

During his visits, Jonothan would head directly to the Children's Bookstore, and after perusing the newest acquisitions, would select and purchase five or six. But the surprise was that they were often the books I had previously chosen for my own work. He knew the potential for drama building that each book held within seconds of reading it. The context, the concept and the content of a selection for his future explorations with students had to demonstrate a drama imperative, a story that would unleash other stories to be constructed together – teacher and students – shaped by an artist/educator who possessed the strategies for developing the deepest thought/felt awareness inside the work. I also watched him interview fifteen senior drama students, and his questioning and listening abilities drew from those young people such insights about their own work and their understanding of drama's significance.

Over the years, in conversations, in demonstrations, on videos and in print, I observed Jonothan continuing to build his philosophy, his personal pedagogy, and his teaching practice. His book, co-authored with Tony Goode, *Structuring Drama Work*, changed our classroom dynamics: teachers now found a way of organising their lessons, a schema for building a program that administrators could understand, that consultants could offer to the workshop participants, that students could record in their notebooks. This handbook of tools held its own dangers, but Jonothan continued to demonstrate through classroom practice and thoughtful talks the qualities that he knew authentic drama represented, and he honed his ideas and his theories, deepened his framework, and moved us into theatre's circle that surrounds our work. In his speech on '11/09 – the Space in our Hearts' – he says 'The difference now is the way we teach. The way students learn. What the human purposes of our teaching are.'

Jonothan's CV profile has certainly changed since I first knew him: he is now National Teaching Fellow, Chair of Drama and Theatre Education, and Director of Teaching and Learning at the University of Warwick, UK. But some things have remained constant: he continues to demonstrate his own teaching practice with classes of students, from primary age children to adults; he analyses the work of those students in shared post drama sessions; he reads widely from a variety of sources, from a wide range of areas inside and outside education; he presents his ideas in speeches internationally in a dynamic and engaging style; he continues to research and inquire about education's fundamental roles in supporting our young people; he works with teachers in both inservice and graduate programmes, supporting them in their own professional growth; he is involved in community and government programmes that offer young students training and scholarships in the arts; he encourages students to be actively involved in their knowledge of theatre, and of Shakespeare in particular; he is a valued member of his university's faculty, and he maintains drama's profile as a significant and worthy educational discipline.

I had the pleasure of acting as the external examiner for both Peter's and Jonothan's doctoral dissertations, and the rich qualities of their writings lifted my spirits as an educator who has worked in drama for many years, who has watched it morph and falter and renew. I was strengthened by their studies, knowing that drama needs and can have professional and academic grounding.

Just this week, I saw a performance of Tom Stoppard's play Rock 'n' Roll, and, as often happens in life, the intersection of this production and the reading of this book pushed me into a wider interpretation of Jonothan's contributions, and Peter's framing of them. In the play, Max, the Marxist philosopher, says that he is 'down to one belief, that between theory and practice there's a decent fit – not perfect, but decent'.

We have spent decades in education and drama struggling towards that fit, and for twenty-five years, Jonothan Neelands has continually provided us with a mindful, intelligent and heartfelt repertoire of experiences, lessons, essays, research, books and talks to support us in our quest to become better teachers in this powerful art form called drama. Read this book, and reflect on drama's journey, on our discipline's history, and on its future. Jonothan Neelands is telling us its story, and we are fortunate indeed.

Professor David Booth
University of Toronto
January 2010

Prologue

Jonothan Neelands

Peter O'Connor has skilfully edited this selection of my writings on drama and theatre education to bring out what he has identified as three key constructions in my work and writing: theatre, democracy and education. The writings themselves are collected from either out of print or hard to find sources and I am grateful for Peter's interest in bringing this collection into being and for his careful appraisal of how the ideas of theatre, democracy and education have developed over time.

I began writing as soon as I became a teacher in 1976. My first job was as an English teacher in a radical and enlightened English Department, led by David Jackson. We were founding members of the Classroom Action Research Network in the late seventies and in *Reflections from an Ivory Tower* I describe how I was encouraged to keep a journal and to research my own practice as a beginning teacher; to make sense of practice through reflective writing.

The writings here stand for themselves of course. My purpose here is to take a more personal voyage through the experiences and relationships which have brought the ideas of theatre, democracy and education to the fore of my thinking and practice.

The circumstances of my childhood were complex and fragmented. Suffice to say that I was born into and soon thereafter adopted into a very privileged up-bringing in London and was from an early age surrounded by theatre. Theatre as culture was part of the culture, in the wider sense, of my upbringing. My natural mother trained at RADA and was working in rep at Chichester when I arrived, unexpected and unplanned. I grew up in my maternal grandfather's house. Long stay guests in the house included Natasha Parry, later to marry Peter Brook, Anna Massey and other, then young and penniless, actors.

My stepfather (through a complex and extraordinary adoption) started his career as an actor at the Ipswich Arts Theatre. After three years in repertory, and an engagement with Brian Rix's Company at the Whitehall Theatre he joined the Stratford Company acting first with John Gielgud and Peggy Ashcroft and then with Laurence Olivier and Vivien Leigh. In 1962 he took over the famous open-air theatre in London's Regents Park and founded the New Shakespeare Company. He produced his version of The Wind in the Willows at the Vaudeville Theatre every Christmas. My first experiences of theatre were as an almost feral child, left to wander amongst the bushes and trees of the park with fairies from A Midsummer Nights Dream in the Summer, and to be chased by 'Ratty' and 'Mole' in costume down the backstage corridors of the Vaudeville in the Winter.

This is where and how the story in these pages begins. I have not told it publicly before now. I have had almost no contact with this side of my childhood since late adolescence, but it is where I began. These beginnings also explain my attraction to the work of Pierre Bourdieu: we have in common that we tried to understand the privileges of our own privileged upbringings in my case this has led to a constant theme in my work to do with democratising theatre by identifying and then reclaiming the culture of theatre associated with the culture of power and seeking ways of making it accessible to all. My own privileged private boarding school education left me, like so many of my generation, well educated but emotionally impoverished and damaged in ways that led to my lifetime as an educator who tries to offer all children a less damaging but equally empowering education. My 'privileged' upbringing and elite education forged my life-long political commitment to challenging the unfairness of the world and equipping the young with the tools needed to transform it.

In the preface to *Making Sense of Drama* (MSOD), I listed those drama practitioners who had shaped and influenced my emerging understanding of the theory and practice of drama-in-education. I was literally 'making sense' of drama at that time. I had just begun life as an advisory teacher for Drama and English in Northamptonshire and *MSOD* began as a set of resources for other teachers to help them begin the same artistic and pedagogic journey that I was also just beginning. I was barely one step ahead of my readers.

I have been very fortunate in having had some extraordinary, often long term, working relationships with friends who have also been my greatest mentors, critics, allies, champions and co-artists. In this introduction, I would like to pay homage again to my own teachers and those whom I have been privileged to work closely with during my life in drama and theatre education. I want to try and tie this to identifying some key formative periods and experiences, both personal and professional. I owe so much to so many people over an already long teaching career. I cannot possibly list everyone who deserves to be honoured for helping me to become the teacher that I am and that I am becoming. I am focusing here on long-term partnerships at crucial stages of my development and beg forgiveness of any reader who expected to find themselves remembered here.

My professional journey towards becoming a drama and theatre educator began in Leicestershire, where I had pretty much bluffed my way into a drama post at an 11-14 High School. Soon after I arrived Robert Staunton, the local drama advisory teacher, came to visit and offered to teach one of my classes. By this time I had already worked out for myself that drama teaching was more fun if the teacher joined in, but I was in no way prepared for Bob's workshop which was entirely participatory and used teacher in role as the means of guiding and shaping a workshop based on David Hare's *Fanshen*. It was a life changing experience for me.

But I was also terrified that I had been rumbled and that rather than drama teaching being easy and fun it was actually complex, sophisticated and based in a deep understanding of theatre and pedagogy – I imagined that all drama teachers worked like Robert Staunton. Robert was one of a team of seven drama advisory teachers working in Leicestershire at that time under the leadership of Maurice Gilmour. Both Robert and Maurice had previously worked for the legendary but often overlooked Silas Harvey in Newcastle and Northumbria. Silas had established drama centres in the most under-served and marginalised communities, that offered a rich diet of classroom drama, youth theatre and performances.

As Robert left my classroom he put a copy of Betty Jane Wagner's *Dorothy Heathcote: Drama as a learning medium* on the table and told me to read it and to start a youth theatre. He was insistent that I needed to provide drama both in the classroom and beyond. That was my job. I make this point here because I was brought up from the start to do drama and theatre; processes leading to curricular and human learning and processes leading to committed and ethical performance.

Leicestershire also encouraged teachers to become their own experts and published *2D*, which became the first series of significant journals of theory and research in Drama and Dance education.

Over the next few years before moving to Northamptonshire, I slowly and often painfully grew my practice as a classroom teacher of drama by studying Wagner's book a page at a time and then trying to make practical sense of it in my classroom and by developing a local youth theatre. My first published piece of writing, in *2D*, was an angsty account of a devised post-holocaust youth theatre production titled *Dust*, at a time when nuclear war seemed inevitable. I was confused to win a local prize for the 'Best Evening's Entertainment' with this Artaud inspired and desperately iconoclastic and nihilistic production.

When I began work in Northamptonshire, I soon realised that I could not expect other teachers to make the same sacrifices of time and effort in order to become drama in education practitioners. I realised that to make the work of Heathcote, Bolton and others possible, I needed to synthesise and demystify the apparent complexities of drama in education. I also realised that if I was to be taken seriously by teachers, I needed to prove my credentials as a teacher who could both demonstrate drama teaching as Robert had done for me and also offer resources for busy teachers to adapt and use for themselves. And so *MSOD* was born. But my point is that from the very beginning there was always the expectation that drama and performance based theatre went hand in hand.

This in part explains my fury at the interventions of David Hornbrook and his creation of the lie that drama-in-education practitioners were as a type anti-theatre and its traditions and against performance of any kind. In my experience these 'folk-devils' did not exist in reality. The strongest centres of drama-in-education in the UK at that time were also the strongest centres of high quality youth theatre and, like Leicestershire, took young people to the Edinburgh Fringe and other European festivals of excellence in theatre for and by young people. Now in his seventies, my first and most significant mentor, Robert Staunton still takes youth theatre to Edinburgh. And Maurice runs a local community theatre in the wilds of Cumbria.

I then worked in Northamptonshire for the remarkable Bill Shaw, who was the Advisor for English and Drama. Bill's loves were literature, jazz and vaudeville and he pursued them with great passion and encouraged and enabled teachers to join in his enthusiasms. But he was also a balanced professional who regularly invited Cecily O'Neill to contribute to residential drama courses in the county. I learnt from Cecily how to structure, how to use theatre elements, how to weave narrative drama, and owe her a great debt. She was also an advisory teacher and experienced at demonstrating drama teaching and successfully led professional development workshops for teachers.

I still look on these years in Northamptonshire as being the happiest and most formative of my working life. We had an extraordinary network of teachers who met weekly in different parts of the county to develop their ideas and share experiences. This was the genesis of the 'conventions approach' to drama-in-education and *Structuring Drama Work* was first published by and for teachers in Northamptonshire. This is where and when I began work and friendship with Judith Ackroyd, and her enthusiasm, criticism, encouragement and creativity have been an important shaping and critical influence on my practice and career.

Through political activities and working for the National Association for Drama Teachers in the UK (NATD) in the eighties I met Warwick Dobson and Tony Goode, who have been my closest friends and working partners for over twenty years. This was an important convergence of influences. Tony ran the BA in Community Theatre at the University of Northumbria, which was arguably the first vocational Applied Theatre undergraduate course in the world. He brought his experiences of theatre with young offenders, tough inner city youngsters, addicts and victims of abuse to my own classroom experiences of drama.

Warwick had been an advisory teacher in the Benwell Drama Centre in Newcastle and had also worked with Silas Harvey. He taught theatre at undergraduate level and was the artistic director of Lancaster TiE and a founding member of the Trotskyist inspired Standing Council for Young People's Theatre (SCYPT) which was an umbrella organisation for the politicised wing of the TiE movement. Warwick is one of the most intellectually and artistically gifted theatre practitioners of his generation and continues to challenge and provoke my own practice and politics. During a period of secondment from Northamptonshire, I developed and wrote the education pack for the Lancaster TiE schools project on the Peterloo Massacre and this experience helped me to understand the political uses of drama and theatre and the necessity of a critical and socially committed theatre to a healthy democracy.

The Structuring Drama Work or 'conventions' approach to teaching drama developed out of my practical work with Tony and Warwick. They shared in the mission to democratise drama teaching by identifying and describing the common techniques and conventions used by the great but often mysterious drama educators. We compared our mission to that of Cecil Sharpe, who had travelled all over England collecting and publishing folk songs and tunes so that they could be enjoyed by all. These conventions were drawn from drama-in-education but also from Moreno's psychodrama techniques, Agit-Prop and other forms of political theatre and the rehearsal techniques of Brecht, Meyherhold. MacColl, Littlewood and other socially committed theatre practitioners.

In 1989, the *SCYPT Journal* first published Dorothy Heathcote's Signs and Portents. This remains my own desert island drama education text – the one article I could not do without. It was written as a statement of the common artistic, semiotic and educational values and practices between Drama in Education and Theatre in Education. It successfully bridged the rehearsal room with the classroom, the work of the actor and the work of the teacher, theatre as performance with theatre as workshop practice.

At the end of the article Heathcote identified a set of 33 role conventions and this, in part, was the inspiration for *SDW*. Whereas Heathcote had confined her selection to conventions for introducing role, we were interested in a much wider set of conventions that did not assume the Stanislavskian 'living through' mode associated with the DiE and Process Drama traditions. In particular, we were interested in taking a more Brechtian or epic realist approach to drama. To use conventions to puncture the illusion of 'reality' in process drama and to make the content of drama strange rather than to make it familiar. The reasons for this shift are explained in *In The Hands of Living People*. But in common with Heathcote we also believed that:

> Most drama that moves forward at seeming life-rate is too swift for classes to become absorbed in and committed to. The conventions offered here all slow down time and enable classes to get a grip on decisions and their own thinking about matters. (p166 in the collected writings)

And in particular we had common cause with Heathcote's analysis that:

> The conventions I shall outline seem to me to be a most useful additive to both types of work (DiE/TiE). Avant Garde theatre has always used them, and film can wonderfully exploit them. I use them more and more in my work and they are comparatively easy to manage with a little care and practice. (p165)

But as central as *Signs and Portents* is to my own praxis, it also represented a parting of the ways. In the final paragraph, Heathcote declared her position as an educator rather than as a drama practitioner.

> Finally, having spent a long time wondering why I have for years been irritated by the cry of 'let's have more drama in our schools'. I now realise why I always wanted to say don't lobby for dramatics, lobby for better learning! (p169)

I have always had absolute respect for Heathcote's decision to turn away from drama as an art to focus on developing a globally and historically significant pedagogic system which uses some elements of drama for other ends. However, my own path has always been as a drama and theatre educator wanting to lobby for more drama in our schools as a means of lobbying for better learning.

Warwick and Tony had studied with Dorothy Heathcote and Gavin Bolton in Newcastle and Durham respectively and during this time Tony formed a close relationship with David Booth from Toronto, who lived with Tony whilst he studied with Gavin Bolton. Through David, we three began to work together in London, running summer schools for the University of Toronto. Later we were frequent visitors to Toronto to work in schools and with teachers.

The Canadian connection is very important to my explanation of myself. One of the few certainties of my childhood was my maternal grandfather, who was proudly Canadian and brought me up to think of myself as Canadian. This is my tenuous claim to Canadian heritage. But Canadian drama educators have had a profound influence on my own development as a drama and theatre educator. Richard Courtney provided the first essential theorising of drama education and I had read his publications alongside those of Heathcote and Bolton. David Booth has been extraordinarily generous in his support, encouragement, care and nurturing. He encouraged me to be brave and make drama popular and accessible for all; he taught me how to speak in public and how to publish.

I became a regular visitor to Toronto, where I met and worked closely with other inspirational and socially committed drama educators, particularly Kathy Lundy, the drama advisor for the Toronto School Board, and Larry Swartz. Here I discovered the delights of teaching drama in the most diverse and richly multicultural classrooms in the world. I also began to teach Summer Schools at the University of Victoria in British Columbia and developed personal and professional relationships with Juliana Saxton, Carole Miller and her husband Harvey. Harvey was the first pure theatre practitioner to take what I was doing seriously as theatre and to guide me and help me to make sense of my work as theatre. He was the mentor for *Advanced Level Drama and Theatre*. He died shortly before publication and Warwick and I were proud to dedicate the book to his life and work.

Carole Miller and Juliana Saxton have also been influential in my practice. Both are generous with their time and productive criticism. More recently, I have been impressed by the critical writings and provocations of Kathleen

Gallagher and once again I have benefited from her generosity in offering feedback and theoretical insights into my own developing practice.

For twelve years I also taught summer schools at Emerson College in Boston with Robert Colby and Bethany Nelson. These intense periods of teaching were a very important kind of laboratory for me to develop ideas and practice in partnership with two outstanding teachers. Much of the work we did was based in social history including the Civil War, the Great Depression and the landmark and brutally suppressed strikes at Lawrence and elsewhere in Massachusetts. Robert was also a fearless critic and restless seeker of new forms of drama which might bring young people closer to the truth of their histories and the practice of authentic democracy. Together we struggled with how to work with class and race in Boston schools and to articulate a democratic pedagogy for drama. Bethany, like Warwick, combines a truly formidable intellect with outstanding practice as an urban drama educator. She brought me back to teacher in role as one of the most effective and immediate tools in inner city classrooms and her recent research into the uses of drama to empower working class students of colour continues to inform my own work.

I have described here some of the important long-term relationships I have gained from over the years. There are, of course, many other drama and theatre educators who have been influential in my own development but at a greater distance – I have always admired and been influenced by the writings of John O'Toole for instance, and recently have had more opportunities to work closely with him. Australian, as well as Canadian, drama educators have had a strong influence on my practice and thinking. Since working at the University of Warwick, I have developed a significant partnership with Joe Winston and we run an international MA together, which we think successfully combines our complimentary skills, interests and experiences. Joe has been a constant source of advice, encouragement and support over the years. The gifted urban teacher Rachel Dickinson, who was also trained by Robert Staunton in Leicestershire, now works with us and my work with her at Shenton Primary School in Leicester led us to co-author *Improving Your Primary School Through Drama* – which brings me full circle back to *MSOD*. This time this introductory drama text book is based in the words and experiences of the teachers themselves as they developed drama as a healing force in a divided community under Rachel's guidance. It is a making sense of drama for the 21st Century.

I have also returned full circle to Shakespeare through my close working relationships with the RSC Education Department. In recent years this has become a powerful and influential relationship that has greatly accelerated my own practice. I am grateful for the support, guidance and models of good practice of Jacqui O'Hanlon, Rachel Gartside and Ginny Grainger and others in this new journey, which has included training the acting ensemble in process drama approaches to workshops for young people. When the new RSC Theatre opens in 2010, 35 per cent of the actors on stage will have been trained for this work. This apple it seems never fell far from the tree.

I suppose that I am surprised by the breadth of my engagement with drama and theatre now. As I write, I'm continuing ten years of research for government into conservatoire level actor and dancer training. I have recently completed research for the National Association of Youth Theatres. My writings are published in journals of sociology, cultural policy and political theory as well as in drama journals and texts.

The beating heart remains of course. That through their artistic transformations of time, space and self in drama, young people can find the voice, confidence and tools to transform their worlds and stories.

Introduction

All drama education involves people learning how to act. It would be a very limited view of drama education to suggest this was only about acting on the stage. A wider view is that in drama in education students learn how to be actors in and for the real world. In creating fictional worlds in classrooms young people take on a wide range of imagined roles to explore what it might be like to be someone else or feel what it might be like in different circumstances. These fictional worlds are created not merely to learn the skills and techniques necessary to construct them, but also to understand their own and other's lives better by trying out real solutions to real issues, looking at the world through different eyes and safely enquiring into issues of deep significance. The worlds of imagined play and the theatre have always served this purpose of creating a space for people to reflect on who and how they are and, more importantly, who they might become. Theatre is a space where the most important issues and concerns of our times are mediated through art into something more than the everyday. The theatre has always been a central market place for ideas, for challenges, for learning, healing and celebrating.

This theatre, which can be recreated with young people in ordinary classrooms with nothing more than the skills of the teacher and the willingness of the young people involved, is a radical revisioning for schooling – and a radical revisioning of theatre.

Theatre belongs to everyone. It is not the preserve of those with acting talent, of a privileged subset of society. It is a joyful place to explore, question and explain our worlds. Theatre has always served as a means for knowing ourselves, and our relationships to those around us. Learning in and about the theatre is about learning how to live. Such thinking lifts drama education from the teaching of acting skills and techniques into a pedagogy that can radicalise and transform the classroom into theatre itself. It creates a pedagogy where young people understand their rights to participate, to make decisions about things that truly matter, and to have their voices heard.

At the heart of democracy is talk. Yet in classrooms around the western world dominated by various forms of literacy strategies, talk seems to have become ever rarer. There is plenty of teacher talk; there always has been. But student talk is a luxury many teachers now feel they cannot indulge in as they teach to the standard that will be tested and tested again. One goal of this book is to remind teachers that talk must win back its central role in classrooms if young people are to see that they live in a world where their opinions, their feelings and their questions are of value. The theatre described in this book shows students engaged in talk that is about things of importance, of substance in the real world we live in day by day. Talk which challenges and questions, talk which at times borders on the irresponsible. And talk that is about how we live together now and how we might live together better in the future.

This book is as much about theatre as it is about education, drama and democracy. It tells the story of a theatre worker who has worked with young people predominately outside theatre buildings in classrooms. Jonothan Neelands' work has been central to the development of drama education around the world. This book explores the journey of his practice and thinking over the past twenty-five years.

The book is divided into three sections. The opening section, *Making Sense of Drama*, looks at how over his career Neelands has sought to make this form of theatre and education accessible for ordinary classroom teachers around the world. Much of his work has in one sense been an attempt to democratise drama in education. In the early 1980s it was about providing the structures that teachers could use to replicate the seemingly magical work that drama education pioneers like Gavin Bolton and Dorothy Heathcote were demonstrating. It has also been about making theatre forms accessible and easy to replicate in classrooms. It was about saying, 'you don't have to be a master teacher like Heathcote or Bolton, nor a theatre grandee, to make theatre with young people'.

In the second section of the book, *The Argument for Drama*, Neelands addresses central issues around the place of drama education within the curriculum. This is informed initially by the 'grand wars' of British drama education of the 1980s and, in particular, the attacks by David Hornbrook and Peter Abbs on drama in education. They called for a return to a pedagogy of educational drama that promoted both high art and a preference for Western theatre forms. It was an assault on the progressive drama education tradition founded in the work of Peter Slade and Brian Way. More personal and wounding was the direct attack on drama in education. Abbs argued that the work

Neelands and others were engaged in was neither of much educational value, nor was it drama or theatre.

The received wisdom of recent years is that the war ended with both sides agreeing that mistakes were made and that process drama now took on theatre forms more deliberately. It wasn't that simple. The Hornbrook devotees had enormous influence over curriculum around the globe. In reality, most classrooms around the world reverted to teaching drama skills, to preparing actors for the stage and, in an ironic and somewhat tragic twist of fate, Neelands' conventions approach became the *de facto* curriculum in many jurisdictions. Here, students now learn individual decontextualised conventions as the content of drama lessons.

For many, the compromise was a messy 'teach the conventions' approach that devalues both process drama and education about the theatre. Neelands himself argues against such an approach. However, the democratising of theatre forms made accessible through *Structuring Drama Work* has been a double edged sword. Neelands argues that the conventions are merely the paint on the palette, and it is the careful sequencing and building within a rich understanding of theatre forms which give sense and meaning to classroom drama.

The final section, *Pro Social Pedagogy*, begins with Neelands' powerful and evocative response to the attacks on the US of September 11, 2001. In these writings, Neelands centrally positions the political implications of his work, and argues most forcefully for drama as a democratising force.

Opening and closing the selected writings with examples of Neelands' practice highlights the fact that Neelands, while a gifted writer about drama education, is first and foremost a practitioner, a master teacher and theatre artist.

I have had the pleasure of watching Neelands teach on numerous occasions. His slow, methodical pace and attention to detail have attracted much comment. So does the richness of the theatre experience, of the deep feeling that flows under and through the work. The image I have of Neelands teaching is the gentle circular rubbing together of his fingers and thumb, as if he were trying to conjure one more miracle of theatre in a place where theatre does not often happen.

I decided very early in planning this book that the articles be republished in their entirety. Many of the earlier pieces are now difficult to access, yet they are seminal documents in the formation of Neelands' approach so deserve to appear in full. The extracts from chapters in books have been only minimally edited to stay as close as possible to the original.

Section One
Making Sense of Drama

This section uses the title of Neelands' first book, *Making Sense of Drama* and the first chapter featured in this section is the opening chapter of that book. It is a transcript of Neelands working with a group of students on the story *Beowulf*. The work marks an important step in Neelands' lifelong quest to demythologise and make accessible to teachers the artistry involved in teaching drama. Many of the key features of Neelands' later work are to be found here.

The choice of *Beowulf* as pretext is typical of the pretexts Neelands has chosen for his work with young people. Neelands has always deliberately encouraged working with art, usually narrative or poetic, as pretexts. He has used the artistry of artists as the basis for drama rather than trying to create characters, plots and settings from scratch.

His choice of pre-existing stories – often from a particular cultural canon – no doubt springs from his early years as an English teacher and his initial interest in drama as a means for exploring literary texts. In our discussions on this section, Neelands suggested that:

> At the heart of drama work is story, whatever anyone else might say about that! It's also about my commitment to theatre, of course. The more I think about it, the more I realise I have always been a theatre rather than a drama educator, and maybe this is why I have always felt on the outside a bit. So in my work there has been Shakespeare, Sophocles, Brecht, Churchill, Bond.

Neelands has been drawn largely to stories of those on the edges, on the margins. As in Beowulf, these are stories with genuine heroic action, of people challenging the social order, often from hopeless positions. Neelands' work has been characterised by a commitment to the idea that the world is an unfair place, and that young people need to be conscious of this to understand how power works in the world. This extract from *Making Sense of Drama* also reminds us that in this choice of pretext, Neelands has also sought an emphasis on role models for young people – fostering faith that individual agency can make things happen, particularly when part of broader social movements.

Neelands has consistently chosen what many might consider to be difficult texts, ones that may not immediately resonate with the everyday lives of young people in classrooms in the later twentieth and early twenty-first centuries. His choice of texts from the classical canon, however, is part of Neelands' belief in cultural democracy: a belief that great literature belongs to everyone. Beowulf is a story rich in dramatic tension, offering themes and ideas that are as relevant today as when it was written. Its difficult language is also beautifully crafted and it is made accessible and powerful through a process that allows students to play inside the story.

Neelands' use of story to open his first book on drama teaching placed him slightly outside the drama in education field in the UK in 1984. The use of story shows the influence of David Booth in this and Neelands' later work. Both Booth and Neelands have, through their careers, fashioned forms of drama education that combine their deep love and knowledge of children's literature and the power of story, with drama in education conventions.

Beowulf as an exemplar of Neelands' work, however, demonstrates its origins in the pioneering work of Gavin Bolton and Dorothy Heathcote. The lived through, unbroken teacher in role work, where everything is mediated through the teacher's dramatic role, was typical of drama education work at the time. The non-naturalistic approaches that have characterised Neelands' practice since *Structuring Drama Work* are not to be found here, except for in the pair work, where students are instructed to improvise or rehearse their farewells before heading off to kill Grendell. Neelands resolutely stays in role as Hygelac, the King of the Geats, and deals with the eager Beowulf who, from the first teacher student interchange, is ready to kill the dragon and end the drama. Neelands stays in role and demonstrates every trick he knows in his attempts to slow the drama down. Those of us who have struggled through the form will remember using lines similar to 'Wait a minute Beowulf, you're too anxious, these things need careful preparation'. It cannot be heard in the written transcript, but I can imagine the rising panic as Neelands could see the drama ending before it had even started. His attempt at a ritualistic ending to the drama now seems somewhat quaint, as the students almost transform into eager musketeers as the great oath is given.

There is a reassuring clumsiness in much of the work in the transcript. When we look at Neelands' teaching as artistry, we can easily see a talented novice in this exemplar. The palette of forms and devices with which he later enriched his work seem to be still unknown to him. Yet flashes of intuition in role mark out great practitioners and we see this in the following interchange when, having asked for stories of recent bravery, Neelands comments in role:

> Ah, times are quiet in Hygelac's court. Nothing ever happens. Anyway, it's a pity those storytellers don't come around anymore – stories to stir your blood [and points to the student who has volunteered to be the story teller].

Remember that at the time, Neelands was an advisory teacher in Northamptonshire. He was trying to make personal and professional sense of the exciting work emanating from Durham and Newcastle, but also to explain it for others. In discussing these times with Neelands, he reflects that he had

> really worked long and hard under Bob Staunton's tutelage to make sense of Betty Jane Wagner's account of Dorothy Heathcote's work and Gavin Bolton's recent *Towards a Theory of Drama Education*. I knew I couldn't expect others to do the same, so I knew I had to 'translate' what I was learning into something more immediately useful. Hence *Making Sense of Drama*, which was, literally, me making sense of drama teaching at a very early stage in my journey – literally one step ahead of the raw beginner. That's the real value of that book. The pedagogy also drew on enlightened English teaching as well as Drama in Education. I was advisory teacher for English and Drama, and at the time as involved in teaching poetry and writing as I was drama.

Finally, opening this book with a transcript of Neelands working with young people reminds us that Neelands is part of the rich drama education tradition that honours theory rooted in classroom practice. Like Peter Slade, Brian Way, Dorothy Heathcote and Gavin Bolton, Neelands has always been prepared to use his practice to inform his theory and vice versa, and he has been remarkably generous in sharing his practice, warts and all, with the world. For Neelands, it is a continuation of the work he was doing as an advisory teacher at the time. We talked about how this shaped his and Cecily O'Neill's generosity in public displays of their work.

> It meant going into schools and putting your practice on the line every day of the week! People wouldn't touch drama unless you could show them how it worked with their kids. The work was always public and high stakes in that sense. I think this shared experience was important in shaping both of us. I'm also of a generation that got their drama training through demonstration

lessons from the great and good and it was natural to continue this tradition. As long as you remember that the work is always bigger than self, ego goes and you just get on with trying to show the power of the art.

Sadly, it is a tradition that is dying. Increasingly, academics in drama education have come through a more traditionally academic route of study. Some PhDs in drama education are now completed by people who have barely worked in classrooms.

The other chapters in this section provide further examples of Neelands' efforts to make sense of drama teaching both for himself and for others.

In *Theatre as a Learning Process*, Neelands' desire to order and systemise an approach to teaching drama sees his development of what was later described as the 'conventions' approach. For Neelands, the conventions provided the key for making teaching drama easier. It is a significant leap away from the 'lived through' approach of *Beowulf* – Neelands recognised that the fragility of the sustained teacher in role work was too difficult for most classroom practitioners.

Yet Neelands acknowledges Dorothy Heathcote's seminal text *Signs and Portents* informed development of this work. However, the thirty-three 'Signs and Portents' conventions are all teacher in role, or role conventions. *Structuring Drama Work* was about drawing from the range of theatrical conventions to widen and grow the forms available to classroom teachers. Teacher in role became one of the conventions available, rather than the signal and defining convention of his work. Neelands suggests that

> All *Structuring Drama Work* conventions are Brechtian in the sense that they disrupt realism and make strange. They came from all over the place and I think Tony Goode is the real architect of the conventions approach. It was the time with Tony (community theatre) and Warwick Dobson (DiE and TiE) that really spurred all of this on. The varieties of dramatic action are the key to it all, of course!

Neelands' frustration over how the conventions approach has since been subverted into a decontextualised learning of conventions is obvious in his comments that...

> *Structuring Drama Works* clearly states that the conventions make the palette, not the painting! It takes skill in using these 'colours'. What is central to my work – and sadly I had assumed this is true of all process drama practitioners but does not seem to be the case – is the idea of the session as a 'journey'

deepening and unfolding as it goes. Like the best theatre and drama on stage and screen, taking us on an authentic experience of theatre even if the lesson is only 35 minutes.

In the extract from *Learning Through Imagined Experience*, we see Neelands defining drama education by looking at its functions. He again asserts its central function as being more than a subject in the school curriculum. This advocacy would be used in the years ahead as evidence that the work Neelands and others were championing was diminishing drama. Clearly, however, Neelands was always interested in creating vivid and exciting theatre. In a time when literacy strategies dominate education systems around the world, this extract also demonstrates the place of both story and drama in language learning.

In the extract from *Beginning Drama* that follows, Neelands addresses the nature of planning a drama lesson by drawing on the notion of the lesson and theatre as montage, the assembly of form and content. He admonishes that

> There must be an aesthetic logic to the montage: it's not enough to simply use a bag of different techniques – taken together the various exercises and techniques used must develop into a complete and satisfying dramatic experience.

He seems to be aware that the commercial success of *Structuring Drama Work* has seen teachers take up the approach without considering the full implications of working in this way. In this extract, we see the beginning of several themes that recur in Neelands' writing over the coming years. The notions around stressing the communal will develop into significant work on ensemble. He is clear too about how he shifts significantly from the work of Bolton and Heathcote, and begins to discuss the non-linear, episodic nature of his own work. The episodic, layered approach is closely aligned to the work of Cecily O'Neill, another who set out to translate Heathcote and Bolton into an accessible form for teachers, and by doing so developed her own unique practice.

Neelands provides details of the content drama teachers need, which includes an understanding about theatre, its history and its cultural practice. Neelands sees drama as powerful pedagogy, but to be powerful as pedagogy and as art form the drama teacher must have a rich and full understanding of the art form.

1
Beowulf – a Sample Lesson

This extract first appeared in *Making Sense of Drama* (1984)
Heinemann Educational Books: 9-23.

Why choose this lesson?

The Beowulf lesson has not been chosen to serve as an exemplar. It is a lesson that is interesting in some ways but as in all of the lessons that we teach there are elements that work well and elements that go astray. There are many ways of using drama and no single sequence of work can be raised up as a model for *all* drama work. Within the lesson described here are a number of strategies, ideas and principles at work that underpin much of the thinking in this book; but the lesson itself could have been organised in a variety of different ways – its construction is not as significant as its *intentions.*

The organising principle of any drama work should not be what other teachers and their groups have done but instead **what's possible?** Of course talking with other teachers and observing their work are invaluable ways of expanding and enriching our ideas about what is possible but in the end the considerations must be:

What's possible for me?
With this group?
In this place?
In the time I have available?

In the Beowulf lesson I had possibilities that would ordinarily be denied to most classroom teachers. (In fact you may well feel that I only scratched at the surface of the possibilities available to me!)

I was working as an advisory teacher. (I had no real knowledge of the group as individuals.)

I was working with only seventeen children. (The construction would have been very different with a larger group.)

I was working in a very small space. (As a result there is little physical action – it's a static, chair-bound session.)

I was able to control the length of the session. (I was not bound by bells, breaks or timetables.)

I am relatively experienced using drama. (I have had the opportunity to develop this experience; I might have handled the King-Beowulf conflict differently with less experience.)

These are the circumstances that defined for me 'What's possible?' and they should be borne in mind when you read the lesson. These circumstances also affected the choice of the Beowulf session as an illustration in the following way:

The lesson is very static in terms of action; it is therefore possible to give a comprehensive picture of the lesson through transcript. Some lessons hang on the actions, or pauses, or symbolic gestures, or facial expressions. Such lessons would be very hard to describe in writing.

The lesson took place in a classroom and is a useful illustration of what's possible if no other space is available. How many of us work in carpeted drama studios?

(The teacher remains in control, acting as chairperson for all that is said, ie, it's a fairly safe structure. In fact, he remains too much in control!)

The lesson was not an easy one for the teacher to maintain and as a result it's perhaps more interesting than a smooth and slick lesson might have been. (Many of the problems stem from the conflict with Beowulf – a girl who totally amazed her teacher with her uncharacteristic defiance. But this conflict was also the mainspring of the lesson.)

Because it wasn't an easy lesson the teacher had to employ a wide range of strategies in his negotiations with the group. If I list the strategies I consider to be at work in the lesson, it might be useful for *you* to tie them into the transcript as and when you recognise them.

1. Using teacher-in-role to initiate the drama; using a leader-authority role.
2. A variety of forms of questioning.

3. Planning both in and out of role.
4. A different but productive teacher-learner relationship.
5. Whole-group interaction.
6. Use of space and time.
7. Coping with responses.
8. Spontaneous development of the drama.
9. Teacher's use of language.
10. Ritual.
11. Using a variety of ways of working.
12. Using and developing children's existing experience – both actual and from story.

The lesson represents one teacher's handling of a theme and his attempts to draw a group into a productive relationship with it. It might be useful for you to consider your own ways into the material: How could the children have been moved into action more quickly? How could the teacher have used the ideas offered by the children more effectively? What other ways could the teacher have found to involve more of the group?

Preliminary work on *Beowulf*
The Setting
Brixworth Primary School: seventeen mixed nine- and ten year olds; one half-day (two and a half hour) session; a self-contained classroom.

The thinking for the lesson came from a personal enthusiasm for Kevin Crossley-Holland's latest adaptation of *Beowulf,* illustrated by Charles Keeping and published by the Oxford University Press. I was impressed by the way the author had managed to make the text more manageable, and more appealing, for younger readers. In doing so he has retained the wonderful aural colour and rich, physical imagery of the verse-story. The text is sensuously matched by Charles Keeping's barbarous and harsh drawings.

I was also interested by the 'old chestnut' reputation that *Beowulf* has amongst drama teachers. It has appeal as a dramatic context for the same reasons, I suspect, as those which made it so popular a spoken story in olden times. For an alternative account of Beowulf as drama see O'Neill and Lambert. There is much to respond to in this epic legend of honour, courage, monsters, duty and sacrifice.

The group had previously looked at *Elidor* by Alan Garner in a variety of ways, including drama, and I thought that drama might again provide a useful tool for them to use in order to penetrate the text more fully and closely.

The Session
In our first meeting we had read slowly the first fourteen pages of the text and stopped at the point where Beowulf and his band settle down in Heorot to wait for Grendel.

I purposefully chose this point because I wanted to work with the *children's* imaginings of what Grendel *might* be like. I wanted to stop before Grendel was defined by the storyteller; this would give the group the chance to consider facing a monster of their own making.

In our reading of the first part of the story I had asked the group to register any signs given in the text as to the nature of Beowulf's world – the customs, the atmosphere, the surroundings. After we had discussed their findings I asked the group to split into fours and to work together on producing a group image of Grendel, using white and black charcoal. At this point I hadn't shown them many of Charles Keeping's drawings because I felt they might inhibit original interpretations.

When the group finished their drawings we sat together and looked at each in turn. We then began to talk abut the tapestries described in the book. Someone remembered that some of those represented monsters also and we talked about what the other tapestries might have represented – kings, heroic deeds, battles, great adventures. I asked them to return to their small groups and to work on preparing tableaux representing the 'golden-eyed tapestries winking out of the gloom'.

When they were ready to show their work we assembled as a large group and I addressed them as the curator of a museum. I explained that we were fortunate enough to have been given a stone casket which had been unearthed near Brixworth Church (a Saxon church). The casket contained tapestries from the time of the Viking raids. I welcomed the group as historians, archeologists and art-historians and asked them for help in deciphering the tapestries and in giving the museum some idea of the significance of each picture – 'What does it tell us about the people who treasured it?'

Each group in turn then showed us their tableau and the experts discussed it as if they were looking at a real tapestry. When we finished, the group asked to take on the roles in the story. They were keen to try out being the Geats and to face their own fearsome Grendels! The following is a transcript of what went on during that role play.

The Transcript

T Teacher; B Boy; G Girl; Be Beowulf; S Storyteller; C Chorus – several voices more or less simultaneously.

T	Where is this happening – the first part of the story?
B2	In England?
T	In what sort of place?
G10	In a big hall.
T	A big hall – how would you imagine that hall?
B1	Heavy wooden tables, big long ones.
G4	And glass chandeliers.
B4	Enormous fireplaces.
T	Anything else? ... would it be a tall, high place do you think?
C	Yes.
T	And would it be all clear and clean?
C	No.
T	How would it be?
B1	Beer mugs everywhere.
B4	Bits.
T	Bits?
B4	Bits of food.
T	Yes ... so we're in the hall of the Geats. How would we be dressed?
G8	Long robes.
B4	Cloaks and big belts with great metal buckles.
G10	Sandals.
T	Sort of sandals yeah – what about our hair, would it be wonderfully clean and...?
C	No.
G4	Dirty.
T	What, sort of long and lankish (gestures) – a bit like mine today?

(*Nods*)

T	And would we be all smooth-faced?
C	No – beards.
T	Sort of rough beards – so we're pretty tough are we?
C	Yeah.
T	How do we think of ourselves then, us Geats?
G8	We think we're the greatest.
C	Yeah.
T	Yes, we're pretty tough eh? We've fought some good battles in our time hmm?
C	Yeah.
T	Nobody dares quarrel with the Geats.
C	No.
T	Right – so I'm going to be Hygelac, King of the Geats – now there are two other roles that we want to use in this opening. The first role is a very difficult one; it's the role of the storyteller. Who thinks they will be able to take the role of the storyteller? (*B1, 3, 4, 5, G2, 1, 3 4, 8 raise hands.*) You do (*indicates G4*) OK. And the other difficult role is ... who thinks they will be able to take the role of Beowulf? (*B1, 2, 3, 4, 5, G8, 3, 1 raise hands.*) Right! (indicates G3) So storyteller, would you like to come over and put this on? (*G4 moves to centre. T helps her to put on a 'Saxon' cloak.*)
G2	She looks like Little Red Riding Hood. (*laughs*)
T	(*To G4*) Would you like to go over there and enter from there? (*indicates doorway*) But give us a chance to settle down. Just wait a while, while we find out what it is like to be Geats. (*G4 looks unsure.*) I'll give you a signal, OK?
G4	Yeah.
T	Ah, well, so Geats, as we're sitting here drinking and eating, what stories does anyone have to tell us? What adventures has anyone had? Anybody done anything daring and exciting recently?
B1	Only thing that's exciting, that's what's happened is ... there've been some good scraps.
T	You have had some good fights then, recently?

B1	Yeah.
T	Who've they been against then?
B	Galactica.
T	Ah, he's been causing trouble again then has he?

(*B1 nods*)

T	And did you sort him out?
B1	Just about, yeah.
T	Good. Anybody else? (*waits*) Any other adventures? (*waits*) Ah, times are quiet in Hygelac's Court. Nothing ever happens. What about you Beowulf, you're always boasting of your bravery.
Be	Too quiet for me.
T	Too quiet, huh, perhaps the young lad wants a taste of adventure, eh!
C	Yeah.
T	You'll soon learn there's more to life than fighting ... there's drinking to be done, too! Anyway, it's a pity those storytellers don't come around anymore – stories to stir your blood. (*gestures G3*)

(*Storyteller knocks*)

G10	There's someone at the door.
S	I come to tell you a story!
T	You've come to tell us a story!

(*Clapping*)

T	We're pretty fierce people you know. I hope you have a story that's suitable.
S	I come to tell you a story about a great big dragon.
T	That sounds like the kind of stuff we like, eh?
C	Yes, yes.
T	Go on then Storyteller, you tell us!
S	Beowulf came to find this dragon. (Stops)
T	Beowulf? Same name as my son here. What sort of dragon was this?
S	I can't explain it was so terrible (*swirls her cloak and turns*) and everyone that came to fight it got killed.

13

(*Reaction of fear*)

T	Where does this dragon live?
S	In a hall, a great hall.
T	And where is this hall?
S	Heorot.
T	In Heorot.

(*Gasps*)

S	In the land of the Danes. It comes every midnight.
T	Midnight? Why don't the Danes sort it out, they're tough?
S	Beowulf (*turns and points with outstretched arm*) you have a go.
Be	(*Jumps up*) Alright, I will. I'll get my men and I'll go. (*Walks off, turns*) Come on!
T	Wait a minute, wait a minute. Beowulf sit you down. (*Beowulf returns to seat.*) Here Stranger have a seat with us. (*Storyteller sits.*) Now this monster he speaks of, this Grendel. He says it frightens the Danes.
Be	We're, we're stronger than them.
T	Well we may be now, but it's not always been that way. Remember we used to have to pay tribute to the Danes?
C	Yeah, yes.
T	We used to have to pay the Danes money or else they would invade our villages. Why should we help them?
B2	We don't even know if there is a monster.
T	No ... what do you say?
B4	I think we could leave it there. Teach them a lesson.
C	Yeah.
Be	(*Stands*) I don't care. I'm going.
T	For what purpose Beowulf?
Be	I want to kill it. (*stamps foot*)
T	Do you think he's the kind of ... will the Danes let him fight the dragon?
Be	I'll prove it.
T	You've got a wild tongue in your head – take a seat.

Be	No.
T	Beowulf, you don't stand in my court.
Be	I want to take my men.
T	Listen to those who are older and wiser than you – talk this through first.

(*Beowulf sits*)

B1	She won't even get in the waters.
T	That's right. Do you think the Danes will even let you land?
G11	I think he should go.
T	Why's that?
G11	Well, he could have a try.
Be	(*Stands*) I don't care if I get killed. At least I will have tried. I want my men. And I want to go.
T	Why do you think you're going to be any better than the Danes who've tried to fight?
G10	Yes.
B4	Yes.
Be	When they came to us ... that were ages ago.
T	And what do you think has happened since then?
Be	I don't know. They could've got weaker. They could have got stronger. I don't know.
T	Well, has anyone else heard? Have the Danes got weaker?
B3	Stronger.
C	Yes, stronger.
Be	They're probably just drunken idiots.
B5	Go and tell that to their Chief.
C	Yes.
T	Anyway, we had to pay the Danes. If we're sending people to help, we should get paid. What do we want from them?
B1	Food.
G4	Food.
G9	Possessions.

Be	Nothing.

(*Long pause*)

T	Nothing?
Be	I'm going whether you want me to or not.
T	Well, wait a minute. We don't know whether anybody is going to go with you.
Be	I'm taking them. I'll have you (*G2*), you (*G4*), you (*G5*).
T	Wait a minute Beowulf. You're too anxious. These things need careful preparations. Ships need to be armed – and food put on board. You need to pick the right people. It's no good picking people who will be no use in such a struggle.
B3	Yeah.
G9	Yeah.
T	Take a seat. (*Beowulf sits.*) First, Beowulf, you tell us what equips you for this task. What have you done in the past?
Be	I don't know. I just want to try it. It could be my first and help me to do others.
T	Olag (*gestures towards B1*) you had the task of training Beowulf in combat, how has he done with his training?
B1	(*Pauses, rubs his chin.*) He's done quite good (pause) I'm not sure if he can go.
T	Now Olag. Beowulf says he is ready for his first task, his first mission – what is your opinion?
B1	(*Pause*) I don't know.
T	What sort of people should we send with him?
B1	Good strong ones.
T	Experienced warriors?
B1	Yeah.
Be	I want to pick my own.
T	You will decide but Olag and the rest of us will guide you in this choice.
B1	I reckon he can go.
T	And he will bring honour back to this hall?

B1	Yeah. Hopefully yeah.
T	And will you go along to protect him?
B1	Yeah.
T	Now who else amongst you has performed tasks that might be useful to us?
Be	Father!
T	Wait a minute, let him speak. (*points to B4*)
B4	Well, the villagers have attacked this place dozens of times. Me and my two fellows here (*puts his hands on the shoulders of B3 and B5*) we've just been throwing boulders about that big (*gestures*) at them. (*B3 and B5 nod*)
B2	Morag.
B3	Yeah.
B5	And the dragon of Troy.
B2	Yeah.
T	Ah, so you have experience in dealing with monsters.
B2, 3, 4, 5	Yeah.
T	And how did you trap this monster?
Be	We made an old Indian trap (*gestures*) and when it was down there we chucked our spears down onto it.
Be	I don't want those three, they're spiteful. (*Stands*)
T	What do you mean spiteful?
Be	(*Stands*) They are always jeering at me. I want him (*G1*), him (*G6*), him (*G7*).
T	Beowulf, you are not yet King. Take your seat. (*Pause, then Beowulf sits.*) You will be guided by your father in this matter. These (*indicates B3, 4, 5*) are three experienced warriors. Now who else?
G8	Us four (*gestures towards G9, 10, 11*) have fought Romans. Many of them.
T	Yes, so you think you are equipped to fight?
G8	Sure we are.

T	Are there any of you who have something to prove, who may wish to risk your lives in this adventure? Any of you who feel there is something to prove?

(*Pause*)

T	Yes.
G10	To prove there is a monster.
T	To prove it's not just a story.
G10	Yes.
G8	So that we can kill it.
B1	Prove who's boss.
B2	We don't even know how big it is yet.
T	We don't even know how big it is.
B1	How do we get into the waters first?
T	We will go by ship. We will prepare a large ship.
Be	(*Stands*) We? I want to go by myself.
T	You will have the lives of many others to consider. You must control your recklessness. Many of those that leave this hall will not come back – and we need to know their blood will bring honour back to this hall; not be lost in a foolhardy adventure.
Be	Yes, father.
T	And Olag. He's not too big for a clip ... What preparations should these warriors make?
B4	We could make deadly spears.
B2	Fireballs.
T	Sorry?
B2	Fireballs.
T	Yes, we could make some tarred fireballs.
Be	I will take a few of everything. We don't know what he's like. So we might need anything.
T	Wise words Beowulf. It's best to be well prepared. Yes?
G4	Poisoned food.
T	Poisoned food? What might poisoned food be used for do you think?

G4	Well it might like to eat ...like some chicken and poison it and leave it for the monster.
T	Right. Yes. Ok.
B1	We'll have to get some wild berries first for p__ pro___ p___ (*struggles for word*) provisions.
T	Yes, and how will we need to prepare ourselves in our heads and in our hearts ... how will we need to prepare ourselves?
B1	(*Without mockery*) I've got some helmets in the back yard.
T	Yes?
B4	Shields.
B3	We'll need the best shields.
G6	And the thickest armour we can get.
T	Yes, any other suggestions?
G2	Train more men.
Be	But father, it will take too long. I want to go now.
T	Well, be patient. Yes?
G8	We'll need fireproof armour just in case this Grendel, as the stranger calls it, breathes fire.
T	That is very wise.
Be	If we fight with anything. I'll fight with my bare hands as well. Bare fight.
T	Brave words Beowulf. Brave words. Let's see how you speak when you face the monster.
B6	We will need mirror shields. Just in case its eyes can turn you into stone.
T	That's right.
Be	(*Stands*) I don't want too much stuff. It'll make the ship sink. I want to go my own way.
T	Be advised Beowulf.
Be	You advise me too much.
T	Will someone speak to my son?
B4	If you get more stuff, you can kill it easier. The ship won't sink because we can make more. Then the ships. The ships can go faster if we make more.

T	Yes.
G2	And he doesn't realise how big the monster is.
T	Olag, perhaps you should remind her what happened the last time we went unprepared to the land of the Danes.
B1	Yes. We were beaten. I still feel the shame.
Be	You think, you think you know everything.
T	Old heads are wiser than young heads Beowulf and you need to rem ...

Beowulf interrupts

Be	Young spirits are stronger than old spirits father.
T	Young spirits may well be stronger. But you need the experience of our years. Our bodies carry the scars of many battles.
B3	If you don't want to listen to us let the Grendel monster kill you.
B1	Stranger, how big is this Grendel?
S	I've heard it's two... well, he's so big it's difficult. He's bigger than this (*points to roof*) – it's two times bigger than this.

(*Gasps, sighs*)

B4	When we killed a dragon that size it took us four hundred men, not thirty.
T	That's true.
G8	When are we going to see this dragon, as you call it?
S	In the Danes' hall at 12 o'clock.
B2	But what if we fall asleep?
Be	I won't fall asleep that's for sure.
G9	Stranger, how many heads has this monster got?
S	Three.
T	Three. So it will see in every direction.
S	And nine eyes.
G1	I will cut off one of its legs.
T	Has anyone else questions about Grendel?
Gs	How tough is its skin?
S	Well, it's as thick as these walls.

(Gasps)

T	Well, swords and poisoned spears will be no good will they?
B2	How fast is it?
S	90 miles per hour.

(Laughter from several)

T	Remember, he is only a storyteller.
C	Yes.
T	As fast as a fast dog?
S	Much faster ... how are we going to trap it then?
B4	We could use nets. So it would run into them.
B6	But if it runs so fast, it could break the nets.
G4	When it comes into the hall, someone could push the table against the door. Then we could surround it and kill it.
B2	Well, if you had nets this monster, if it is true, could just pull them apart.
T	Yes, what about the suggestion we've just had over there? Yes?
G10	If it turns around its tail will kill all of us.
S	And he's ninety-nine stone.

(Gasps)

B4	He'll break the table.
T	So has anyone else any suggestions? The Danes must have had ideas that haven't worked, so we need to go with a good plan. Olag, yes?
B1	If we get a big log and trip it over, then we can get a big boulder and smash it on its head.
G6	It might run straight through it.
B3	Go for its legs.
G2	Storyteller, does it eat actual human beings?
S	Pardon?
G2	Does he eat actual people?
S	Yes.

(Gasps)

G8	We should heat up iron and push it in his eyes.
C	Yes, yeah. (*Some clap*)
T	That idea finds favour with you does it?
C	Yes!

The planning continued for another ten minutes, then I asked the warriors to return home to prepare themselves. In pairs, they improvised their farewells with an emphasis upon reassuring and explaining. The partners who were being left behind reported back about their feelings and anxieties at that moment – was it fair to them for their partners to go on such an adventure?

The group again took on the roles of warriors and assembled on the dock, in the early morning, ready to board ship.

| T | Stand in a line, warriors. (*They assemble carrying spears and bundles.*) Four in a rank! Space out so that I can inspect you. Now, the other Geats are all around you watching. So stand and show them you are ready for this mission. |

(*Teacher inspects the warriors, slowly. There is silence. Voices are very quiet. The conversation is private.*)

T	Are you prepared, Storyteller?
S	Yes. (*T moves on.*)
T	And you, are you prepared?
G2	Yes.
T	And have you brought anything special with you?
G2	Yes, my axe. (*T moves on.*)
T	Are you going to be warm enough?
G1	Yes.
T	Right. (*Moves on.*)
T	And you, you're young to be on this mission. Young to die. Have you thought about that?
G4	Yes.
T	And why are you so keen?
G4	To help get rid of the monster.
T	And have you brought anything special with you?
G4	Yes, a large spear my grandad gave me.

T	And have you said your farewells to your father and mother?
G4	Yes.

(*T carries on talking with every child.*)

T	Well Geats, you'll be boarding and leaving soon, taking the honour of the Geats with you. Now some of you have not been before. You may not know that we always speak the great oath of the Geats before we go. Perhaps some of the more experienced, of the oath ... who can remind us? ... perhaps you remember parts of it only? ... it's a long time since we set out like this ... Yes?
B2	A part of it is, we will bring back the oaths of the giant creatures.
T	We will bring back the oaths of the giant creatures – can anyone else remember?
B3	We shall trap them.
T	We shall trap them – and can anyone remember the parts that are to do with honour and courage that we are looking for?
G10	And wisdom.
T	And wisdom. What is the one motto we have, the motto we always say?
B2	Go proudly.
G8	Never boast.
T	Go proudly, never boast.
B1	All for one, one for all.
T	Yes. Go proudly, never boast. All for one. One for all.
C	Yes.
T	Let us hear you say it – and let's see you raise your weapons and shake them as we speak. GO PROUDLY NEVER BOAST.
All	(*Raising weapons*) GO PROUDLY NEVER BOAST.
T	ALL FOR ONE. ONE FOR ALL.
All	ALL FOR ONE. ONE FOR ALL.
T	Good luck, warriors!

Session ends.

Bibliography

Crossley-Holland, K (1982) *Beowulf.* Oxford University Press

Garner, A (1965) *Elidor.* Collins

O'Neill, C and Lambert, A (1982) *Drama Structures.* Hutchinson

2

Theatre as a Learning Process

This extract first appeared in *Structuring Drama Work*, Co-edited with Tony Goode: 2nd Edition (2000) p105-112

An active inquiry using theatre involves students engaging with complex areas of human experience in order to discover the questions and issues which are relevant to their needs and level of experience. The process of inquiry is cyclical and ongoing because the nature of theatre is to discover and rediscover new depths in the material in focus. An actor may have played Ophelia several times, but work on a new production offers the opportunity to discover new facets and ambiguities in the role. A group of students may often have worked in drama on the theme of families but a different starting point, or a fresh match of convention to theme, offers the possibility of new areas of inquiry and understanding. Because theatre is essentially concerned with the sweep of human experience it tends to prompt new levels of questioning rather than to promote answers.

This educational process can be viewed as a cyclical model based on certain key stages in the development of an active inquiry through theatre.

1. Experience/source → issue

Discussion and responses to the source will move towards the identification of those content-focused issues which will form the basis for the inquiry through theatre. The issues may relate to:

    (a) *Problems of meaning – how to find depth in the source*

    –   questions about the logic and sequence of events described in the source

- speculations about the wider context of the source
- personal and social issues triggered by the source
- questions about motivation, intentions, consequences of actions referred to in the source
- curiosities about the people and events described in the source

(b) *Problems of form – how to translate the experience into theatre*
- how to stage or how to re-enact events described in the source
- how to set up a situation for improvisation which will relate to the experience described in the source
- how to apply techniques, skills and conventions in order to open up the material
- how to find and exploit the dramatic potential in the material in order to realise and convey symbols, atmosphere, metaphor and tension

2. Framing action through convention

This stage in the process is reached when there is sufficient commitment to the idea of exploring further the area of experience identified through the source and the group's initial responses to the source.

The transition from discussion about the issues involved to behaving and talking 'in context, in action' is a delicate shift into theatre. The success of this transition is likely to be determined by an agreement amongst the majority, if not all, of those present, to *observe the constraints* of the conventions on role behaviour and the imagined uses of time, space and presence.

Making an effective match depends on a careful consideration of a variety of factors relating to the personal, social and aesthetic needs of the group and the teacher/leader, as well as to the issue arising from the content. The choice of convention will seek an appropriate match with the issues identified but the choice will be limited by:

- the values the teacher/leader seeks to promote or exclude from the inquiry
- the value the students place on the process of theatre as a form of inquiry and their willingness to participate as actors and/or spectators
- the learning intentions underlying the inquiry
- the mode of action which is appropriate to the personal/social needs in the group and the aesthetic development of the inquiry.

Observing the constraints – agreeing to suspend disbelief

For dramatic activity of any kind to take place, participants need to agree to behave in ways which make it possible for theatre to happen. The dominant performance tradition in Western lyric theatre, for example, requires an audience who agree to remain silent, fixed and virtually invisible for the duration of the performance, and in return actors agree to confine their behaviour and talk to that which is consistent with the imagined experience they are representing for the audience. The audience agree to discuss and comment after the actors have signalled the end of their work. Each of the conventions described in this book requires participants to agree to constrain their behaviour in specific ways and to adopt roles which reflect the roles of spectator and actor.

The nature of the agreement required will vary from one convention to another; some conventions will require subtle and complex agreements:

- In Hot-Seating, for instance, an agreement is made that one or more of the group will speak and behave as if they were roles and characters involved in the drama. The rest of the group agree either to behave as spectators by allowing the characters to speak or to ask the characters appropriate questions without challenging the illusion. The agreement may also include the idea that other participants can only ask questions which are appropriate to a particular role or viewpoint, such as scientists, detectives, newspaper reporters, etc.

- In whole-group dramas supported by Teacher-in-Role, participants agree to fuse the roles of actor and spectator so that a participant restricts herself to talk and behaviour appropriate to someone who is part of the fictional experience – even if, psychologically, she is more of a detached spectator watching and following the fictional behaviour of others who are more involved as actors. An agreement is often made to hold questions and comments belonging to the real dimension until the symbolic dimension offered by the role-play is suspended for discussion and reflection.

The agreement required by a theatre convention is more easily secured if those taking on the roles of spectators and actors have elected to be present through choice and have an inquisitive interest both in the content and in the form of the performance or dramatic experience. In educational contexts, however, this is often not the case. Within any group there may be a range – from those committed to the drama, through those who are uncomfortable with the idea, to those who are only there because they are forced to be so.

The decision to proceed into dramatic action in certain educational contexts is, therefore, a difficult one to make. The decision might be influenced by evidence that:

- the source has aroused sufficient enthusiasm to consider suggesting theatre as a way forward
- a workable proportion of the group feel ready to observe the convention that is suggested as an introduction to the dramatic work
- moving into theatre is likely to increase rather than diminish a possibly low level of initial commitment to the project
- an appropriate match of content and convention can be made
- preliminary discussion has allowed participants to make choices between conventions suggested as starting points for the action and also to make choices about whether they wish to participate as spectators or actors
- participants are clear about the intentions of the work in terms of how it might develop understanding of both convention and chosen content

Teacher/leader values on content

An active-inquiry mode of working suggests an openness to the idea that students should discover and make their own meanings out of the content as a result of their work in drama. In practice, the range of available meanings is likely to be constrained by teacher/leader concern to filter choices about the match of convention to content in order to promote certain values through the work and also to resist the emergence of other values. There is, of course, a tradition in theatre of the voices of the playwright and director dominating the work of actors and others involved in the performance and, as a result, also dominating the range of meanings communicated to the audience. The same is inevitably true for the teacher/leader involved in the process of matching convention to content.

Improvised drama tends to allow participants greater freedom to be actively involved in the matching process but even so the teacher/leader may wish to avoid a match of convention to content which might produce responses which will ultimately deny the dignity of, or exclude, individuals in the group of the people they represent in the drama on the basis of gender, social class, ability, sexuality, ethnicity or age. In preventing the portrayal of deficit images the teacher/leader is also positively promoting values such as tolerance, fairness, justice, compassion, respect for others. The force of teacher/leader involvement (or lack of it) will be influenced by his/her own moral and political ideologies.

The choice of convention may also be limited in instances where the teacher/ leader gauges that the material is becoming uncomfortable and over-threatening for individuals in the group, and that the use of certain conventions may increase the problem.

In very general terms, narrative-action conventions, because they emphasise events and work at a relatively fast pace, may encourage superficial or poorly considered responses, whereas well-researched context-building action and the controlled pace of reflective action may produce challenges to assumptions and prejudices.

The process of matching convention to content to the needs of the group is underpinned by the assumption that the teacher/leader is working with a consistent and explicit set of principles which check and guide teacher/ leader intervention in the students' choice of convention, and also that the teacher/leader is planning to ensure that an improvisation allows for fresh insights to be developed within a framework of constraints.

Teacher-in-Role is a particularly sensitive way for the teacher/leader to initiate changes in the direction of the drama, challenges to thinking, shifts in action and new conventions from within the symbolic dimension, ie, to manage the real needs and concerns of the group from within the drama. In an active-inquiry mode of working it is particularly important to make reference to reflective/evaluative questions which clearly indicate the level of advantage the teacher/leader is taking in the drama through Teacher-in-Role, and to ensure that responses to the questions are consistent with the principles.

The following questions are designed to assist teachers and students who wish to use a Teacher-in-Role convention as a central resource for initiating, developing and managing a drama:

What information is being given?
– about the context
– about the situation
– about the roles the group are being invited to adopt

What atmosphere is the role generating?
– through selection of: vocabulary; register (linguistic); tone; category of action; volume; costume/props; spatial relationships

What doors are being opened to the group?
- clues as to what needs doing by whom
- a definition of the problem
- possibilities for interaction
- what human themes and issues are being introduced
- indications as to what sort of 'destinations' the group might travel to in the drama

What doors are kept closed?
- parameters of the action defined by role
- decisions made by the teacher/leader rather than by the group in response to the role
- clues as to who will hold the balance of power in the interaction

Where is the challenge?
- Is a task being set?
- Is the role going to cause a disturbance within an existing situation?
- Is a request for help being made?
- What demands are going to be made on the group?

What tension is being created by the role's presence?
- What affective tension will hold the 'game' of the drama together and provide a motive for joining in? Possible tensions might include:

  tension of secrecy
  tension of mystery
  tension of an obstacle to overcome
  tension of time
  tension of dare/personal challenge/test
  tension of dependence on another
  tension of status to be challenged

What controls are within the role's behaviour?
- Are implicit/explicit 'rules' introduced by the role?
- How is the group's attention held?
- What attempts are made to focus the group's activity or verbal responses?
- Where is the source of the role's authority?

  in its status
  in its situation
  in its spectacle

Group values on theatre as a learning process

The match of convention to content also depends on the value the group place on dramatic activity as a useful and meaningful means of handling the source material. Because theatre uses the whole person for expression, there is a considerable risk for participants who cannot, without feeling threatened, let go of their concerns and pressures in the *real* dimension in order to move into the exposure of the *symbolic* dimension. Equally, individuals may be conditioned to expect theatre to be a low-level learning activity to which they find it difficult to give commitment. *Matching requires negotiation over the level of risk and commitment for which a group are prepared.*

The conventions allow for considerable flexibility over levels and degrees of involvement. Certain conventions often assume whole-group participation by limiting responses to the symbolic dimension of the drama (by only allowing responses-in-role).

Teacher-in-Role	**Meetings**
Still-Image	**Mantle of the Expert**

Other conventions allow for a small group of 'actors-by-choice' and a larger group of 'spectators-by-choice' to be involved in the direction and improvisation of the drama; they also allow for the roles of spectator and actor to be picked up, exchanged and dropped when participants choose to do so:

Forum-Theatre	**Hot-Seating**
A Day in the Life	**Voices in the Head**
Narration	**Moment of Truth**
Giving Witness	**Tag Role**

Within each convention there are further variables. For example, Hot-Seating often suggests the idea of there being one or more actors sitting in a chair, responding to questions from a group of spectators who may or may not be in roles themselves. There may be a reason why a group does not produce any volunteers for hot-seating. If so, there are a number of variables which may assist the group's use of the convention:

– The teacher/leader can take the role and be questioned by the group as themselves

– An empty chair can symbolise the role and the group can collectively respond, in the role's words, to questions asked

– The teacher/leader can put the questions to the empty chair and then ask the group to respond with what they think the role's thinking might be, or what their own response might be

Experimenting with the use of conventions and the roles of actor and spectator allows the group to control a subtle and gradual shift from the real to the symbolic. For example, action can grow from the group using furniture and other objects to represent the place where they imagine the drama is taking place and from them talking about the space, its atmosphere and what is in it. Figures can be placed in the space to represent where characters might be at a particular moment in the drama – conversation about placing the figures will start the process of theatre-action for the group. The group can suggest motives, thoughts and words for the figures, as themselves or symbolically through conventions such as Voices in the Head or Thought-Tracking. As interest grows in the context, the group may feel ready to enter the scene and interact together. But even if they do not, they have already begun to engage with theatre whilst appearing only to be commenting on the way in which they have visualised the scene of the drama.

Intentions for the work

A further consideration in the matching process is the short- and long-term intentions of the work; the purposes underlying the group's use of theatre. The historic functions of theatre as an educative medium demonstrate that it is used in a variety of contexts which, briefly summarised, stretch from the psychotherapeutic through documentary, satiric and didactic to cathartic entertainment. In educational contexts there is is evidence that theatre is used for a wide range of purposes – often as part of a structured developmental programme that organises learning purposes in the form of a syllabus to be followed or as programmes of study leading to specified attainment targets. In common with other art forms, both the long- and the short-term educational objectives for theatre work can be classified within a compass-type model which has four points of reference:

- **Instrumental objectives**
  Specific, measurable goals relating to skill development, conceptual development and knowledge.

- **Expressive objectives**
  Unspecific, indeterminate goals relating to the student's development of attitudes and values which may, or may not, occur through involvement in the dramatic action.

- **Aesthetic learning**
  Skills, concepts and knowledge relating to the art form.

■ **Personal and social learning**

Skills, concepts and knowledge relating to self and the 'self/others' areas of learning provided in both the symbolic and real dimensions of the drama.

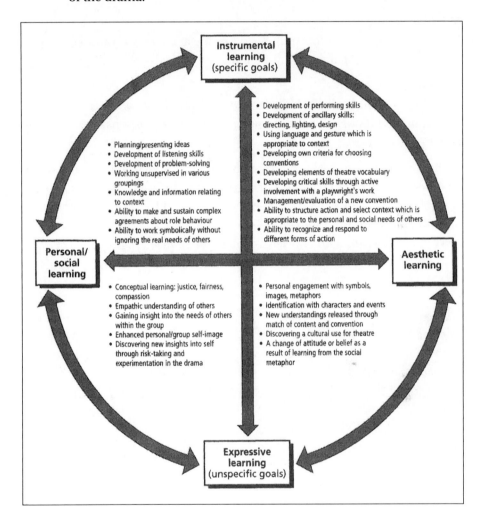

Categories of action

It is important to consider the category of action best suited to the issue which is to become the focus of the drama.

● **Context-building**

Does the space need re-arranging to represent the context for the action physically? Do characters need creating or fleshing out? Is any additional contextual information necessary?

◆ **Narrative**

Is there a need to clarify the story or to move it on through action? Will narrative action breed commitment to the drama through the strength of the story-line?

▼ **Poetic**

Does the group need to concentrate on making and communicating the symbols and images which represent their responses to the drama?

■ **Reflective**

Are things moving too quickly? Is there a need for action which requires consideration and thought? Is there a need for clarifying responses through the action?

Within each category, a further set of choices is available according to whether a direct or indirect form of entry is appropriate and what balance of spectators/actors is required either by the content or by the group. *Part 1 provides detailed information about the conventions within each category according to their uses and the level of demand made on participants in order to assist in making a choice of convention at this level.*

The challenge, and the satisfaction, for the teacher/leader lies in the level of creativity required to establish a priority order for the factors which will determine the appropriate match of convention to content for a group at a particular stage of its personal, social and aesthetic development.

3

Learning Through Imagined Experience

This extract first appeared in *Learning Through Imagined Experience* (1992) Hodder and Stoughton: 3-15

Drama is not simply a subject but also a method ... a learning tool. Furthermore, it is one of the *key* ways in which children gain an understanding of themselves and of others.

Planning for drama in the classroom requires a clear understanding of its nature and the contribution it can make to children's learning. Drama is not simply confined to one strand in the statements of attainment which ceases after level six. *It is central in developing all major aspects of English. (English for ages 5-16)*

Definitions and Challenges

This book aims to help teachers [in England and Wales] working in Key Stages 2 and 3 to make the most of drama's potential to enhance a range of curriculum experiences, including language activities, for young people. The book is written partly as a practical response to the important and far ranging references to the need for drama in the national curriculum documentation and partly in the knowledge that many teachers remain hesitant about initiating drama activities even though most would credit its value in learning. This paradox deepens when one considers that it is often the most valuable facets of drama which lead to the greatest hesitation on the teacher's part. The purpose of this introduction is, therefore, to clarify the value of drama, address the difficulties many teaches encounter in using drama and analyse what drama represents as a way of learning.

Many teachers remain confused about what actually 'counts' as drama, there is an apparently bewildering range of activities from staging plays, through games and improvisation to the kind of simulation or roleplay encountered in INSET and training which also claim to be 'drama'. Some clarity of definition is to be found in the HMI document *Drama 5-16*:

> Drama in schools is a practical artistic subject. It ranges from children's structured play, through classroom improvisations to performances of Shakespeare. It relies on the human ability to pretend to be someone or something else. Through this act of the imagination, pupils can explore how people in particular circumstances might behave now and at different times and in different societies. Though imaginary, the exploration can be experienced and shared as if it were real.

> Through drama we recreate and examine people's actions, including our own, and see both how they might have come about and where they might lead. We test our individual viewpoints against those of others; this is what happens as soon as two people take on different roles in a drama. They are placed in opposition or at the very least they represent different points of view. The conflicts at the heart of drama carry the process forward. By testing and, where possible, resolving human predicaments, drama helps pupils to face intellectual, physical, social and emotional challenges.

It follows from this definition that drama is a broad and encompassing term that associates a rich variety of ways of working which have as their common element the human ability to imagine and recreate other people's behaviour at other times and in other places. The definition itself prompts a list of the features of drama most frequently considered valuable by teachers and students alike.

Drama is a practical activity

It allows young people the opportunity to use space and movement, in addition to speech, in order to make meanings. It is not desk bound or dependent on the ability to write for its expression. It is an apparently loose and fluid form which in fact requires discipline and constraint for its execution.

But ... because it is practical and tends to use large spaces the problems of management and control are more complex than in conventional 'desk-and-text-book' approaches to teaching.

Because drama uses words and human actions for its expression there tends to be no written record as evidence of 'work'. *Even though follow-up work in other curriculum areas may serve as evidence that the drama has enhanced young people's understanding,* many teachers are pressured to produce written outcomes or results for all classroom activity or to look upon learning which is difficult to assess precisely as being of secondary importance.

Drama is a form of shared cultural activity

It is part of an unbroken cultural tradition which has been present in all civilisations throughout history. Sharing in cultural experiences is one way in which the young become initiated into the values, traditions and identity of their society. This has become an increasingly urgent argument for drama, and other arts, in schools given that technological progress has generally led to a decline in opportunities for shared cultural activity in society as a whole. The effects of television, changes in food technology, the dangers of being on the streets, the prevalence of recorded music in public places and the automation of retailing and industry have all resulted in: less playing and singing and dancing and storytelling in the home and in public places; less live community culture; less human interaction in the home, streets and shops; less distinctive, cultural representation for minorities and local communities.

But ... the notion that schooling provides young people with an induction into society through cultural involvement is not a priority for the present government and its educational legislation. It is therefore difficult for teachers to argue this cultural priority against the government's priority of basic and vocational training in preparation for fulfilling an economic role.

Drama provides a vehicle for exploring human nature and experience

It does this through accessible and concrete examples ('stories-in-action') which serve to provide young people with the means to express their own experience and to develop central societal concepts such as democracy, justice and freedom as well as personal concepts such as love, relationships, and family. Because the 'stories-in-action' which are the content of drama are composed out of the negotiations and understandings of those taking part, the teacher needs to develop the skills of a storyteller who is able to select content, form, register and tone and develop a story from the responses of the group and her understanding of their potential for achievement.

But ... language specialists, in particular, are often trained in and attracted to more private forms of fiction making, reading, writing, etc, which do not involve the same level of social interaction and teacher responsiveness. Drama is a *social and collective art form* with very different demands for students and teachers alike.

Drama involves taking on roles and adopting different viewpoints in 'real' experiences

Encouraging students to work through dramatic situations, in fictitious roles, enables them to view their own behaviour, and other people's, from unfamiliar perspectives. The emotional experience is real for the students even though the activity is fictional (think, for example, of the real sadness that may move us when we read a story). As a consequence, the students can be helped to reflect on their behaviour in the drama from 'another' person's point of view. The right choice and management of situations, contexts and stories relating to the environment, for instance, can provide young people with authentic experiences of what it would be like to be in a threatened environment which may be far removed in time and place from their own immediate and protected environment. This is useful in overcoming the detached climate of the classroom by helping students: to see the underlying human significance and themes in their learning; to explore prejudices and stereotypes; to develop empathy and respect for others who are culturally, historically or socially different from themselves.

But ... because drama often uses 'stories' in order to look at reality (history, social issues, relationships), there may be some concern about the legitimacy of what is learnt through drama which may be more to do with subjective responses and 'feelings' rather than acquiring hard, objective facts. Some teachers are also concerned about the depth of feelings some young people may experience through drama which may touch upon realities in a young person's life that the teacher is not trained to support. As the definition from *Drama 5-16* suggests, drama inevitably pivots around conflicts of principle, values, attitudes. This means that, quite rightly, the stories in drama often provoke discussion about morality and reality. Often students will take a strong stand in relation to their feelings about justice and fairness in the 'stories' they engage with.

There is understandable concern about what might be the most supportive teaching strategy for dealing with the expression of a range of deeply felt values and convictions in the classroom. This is particularly important at a time when there are so many divisions in society, represented within our classrooms, which occur on the basis of gender, race, class, creed and belief. There is also constant concern about ideological bias, partisan imbalance and teacher accountability which are all associated with learning about reality through fiction.

Drama generates vocal and active responses to fictional situations

Learning in drama results from facing the challenge of behaviour realistically in a fictional situation and then being pressed by the circumstances of the fiction, as it unfolds, into finding and using appropriate vocal and active responses. It is this 'realness' of drama, in which roleplayers give and receive (write and read) each other's messages simultaneously, which makes drama a unique form of literacy. In conventional reading and writing activity, fictional situations are unalterable, recorded and described; students are either fixed in the role of spectator, observer or reader, or in the role of writer. In drama the same fictions may be transformed by the students' responses and the fictions are entered into and lived as a 'here and now' experience. This immediately prompts new understandings and uses of language as a direct result of the active experiencing of the fiction.

But ... the potential contribution of drama to literacy development has tended to be ignored beyond Key Stage 1. The Statutory Orders for English make only token reference to drama's usefulness in providing practice for oracy skills whilst legislating for a plethora of conventional approaches to language development which may break literacy into discrete areas such as spelling, reading, etc.

Each of these areas has its packages of skills and programmes of study which do not sufficiently stress whole-language experience or integrated approaches to literacy. Faced with the weight of detail in the Statutory Orders, and uncertain about drama's potential, many teachers are reluctant to take time from what they must teach, by law, in order to teach as they might want to, ie, by using ways of working which are non-statutory.

Drama develops the imagination's ability to 'make believe'

Drama develops the imagination's ability to construct and 'make believe' unfamiliar contexts and situations; it demands that we respond to them as if they were actually occurring. In drama young people are able to take satisfaction in creating credible and coherent, alternative worlds and experiences through their own imaginative efforts. In so doing, young people are realising and extending their ability to imagine new futures and alternatives, new problems and solutions, a world beyond the street corner. Drama encourages creative ways of understanding and offers young people an opportunity to express their developing view of human experience.

But ... again the present climate of legislation tends to ignore the importance of the imagination in young people's learning. In an effort to create a skills-centred approach that will prepare young people for their economic roles after schooling, the National Curriculum pays scant attention to the importance of providing for the imaginative needs of young people as they are developing through childhood into adolescence. In so doing, the curriculum is in danger of being presented to young learners as stale facts and skills to be drilled in. Without due attention to the imagination, young learners are denied the sense of conflict, excitement, anticipation and satisfaction which accompanies both the discovery learning and the difficult psychological passage from Key Stage 2 to Key Stage 3.

A Model for Language Learning Through Story and Play

Drama is essential to the development of speaking and listening skills as well as providing a bridge for other forms of learning in literacy such as reading and writing in a wide range of registers for one's own purposes. The role of drama in relation to reading fiction is well put in the DES document, *Aspects of Primary Education: Language and Literature*:

> ... effective work in drama often uses literature to enrich children's first hand experience in imaginary situations, the immediacy of which stimulates them to adapt their language to their roles. Through drama, the children's language repertoire and their understanding can be extended in a unique way.

There is growing evidence which testifies to this power of drama in offering young learners a unique relationship with literature and talk. Using drama, a child is able to enter into the world of a book or story and behave as one of its characters, free to ask other characters (taken on by the teacher and others in the group) the questions that they want to ask and free to attempt to negotiate alternative choices to those given in the original. The difference in comprehension is similar to the difference between hearing about an event and actually being there at the time. Drama therefore complements and enhances other creative forms such as reading and writing, and by including drama with other creative forms a teacher is able to offer all young people a tool for expression. This enhancement means that a broader range of ability has access to an expressive form.

However, in terms of the whole curriculum, – which includes language – this book claims that drama is an important way of enhancing classroom learning: it is not a substitute for analysis, objective learning and pastoral counselling; rather, it provides a bridge between the unfamiliar world of concepts and data and the recognisable world of human experiences and endeavours. The argument for drama in the classroom is like the argument for fiction, generally, which Harold Rosen expresses as:

> Narrative [*drama*] must become a more acceptable way of saying, writing, thinking and presenting. I am not proposing that anecdote [*drama*] should drive out analysis but that narrative [*drama*] should be allowed its honourable place in the analysis of everything, that stories-in-the-head [in action] should be given their chance to be heard. (*Stories and Meanings*)

Despite the strength of these arguments in favour of drama as an active learning tool with a broad range of applications within and beyond the language curriculum, there are apparent 'risks' involved in using drama. As teachers, we all face this dilemma of wanting to work in lively and inspiring ways with young people whilst also needing the professional security of remaining responsible and in control over classroom management. Many teachers feel unsupported by pre-service and in-service training in the non-specialist uses of drama.

Risk 1   Whether or not the cost in time and energy expended in developing drama will find a return in improved standards across a broad range of activities.

Risk 2   Whether using drama might lead to a feeling of losing control and purpose.

Risk 3   Whether or not, as experience of using drama grows, the teacher and groups will become more effective at encountering the problems of planning and managing the drama together.

Whilst suggestions can be made as to how the risks identified above can be reduced, and gaps left by inadequate training opportunities can be plugged, the problem of 'cost' – the time and energy expended in developing drama opportunities – remains. As with other forms of innovative and active learning, a teacher's decision to adopt drama into her repertoire of teaching styles will largely depend on the teacher's own value system. There are clear similarities between drama and the kinds of approaches associated with 'real' reading, developmental writing and the best practice in early-years education.

These approaches are characterised by a view of language learning which goes beyond the superficial acquisition of skills and linguistic conventions and terminology to consider the context of learning and thought, language and social context and language and identity. In other words, they amount a view of learning which recognises the centrality of language to all human activity and which seeks to develop a young person's language as a tool for socialising, thinking, communicating, expressing emotions, forming ideas and action, etc.

Within this view, drama is an important means of constructing and ex-periencing the social contexts within which the different functions and uses of language can be identified and developed. The practical advice offered in this book is generally to do with building and working in dramatic 'social con-texts' which offer the possibility for a richer variety of language and learning experiences than would be possible in a 'skills-and-drills' approach.

The view of language learning outlined in Figure 1 is considered in relation to Key Stage 2 and Key Stage 3 but it is influenced by understandings about the nature of language acquisition which have their widest currency in ap-proaches to Key Stage 1.

■ **Dialogue with an empathetic adult**
Through drama the teacher is able to engage in dialogue with chil-dren in a variety of adult roles other than 'teacher': as someone who needs help; as someone who has had a special and exciting ex-perience; as someone from a different culture or time; as someone who is struggling with a disability, etc.

■ **Opportunities for imaginative play**
The spontaneous and unformed play of Key Stage 1 becomes more conscious and crafted through Key 2 – Key Stage 3 so that whilst re-taining some of the spontaneity of infant play there is a growing awareness of the art form and its possibilities.

■ **An enabling environment that provides a variety of language experiences**
Drama offers the possibility of building and working in a variety of different roles, situations, places, each of which provides new and authentic language demands within a secure environment.

Together these three conditions for learning seek to recreate in the classroom a model of learning which has been successfully operated by most preschool children in acquiring the basics of a 'mother-tongue' (here used as a nurtur-ing term, quite literally learning to use mother's tongue!). Researchers like Joan Tough have sought to understand the means by which young people undertake the most sophisticated and complex of all human learning achievements. In doing so, they have discovered that preschool children use

Teacher/learner relationships

■ Teacher sees her role as an enabler of learning rather than as a controller of knowledge.

Emphasis is on discovery through structured experience rather than instruction through telling.

Learner's personal growth and self-esteem are seen as central to achievement.

■ Responding to a child's present needs takes priority over vocational preparation for the future.

■ Enjoyment and fun are seen as legitimate and necessary elements in learning.

Relationships between learners

■ Learning occurs through interaction and collaboration leading to individual achievement.

■ Every child has a responsibility for herself and for her learning group.

■ Team-building and group skills are important to all curriculum areas.

Meaning and relevance in language learning

■ Learning to use language effectively should be an empowering and enjoyable journey rather than a chore – technical skills and accuracy are developed out of need, the need to communicate successfully rather than through fear of censure.

The learner should have integrated experiences of the NC Profile Components.

Motivation and relevance are essential to successful language development.

Introducing language contexts which encourage the learner to pursue personally relevant meanings and understandings leads to the development of skills-decontextualised skills training hinders development.

Language development requires a range of assessment and evaluation strategies which include: holistic/ impression marking; peer-group assessment and self-evaluation through diaries and journals.

Success in all other curriculum areas is dependent on developing reading, writing and speech as effective forms of meaning-making.

Figure 1

The social health of a group will affect individual progress.

■ Issues of race, gender and cultural differences need to be continually addressed through the curriculum.

The role of the arts in learning

■ Art forms of the theatre and literature have recognisable origins in a child's natural uses of story and play.

The arts provide the bridge between knowing and feeling.

The arts enable a child to symbolise, capture and access abstract meanings.

■ The arts are vital to the life of the school and of the child.

A set of values for drama in language development

Figure 1 (continued)

a range of behaviour and processes in order to satisfy their basic need to communicate with others and understand the world around them. The apparent success with which most of us manage this early learning has prompted attempts to preserve and develop the mother-tongue learning model into formal schooling. Here, for instance, is an extract from a document on assessment issued to schools by the Ministry of Education in Ontario, Canada:

> Today there is a growing conviction that 'most learning occurs not as a private, interior experience but as an interactive one, socially shaped. Knowledge is less a personal acquisition than an inter-personal production: relational, collaborative and more specifically a matter of exchange. In fact the way children learn their mother tongue is seen as a potential model for all learning and schools in many countries are now beginning to institutionalise this model. It places students at the centre of activity in the curriculum, and it emphasises learning not teaching. (*Does This Count?*)

In the present educational climate in this country, it is hard to imagine that governments in North America are beginning to put forward the view expressed above as a rationale for re-organising schooling. The example given above arrived in schools after seven years of working with a Provincial curriculum and testing system much like our own National Curriculum.

In these countries and others, there is a growing belief that too much emphasis has been given to what must be taught in schools and too little to understanding the processes which separate successful learners from less successful, and, in turn, to what are then the most effective processes for learners to use. This commitment to change the emphasis of government thinking results from a growing awareness that education cannot have the single aim of preparing young people for an economic role. For children's and society's sake, it must also prepare them for a broader social role; education must have an instrumental value but not at the expense of its intrinsic value.

The model of mother-tongue learning is often echoed by language specialists writing about the organisation of language learning in later stages of education. Here is Nancy Martin talking about learning in Key Stages 2/3:

> In coming to understand how children learn language we have come to understand that this is also the way of much other learning. In taking part in rule-governed behaviour – a meeting, a party, group discussion, dramatic improvisation and so on – a newcomer picks up the implied rules by responding to the behaviour of others and quickly internalises them. Becoming literate operates in a similar way. We learn what stories are by reading and telling and

writing them; similarly with other genres. There is, of course the alternative, traditional mode by which teachers analyse the rules and teach them as pro-cedures of models. (*The Word for Teaching is Learning*)

In her analysis, Nancy Martin is arguing for an interactive, contextual and social mode of language learning which seeks to develop the mother-tongue model. Figure 2 attempts to represent this model graphically so as to remind us of the key features of leaning:

- The child is at the centre of her learning; there is no formal external curriculum for her to comply with. The motivation and purpose for learning is borne out of her need to communicate not just her im-mediate physical needs, but her thoughts, dreams, fears and hopes.

- The child learns through interaction with those around her – parents, siblings, peers, the wider community, etc. She also learns through interaction with television, books, pictures, songs and rhymes, pets, etc.

- The child uses a range of real behaviours in her learning, named in the upper semi-circle of the diagram. But she also uses a range of symbolic or representative forms in her learning which are named in the bottom semi-circle. It is this use of story, imaginative play, rhythm and other cultural activity in making sense of and explaining the world around her which is of particular significance in relation to drama and language development.

- Alongside the skills acquired in mother-tongue learning, children also develop knowledge about human nature. They are skilled ob-servers whose principle concern is to understand how people behave, how to gain reward, how to get what they need and what happens when they or others behave in certain ways. *They are used to learning about the world from within the context of human be-haviours.* They may also develop a strong affinity with the animal world through observing that animals too are in the power of adults and not always successful in communicating their needs!

Readers of this book will undoubtedly be familiar with the importance of story and play in early-years learning but may be quizzical about the continu-ing significance of these forms in Key Stages 2/3.

Pre-school learning, despite its complexity, is concrete, actual and context bound. The types of real behaviour identified in the diagram are used to deal with what is actually present within the child's immediate horizons. The sym-

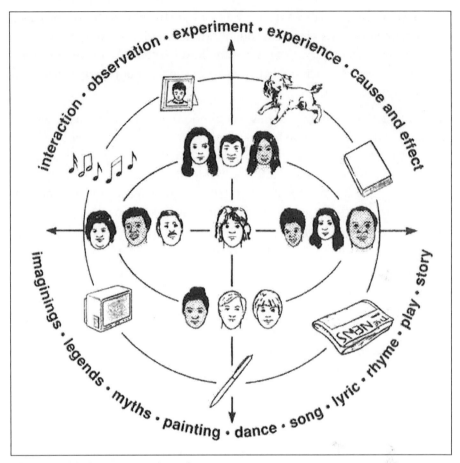

Figure 2 Mother-tongue learning

bolic forms identified are used to help the child to begin to use language and behaviour to represent concepts, attitudes, behaviour, moods and feelings which are not concrete or present – in other words, to deal with the abstract world.

Through story and play, children can begin to make sense of a world which is invisible and distant until it is brought into the child's experience through symbolic language and action. Stories and play offer the child concrete examples of ideas and experiences, embedded in recognisable human situations, which they are too young to deal with through conceptual language and discourse.

In a conventional, transmission model of education, story and play are relegated to the sidelines when the curriculum begins to deal with increasingly abstract concept and skills. Yet story and play are the natural means by which young people process abstract thought. An alternative argument, based on common sense, would be to preserve the importance of story and play precisely because the curriculum becomes increasingly remote from real actions and concrete situations.

The more the curriculum requires children to operate at a symbolic level of concepts and generalisations which are divorced from particular situations or from human experience, the more need they have for the support of story and play to help them understand and see the significance of their learning in recognisable contexts. In adult life we still have this same need for concreteness – think how much we communicate through story; how we prepare for difficult events by 'role-playing' the event in advance in our heads; how we would rather be shown how to fix our car than be told the theory of internal combustion!

The view of drama in this book is therefore rooted in a mother-tongue approach to learning in Key Stages 2/3. The content of the drama may be the key concepts, principles and generalisations which form the language curriculum and much more. The mode of learning attempts to recreate the need to learn through providing concrete examples of situations in which people find themselves actively using or discovering the importance of the content so that:

- content relating to the theme of buildings is taught through the situation of being builders needing to finish a construction
- content relating to the theme of democracy and the difference between cultures is taught through the situation of the crowds standing for freedom in Tiananmen Square
- content relating to the environment is taught through the situation of scientists travelling to the North Pole to conduct experiments.

4

Structuring to Begin

This extract originally appeared in *Beginning Drama:11-14* (1997).
David Fulton Publishers: 58-70

S ome of the work that a drama teacher does will be in the form of lessons that are planned in ways which would be familiar to teachers of other subjects – lessons on aspects of theatre history, stage craft or technology for instance. But, as we noted in the discussion of the teacher's role as dramaturge, there is an expectation that making and experiencing drama is at the heart of the drama curriculum.

The quality of the making and experiencing is, at first, dependent on the teacher's skills of structuring. During KS3, the teacher's modelling of structure and the choices that are available in structuring a dramatic experience will merge into the expectation that the students will become increasingly confident, knowledgeable and responsible for their own structuring.

In a conventional lesson plan, activities are organised so that students can understand, internalise and apply the particular skill, concept or knowledge that is contained in the lesson's objectives. On the surface a planned drama experience may look like a conventional plan. The teacher will have aims and objectives for the session and will also have a list or sequence of activities for the students to engage with. But, in addition to satisfying the curriculum objectives for the lesson, the sequence must also provide students with a living experience of drama – an analogous experience to being in or at a play or watching an episode of drama in some other form. The sequencing of the lesson needs to be as subtle and as crafted as any other dramatic sequence that is planned to unfold its meanings or theme in time and space and which moves the audience, progressively, towards a new-felt understanding of the human issues and themes that are being dramatised.

In this sense the structure of the classroom drama is in the form of a montage: a construction of meanings which is a specific result of the assembly of form and content during a drama. The montage, or the juxtaposing of the 'pieces' used in the drama, also guides students through the dramatic event of experience. The montage is more than the linear sequence of events in the narrative. In theatre the events of the story are only one dimension of the presentation. Theatre is a spatial as well as a temporal art. What happens in the theatre space in terms of objects, design, lighting, sound and the physical arrangement and gestures of the players also contributes to our understanding of what is happening. The montage that comprises the practical component of a drama lesson, then, refers to the totality of all the actions in the lesson and it is assembled, as in any dramatic event, to produce specific effects.

In some lessons (particularly in early KS3), the students may be aware of following a story where the sequence of the lesson is tied to the stages of the story – beginning, middle and end – and which focuses on causal relationships between people, contexts and events in the story. In other lessons the story may already be known or the source material for the lesson may not be in the form of a narrative. In such cases the structure of the dramatic montage is more visible. The various activities and tasks are assembled in such a way that students' attention is drawn to themes or ideas which develop and deepen as the work progresses but without being driven by a narrative logic. A tableau representing a particular moment in the story might be followed by students giving 'thoughts' to the characters in the tableau, or rearranging the figures in another group's tableau to demonstrate an alternative perspective – this sequence is designed to develop understanding of the human themes and issues without moving the narrative forward. The actions extend out from a moment suggested in the narrative, the lesson progresses in time but the dramatic exploration is held to this moment in the narrative.

In most forms of drama the montage is notated or recorded as a sequence of scenic units. These units may correspond to the playwright's own division of the play into scenes. They may also correspond to the director's or actors' performance or the emotional rhythms of the play. The study of the different ways in which theatre practitioners have and do construct montage and the relationships between different genres of theatre (comedy, tragedy) and different approaches to montage will be the focus in drama for students in KS4 and beyond.

However the montage is made, the scenic units must have meaning in themselves and also contribute to the complex meaning of the play as a whole. In other words, each unit must have its own logic for performers and audience but also contribute to the logic of the whole performance. The concept of 'episode' is a useful construct for students to understand. They will know, from their experience of TV drama, that an episode of a TV series should make sense in itself but they also know that their understanding of characters and the 'meanings' the producers want to communicate accumulate over a number of episodes. So there is the sense of the episode both having its own shape and logic but also contributing to a developing understanding which will only be complete when all the episodes have been watched.

Each scenic unit or episode of the montage (shown overleaf) provides a three dimensional experience for actors and audiences – it is not made of a single action such as a change in space or a line spoken, it is a complex of simultaneous actions that together offer meaning.

In most forms of drama there is a specific requirement that each scenic unit will be played in the dramatic present. The dramatic present refers to the particular quality of time in drama. We appear to be producing, or witnessing, a 'here-and-now' representation in which events unfold as we see them – they are not reported past events, as they are in story. But in effect the 'here-and-now' of drama must be linked to what has already happened or what we already know prior to this moment in the performance. The 'here-and-now' of drama must also imply a future or cause an audience to question how the events we are witnessing now will create future events. It is this sense of an implied future (or destiny), which is connected to past events through what is revealed in the events that are happening now on stage, that differentiates the dramatic present form the 'here-and-now' of everyday life. The present in drama is always in the margins between a tangible past and future.

The linking between the past and an implied future in each passing moment of the drama causes the audience to extend and deepen their understanding of the play's theme. Each passing moment should build on and clarify what has happened and clarify, through implication, our expectations of what will happen next.

There may be further aesthetic considerations in making the montage. The relationship between scenic units may be used to create different kinds of rhythm. The **rhythm** of a drama may be tied to an emotional score – a balance of 'highs and lows' – or to the tensions in the relationships and events that are being represented. The rhythm in school drama, as in some forms of theatre, may create a balance between **efficacy** (where the purpose of the drama is to bring about some kind of change in understanding and attitude or to create

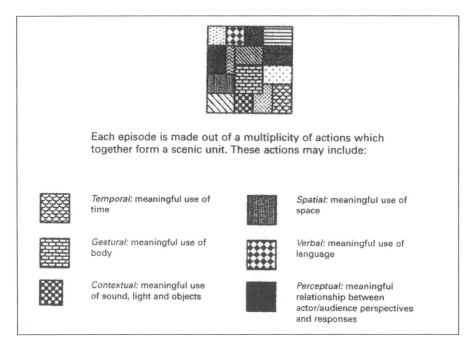

Each episode is made out of a multiplicity of actions which together form a scenic unit. These actions may include:

Temporal: meaningful use of time

Spatial: meaningful use of space

Gestural: meaningful use of body

Verbal: meaningful use of language

Contextual: meaningful use of sound, light and objects

Perceptual: meaningful relationship between actor/audience perspectives and responses

lasting results for the participants) and entertainment (where pleasure and fun are given precedence).

The use of the elements of drama (time, space, people, objects, sound and light), the structuring concepts of 'montage' and scenic 'units', and the principles of playing a 'dramatic present' are common to both conventional theatre presentation and to curriculum drama at KS3. However, the drama teacher has additional concerns that guide the structuring of curriculum drama and which, inevitably, make such drama appear 'different' from some other forms of non-school theatre. These considerations include:

Working positively with the constraints of time, space and numbers

Drama is a very flexible art form but even so, drama teachers often work with constraints that are quite unique to the school situation. The time allowed may vary from regular weekly slots between 45 minutes and an hour or more in length to shorter and/or less frequent periods. It is difficult in such circumstances to maintain the progressive experience of a montage. The time constraints may mean that students are forced to engage and work with drama more quickly and sketchily than in other forms of non-school drama. The spaces that are used for drama may vary from custom-built studios to corridors! The drama teacher is also working with a large number of actors who can't be expected to be mere extras to the work of star individuals – they must all be offered a meaningful and varied experience of producing drama.

Managing the planned with the lived

We have noted that curriculum drama differs from other forms of drama in the sense that it is not 'by choice'. Engagement has to be negotiated. Structuring in curriculum drama must take the lived experience of students into account in terms of their inhibitions, differing abilities, peer-group dynamics. The need to deliver a planned curriculum in drama that is related to the school curriculum and ethos as a whole is also a constraint on structuring. The teacher does not have a free rein. She is responsible for ensuring that lessons are productive, well ordered and supportive of the school's ethos. There is often a greater emphasis on the efficacious uses of drama (to produce specific results) than on providing entertainment (as important as the experience of pure pleasure in the theatre is).

Working with two aesthetic traditions

The principles and concepts of structuring that we have discussed are derived from the restricted art of literary theatre. They describe the way in which practitioners in conventional, 'serious', theatre approach their work. But, as we have noted, most students' aesthetic experience and knowledge is derived from the oral and communal aesthetic of film, TV and other forms of popular entertainment. Structuring in drama should not alienate students from their own cultural knowledge and practice – it should seek to build bridges between aesthetic traditions.

The principles that follow may help you to positively address these considerations – which are particular to the local context of making, performing and responding to drama within the curriculum.

Teach structuring through the experience of structure

Make the montage – the assembly of form and content – visible to students; discuss the choices that are being made; encourage students to use, and reflect on the use of, the full range of drama elements so that their own group work is three-dimensional.

Co-author to create co-ownership

Encourage suggestions about how to develop both the plot and the montage of the drama; work with and from the students' questions about the themes and ideas that are being dramatised. Use (and therefore pass on) your own skills and knowledge to enhance students' work – sound, lights, choreography and direction where appropriate.

Introduce and use a diversity of conventions and traditions

Introduce and blend together conventions from other cultures and from film/TV. Avoid suggesting that there is a hierarchy of conventions in which the conventions of Western theatre have a 'natural' superiority over other traditions.

Prohibit unacceptable images

Art in school is restricted to representations and messages which are acceptable to the whole school community – student-artists are not free from censorship. Have no concerns about either banning or confounding prejudicial images and characteristics.

Use an episodic structure

This needs to be open-ended like the episodes of a TV series; each episode speaks for itself. Don't be tied to having to finish the story or to complete all the stages of a planned sequence. An episodic structure gives greater flexibility – you can extend or shorten the sequence of episodes according to the needs and interest of the group. Episodic structures are a familiar means of bridging the time gap between one episode and the next, of TV series, soaps, etc.

Use group work to cover more ground

Whenever possible give groups *different* tasks or scenes to do in order to cover more ground; stress difference; make watching more interesting. Encourage groups towards diversity of meaning rather than conformity. In terms of the response to group work, encourage students to extend their sense of 'possible meanings' rather than to reproduce the same ideas.

Stress the communal rather than the individual, and structure accordingly

Draw attention to the means and meanings used in group work rather than to comments about individual contributions and skill levels. Structure for ensemble work rather than principal characters – think of groups of characters rather than individuals. Run group presentations as a single performance sequence so that reflection is on the *whole* experience created by the group as a whole.

Practical drama work in schools often takes on a conventional structural shape (genre). For instance, when I was trained to teach drama the genre we were given followed a conventional pattern of games/ice-breakers, short improvisations or scenes, followed by debriefing and relaxation exercises. Whatever the content or objective for the lesson we would try and fit what we were doing into this pattern. Nowadays there is a greater variety of genres of practical drama to be found – greater variety means greater choice for teachers and students. In the table that follows I have tried to identify some common genres of drama work and to offer some advice on structuring within each genre. I have tried to avoid creating a hierarchy of genres by giving greater value to some rather than others. It is my belief that all of these genres are needed in order to effectively deliver the practical component of the KS3 drama curriculum. I have, however, given extra consideration to the conventions approach because it is the genre that works best for me and I believe it to be particularly appropriate to KS3.

Knowledge

This will be the shortest of the sections even though it ought to be the longest! It isn't possible to 'give' the knowledge that a drama teacher needs in these few pages. I am restricting myself to describing the different categories of knowledge and giving some sense of what might be included in each. (I have included only knowledge that is specific to drama teaching – not the basic body of pedagogic knowledge that all teachers need to acquire). Part of my own pleasure in teaching drama is knowing that I will never know enough – I need to constantly seek new knowledge that will enhance my practice. The breadth of knowledge that I describe here will take experience and time to gain. The knowledge is to be found through reading the books suggested in the annotated bibliography and beyond. It is to be found through going to the theatre and cinema as often as possible and through going to workshops. It is also to be found through experience, both of teaching drama and of being attentive to the world around us.

In order to be an effective subject specialist in drama at KS3, a teacher needs to acquire knowledge in these five categories: practical, theoretical, technical, historical, cultural. There will of course be overlap between these categories – masks are placed in practical knowledge because there are traditions and particular uses of masks that teachers should know about, but technical knowledge is needed in order to teach mask-making.

At first glance the knowledge that is described may seem to go far beyond the requirements of the KS3 curriculum. Certainly, you don't need everything that

small group play making

Students prepare their own scenes based on a title or theme. The work is performed to the other groups.

■ Break the production process of the scene into stages (beginning, middle and end, for instance) and give instruction and feedback at each stage

■ Give opportunities for reworking scenes after feedback

■ Focus on helping groups to clarify *what* is being communicated and *how* it might be communicated more effectively

■ Encourage students to explore non-naturalistic conventions in their work, eg, dance, masks, narration

rehearsal

Students work on extracts or whole plays and are given responsibility for a full realisation, or performance, of the playwright's work. Through a process of rehearsal students are expected to explore the meanings communicated by the playwright and how to codify those ideas in theatre form.

■ Encourage creative approaches to rehearsal by using other drama conventions such as improvisation, sculpting, 'tableau' or 'hot-seating' to research character, setting and language

■ Don't leave it to the students – they need direction and knowledge from you! The students rely on you to make sure the finished work will not embarrass them!

■ Be flexible with casting, use multiple characters or double-up or have different actors for different scenes

■ Encourage students to use the full range of the elements of drama – light, space, objects – to comment on, or reinforce, the verbal playing of the text

skills development

A particular skill, such as movement, voice, dance, mask-work or improvisation, is isolated and taught to students who then practise in order to improve their expertise. Practising may involve following the teacher/trainer, private or group practice and applying the skill in a short game or exercise.

■ Establish the relevance of the skill to the drama work; how students will use it, how the training will help them to do better drama

■ To feel comfortable in a skills-based exercise (such as learning to move in a mask so that the mask is always facing the audience), students may still need some sense of context and content. Drama is a concrete art in which players need a sense of real-life motive and purpose

■ Use the students' strengths, focus on skills of agility, speed, dexterity and imaginative response – but avoid the fear of physical embarrassment!

■ Use popular cultural forms as vehicles for skills development: rap, juggling, acrobatics, dance, ball games

living through

Students, working with the teacher-in-role (a player in the drama), place themselves in an imagined situation and then, through making and taking characters, they behave as if they are living through the imagined experience as it unfolds. How they act and react is determined both by the 'culture', or given circumstances, of the situation and also by agreed narrative characteristics such as elements of fantasy or an intensifying of the potential 'drama' of the situation.

This is a very action orientated genre. Quite literally, nothing will happen unless the participants take action themselves. In this way students are very conscious of forging their own histories through their actions, just as Shakespeare's characters were.

The development of this genre of theatre experience is closely associated with the work of Dorothy Heathcote and Gavin Bolton, but 'teacher-in-role' is also linked to the 'joker' in Augusto Boal's 'forum theatre' and to the old tradition of adults joining in and enhancing children's fantasy play. This genre is often used as a model for drama in KS1/2

■ Spread time constructing the context of the imagined situation – the 'W' questions

■ Use teacher-in-role to initiate, model, guide and control students' behaviour; weave together the students' responses; build atmosphere; work as a storyteller within the story

■ Encourage students to create and try roles and role responses that are different from their own daily roles and behaviours

■ Break the work up and include reflection, exercises and other conventions in the montage so that both the theatre and the analysis of behaviour offered by the imagined experience is not forgotten

conventions approach

A 'laboratory theatre' approach in which some aspect of human behaviour or experience is isolated and selected for close exploration. The aspect may be contained in a playscript, a literary source or any text that comments on human nature/culture. The montage is made of episodes in which students use a variety of techniques or conventions to illuminate the content. An initial tableau of events may be followed by hot-seating characters or providing inner monologues for the initial tableau. The techniques used are derived from conventions which are local to curriculum drama – teacher-in-role – as well as from post-naturalist theatres – alter-egos, Brechtian devices, forum theatre

■ Look for opportunities to layer the work by combining conventions or reusing earlier work. We might provide the soundtrack of memories for a poignant moment that is caught in tableau, or repeat lines spoken earlier as we watch characters react to hearing them again

■ Don't move too rapidly from the use of one convention to another. Look for opportunities to use new conventions to further develop or investigate the students' work; rearrange the spatial relationships in a tableau, for instance, to see how the meaning changes, or, focus on a particular action or gesture and isolate it for discussion or as the basis for further creative extension

is here to be a drama teacher at KS3. But the more knowledge you have of drama yourself the more you have to draw on and inform your teaching at any key stage. In the English educational system, a drama specialist is required to have knowledge equivalent at least to A-level.

Practical knowledge

- dramaturgy; the use of the elements of drama to communicate meanings
- acting styles, dance, masks and other relevant aspects of stage craft
- management of personal and interpersonal behaviour
- project management (production)

Theoretical knowledge

- specific to teaching drama in schools (books like this one, for instance)

- dramatic theory (which might range from the works of Aristotle to Raymond Williams and the theoretical writings of Brecht, Stanislavski and others)

- semiotics of drama (how meanings in theatre are constructed, communicated and reconstructed by audiences)

- theatre anthropology (the different cultural uses and manifestations of performances in other times and places as well as our own)

- the theoretical writing of key twentieth century theatre and school drama practitioners (which might include Slade, Way, Heathcote and Bolton but also Stanislavski, Meyerhold, Brecht and Boal)

- awareness of relevant critical theory – feminist, post-colonialist, performance, literary

Technical knowledge

- sound and light technology

- use of IT as control system for above and for use as part of drama (using the World Wide Web for research, for instance)

- scenic design and construction (including costumes and properties)

Historical knowledge

- major periods and styles of Western theatre – Greek, Elizabethan/ Jacobean, Realism/Naturalism, Symbolism and Expressionism

- twentieth century and pre-twentieth century playwrights, eg, Shakespeare, Jonson, Brecht, Miller

- genres of tragedy and comedy

- key period of social history, eg, Athenian and Elizabethan societies, Industrial Revolution, 1930s and 1960s

- popular theatres and entertainment, eg, mysteries, commedia, melodrama, vaudeville, federal theatre project, musicals

Cultural knowledge

- major non-European performance traditions, eg, Kathakali, Noh, and Kabuki, Carnival, shadow puppets

- contemporary trends in writing and performance styles

- media and representation

- major cultural movements such as modernism and postmodernism

- the oral and communal aesthetic tradition

Section Two:
The Argument For Drama

This section of the book opens with impassioned and, at times, angry responses to the attacks on drama education from what Neelands describes as the 'new saviours of drama'. He positions the new saviours as those who wanted to save drama from the 'misguided' notion that it was a pedagogy and not a discrete art form. The *de facto* leaders in the charge were David Hornbrook and Peter Abbs. The binary nature of the criticism was particularly galling to those who worked in and across the art form, such as Neelands. Eighteen years later, it is difficult to imagine the passion with which this debate was conducted.

It is hard, too, to imagine the ugliness of Thatcher's Britain without living through it. It was a place where wars were fought, won and lost on many ideological battlegrounds. Neelands argues that the new saviours recreated the 'Theatre vs Drama' debate for their own ends and their arguments saw theatre and drama become locked in mortal combat. Although saying he does not want to join the battle, Neelands does exactly that. He argues passionately that improvisation is an art form, and that acknowledging drama as an effective pedagogy that all teachers can use does not limit or diminish drama as an arts discipline with its own body of knowledge.

The Meaning of Drama, written in the height of the territorial battles that nearly derailed the progressive movement of drama education, is a valuable historical document. Internationally and especially at secondary level, drama curricula have retreated into the study of text and preparation for a Eurocentric view of theatre. This extract will therefore resonate with many drama teachers too young to remember these turf wars of the 1980s. Neelands' notion of a curriculum that is child-centred rather than economic-needs centred should also resonate in jurisdictions such as in the UK, Australia and

New Zealand, where clear choices about national curriculum directions have recently been forged.

In *Theatre Without Walls*, Neelands continues the defence of educational drama. He goes further than suggesting it teaches about the art form, to arguing that it is a form of theatre in its own right. He maintains that educational drama has its genesis in an alternative, globalised, aesthetic performance tradition which complements, rather than excludes, the Euro-American theatre tradition. Neelands suggests that metaxis, which sits at the heart of educational drama, is not in opposition to the mimetic art forms championed by the new saviours. He argues passionately that educational drama should include, legitimise and make use of those other fluid forms of dramatic experience in young people's lives that are outside of the Euro-American tradition.

This too should resonate yet more strongly in the age of digitised performance and as new theatre forms are created in virtual spaces almost daily. Educational drama must be inclusive and not restrict itself to the teaching and privileging of one performative tradition. Neelands argues for a more democratic form of theatre, one that is not for the privileged few with talent, nor simply to tell the stories of those whose stories have already been written by others. The tradition of improvisation, which sits at the heart of educational drama, is based on an understanding that everybody can – and has the right to – make artistic statements about their own lives. These artistic statements are merely different, not inferior to those of high art practitioners. When Neelands asserts that he is essentially a theatre worker, he places himself within this tradition.

The Hands of Living People is a more reflective piece than the two earlier extracts in this section. In selecting this piece, Neelands suggested it was the publication closest to his doctoral thesis. Again, he is arguing against binaries. This time it is to articulate a new hybrid concept of drama education that is between the old imaginaries of 'process' and 'curriculum' as they have been historically used – often divisively – in drama. In theatre terms, he attempts to broach the distinctions between the presentational and the representational, and considers how the conventions approach, in its use of Brechtian devices, achieves this. It is a genuine and sophisticated attempt to marry drama in education and the demands of curriculum.

In the journey beyond Beowulf, Neelands argues for convergent but different dramatic responses, rather than the whole class conforming to a monolithic 'consensus'. Here, the participants are not bound by the space and time of a singular drama world. In 'moving beyond', Neelands is suggesting that the curriculum demands a different approach to learning in, through and about drama. Drama experiences are no longer enough, and he acknowledges that teachers now need to meet a complexity of objectives, in both performative and pedagogical terms.

5

The Meaning of Drama

This extract originally appeared as 'The Meaning of Drama' in
The Drama Magazine. November 1991. 6-9

Two old bogies are back to haunt us; confuse us; divide us. The first bogie is the resurrection of the Theatre vs Drama controversy. The second bogie is the 'fear' of English as the monster that will consume drama as a specialist activity. Two old bogies because both issues are ideological and political in origin and therefore the presentation and argument of both issues tends to be contradictory, selective and distorted by propaganda.

The purpose of this article is not to join the debates but rather to ask why these bogies should have returned at this point in the development of drama and its relationship with the curriculum. The debate itself has already been well tackled in a spate of recent articles in *The Drama Magazine* (Clarke, Goode; Haseman; July '91) which have restated and developed the commonly held view that theatre and drama are inter-related and inter-dependent dimensions of the same art form. Geoff Gilham's incisive analysis of the dialectical relationship between theatre and drama contained in his review of Hornbook's *Education and Dramatic Art* is particularly helpful in placing the issue in the broader context of the ideological struggle for control of the curriculum (*SCYPT Journal* no.21).

The new saviours of drama

The articles cited above have a common feature. A frustration that the 'new saviours' (Hornbrook and his adherents) of drama (or is it theatre?) have chosen to attempt to either ridicule or suppress any theoretical and practical developments in drama prior to the introduction of the Education Reform Act and the simultaneous publication of Hornbrook's work. I am not concerned in this article to further review Hornbrook's work other than to say that, for me, there is much to learn from his writing. But the style of his discourse – dismissive, sensational and polemical – buries the contribution he makes and, unfortunately, his message has become ideologically hijacked and turned into a crude Theatre vs Drama argument of tabloid simplicity.

I have dubbed Hornbook's clique the 'new saviours' because that is how they represent themselves and that is how they are being courted by state agencies such as the National Curriculum Council and the Arts Council.

Both agencies have picked working parties 'on behalf' of drama – these 'official' voices continually promote Hornbrook's thesis as a means of justifying their willingness to conform to the government's ideology of education. By being apparently progressive and up to date in using Hornbrook's work the working parties attempt to persuade us that the future of drama depends on burying its past. And here lies the greatest contradiction; that a 'Marxist' critique of drama should have become the acceptable model to a far-right conception of the curriculum. Have the 'new saviours' been selected to serve on government working parties on the basis of their allegiance to a Marxist view of drama and education? Of course they haven't. This is an important contradiction which I will deal with at length later in this article.

Twelve years of Thatcherism have taught us that opponents to the government's ideology are not given an official voice and where there are opponents already in office they are generally removed or displaced – witness Thatcher's cabinet 'reshuffles'. No, the working parties have been chosen because of their willingness to express drama in the government's terms. As far as I am aware, from recent drama publications, courses and conferences, Hornbook's work only finds material support in these working parties. The majority of practising teachers seem more concerned that the great advances in drama prior to ERA are being eroded and denied. So what is the attraction of Hornbrook's work to the government and why is it so feared by teachers?

The 'new saviours' have recreated the Theatre vs Drama debate in a very particular way. They drive a deep, hard, wedge between the words theatre and drama – 'theatre' and 'drama' become enemies locked in combat. They characterise drama as an eccentric form of alternative teaching based on an eclectic and misguided set of theories which have, in their view, nothing to do with the ART of theatre; drama, in their view, has been over concerned with content and experience at the expense of form and grammar. They are 'new saviours' because they seek to 'rescue' the status of drama by redefining it as a subject for academic and vocational study rather than as a process for learning. The argument is that by establishing a discrete body of knowledge, defining theatre skills and a canon of dramatic literature, drama can once again become a recognisable, and respected, curriculum OPTION.

Within this argument there is an implicit assumption that craft and art are the same thing. By this I mean that when the 'new saviours' talk of art they are really talking about the theatre-craft; the skills, knowledge and techniques used in the making and appreciation of theatre. Art, on the other hand, is the effective application of craft to content in order to realise meanings. The application of craft in order to make art requires imagination, perception, sensitivity and purpose. In this sense I am strongly drawn to Maggie Semple's process – definition of art as the action of making communal meanings out of human experience; in other words art becomes the synthesis, or concretisation of form (craft) and content (human experience) in order to crystalise meaning. A craft view of theatre avoids the issue of content, the issue of ideological and cultural bias in terms of the meanings produced and the possibility of theatre being used as a means of opposing, and exposing, the consequences of ideology.

A craft view of drama is feared by teachers because it is a betrayal of all children's entitlement to an immediate and accessible arts process which allows them to apply symbolic form to those areas of curricular, cultural and social content which have significance for them. Teachers understand that what you do your drama about is as important as how you do it. They also understand that craft develops alongside the children's desire to make meaning; that craft develops from a child's existing play, story and media experience; that you don't have to learn and practice new skills before you can begin to dramatise human experience.

There are two important contradictions in the position taken by the 'new saviours'.

The contradictions
In order to justify their position they have become increasingly selective in their aesthetics of theatre. Whilst apparently 'replacing' theatre into the drama syllabus, they end up ignoring, or attacking, some fundamental aesthetic assumptions about theatre. In the last issue of *The Drama Magazine* a prominent 'new saviour', who is also a member of the working parties, gave us some interesting and largely unsubstantiated evidence of this new conception of theatre. The interview makes these points:

■ that the dramatic curriculum has been too narrow because it has not been concerned with text. But, apparently, it has also been too broad and unfocussed because it has been over-concerned with personal and social learning. And yet, traditionally and in every culture, theatre manifests because 'Society needs drama.....because in it it seeks the human image'. Drama teachers who ... attempt to form a text out of children's expressive responses to the content of their personal and social education are referred to as simulation and a waste of time which 'needs to be used for drama'.

■ that the National Curriculum is all about assessment which is combined, in the interview, with a stress on the importance of objectives and criteria for drama, so that children are clear from the outset about what they can expect to learn and how their learning will be measured. This is very tidy. But as Eliot Eisner has shown in his research, combining objectives with assessment is only useful when the objectives define something which can be objectively measured and when the form of assessment is an efficient and appropriate form of measurement.

Objectives in science and maths are frequently measurable and open to objective assessment. You either learn $2 + 2 = 4$ or you don't. Can theatre be reduced to that which is measurable? Do artists know from the outset precisely what they are going to learn from their symbolic activity? We may have the means of assessing theatre-craft objectives in a way which is more or less consistent with the government's view of objectives and assessment but we certainly cannot assess theatre-art in a manner which is consistent with the testing of skills in science and maths.

■ drama has more in common with the other arts than it has with other subjects in the curriculum. Why? From a craft point of view it may make sense to lump drama in with other crafts. It fits with the craft view to uncouple drama, as a process, from subjects which offer a content relationship to drama such as history, literature, religious and moral education. When the 'new saviours' talk of the arts they generally don't include verbal arts within that generic term. They adopt the thinking in the 'Arts in Schools' documentation which has become a second reference work for the 'new saviours'. Hornbrook, in particular, even claims to be rescuing drama from English.

And yet, the simple truth of the matter is that there would be no drama in our secondary schools if English hadn't given time for it in the first place, much primary drama is taught by teachers who believe in the centrality of story and literature in the curriculum and if it hadn't been for Richard Knott, an English adviser, there would have been no NCC drama working party.

Teachers may, understandably, fear territorial and boundary warfare with English in terms of their specialism and career opportunities. It is cynical to exploit this fear when in reality what is being proposed is a performing/visual arts ghetto within the curriculum which is weak and powerless because it does not include the core of the core subjects – English (verbal arts). It is also the case that there is a long tradition of radicalism in verbal arts teaching as there is in drama (cf Williams, Freiere, Rosen, Britton, Eagleton, Craig etc). By severing the links drama becomes bound to the traditions of art teaching rather than to the progressive movement amongst verbal arts teachers.

The second contradiction within the 'new saviours' position lies in the results of the working party's endeavours. The 'new saviours' have had an unrepresentative influence on these working parties. They have claimed to be restoring drama to its proper position as a distinct arts subject with its own syllabus. Yet the only publication we are likely to receive – *The Drama Poster* – makes no reference whatsoever to the art form, the subject, the dramatic syllabus. Instead it catalogues a mind deadening list of cross curricular references to the possibility of drama in examples which invariably include 'eg, role play' or 'eg simulation'. The very forms of drama, dissipated across the curriculum, which the 'new saviours' claim have lead to drama, as a serious curriculum area, falling into disrepute! Whilst crusading for drama as a subject in its own right the 'new saviours' have, in fact, reinforced a view of drama as a servicing agent for 'important' subjects.

Two views of the curriculum

I want to return to a point I made earlier in this article. Why should Hornbook's 'Marxist' critique of drama in education be so attractive to the educational bureaucrats and ideologues of the right? To answer this question we need to look for a broader overview of the ideological battle that is being fought for control of the curriculum. All teachers now find themselves locked in this battle. Indeed, many of the 'new saviours' carry the scars – privatisation of drama services in Hampshire, slashing of funding for the Holborn Performing (sic) Arts Centre, etc.

For teachers the battle is to try and reconcile the values and practice which brought them into teaching with the values and practice imposed through the National Curriculum legislation. For many teachers there is sense in the concept of A National Curriculum but there is, also, increasing concern about the ideological content of THE National Curriculum. I am not clever enough to explore the full intent of the government's ideological position. But I can identify the educational origins of the government's approach to curriculum control; it is based on two premises which Frank Smith has identified as being prevalent in many advanced technological societies' attempts to redefine the curriculum.

- justification for the 'new' National Curriculum is based on the 'bureaucratic myth that learning can be guaranteed, if the instruction is delivered systematically, one small piece at a time, with frequent tests to ensure that students and teachers stay on task'. A recent research project undertaken by the Ministry of Education in Ontario concluded that: 'When we examine the evidence from our schools, we must conclude that the myth is widely and often unconsciously accepted. Yet the evidence in this survey leads us to conclude that such a view of human learning is profoundly mistaken'.

- promotion of the notion of 'accountability' in order to erode trust in progressive child-centred teaching programs (which includes the best D.I.E. surely?) which in turn leads to insecurity within the profession and the community. Frank Smith again: 'There is one reason only for the insistent control of programmatic instruction and tests in classrooms. That reason is lack of trust. Teachers impose programs and tests when they do not trust children to learn, and politicians and administrators impose programs and tests when they do not trust teachers to teach.....

  Teachers are given responsibility without autonomy; they are expected to teach according to schedules of tests and examinations. The tests control teachers far more effectively than occasional visits from inspectors and other supervisors. Through tests, teachers can be controlled without anyone ever entering their classrooms'.

Remember the words of the 'new saviour' quoted earlier in this article? – the National Curriculum is all about assessment. Chilling stuff.

Frank Smith concludes: 'Ironically, the procedures that are supposed to ensure that teachers teach effectively prevent them from doing so. Control through tests is lowering standards and reducing expectations.' If this all sounds like some remote North American nightmare talk to those teachers who were forced to abandon teaching their seven-year olds for five weeks or more of this past term.

Why does the government seek to control teachers and what they teach? Because they do not trust teachers to deliver a curriculum vision generated by a combination of far-right politicians, financiers and businessmen. Their vision is of a curriculum tailored to the 'needs' of the market, the creation of an acquiescent work force and the de-humanising effects of technological progress. I have tried to characterise, simply, the two visions of the curriculum which teachers are struggling to reconcile below:

Economic Needs Curriculum

- the purpose of the curriculum is to prepare the child for a future economic role in society
- curriculum consists of training in skills required for future economic role; skills tested by outcome
- rigid curriculum framework which the child must adapt to in order to succeed

Child Centered Curriculum

- the purpose of the curriculum is to respond to a child's present and developmental needs
- curriculum consists of meaning-making activities and experiences; assessment of processes used, by child, to make meaning
- flexible curriculum framework which is adaptable to individual needs

From this sketch it is possible to outline some points of conflict between the two models:

- the Economic Needs Curriculum is based on the assumption that employers at the 'receiving end' of education are better placed to determine curriculum design than educationalists. So now, the NCC and SEAC are controlled by a top industrialist and a banker respectively. Both have an 'open mind' because they have 'no previous experience of education' (*sic*). The Child-centered Curriculum, on the other hand, must be controlled by a partnership of teachers, parents and young people if it is to accurately determine present and developmental educational needs
- The Child-centered Curriculum assumes that it is important to respond to a broad range of needs; including the need to prepare young people for a future economic role. This broad range of needs typically includes cultural, religious, emotional, personal and social needs.

These needs are not necessarily considered relevant to an Economic Needs Curriculum

■ the Economic Needs Curriculum is always concerned with what children will need at their point of entry into the market place. The curriculum for seven year olds reflects this central concern as much as the curriculum for fifteen year olds must. In a Child-centred Curriculum, the curriculum is designed for the developmental needs of seven year olds – it aims to reflect the skills, interests and meanings which are relevant to that particular stage in a child's development. In this way the curriculum is made meaningful for children as they presently are. It is not made distant by being based on a developmental stage which is still a long way off for most seven year olds

■ the design of the Economic Needs Curriculum is made simple by defining the work-related skills needed at the point of entry into the market place. These skills can be listed, bunched together, spread out over the years of schooling and taught one by one. Assessment is made easy – you give training in the skill, you give a task which requires competence in the skill and children either succeed or fail in doing the task set. The design of the Child-centred Curriculum, on the other hand, is highly complex because it rests on the assumption that children learn when they comprehend what they are learning and that they are able to construct and understand meaning. 'The struggle to learn is usually a struggle to comprehend. The moment of comprehension is the moment of learning. Learning is a smooth, continuous flow from one understanding to another, not a series of sporadic lurches from confusion to confusion'[1].

Assessment is equally complex because it is concerned with the processes used by the child in order to make meaning – it is not concerned so much with outcomes as with journeys. We are talking about sophisticated tools such as observation, tracking, profiling, log keeping. We are not talking about tests which can be simply administered to a whole class at one sitting.

■ there are at least two senses in which the Economic Needs Curriculum can be seen as manipulative and the Child-centred Curriculum as being empowering

Firstly, the Economic Needs Curriculum asserts that skills must be acquired before meanings can be made. NB: the obsession with phonics – you are not allowed to make sense of print until you have received training in the forty five rules of phonics. The Child-centred

Curriculum empowers by suggesting that skills are developed in the pursuit of personally relevant and useful meanings – if the story holds enough promise you'll crack how to read it.

Secondly, the Economic Needs Curriculum manipulates by legislating the same curriculum for all children regardless of whether they live in an isolated mono-ethnic rural community in Cornwall or a multi-ethnic inner city housing estate in Bradford. Children must conform to the curriculum. The Child-centred Curriculum empowers by remaining flexible to individual, local and cultural variations. It is locally determined within agreed guidelines.

■ The Economic Needs Curriculum is antagonistic towards the development of meaning making processes, particularly processes such as drama which place technical and scientific skills within the context of society, history and humanity. For industry in a technological society to be successful there can be no questioning of the impact of technology on the environment, culture, humanity. Industry requires young people who are skilled enough to build and drop 'smart bombs' but not educated enough to question their existence.

The relationship to other child-centred literacy teachers

Many of the most important developments in drama in education in the last thirty years have been firmly rooted in a Child-centred Curriculum model:

- the importance of story and play as means of making sense of the world
- teacher in role as an empowering model of subjective meaning for young people
- working in dramatic context as a means of making science, history, social studies skills and concepts relevant, meaningful and accessible
- dramatising human experiences in order to challenge race, gender and class oppression in society
- understanding the cultural and educational *continuum* between informal play for self and the formal presentation of plays for others (which Hornbrook, in his selectivity, chooses to ignore together with the whole body of psycholinguistics and cognitive development theory which supports this aspect of drama in education)

The list could go on. Many of these developments have resulted from the earnest desire of teachers to make learning activity more meaningful for young people and from a growing understanding of how young people learn.

> 'just as concepts and theory serve to connect the facts of observation and experiment ... so the great dramatic themes and metaphors provide a basis for organising one's sense of humanity
>
> ... for bringing some unity into the scatter of our knowledge as it relates to ourselves'

These developments have been mirrored by similar developments in the teaching of literacy. Gordon Wells provides, from his research, two useful views of literacy which relate closely to what 'meaning making' in drama has been about in the last decade or so:

> 'literacy is the ability to exploit the symbolic potential of language for one's own social and personal uses'.[2]
>
> 'to be literate is to have the disposition to engage appropriately with texts of *different types* in order to empower thinking, feeling and action in the context of purposeful social activity'[3]

Literacy teachers know only too well what the cost is of continuing to pursue a meaning-making, child-centred curriculum. In the face of naked ideological prejudice they have, this year seen: media and political hysteria generated by propaganda about the evils of 'real' reading; right wing MPs trying to block Frank Smith's visa to attend the International Literacy Conference in Norwich; the suppression of the language in the National Curriculum project materials – which involved hundreds of teachers in several years' work attempting to reconcile the two curriculum views. Are these 'English' teachers the monsters we fear? At least literacy teachers had powerful voices who were not prepared to give up on the gains already made. At least the various working parties fought, to the point of suppression to include elements of a Child-centred Curriculum approach in official reports.

The real theatre vs drama debate

Rather than being supported by attempts to help drama teachers work effectively within the law whilst maintaining their values and principles drama teachers have, instead, been returned to the old nightmare of the debilitating theatre vs drama debate. Only this time the real debate is hidden. For, in terms of the 'new saviours', theatre vs drama really means a view of theatre that conforms to the Economic Needs Curriculum vs a view of theatre (which they call drama) which conforms to a Child-centred Curriculum.

All the interviews, briefings and the infamous poster itself show us that the official drama working parties – thanks to the influence of the 'new saviours' – have started from a consensus approval of Hornbrook's thesis and the *Arts*

5-16 publications. In that thesis Hornbrook ridicules the advances in child-centred, meaning-making drama. He creates the child-centered drama teacher as a shaman leading the ignorant astray. He dismisses the developments in drama in education listed earlier under the heading of 'platitudinous improvisations' and improvisation itself as '... the uninhibited manifestation of the creative spirit'. The *Arts 5-16* is equally cursory before moving quickly to detail Hornbook's 'contribution'.

By denying the art in improvisation, by downgrading drama's value as a learning medium and by attempting to define a fragmented, skill-centred theatre subject, the 'new saviours' become people the government can deal with. It becomes possible to reduce improvisation to the absurd depths of the drama poster, eg role play, eg simulation. It becomes possible to redefine the essence of progressive drama as useful active learning strategies any teacher could use. It becomes possible to divorce craft from meaningful content eg make puppets eg build a set.

Most ironically what started as a 'Marxist Critique' ends up being the rationale for suggesting, as the poster does in the technology section, that, eg role play is a good way of teaching that people are an 'important resource that needs organising, training and managing'. If that's not evidence of the ideological content in the Economic Needs Curriculum then find me a better one! It's the same ideology that later converts dead people into 'collateral damage'. And our 'new saviour' in his interview reminds us that drama teachers *must* work with the head teachers who are grasping the value of the arts in terms of marketing their schools.

The report from the NCC working party will inevitably be disappointing I'm afraid. Nor, do I think it would have made much difference who had been called to represent drama. Being constrained to express drama as just another element in a ruthlessly narrow Economic Needs Curriculum must lead to a betrayal of child centered practice. I just find it hard to believe that the task of shifting the 'official' view of drama from one curriculum vision to another was made so easy.

Notes
1 Bruner, J (1974) *Towards a Theory of Instruction*. Harvard
2 Wells, G (1988) *Children as Meaning Makers*. Heinemann
3 Wells, G (1991) Talk and Text in 'The Talk Curriculum. Pembroke

6

Theatre Without Walls

This extract originally appeared as 'Theatre Without Walls' in *Drama* Vol.2 No.2. Spring 1994.

Alternative aesthetics in educational drama

Those who embrace difference will always be in danger from the apostles of purity. (Salman Rushdie)

I do not want my home to be walled in on all sides and its windows to be stuffed. I want cultures of all lands to be blown about my house as freely as possible. But I refuse to be blown off my feet by any. (Mahatma Gandhi)

A conflict of traditions?

The purpose of this article is to respond to a growing tide of criticism of the educational drama tradition. A tradition which has drawn its inspiration from the pioneering work of Way, Courtney, Heathcote and Bolton. In simple terms, educational drama is a genre of theatre which is characterised by its emphasis on a variety of forms of improvisation and its claim to be a powerful medium for learning. On both sides of the Atlantic there are suggestions that educational drama is opposed to the 'traditions' of theatre and damaging to the future of theatre as a subject in the curriculum.

These criticisms, as we shall see, are often supported by the assertion that educational drama may serve useful educational and pedagogic purposes but it cannot be legitimised or considered aesthetically as art. In response, exponents of educational drama have tended to defend their practice by referring to educational arguments and theories of cultural psychology and child development. They have not responded, as I intend to, by theorising the aesthetics of their practice.

I want to suggest that criticisms of educational drama often stem from a tension between 'progressive' and 'cultural conservationist'[1] views of what theatre is. This tension is based, I believe, in a perceived conflict between different performance traditions which do not need, in practice, to be oppositional or exclusive. I use the word 'traditions' carefully. I want to suggest that educational drama has its genesis in an alternative, globalised aesthetic performance tradition which complements, rather than excludes, the Euro-American theatre tradition.

Who said that!

I am unable to precisely reference the domestic criticisms of improvisation made in the American educational system. But, at a recent AATE Conference (Boston, 1993) I was struck by the number of panels and discussions which adopted a hostile stance towards educational drama. The suggestion seemed to be that educational drama represents an unfortunate aberration in the development of school theatre programmes and that the time had come to 'move back' into a more substantive and traditional form of practice. My own anecdotal experience of these discussions suggests that the 'ephemerality' of improvisation is a key concern for the American critics of educational drama[2]. Dramatic literature has a permanence that improvisation hasn't. As long as there continues to be a literature of children's theatre, the argument goes, its status as a subject is secure.

The concern seems to be that if improvisation takes a hold in school drama programmes then the literature of children's theatre will diminish and be impoverished as a consequence. The critics of the uses of improvisation in educational drama also seem fearful that the understanding and valuing of theatre is threatened.

I am conscious that the role of improvisation in educational drama is framed differently in the States. In my very limited experience I find that in the USA improvisation tends to be explicitly focused on pedagogic and personal and social functions – 'conflict-resolution', 'critical thinking', 'story building' – rather than on aesthetic or social/philosophical function as tends to be the case in the UK. From a personal perspective I also have some problems with explanations of improvisation that play down its symbolic creativity.

In the UK there has been an increasingly bitter exchange between the critics and exponents of educational drama. The most vocal and articulate of these critics have been Peter Abbs and David Hornbrook. In essence the substance of their criticisms are analogous to those made in America. Abbs in his preface to Hornbrook's *Education in Drama* claims that educational drama is: 'Devoid of art, devoid of the practices of theatre'. Hornbrook (1992) in a recent article in *The Drama and Theatre Teacher* suggests that educational drama goes against 'all commonly held views of theatre'. He goes on to say:

> A country with one of the richest theatrical traditions in the world has suc-
> ceeded in turning out a generation of students who are, in effect, dramatically
> illiterate.

In fact, the number of students entering and achieving high grades in public theatre studies exams in the UK has risen by 25 peer cent in the last five years. The hard evidence shows that more children gain high grades in public examinations in drama than in any other art form.[3] The evidence is that exposure to educational drama increases the number of young people who understand and value theatre, including the great dramatic literature of the Euro-American tradition.

Beyond the Euro-American Tradition: The influence of performance theory and post-structuralism

On both sides of the Atlantic the critics of educational drama have appropriated terms like 'aesthetic', 'art', 'commonly held views of theatre' to support their position. In doing so they assume that these terms have neutral universal meanings. In their rhetoric, they appear to cast themselves as cultural warrior heroes battling to preserve 'our' values, representing what 'we', 'right-minded', people believe. They fight to preserve 'art', 'aesthetics' and 'theatre' from the barbarians at the gates. The assumption is that there is one, globally accepted, natural ideal of 'art' and 'theatre'. That the global prominence of the Euro-American theatre is unquestionable[4].

Cultural conservationists also argue that there is a clear line dividing the 'high art' of classical theatre from the 'low art' practices of educational drama (Hornbrook, 1992); that theatre is a 'natural' hierarchy of aesthetic experience in which the institutions, practices, genres and terms of 'high art' have an undisputed prominence[5]. They believe that the conventions and literature of the Euro-American theatre are 'naturally' the most civilised and represent the highest expression of the art form. Indeed, they seem to suggest that Euro-American theatre is the art form and that preserving the integrity of Euro-American theatre from the corrupting influences of 'lesser' genres of theatre and popular entertainment is the proper work of the drama teacher[6].

As Paul Willis (1990a) has demonstrated:

...the terms of high art are currently categories of exclusion more than of inclusion.

Rather than celebrating the rich aesthetic diversity to be found in different forms of theatre, the critics encourage us to exclude any form of theatre which doesn't coincide with their conception of theatre. The damage that such a view of art can do to the future success of theatre as a vital and relevant passion in young people's lives is eloquently argued by Willis (1009a:3)

...the complete dissociation of art from living contexts. This is where the merely formal features of art can become the guarantee of its 'aesthetic', rather than its relevance and relation to real life processes and concerns: religious art installed in the antiseptic stillness of the museum.

As in so many spheres the blame for the rot that has set in drama is placed firmly on the shoulders of the 'progressive movements of the sixties'.

I would argue that the methodology popularised by Heathcote and her amanuenses has inherited all the worst characteristics of school drama's progressivist legacy. (Hornbrook, 1992)

In England, at least this is a familiar witch hunt. Everything from rising crime to one parent families is blamed on the 'progressive movements of the sixties'. Educational drama, in its present form, was indeed born in the sixties and is now being enriched by other aesthetic and cultural projects which have their genesis in the same rich period of recent history. I want to focus on two such projects – post-structuralism and performance theory – and discuss their relationship to educational drama.

Post-structuralism emerged in response to those minority and alternative voices that began to be heard within the 'progressive movements of the sixties'. Voices which continue to be politically and culturally marginalised in our society began to be successful in challenging the politics of cultural representation and the false stories which sustain the powerful at the expense of the weak[7]. Women, gays and lesbians, native peoples, postcolonial writers, the physically and developmentally challenged and many other groups have transformed ideas of what is presented as 'natural' in our society by exposing the ideological nature of the stories and representations that are used to try and persuade us that we all want to live in a world which is 'naturally' ethnocentric, phallocentric and heterocentric[8].

This critical attitude to the sexist and racist images that surround us is commonplace in most teachers' practice – we avoid perpetuating stereotypical images of minorities for instance. Do we want to be restricted to teaching stereotypical images of theatre?

When critics of educational drama talk of 'commonly-held views of theatre' we need to ask by **whom** are these views commonly held? When they talk of 'aesthetics' we need to ask **whose** aesthetics? Is a definition of theatre which excludes educational drama the only possible definition – the natural definition?

As a form of 'cultural analysis' post-structuralism seeks to destabilise our sense of what is 'natural' and what isn't. To remind us that 'our' view of the world is just that and no more – it would be a different view if we were standing in another place at another time. The idea that investment in western science and technology will solve all human problems, for example, may appear natural to us. In some other cultures western science and technology are seen as being the problem.

In the same way the meaning that we attach to words like 'theatre' and 'aesthetics' is culturally and therefore ideologically produced there is no definition of theatre which is above ideology. As Althusser (1963:46) suggested: 'ideology has no outside'. There is no 'neutral' definition of theatre, for instance, any definition is ideologically loaded. From this perspective, the criticisms of educational drama tell us more about the ideology of the critics than they tell us about either theatre or educational drama.

The influence of the 'progressive movements of the sixties' has also been alive in mainstream Western theatre. The late 1960s and early 1970s were a period of experimentation in theatre – new forms of performance were developed and many of the classical conventions of acting and dramaturgy (Barba, 1992)[9] were put to the test. *La Mama, Squat, TPG, Gay Sweatshop*, Brook, Marowitz, Mnouchkine, Grotowski, Wilson and others moved towards forms of performance and research that rejected the dominance of dramatic literature in favour of an emphasis on the 'event', the live **actions** of theatre.

> ...situate theatre where it belongs: among performance genres, not literature. The text, where it exists, is understood as a key to action, not its replacement. Where there is no text, action is treated directly. (Schechner, 1988:28)

> Theatre anthropology seeks useful directions rather than universal principles ... it is the study of human beings' socio-cultural and physiological behaviour in a performance situation. (Barba, 1991:8)

These experiments in theatre met with the same critical reaction that has characterised the conflicts surrounding educational drama. Susan Bennet (1992:28) describes the origins of 'performance theory' in these terms:

> Performance theorists responded to mainstream North American theatre theorists who berated the devaluation or even total rejection of text by performance artists. Traditional theorists saw this as the final straw in the alienation of audiences, sending them to the 'culturally inferior' entertainments of cinema and television.

Faced with a critical and hostile theatre establishment, the innovators began to theorise their position. What kind of theatre were they producing? Clearly not the theatre of the mainstream critics. A new trans-cultural definition of theatre was needed that would encompass the work of the innovators within a broader field of theatre which acknowledged not just the Euro-American performance tradition but other 'rich traditions' as well – Noh, Kathakali, Topeng Pajegan.

The journey beyond the forms and conventions of Euro-American theatre inevitably led to interest in the non-mimetic performance traditions of the Oriental, African and Islamic worlds[10]. This journey was not merely aesthetic in nature. Working with teachers from other cultures exposed Western artists to alternative philosophical traditions – different systems of thought and belief, different aesthetics. As a result, performance theorists (Schechner 1988, 1989, Barba and Savarese, 1991) began to question those fixed and exclusive definitions of theatre offered by the mainstream theatre theorists in the Western world and which have held dominance since the time of Aristotle.

Rather than seeking to further reify the distinctness and impermeability of concepts and roles such as actor, audience, theatre space, director, producer, text; performance theorists moved, instead, towards a more fluid analysis of theatre experience as a genre of human performance framed within a trans-cultural perspective. The walls of culture, the walls of convention and tradition, the walls between theatre and life began to be taken down. Through performance projects and training they evolved alternatives[11]. Increasingly, performance theory has created a hybrid of aesthetic and anthropological interests – researching, learning, transforming and performing.

The criticisms of performance art and of experimental forms of theatre, like the criticisms of educational drama, rest on a perceived conflict between different performance traditions; Western and Oriental/rural-tribal. But there is also a conflict between philosophical traditions. On the one hand there is the Western philosophy of dualism – the rigid separation between mind and matter which dominates the Western world view. This view is deeply embedded in the Western consciousness to the extent that we often assume that the divisions we make between animate and inanimate, nature and humanity, art and science, religion and daily experience are natural and globally recognised. On the other hand there are the Oriental and Native philosophies which strive for wholeness; which look for connections rather than boundaries – philosophies which do not recognise or submit to Western forms of categorisation – which do not separate art from life, nor artists from other kinds of people.

By examining and then celebrating their position on the 'margins' of mainstream theatre, performance theorists became more interested in exploring and crossing the permeable boundaries between: theatre and other genres of performance – ritual, play, games, sports, dance and music; Occidental and Oriental aesthetics; aesthetics and social rituals and dramas; actor and audience relationships:

> Performance is no longer easy to define or locate; the concept and structure has spread all over the place. It is ethnic and inter cultural, historical and ahistorical, aesthetic and ritual, sociological and political. Performance is a mode of behaviour, an approach to experience; it is play, sports, aesthetics, popular entertainments, experimental theatre, and more. (McNamara, 1982:2)

Performance theorists abandoned the security and false certainties of the Euro-American playhouse and worked in the marginal, and indistinct, areas between theatre and other forms of human social and aesthetic experience. Just as educational drama practitioners seek to do.

In theorising their position on the fringe of mainstream theatre, Schechner and others have broadened our conception of theatre so that it has lost some of its ethnocentricity and begun to be inclusive of a multiplicity of forms and conceptions of theatre. They have succeeded in de-stabilising the fixed categories and concepts that comforted the mainstream theorists. The voice of a marginalised group seeks recognition not just for itself but on behalf of the marginalised, the voice of the institutionalised centre tries to shout down those who challenge its power.

In trying to develop trans-cultural understandings of performance, performance theorists challenge those who, like the critics of educational drama, tend to the Aristotelian belief that there is a transcendent ideal and unified form of theatre which we should aim for in our work. That we should strive, in our work, towards an unobtainable ideal form of theatre – which closely resembles Euro-American theatre, of course! For the conservative likes to know that there is a clear evolutionary progression from the 'primitive' to the 'civilised'[12].

This narrow evolutionary model of theatre depends on the discredited, but still influential, theories of the 'Cambridge Group' – who proposed that the origins of theatre were to be found in the *sacer ludus* – sacred ritual – of the ancient Greeks (Murray). The theory is that *sacer ludus* evolved into dithyramb – odes or epic poems – and subsequently into tragedy. The fact that no evidence has been found to substantiate the existence of the *sacer ludus* and that the theory rests on trusting Aristotle's dubious skills as a professional ethnologist does not preclude Hornbrook (1991:25) from perpetuating the myth that **all** theatre has its origins in mystical religious experience:

> it is widely accepted (*sic*) that the origins of drama and indeed all art, lie in the religious rites of our ancient ancestors

However, as anthropologists have begun to question the ethnocentric bias within their work and to accept that cultural definitions are ideological rather than autonomous – summarised in Street, 1993 – they have abandoned 'originary' and hierarchical theories of aesthetic and social experience. It has become clear that theatre inter-links, and shares its roots with, games and sports and a number of other genres of aesthetic and social performance as much as it does with religious experience (Turner, 1992).

> There are only variations in form, the intermixing among genres and these show no longterm evolution from 'primitive' to 'sophisticated' or 'modern'. Sometimes rituals, games, sports and the aesthetic genres (theatre dance, music) are merged so that it is impossible to call the activity by any one limiting name. That English usage urges us to do so anyway is an ethnocentric bias, not an argument. (Schechner, 1988:6)

It is clear that there is no single and pure evolutionary route in the historical development of theatre; it is and has always been influenced by a range of social, aesthetic, technological and economic developments. An 'originary' theory of theatre would have to prove that the sacer ludus was the original Greek theatre rather than, say, the Olympic Games. Needless to say no such proof exists.

> The relation among genres of performance that I will explore is not vertical or originary **but horizontal**.... If one argues that theatre is 'later' or more 'sophis-

ticated' or 'higher' on some evolutionary ladder and must derive therefore from one of the others, I reply that this makes sense only if we take fifth century BC Greek theatre as the only legitimate theatre. Anthropologists with good reason, argue otherwise, suggesting that theatre – understood as the enactment of stories by players – exists in every known culture at all times, as do the other genres. These actions are primeval, there is no reason to hunt for 'origins' or 'derivations'. (Schechner, 1988:6)

The shift from a vertical to a horizontal relationship between performance genres is essential to understanding the central place of improvisation in educational drama. Aristotle maintained that both tragedy and comedy had their **first beginnings** in improvisation. *'men eventually created poetry from their improvisations'* (Poetics chap 4). Criticisms of educational drama are often based on this idea that improvisation is a 'primitive' or 'undeveloped' form of theatre. In a horizontal paradigm, improvisation is not 'lesser' or 'cruder' – it is different from and parallel to other forms of theatre.

By exploring the horizontal relationships between different forms of aesthetic and social performance, Schechner and others have drawn attention to the important aesthetic differences between the Euro-American theatre and more informal community art-making traditions which have always been alive both within European cultures and beyond.

The alternative tradition

At the level of daily, community aesthetic experience there is a remarkable consistency between different cultural traditions. A consistency which contrasts with the dominant Aristotelian conception of theatre.

This consistency of experience challenges the Aristotelian premise that art and life must be consequent, never co-extensive. It also challenges the relatively recent European idea that art and artists are isolated from life and our daily work (Williams, 1976; Gimpel, 1961)[13].

In Aristotelian aesthetics, life is raw, art is cooked. Life is 'transformed' into something more perfect through the representative, or 'art-making', processes of mimesis; we make a representation of a real situation and in so doing we create something which is different from a real situation. In the Aristotelian sense (Fergusson, 1949) the process of *mimesis* will result in an artwork which takes on its own independent and separate life[14].

Mimesis takes as its origin an 'action' in the real world but through the processes of aesthetic crafting and shaping the representation – art-work – of the real action begins to take on a life of its own – it is no longer a mere imitation; it has become transformed into a piece of art with its own independent validity and existence[15]. For Aristotle, art was essentially and qualitatively different from life and must follow from it – the two cannot exist as a single experience. He denies the Platonic principle of *metaxis*[16]. Boal translates Aristotle's position as:

> The **metaxis**, that is, **the participation of one world in another**, is unintelligible; in truth what has the world of perfect ideas to do with the imperfect world of real things? (Boal, 1979)[17]

Educational drama is mimetic but it doesn't deny the possibility of there being a *metaxis* between the dramatic and the real. Participants use representative actions in order to make a living representation of real actions in other times and places. But the idea that life and art are rigidly separate areas of experience and cannot coincide is challenged in educational drama (Bolton, 1992 chap 1)[18].

> The separation between art and life is built into the idea of mimesis. It is this coming after and separation that has been so decisive in the development of Western theatre. ... In non-mimetic art the boundaries between 'life' and 'art' are blurry and permeable. (Schechner, 1988:38)

In contrast to most other forms of Euro-American theatre, educational drama does not seek to separate out the symbolic context of the drama from the real context of the audience through space, time or role[19]. The 'live' theatre of educational drama acknowledges and involves all who are present as fellow participants in the creation of a performance which is based in the 'here and now' experience of those present. You have to be there and be involved in the making, as well as the observing, to experience it. In educational drama the formal divisions between actors and audience functions are consciously blurred so that:

> The participants in drama are not just construing but actively creating the imaginary world. The audience in the theatre waits for something to happen, but the participants in a drama session make it happen. (O'Neill, 1989:20)

In the Euro-American tradition, 'live' usually means actors pretending they can't see the audience and an audience which pretends not to be there – there is no direct, interactive relationship between the experience on stage and the experience of those present as audience. In Euro-American theatre we are accustomed to the physical separateness of stages and auditoria, of actors and audiences, of playwrights and actors and the idea that art comes after experience not as part of it. In contrast, educational drama is actual and existential.

In educational drama the metaxis between the drama and participants' actual experience, which is scrupulously avoided in Euro-American theatre, becomes the central aesthetic principle. Participants are encouraged to shape the symbolic action of their drama, *as they proceed*, responding to each other and negotiating the meaning of their work at both a symbolic and an actual level. In educational drama, life and art become co-extensive – we cook it as we live it.

And it is this challenge which is based both on the experience of non-mimetic aesthetic traditions and daily, community aesthetic experience, which is most feared by the critics of educational drama[20].

The aesthetics of actualisation and orature

The anthropologist, Mircea Eliade (1965) has investigated the structures of non-mimetic art forms amongst rural-tribal societies and concludes that *metaxis* is central to what he calls *actualisation* in which reality and a symbolic reality are experienced in the same breath

> ...rites the **actualisation** is a making present of a past time or event

Actualisation, which is a common feature amongst non-European aesthetic traditions (Schechner, 1988), is defined as a special state of being in which life and art become co-extensive, in which we do not create after nature but like nature[21]. In this sense the concept of *actualisation*, the dream state of shamanism and acts of ritual are brought close to *metaxis* – the state of being in the act of representation and being in the real actions of the world at the same moment.

> The rite makes the myth present. Everything that the myth tells of the time of beginning, the 'bugari times' (Dreamtime), the rite reactualises, shows it as happening, **here and now**. (Eliade, 1965:6)

For those peoples whose art is a process of 'actualising' there is the assumption that experience cannot be segregated into hierarchical planes: spectating, participating, worshipping, loving, learning. It is not, as Schechner (1966: 219) explains, that every experience is the same, but that all things are part of one wholeness, and that within the range of our lived experience unlimited exchanges and transformations are possible. Schechner quotes from Levi-Strauss' conceptualisation of the 'Savage' mind:

> This is the case of art ... savage thought is definable both by a consuming symbolic ambition such as humanity has never again seen rivalled, and by scrupulous attention directed entirely towards the concrete, and finally by the implicit conviction that these two attitudes are one

'Actualising' also assumes that there is a mass participation in symbolising actions – art-making. That there are no divisions between 'artists' and 'spectators'. The act of 'being there' *and* participating in the social production of meaning is the important feature. Kwesi Owesu (1986:127) uses the term orature to describe the trans-cultural social and aesthetic dynamics of tribal-rural art:

> These cultures evolved many complex and innovative forms as well as special characteristics and qualities. The symbol of appreciation, a V-sign above the head of a dancer in Akan culture, the sophisticated facial expression of a Kathakali dancer, Yoruba mask-making, Inca painting or Mbira music ... between them they share certain common dynamic values and traditions of aesthetics relating to the structures, relations and processes of creativity. It is the sum total of these that we call orature.

Owesu (1986:130) argues that the dominant concepts of the arts and culture, in Euro-American societies, are inappropriate for describing the aesthetic aspirations of those whose roots are in the Asian and African diasporas. Like Schechner, Owesu is frustrated by the difficulty of trying to articulate an alternative world view from within the language of artistic compartmentalisation developed in bourgeois Western art circles. But, nonetheless, he provides an eloquent description of 'actualisation':

> In orature, the most important 'actors', 'poets', 'directors' and 'painters' are the people, the masses **living out** their life dramas and expressing them through cultural media and institutions ... A participant in a maize dance does not merely mimic the plant and its phases of growth. He or she creates social meaning, re-enacting social relations with other dancers in the process of articulating determinant social experience.

How different is Owesu's description from the lived aesthetic experience still alive in our European urban communities? Alongside the minority experience of 'high-art' there is a complimentary source of aesthetic 'actualising' to be found in parades, ceremonies, pub singalongs, dances to soul and rock music, karaoke, storytelling, dressing up and going out, chanting.

Even amongst the 'indigenous' Euro-American communities there has always been and continues to be a tradition of 'actualising' with similar principles to those identified in orature and non-mimetic art forms. Country dances, festivals, celebrations all involve some element of metaxis – being there and symbolically behaving in the same moment.

Drama as the art of the moment

Educational drama seeks to evolve a practice that reflects the forms, traditions, values and spiritualities of the globalised, multicultural societies that exist in most Western countries. It also seeks a practice that takes on new aesthetic forms and purposes in response to young peoples' increasing access to dramatic experiences through film, TV, ritual, ceremony, games, sports, dance, music and the social dramas of living at the tail end of the 20th century.

Young people's dramatic experiences are not confined to the stage. Richard Schechner (1989:311) argues that the inter-generic and inter-textual exchanges between theatre and other forms of entertainment and social representation have become so frequent and pervasive that we can no longer isolate a theatre box in any credible or useful way:

> So there is theatre in the theatre; theatre in ordinary life; events in ordinary life that can be interpreted as theatre; events from ordinary life that can be brought into the theatre where they exist both as theatre and as continuations of ordinary life.

It has become commonplace to notice the appropriation of elements of theatre not just in film and TV drama but also in sporting events, news media, political rallies and advertising. Any account of theatre must now include the 'theatricalisation' of news, entertainment and sport.

The paradox is that we are now living in the 'dramatised society' that Raymond Williams (1976) identified[22], but as Paul Willis's (1990a) detailed ethnographic research in the UK shows, only 7 per cent of young people go to conventional Euro-American theatre. A percentage which has been consistent over many years.

Educational drama now seeks to include and legitimise and make use of those other fluid forms of dramatic experience in young people's lives that are outside of the Euro-American tradition. Dramatic experiences which are not bound to the same actor, audience, space conventions. Experiences which are interactive, existentialist and often ecstatic – so drama borrows:

- the self-absorbed experiential quality of play
- the tension of rules and unknown outcomes from games and sport

- the social and cultural assertiveness of ceremonies and rituals
- young people's own life 'scripts' learnt from the social dramas of their own lives and of others, often based on social dramas represented through TV and film
- the sensuous intensity and spectacle of live entertainment events
- the visual and physical expression of dance and personal fashion (costuming?)

The important consideration here is that what is borrowed changes the forms used. Educational drama is concerned with the experience rather than the study of alternative cultural forms and concepts; the effect and affect of symbolic actions rather than a distanced appreciation of them. As a consequence, the forms of improvisation and representation that characterise educational drama are evolving away from the forms of rehearsal, study and performance which have become conventionalised in the Euro-American theatre tradition.

This evolution is in some part based on a search for a form of theatre which gives value to young people's commonest dramatic experiences rather than continuing to restrict itself to forms of practice which are only enjoyed by 7 per cent of young people. Willis's research shows that these alternative symbolic experiences tend to be social, interactive and existential in nature. They are closer to *orature* and the symbolic ambition of the rural-tribal tradition than they are to the conventions of Euro-American theatre. As Paul Willis (1990b:15) suggests, they offer an alternative aesthetic:

> ...It is the practical activity of this cultural **work** (quite literally) which we wish to hold and highlight as an everyday accomplishment in our notion of the grounded aesthetics of common culture.

> This cultural work may involve no texts or artefacts, no 'artistic things' at all. There is, for instance, a dramaturgy and poetics of everyday life, of social presence, encounter and event ...They (young people) are the practical existentialists. Inescapable, sometimes excessively, **they live in the moment**[23].

Because educational drama respects, values and uses a range of aesthetics it can bring both familiarity and **difference** to young people's own daily grounded aesthetics. The difference is that the existential and interactive experience of social improvisation is mediated through the symbolising and transforming languages of space, time, human action, words, sound, lights and objects. The same symbolising languages used in the dramaturgies of the Euro-American tradition; and all other performance traditions. The lived experience of educational drama combines the reflexive and existential qualities of actualising with the reflective and self-conscious processes of mimesis.

Educational drama combines aesthetic purposes with specific pedagogic purposes and this duality has also influenced the forms used in educational drama. Educational drama adopts the principle that if your own 'grounded aesthetics' are being valued it makes you more open to the possibility of discovering and using other formalised aesthetic traditions; including the Euro-American tradition.

The aims of educational drama are justifiably broader than the production of actors, directors, theatre historians, critics and writers. For young people the art of theatre, as Artaud suggested, is the art of the moment.

Finally...

I have suggested that inclusive definitions of theatre which restrict us to 'high-art' histories, artefacts and practices blind us from seeing the aesthetic and social potential of educational drama; which is closer to the communal 'actualising' of both rural-tribal societies and our own – Euro-American – community experience of symbolic creativity. This 'other' form of art making is not superior or inferior – it is different. 'Similar principles; different performances' (Barba, 1992).

I have suggested that in Euro-American societies, there is a **duality** of aesthetic experiences, sometimes termed as 'popular' and 'high', and that both have a long historical tradition[24]. There is no historical evidence to support the idea that participation in 'popular' forms of aesthetic experience leads to a decline in appreciation for 'high-art' forms. They are on different planes of aesthetic experience. It is only recently, and for economic reasons, that the nature of this duality of aesthetic experience has begun to radically alter.

In the late 20th century the explosion of mass media has resulted in an appropriation of aspects of popular culture by an increasingly small group of entrepreneurs whose motive is to make economic profit out of mass programming for a mass audience. The experience of popular culture in Western society is forever bound up with: the essentially passive response we make to film and TV; advertising; sponsorship; personality cults and sectarian political manipulation[25].

If educational drama, through the medium of improvisation, seeks to capture some of the qualities of 'actualising' then it does so in order to oppose and subvert the new mass forms of popular 'entertainment'. It is not in opposition to the Euro-American theatre tradition with which it shares a long and dignified history because it exists on a complimentary but different plane of aesthetic experience (Willis 1990b). Film and TV have not taken away from mainstream theatre audiences. But they may be taking away the value we place on communal singing, dancing, music-making, storytelling, celebration and merry-making. Those aesthetic experiences which symbolise our togetherness whilst we live, make and shape together.

Notes

1 The term 'progressive' is used to describe practice which seeks to transform the traditions of Euro-American Playhouse theatre; 'Cultural Conservationist' describes practice which is, firmly, rooted in the same traditions and which preserves rather than challenges the conventions of the Euro-American tradition. Perhaps the most obvious difference lies in attitudes to playtext – for conservationists, the literature of theatre is central to its study and practice; for progressives it is the act of theatre which is central.

2 There is a much richer tradition of children's theatre in the USA than in the UK. The emphasis on process rather than product within the discourse of educational drama is a justifiable concern for children's theatre practitioners. I want to suggest that crude divisions between process and product tend to exist in the rhetoric rather than in the practice of educational drama. Lowell Swortzell provides a useful summary of his concerns as a leading children's theatre practitioner in Jackson, 1993.

3 Data provided by SCAA and AEB, high grades = A-C. The biggest increase is at 'A' level, taken at 18. The questions require a detailed knowledge of the Euro-American tradition.

4 In this sense the critics are part of a long 'cultural conservationist' tradition; they are fellow travellers with Arnold, Eliot, Leavis, Richards and, more recently, E D Hirsch and Allan Bloom.

5 These arguments are often supported by emotive comparisons between the 'quality' of improvisation compared to *King Lear*, for instance. In fact, these two theatre events are separated by a degree of difference rather than by a degree of quality. They are alike in using the common elements of theatre but entirely different in a number of key respects (Bolton, 1992 chap1). You could argue that *Macbeth* is a better Shakespearean tragedy than *King Lear*. You wouldn't argue, beyond personal preference, that baseball is higher on a scale of quality than cricket.

6 In 1993 the Arts Council in the UK published its guidance to schools on drama – the suggested curriculum was depressingly reductive in its emphasis on training young people in the skills of using Euro-American forms and conventions.

7 See *Voices for Change* ed. Lawrence, 1993, particularly Neelands, J. 'The Starry Messenger' for a more detailed account of the influence of post-structuralism and post-modernism within educational drama.

8 In which the dominant powers seek to persuade us, just as the critics of educational drama do, that certain definitions of theatre are 'natural' and others aren't.

9 Dramaturgy is the term used to describe the performance text, ie, all the stage actions which together provide a record of how a performance is structured: *The word text, before referring to a written or spoken, printed or manuscript text, meant a 'weaving together'...That which concerns the text (the weave) of the performance can be defined as dramaturgy, that is, 'dramaergon', the 'work of the actions' in the performance.*

10 Western forms of aesthetic performance, with the exception of ballet, are mimetic in the sense that the actions and symbolism are based on real life actions.

The actor makes special use of familiar gestures in performance. Non-mimetic forms of performance, such as Kathakali, use codified gestures and symbols which are not based on real life gestures; they are special languages learnt by performers and audience alike. This explains why Western performance strive towards 'realism' and 'naturalism' whilst non-mimetic forms strive towards perfect technique and mastery of ancient codes.

11 This, of course, has been a long journey. The 20c history of theatre shows that Craig, Artaud, Brecht, Grotowski and Brook in particular, integrated aspects of Oriental theatre forms into their work – or, at least, took what was useful to them (Bharucha, 1990). Performance theorists are more concerned with developing a new conception of performance which is neither of the west nor of the east but made of both; a trans-cultural form of theatre often referred to as 'third theatre' (Sircart 1986, Barba, 1991, Watson, 1993). Barba and others are not concerned with imitating or appropriating the outer form of different cultural genres of performance. They are concerned with understanding the underlying, trans-cultural principles, codes and behaviours of aesthetic and social performance.

12 These are categories which assume that Western civilisation is civilised in relation to primitive rural/tribal and Oriental civilisations. Post-structuralism, performance theory and educational drama share a healthy disrespect for these categories. Civilised/primitive distinctions belong to the Victorian obsession with Social Darwinism (Lane, 1982). In terms of the future of the environment which cultures are primitive and which civilised?

13 This idea first took hold during the Renaissance. Michaelangelo, it seems, reckoned he should be paid a better rate for the Sistine Chapel than for painting donkey sheds. It became fully developed in the 18th century, see Williams 1976 for the story.

14 *Mimesis* is often taken to mean the imitation of an action. This is, of course, central to any concept of **Western** performance. In common parlance we often refer to the Aristotelian axiom that 'Art imitates nature'. In fact, this is a distortion of Aristotelian aesthetics. Read within the context of the *Poetics* the axiom is more accurately put as 'Art **recreates** nature'. The process of *mimesis* (aesthetic imitation) produces a 'likeness' not a simulacrum. In Aristotle's view the 'likeness' should show us the world as it should be, *not as it is*.

15 A mimetic representation – a play, dance, song – is based on real actions but it also becomes a thing in itself. The play exits independently from the real life action at its source. The play is a representation of real actions but it is also an art-work which is complete in itself. Shakespeare used a variety of folk stories and histories as the source of *King Lear*. But the play has integrity and life of its own which goes beyond being an imitation of those stories and histories. In the Aristotelian sense the play represents real actions taking place in another time and space – but the play also exists in the time and place in which the play is being performed. It has become temporarily and spatially removed from the real actions of life.

16 See also Boal 1979:1-50 Boal's critique emphasises the disempowering quality of Aristotelian theatre. By separating art from life, Aristotle also separates art from politics – aesthetic action from political action. An aesthetic principle much in favour with the emerging Athenian Aristocracy which patronised Aristotle.

17 At the time of writing (12/93) an exhibition, *Europe Without Walls*, is being held in Manchester of art produced during the revolutions in central Europe in 1989/90. A review asks the question whether posters and pamphlets produced during the revolution, ie, as part of it, can be considered ART in the same sense as sculptures and paintings produced **after** the revolution! In my argument both are art.

18 In fact, as we shall see, the idea and possibility of *metaxis* is a defining principle of educational drama.

19 A courtroom improvisation might be raising and quoting from real issues about fairness and justice in the context of the children's classroom. We all have examples of young people who have used their role in the dramatic context to speak, symbolically and eloquently, about their actual concerns and relationships within the real-world contexts they share with their family, friends and classmates.

20 Attempts to redefine and experiment with audience/actor relationships in mainstream theatre meet with similar hostility:

> under the pressure of attempts at audience participation, the theatre splits into a physical life without imaginative dimension and an imaginative life incapable of presence (Cole, 1975).

21 It is defined in the same terms as metaxis – on a global scale Plato seems to have got it right and Aristotle wrong!

22 The idea of a 'dramatised' society in which our perceptions of the world have become 'dramatised' by the media is not abstract for people living in Northern Ireland, for instance. The perception that people in mainland Britain share is that violence, death and bombings occur on a daily basis. That is not the lived and actual experience of people living there.

23 See above!

24 It is only the imposition of a class structure which attributes one form or aesthetic experience to the middle and ruling classes and another to the working classes which has led to the prejudicial separation between 'high' and 'popular'.

25 Neither Barba nor Schechner make the point that one fundamental difference between Western and other aesthetic traditions is the extent to which technology has determined the development of performance in the West – film and TV are of course obvious examples of art forms born of technological progress. In Oriental and Native performance, technology has had a negligible influence on the aesthetic development of traditional forms.

References

Barba, E and Savarese, N (1991) *A Dictionary of Theatre Anthropology; The Secret Art of the Performer.* Routledge: London

Bennet, S (1992) *Theatre Audiences.* Routledge: London

Bharucha, R (1993) *Theatre and the World; Performance and the Politics of Culture.* Routledge: London

Bolton, G (1992) *New Perspectives On Classroom Drama.* Simon and Shuster: London

Cole, D (1975) *The Theatrical Event.* Wesleyan University Press: Boston

Cornford, F (1914) *The Origin of Attic Comedy.* Edward Arnold: London

Eliade, M (1965) *Rites and Symbols of Initiation.* Harper and Row: New York

Fergusson, F (1949) *The Idea of a Theater.* Princeton University Press: Princeton

Gimpel, J (1961) *The Cathedral Builders.* Grove Press: New York

Hornbrook, D (1989) *Education and Dramatic Art.* Basil Blackwell: Oxford

Hornbrook, D (1991) *Education in Drama.* Falmer Press: Brighton, England

Hornbrook, D (1992) 'Can we do ours Miss' in *Drama and Theatre Teacher.* Vol 4 no 3.

Jackson, T (1993) (Ed) *Learning Through Theatre.* Routledge: London

Lane, J (1982) *The Death and Resurrection of the Arts.* Green Alliance: London

Lawrence, C (1993) (Ed) *Voices For Change.* National Drama Publications: Newcastle upon Tyne

McNamara, B in Turner, 1992

Murray, G (1912) *The Four Stages of Greek Religion.* Oxford University Press: Oxford

Neelands, J (1993) 'The Starry Messenger' in Lawrence, C (*op cit*)

O'Neill, C (1989) 'Ways of Seeing; Audience Function in Drama and Theatre'. In *2D* Vol 8 no 2

Owesu, K (1986) *The Struggle for Black Arts in Britain.* Commedia: London

Schechner, R (1988) *Performance Theory.* Routledge: London

Schechner, R (1989) *Between Theater and Anthropology.* University of Pennsylvania Press: Pennsylvania

Street, B (1993) 'The New Literacy Studies' in *Changing English* Vol 1 no 1. Institute of Education: London

Swortzell, L (1993) 'Trying to Like T.I.E.' in Jackson, T (1993)

Turner, V (1992) *From Ritual to Theatre; The Human Seriousness of Play.* PAJ Publications: New York

Williams, R (1976) *Keywords.* Penguin: Harmondsworth

Willis, P (1990a) *Common Culture.* Open University Press: Milton Keynes

Willis, P (1990b) *Moving Culture.* Calouste Gulbenkian Foundation: London

7

In the Hands of Living People

This extract originally appeared as 'In the Hands of Living People:
Between the ideas of process and curriculum' in *Drama Research*
Vol. 1 – March 2000: 47-63

We shall make lively use of all means, old and new, tried and untried, deriving
from art and deriving from other sources, in order to put living reality in the
hands of living people in such a way that it can be mastered. (Bertolt Brecht
1938)

Imagining Drama

In the conference publicity, I was interested to discover that I was positioned as a '....practitioner and writer on **both** process **and** curriculum'.
These terms, 'process' and 'curriculum' are not conjoined anywhere else in
the publicity. Gavin Bolton and Dorothy Heathcote are both associated with
the term 'drama-in-education' for instance; no mention of both 'process' and
'curriculum' there.

Now I understand that the conference organisers' straightforward and honest
intention was to draw attention to the fact that I have, as one of them explained in an e-mail: 'written on both the process of drama and on its role in
the curriculum'. And the proof is apparently in the books that I have written.
I am not suggesting that the conference publicity actively seeks to create a
division between 'process' and 'curriculum'. Indeed, it is clearly an attempt to
bring these ideas, or imaginaries, together. But I want to do some necessary
nit-picking around this seemingly uncontroversial idea that my work reflects
the imaginary that there is such a thing as 'the process of drama' and that 'the
curriculum' is, firstly, not a process and secondly, that drama has a role in the
curriculum, rather than being a 'curriculum-as-live(d)-process' in its own

right. In other words, I am not at all comfortable to subscribe to either of the imaginaries of 'process' and 'curriculum' or the implied opposition between them, which are implicitly, at least, contained in the publicity.

This discomfort is exacerbated by the fact that I suspect, and will hope to demonstrate, that the origins of the imaginary of 'process' are to be found in the position-taking of those in the field of drama who describe their work as 'process drama'. I also believe that the origins of the imaginary 'curriculum', lie in the old familiar binaries of 'method/process' and 'subject/product'. Historically, of course the progress of drama in schools has been hindered by this either/or conception of practice as either 'method' or subject' either 'process' or 'product'. Historically, human progress of any kind in schools has been hindered by the acceptance of 'the curriculum' as some sort of monolithic, dehumanised, inert *structure*; the curriculum-as-grand-plan, rather than as the multiple curricula of live(d) experience.

In this paper I want to offer a critique of the idea of 'process' in drama as it is currently imagined in the practices and discourses of the 'process drama' position in the field. I also want to critique the imaginary of 'curriculum' when 'curriculum' is placed in opposition to 'process'. If this all sounds unnecessary and complicated, give me indulgence! In writing about both process and curriculum it has not been my intention to straddle two 'camps' or to dip into different ponds. I may have failed, but my intention has been to try and articulate a new hybrid concept of drama education that is 'between' the old imaginaries of 'process' and 'curriculum' as they have been historically used, often divisively, in drama. If I suggest that my work is 'process-curriculum' then in actuality what I am suggesting is that I am working under the hyphen. The hyphen rather than the conjoined concepts/positions/histories of difference is the site for a new imaginary of drama education. Or at least, that is what I will try to argue here.

The Defining Characteristics of Process Drama

So, how am I imagining 'process drama'? What do I imagine its defining characteristics to be and how might my own imaginary of drama seek to go beyond the boundaries of this position? There are, of course, some quite precise definitions of what 'process drama' is and is not. For instance, Cecily O'Neill describes 'process drama' thus:

> Process drama is a complex dramatic encounter. Like other theatre events it
> evokes an immediate dramatic world bounded in space and time, a world that
> depends on the consensus of all those present for its existence. Process

> *drama proceeds without a script, its outcome is unpredictable, it lacks a separate audience...*

Later she writes:

> *The book is specifically aimed at drama teachers and makes close connection with a range of curricular material, including history, social studies and literature, but the experience of the drama is also valued for its own sake. The significance of theatre elements ... within these drama structures is acknowledged, but it was not part of our purpose to explore their operation in any detail.*

They also help me to discover, therefore, what is implied in the different imaginary of 'curriculum drama'. Process drama is an 'encounter', an 'event', an 'experience'. It is connected to other subjects in the curriculum like history, social studies and literature but it is not a subject itself; 'theatre elements' and how they are used will not be explored in detail. Interestingly, 'process drama' is said to '**lack**' an audience. It proceeds without a script and its outcome is unpredictable. O'Neill accepts that 'Process drama is almost synonymous with the term *drama in education.*'

What does O'Neill's conception of 'process' share with the drama-in-education tradition? At one level, there is a shared belief in the primacy of 'dramatic playing' and in the 'representational' mode of theatre-making. There is an implicit and shared sense in both that working in the dramatic playing and representational mode of theatre is 'better than' and more 'authentic' than working in a performance and presentational mode.

In contemporary performance theory, the 'representational' mode describes any performance that seeks to create a 'virtual' or 'parallel' reality, which co-exists with but does not inter-penetrate the audience's reality. The actors appear to ignore the presence of an audience. In theatre, the representational mode includes 'realist' or 'naturalist' styles of theatre in which the actors appear to be actually inhabiting the drama world represented on stage.

Conversely, 'presentational' theatre offers no such illusion. The dramatic world is not evoked but demonstrated, it is not experienced as a 'reality' but shown to be a version or interpretation of actuality; it is closely associated with the work of Brecht and so-called Brechtian styles of theatre. In presentational performances, the actors will acknowledge the audience and communicate directly to them.

'Dramatic playing' is the acting style most often associated with representational forms of drama and theatre. It is interesting that 'dramatic playing' is often described in Stanislavskian terms as 'living through'. The idea being that the participants in process drama, like Stanislavski's actors, are 'living through' the given circumstances of the imagined situation 'as-if' these events were actually occurring to them; they are 'being' in role, or character. In process drama, there is a 'consensus' that all those present exist, temporarily, within the immediate dramatic world. They are bound to its parameters of space and time rather than their own actualities. In 'process drama' we can be denied any social space, outside of the bounds of the drama world, in which to comment and reflect from within our own parameters of existence and difference – it lacks an audience; or at least it imagines that it does. In order to participate I must accept the circumstances of the fiction as unchangeable and the outcome as being unpredictable. Unless I speak, in role, from within the bounds of the 'consensual' drama world I can have no other voice. In process drama, participants learn from the 'real' experience of 'being' in the dramatic world; it is a psychological and private mode of learning based on how we feel as a result of our drama experience.

In the presentational mode of theatre-making, associated with Brecht but also characteristic of the great non-European performance traditions and other popular forms of entertainment, experience is shown rather than lived. We demonstrate through dramatic representations, or depictions, the way the world is and how it works. We illustrate, rather than illude, our understanding of human behaviour and experience. In the presentational mode, there **must** be an audience who respond as themselves to what is being demonstrated and who are aware that the 'dramatic world' is nothing more and nothing less than an imaginary construction; a hermeneutic that needs constantly testing and modifying against our existing (or becoming) imaginaries of the world. Learning in the presentational mode is through public discussion, comment and the voicing of different conceptions of the world; it is sociological and public, based on what is actually said and done rather than on what is 'felt' or 'experienced'. The purpose of Brecht's theatre was to show the world, and therefore the circumstances of the drama world, as changeable and to show that the outcomes of the drama may well be predictable according to political principles and the logic of human history. It is a theatre of knowing, rather than a theatre of cathartic understanding.

Moving Beyond the Boundaries of Process Drama
So Let us March Ahead! Away With All Obstacles!
In England we have been developing a way of working in drama that has sought to include both the presentational and representational modes. This

way is often referred to as the 'conventions' approach, because it employs a wide range of 'means' drawn from both the representational and presentational traditions. Following Brecht's advice we have sought to make lively use of all means. The emphasis in the conventions approach has been on giving students the means to make their own dramatic representations by introducing them to increasingly wide and complex choices of 'means' for depicting the world; old and new, tried and untried. In this sense, the conventions approach does seek to explore in detail the significance of theatre elements; their historical and contemporary uses and the cultural traditions that they represent. It is an approach to drama that may well connect with other subjects in the curriculum, but it also makes drama itself a subject for practical study by students. Putting living reality in the hands of living people.

There are fewer rules and artistic restrictions in this way of working. There will always be an audience, or a sense of an audience. There may well be scripts. Because of the emphasis on groups developing convergent but different dramatic responses rather than the whole class conforming to a monolithic 'consensus' the participants are not bound by the space and time of a singular 'drama world'. Although, of course, at times they might be!

Crucially, perhaps, in the conventions approach there is a more complex understanding of 'participation'. In process drama, as we have seen, there tends to be an emphasis on total participation in an event that unfolds as a result of the actions taken within the drama world. In process drama this degree of participation is often crudely opposed to the total lack of active participation in some other, mainly historical, genres of theatre in which the audience appear to be nothing more than passive voyeurs of the stage-action; an audience of 'peeping toms' as Artaud famously described them. Because the conventions approach embraces both presentational and representational modes and because it may also lead to orthodox performance of some kind it tends to operate with a subtler sense of degrees of participation. Below I have characterised a **Scale of Formal Participation**, which seeks to describe six degrees of participation between the poles of total and passive. The examples are designed to illustrate the range of possibles not just in classroom drama but in performance events as well. In the conventions approach, students and teachers may well play the whole scale even within a short period of drama.

1 Players
Participants are physically and psychically engaged in the dramatic action, which requires actions-to-be-taken in order to progress. 'Dramatic playing' is

the exemplary form of this level of participation. Dramatic playing often corresponds to the conventions of psychological realism in observing a 'natural' use of psycho-physiological gestures in real time and in one place. In Schechner's anthropology of performance, 'ritual' is the exemplary form of this level. In both 'dramatic playing' and 'ritual' everyone who is present is assumed to be a part of the dramatic action. There is no outside. Participants are only able to effect events through dramatic action; the real life context and channels of communication are suspended. At this level of participation there is the illusion, at least, of total transformation; the intention is that the participants will be personally transformed by the activity and they are re-warded for exhibiting responses and behaviours that conform to the 'illusion of transformation'.

2 Social Actors
The space is informally divided into 'stage' and 'auditorium'. Participants have the choice of commenting on and criticising the actions of the actors or of moving into the stage and offering alternative actions for themselves. There is, therefore, the choice of participating in a social discussion about the actions on stage or participating directly, oneself, in the stage action. This level of participation is closely associated with the work of Augusto Boal and with the 'conventions approach'. Its dramaturgy tends to stress the aesthetic plasticity of time, space and physical presence. It is concerned with making the world that is external to us all, visible and discussible, through the con-creteness of dramatic representation, rather than with dramatising the internal and private experiences of the participants. At this level there is a clear distinction between the 'stage' – a public sphere – and the private space of the audience. The 'transformations' of the stage are partial at this level. The actors do not try to create the illusion of total transformation.

3 Framed Witnesses
The audience participates psychically in the stage actions by adopting a role-perspective, or 'frame' in Goffman's sense, in relation to the dramatic action. They are asked, to watch the actions on stage 'as-if' they were involved in, or socially responsible for, what happens. The audience may, or may not, parti-cipate physically and vocally in what happens even if they are addressed directly by the actors – they witness the event as a jury, as guests, as decision makers. This form of work is associated with theatres of Meyerhold, Brecht and Grotowski. It is independent of any specific dramaturgy, except that it implies that a physical and psychic relationship is created between the

'actors' and the 'witnesses'. Again, transformation is partial and reflexive. The actor of Brecht's Epic Theatre is an exemplary model.

4 Active Witnesses

There is a clear and formal separation between the audience and the performers. The audience remains in its own 'reality' but they are either encouraged or allowed to make their response public through cheering, discussing, commenting amongst themselves as the performance progresses. This form of participation is associated with popular entertainment (pantomime for instance), sports and other spectacles that are primarily visual and spatial rather than verbal. It is also associated with Didactic and Agit-Prop theatres.

5 Passive Witnesses

The audience may be placed in a close physical relationship to the action, and some elements of the action may be addressed directly to them. But the audience minimises its presence through a 'learnt' disposition for stillness and silence. Aesthetic appreciation of the professional skill of the producers, becomes more important to the audience than its direct participation in the process of production. It is, therefore, the point at which the work is primarily 'aesthetic' rather than social in its intent. But there is still a sense of an 'event' that is socially shared. This form of 'witnessing' is associated with most contemporary Western 'serious' theatre and many school performances for a community audience.

6 Observers

There is no social contact between the audience and the actors. The privacy of the individual voyeur is emphasised through darkening and deepening the auditorium. The actors create an autonomous illusion, 'as-if' no audience was present, and the individuals in the audience make no recognition of the presence of others. This form of theatre belongs to the relatively brief period of Naturalism and the proscenium arch theatre.

In seeking to describe some of the characteristics of the 'conventions approach' I am not seeking to distance myself from 'process drama' or to denigrate the tradition that it draws on. Rather, I am urging us to go 'beyond'. I am using the imaginary of 'beyond' that Bhabha has described so well:

> The 'beyond' is neither a new horizon, nor a leaving behind of the past ... Beginnings and endings may be the sustaining myths of the middle years; but in the fin de siecle, we find ourselves in the moment of transit where time and space cross to produce complex figures of difference and identity, past and present,

inside and out, inclusion and exclusion. For there is a sense of disorientation, a disturbance of direction, in the 'beyond; an exploratory, restless movement...

The State of Drama in the State of England
A Disturbance of Direction

There are other characteristics of drama in England which begin to inform my understanding of the imaginary 'curriculum' when it is used to distinguish 'process' from other orientations in drama. Despite the jeremiads of influential voices on both the left and the right in drama at the time, drama has flourished during the last decade rather than withered on the vine as they had predicted. There are of course exceptions – for example, the destruction of TiE and the temporary difficulties for drama in the primary curriculum caused by knuckle-headed interpretations of the National Literacy Strategy.

Through the darkest days of state intervention and centralised control and policing of the curriculum, drama has taken root in most of our schools almost in spite of its exclusion from the National Curriculum. For most of this period the values and practices of drama that have been prized in schools have been firmly rooted in the Drama-in-education tradition which underpins the process drama model. The recent Secondary Heads Association publication *Drama Sets You Free* is a clear endorsement of that tradition's claim to offer a powerful, motivating and integrated approach to learning which foregrounds the personal, moral and social and community-making benefits of 'process drama'. Indeed, this publication concludes with the memorable assertion that: *A school without drama is a school without a soul.* In the same spirit, the new Curriculum 2000 for England makes it a legal requirement for schools to use drama, not just in English, but for a wide range of purposes including spiritual, moral and social and cultural development, the development of inter-personal and problem solving skills and the active exploration of the Statement of Values which is the foundation of the new curriculum in England.

Taking root in schools means being provided with a space in the curriculum and increasingly this space is a drama space rather than a space borrowed from other curriculum subjects. Once a space is reserved for drama it raises the issue of how this space will be used; this implies a Plan. And this is, I think, at the heart of the distinction that is being made in the 'process' and 'curriculum' divide. For an increasingly large number of students in English schools and colleges the possibility exists for a child to have continuity of drama provision from 5-18. In Secondary schools at least, this drama provision is likely to be managed by a specialist teacher with a degree in drama and theatre who may also have experienced drama at school themselves. In England, this same teacher is also likely to offer drama as an extra-curricular activity and to organise a performance schedule. And the potential space for drama is considerable. Imagine a child whose first experience of drama is at 7. Say, and it's possible, that this child has drama for one hour once a fortnight for the rest of their days at primary school. Say the same child then has regular drama, as most children in England now do, once a week between the ages of 11-14. Say that this child now goes on to study drama at GCSE and AS/A level. This child may over the course of 11 years of schooling experience something like 1,700 hours of drama, or 70 days! Now add to that the hours of extra-curricular and rehearsal time which are also available to this child.

When you are given this kind of space for drama you cannot afford to think of drama as a series of 'events' or 'encounters' which are autonomous and independent of each other. You cannot think in terms of isolated episodes. You have to conceive of some sort of temporal map that will ensure progression and continuity and which presumes that the child will want and can expect to 'get better' at drama. How will the experience of drama at 14 be different from at 7? What is being built on and what is it building towards? There is the space not just to use drama to provide 'experiences' for students but also to teach drama to students so that they can use it better for themselves. You cannot exist on a diet of imaginary whole class meetings with mysterious strangers bound in a 'drama world' – the novelty of 'process drama' wears off, you will soon crave variety and difference in your drama. You will want access to all that drama and theatre can do in all of its manifestations. You need, in short, a curriculum. I think it is no accident that in England we have quietly dropped the term Drama-in-Education and adopted instead the term Drama Education which implies a broader range of traditions, functions and practices which include 'process drama'.

Does having a drama curriculum mean abandoning the values and goals of 'process drama'. Well, I think that suggestion is imagined in the phrase 'both process and curriculum'. The idea seems to be that the 'plan' for drama will become more important than the lived experience of drama – the process. This *is* a real danger. We live in an age in which the 'curriculum-as-planned' has overshadowed the vitality of the 'curriculum-as-live(d) experience'. We live in an age of a state-centred educational system, rather than in the child-centred imaginary of the 'process drama' tradition.

In a state-centred system, those in temporal power can comfortably imagine that the folders and ring-binders that contain the Plan for the curriculum in every school actually represent the curriculum as it is lived by children and teachers. It is a neat and tidy view, which assumes that as long as everyone is getting on with the Plan in the same way, at the same time, everything is well in the State of England. The consequences of working in an educational system that is dominated by this imaginary of the curriculum as a Grand Plan are exquisitely described by the Japanese-Canadian educator, Ted Aoki, in these terms:

> *What we see here is the conventional linear language of 'curriculum and instruction' of 'curriculum implementation' of 'curriculum assessment'. This is the world in which the measures that count are pre-set; therefore ordained to do the same – to dance the same, to paint the same, to sing the same, to act the same ... where learning is reduced to 'acquiring' and where 'evaluating' is reduced to measuring the acquired against some preset standardised norm. This metron, this measure and rhythm, is one that in an overconcern for same-ness fails to heed the feel of the earth that touches the dancing feet differently for each student.*

Aoki argues for a different and multiple conception of the curriculum that includes the idea of the live(d) curricula of students and teachers. By this he means a view of curriculum that is based in the situated pasts, present and emerging life experiences of students and teachers. It is a view that recognises the multiplicity of the living experiences shared differently in different class-rooms, by different students and different teachers – it is not quantifiable; it cannot be bound in ring binders; it is lived. Now for those observers on the outside of the English education system it may look as though drama in this country has succumbed to the curriculum-as-planned view. We have been engaged recently in trying to establish a coherent plan for drama, with aims and objectives, schemes of work and assessment systems. We do set targets for our students and keep records of their achievements in drama. We may even have drifted too far in this direction; becoming temporarily obsessed with the detail of the Plan. And it may appear because of this attention to a Plan for drama that we have abandoned a 'child-centred' view of the curri-culum. But Aoki is not urging us to drop one view for another, he is arguing for a 'multiplicity' of meanings of 'curriculum'. He compares this multiple imaginary with Chinese ideograms in which a single word is graphically rendered into its multiplicity of origins, nuances, orthodox meanings and im-plications.

In order to make the most effective use of the space given to drama we need a plan of where and when and why we are going with our students, but every drama teacher knows that the true art of teaching lies in the complex tempering of the planned with the lived. Whatever the plan, it is not complete until it meets with and is mediated by the different live(d) experiences of the students who enter the drama space. We recognise that these students do not come to us as 'human beings' but rather as 'human becomings' – we believe that what we do is planned to help them in this journey of becoming. We try, by all manner of means, deriving from art and deriving from other sources, to put living reality into the hands of living people. The curriculum is the necessary map, it is not the journey itself.

Managing the planned with the lived implies working with what I will describe later as a 'complexity of objectives'. In the process drama and drama-in-education tradition teachers tend to work with a 'density of objective'; their purpose is to provide an 'event' in which some aspect of human experience is explored in depth through the means of dramatic playing. As a result of this episode, participants may come to know a great deal about a particular episode of human experience and its human significance for them at that time.

When these singular events occur in a drama curriculum that has a longer-term plan and strategy, the teacher will inevitably work with a range of objectives, which might span diverse domains of educational, personal, artistic and cultural learning. These broader objectives of the planned curriculum, will include but go beyond the particular objective of a single drama event. This teacher will also be working within longer-term systems of accountability and assessment. The teacher will also be working within the personal and social politics of the group over time; seeking to have a positive effect in their lives if given time. The inter-weaving, juggling, structuring, balancing that needs to be done in order to knit these long-term concerns into the space and time of a planned curriculum, takes skill! That is why I refer to the 'complexity of objectives' which characterises drama in many English schools today. Drama teaching which is increasingly able to consider the whole effect of the 'bits', rather than focussing on the 'bits' as individual events.

Drama teachers are expected to do a lot for their money in England as elsewhere. Here a drama teacher may be responsible for teaching drama as a discrete and officially invisible subject in the curriculum including teaching examinations at 16+ and 18+. They will also organise extra-curricular clubs, theatre visits and performances. The most visible face of drama, within the statutory orders for English, has to be understood and delivered and this may also include preparing 14 year olds for their national Shakespeare tests. English, as do several other subjects, also rely heavily on drama methods in the new requirement, in Curriculum 2000, that each subject must state how it will teach spiritual, social, moral and cultural developments and the transferable skills of problem solving, communication and inter-personal relationships. If this drama teacher has some experience they are also likely to hold a position of pastoral responsibility and want to promote, or more importantly dramatise, some of the values in the new Statement of Values. Let me quote briefly from this Statement, so that you can hear for yourselves the extent to which the agenda of many drama classrooms has now become a new national agenda for education:

The Self
We value ourselves as unique human beings capable of spiritual, moral, intellectual and physical growth and development

Relationships
We value others for themselves, not only for what they have or what they can do for us. We value relationships as fundamental to the development and fulfilment of ourselves and others, and to the good of the community.

Society
We value truth, freedom, justice, human rights, the rule of law and collective effort for the common good...

The Environment
We value the environment, both natural and shaped by humanity, as the basis of life and a source of wonder and inspiration.

Rhetoric maybe, but it creates the chance for us to actively insist on these shared values in schools and to use drama to actively promote them. For those of us more familiar with directives that begin, *the child should* or *the child must*, the use of an inclusive *we value* is refreshing. Schools are of course communities and in our new curriculum there are at last signs that the quality of community and communal life are being given greater priority. And in communities in our time, in other times and in other places performance functions in different domains of community life just as it does in the community life of the school. Richard Schechner bases his anthropology of performance on the idea of four inter-related domains; healing, education, ritual and entertainment. In the 'complexity of objectives' which drama teachers work with it may well be that, over time, the curriculum in drama will serve therapeutic, educational, community and pure entertainment needs in the school community. In order to operate in these different domains, drama teachers will draw on whatever means necessary; they cannot, and will not, restrict themselves to a single restrictive method of working.

I have restricted this account of the 'shape of things to come' to England for a particular reason. Drama is now well established in our schools, but it is still free of the 'strait-jacket' of a National Curriculum Subject. This is not necessarily the case in other national communities. It may well be that restricted models of drama practice like 'process drama' and Boal's arsenal of the 'Theatre of the Oppressed' are entirely appropriate in situations where drama has not taken root in any significant way. In many countries, drama is in what we might call an 'advocacy' phase. In this phase the arguments need to be made and won for drama; its claims have to be clearly demonstrated and the distinction between participatory forms of efficacious drama and orthodox forms of theatre for entertainment has to be established. In these circumstances, each 'event' will have significance because there may be no other secure space or time for subsequent 'events'. But of course, the goal in this advocacy phase is to win a stable, constant and secure place for drama in the education of all children. If the advocacy phase is successful this space will be awarded and a new phase of implementation begins. Implementing drama creates the possibility of carefully mapping out the Plan for drama and extending the possibilities for teaching and learning in drama. In this sense, because I am privileged to work with those in both phases of development, I am involved in **both** process **and** curriculum depending on audience and local circumstance.

Contract
The necessary framework of negotiated and public 'rules' which govern all our behaviours in drama. This framework is there to protect students and teachers and to provide an explicit regulated public arena in which, just as in a game, the students and their teacher are clear on what is allowed and what is not allowed. Neither the teacher nor the student is free, for instance, to make racist or sexist comments gratuitously if that is prohibited in the contract.

Given Circumstances
What a student says and does is further limited by the 'given circumstances' of the lesson. These might be the given circumstances of the imaginary drama world as in 'process drama'. (And why on earth are we so reluctant to use this language of given circumstances and objectives in 'process drama'?). It might be the given circumstances of a playtext, or pre-text; characters, situations, historical context. It might also be the given circumstances of the curriculum; we are limited to the boundaries of a particular planned objective. To make matters more complex in the social reality of the drama the given circum-

stances will also include constraints of time, mood, space, who's up and who's down – you name it!

Convention

What we say and do in drama is further restricted by the 'means' that are employed to realise the given circumstances. In 'still image' for instance we are not free to say anything! Utilising a broad range of conventions appropriately and effectively, provides students with different experiences of form and therefore of content. It also provides them with the knowledge to make more effective and complex relationships between 'means' and 'meanings' in their own drama-making.

Knowledge and Experience

Clearly our existing knowledge and experience further limit us. Again this is a broad concept that would include knowledge and experience of the given circumstances, of the conventions being used, of the skills needed to realise the work dramatically. We add to the students' knowledge and experience of the world and of drama in our work with them but we also need to accurately assess and then use their prior knowledge and experience and manage the other frames appropriately.

Personal Boundaries

What we say and do will also depend on our emerging sense of self – our bodies, our cultures, our sense of 'difference', our histories, our lines between intimate and public domains of behaviour, our level of self esteem. In some situations this frame may encompass the others. In other words we may find ourselves in situations where we cannot even move to contracting without sorting through issues of personal and inter-personal boundaries in the group.

My suggestion is that when things go well and when things, as they often do, go less than well we can return to these frames and assess how effectively they were matched and managed. Are there problems with the contract? Were the given circumstances explicit and concrete enough? Was this the right convention to use, might another have worked more effectively? Did the students have sufficient knowledge and experience to feel free to participate? Was the work too challenging to the student's personal boundaries?

Have I defined 'curriculum' drama? We are defining it and refining it – it is not a rupture with the past, it is not a rejection of those constant values that have guided drama education, in all of its manifestations, in the past fifty years. But just as Edward Bond urges us to remember that every child needs a map of the world, so too does every drama teacher need a map of their own *teatrum mundi!*

References

O'Neill, C. (1995) *Drama Worlds* Heinemann (U.S.). Portsmouth

Bolton, G. (1992) *New Perspectives in Classroom Drama.* Simon and Shuster, London

White, R. Kerry (1995) *An Annotated Dictionary of Technical, Historical and Stylistic Terms Relating to Theatre and Drama.* Edwin Mellen Press, Lampeter

See, for instance, Neelands, J. and Goode, T. (2000) *Structuring Drama Work,* 2nd Edition. CUP, Cambridge

Schechner, R. (1993) *The Future of Ritual.* Routledge, London

Bhabha, H. (1994) *The Location of Culture.* Routledge, London

SHA (1998) *Drama Sets You Free!* SHA. Leicester

Aoki, T. (1996) Spinning Inspirited Images in the Midst of Planned and Live(d) Curricula in *FINE; Journal of the Fine Arts Council, The Alberta Teacher's Association* Fall 1996. Edmonton

DfEE and QCA (2000) *Curriculum 2000.* HMSO, Norwich (www.hmso.gov.uk/guides.html)

Schechner, R. (1993) *The Future of Ritual.* Routledge, London

Section Three
Pro-Social Pedagogy

This section of the book features four articles in which Neelands' political motivations are at their most obvious and their most inspiring. *11/09 Space in our Hearts* is, quite simply, an extraordinary piece of writing. Written just after the terrorist attacks on the World Trade Centre and the Pentagon, and originally presented as a keynote, Neelands makes a potent case for the place of drama education in a world seemingly at war with itself. The human need for art at times of crisis and drama's ability to allow people to act as if they are other than themselves provides us with the opportunity to temper imagination with empathy. The events of what he call 11/09 seem to have jolted Neelands from the optimism of *In Living Hands* to suggest that the debates over curriculum had been a distraction from the more important issue of what drama does for students. The urgency of the situation at the end of 2001 provides the chilling backdrop to Neelands' plea that for drama teachers the response to the world post 9/11 must be a vital reaffirmation of the principles of drama in education. Where *In Living Hands* Neelands had been willing to see the term drama in education disappear, he argues now for retaining the nomenclature and also its defining legacy. Again refusing a binary view of the world, Neelands posits drama in education's pedagogic context as living betwixt and between a set of dialectics.

Drama in education is seen as a humanising and democratising response to the events of 2001. Neelands reminds us that although these events were extraordinary in their imaginative power they too are informed by a legacy: a legacy of the abuse of power. His refusal to Americanise the date is in deference to the murderous events of September 11 1973 in Argentina, which were supported by the Nixon regime. Neelands argues the humanising force of drama in education is the 'new basic'. The intervening eight years suggests we ignore the plea for a curriculum with empathetic imagination at our peril.

Since 2001 the American foreign policy response has been to introduce democracy at the end of a gun. Under the Bush regime the world was divided into simple binaries. For us or against us; American or Freedom fries. Education as a force to humanise, to feed and to nurture the compassionate potential of the imagination stands as a direct challenge to the divisive policies of the wars on and of terror.

In *The Art of Togetherness*, Neelands reminds us 'that action and acting are at the heart of the process drama tradition as well as the processes of professional rehearsal. In drama nothing can happen unless young people take action.' It is in this participation and this acting in the world of fiction that Neelands sees the possibility of young people actioning a better world for themselves.

Neelands sees his work and the potential of drama in education as belonging to, if not betwixt, two traditions. It falls within the pro-social pedagogy of John Dewey and Paolo Friere, and their notions of participatory democracy. It also falls within the modernist aesthetic tradition represented by dramatists such as Ibsen, Brecht and Bond, who saw that from transformation through and on the stage, real world change could occur.

In yet another shift of nomenclature to describe his practice, Neelands now refers to his work as ensemble theatre. In the ensemble-based model the effects of drama go beyond the boundaries of the subject and the classroom. It has the ambition of impacting on young people's quality of life and learning in the wider community. Neelands argues that 'ensemble-based learning' is a bridging concept between those pedagogies of the rehearsal and the classroom. This pedagogy centres on democratisation of learning and artistic processes through high quality relationships for learning and living together. Interestingly, Neelands now considers bridging the pedagogies inherent in performative tradition and the theatre of the classroom rather than bridging the aesthetic. Neelands has used this bridging approach with actors and educators at one of the world's most famous acting companies, the Royal Shakespeare Company. It is refreshing to see the bridge can hold two-way traffic.

In the third piece in this section, a written version of the Seamus Heaney address Neelands gave in Cork, Eire in 2005, we bring the journey that began in 1984 almost full circle. Neelands again rehearses the notion of drama as a lens to replace the mimetic notions held in much Western art. He aligns his work alongside that of Brecht, seeing ensemble work as theatre acting as a dynamo. Like Brecht, Neelands see the potential of theatre to be a catalyst for the wider human struggle to determine the world, rather than be determined by it. Such work for Neelands is the 'creation of egalitarian democracies to replace the aristocratic and totalitarian systems of governance which continue to dominate our age and place'.

Ensemble theatre is not merely a model of participatory democracy; it is participatory democracy in action. Here, Neelands often uses the word belief: either his, Shakespeare's, Brecht's or of his fellow theatre workers such as O'Toole and Dunn. In the end I believe Neelands' work is not about academic argument, empirical evidence, or carefully calibrated scientific proof. It is about belief, which is rooted in the soul of humanity. Believing that the world can be different, can be better, is harder when all the evidence says otherwise. But it sustains a career in the most human of all art forms, the art of living together and imagining how we might live together better in the future.

The final extract is an unpublished lesson plan based on Shaun Tan's picture book *The Arrival*. As an example of ensemble-based theatre, it demonstrates much that has changed in Neelands' practice since 1984, and also highlights that which has remained constant.

Neelands' lesson plan, given to participants at workshops he runs, is still part of a life-long mission to make the teaching of drama and the making of theatre in classrooms accessible to everyday teachers. The structure that provides entry into rich and layered theatrical experience requires careful attention to the dramatic form, but Neelands would argue this is within the provenance of every teacher. The plan becomes a blueprint for the making of theatre by others, and Neelands strives to make the instructions clear and stepped for ease. It is easy to imagine beginning teachers and theatre workers trying to follow it exactly, while more experienced practitioners opt for using the outline to improvise their own work.

The lesson plan is rich in theatre making opportunities. The postmodern eclectic use of pedagogical and theatrical conventions are Brechtian in making the familiar strange, and the strange familiar. The task of arranging the hands on the suitcase reveals the teacher-artist that Neelands has become. It demonstrates Neelands' acute awareness that most meaning is made in the aesthetic detail. The reliance on teacher in role as a central device has disappeared but the teacher role remains essentially the same. Neelands can still be seen as the central figure, constructing and layering dramatic experience for wider learning by using all the elements of theatre at his disposal.

Students are now labelled as learners, and one imagines this work could find its home as comfortably in the rehearsal studios of the Royal Shakespeare

Company as in a secondary school in Auckland or Tokyo. The bridge between the two theatre traditions means the use of both presentational and representational forms are sequenced in subtle and layered ways. Learners are directors, writers, actors, and also live through moments of the story.

The plan uses an artistic pretext that is rich, complex and politically charged. It deals with issues of importance and of consequence. They are issues of social justice and call on participants to act.

Neelands' handout from Migrants Rights International reminds us that if the work is postmodern in its eclectic use of conventions, it is unreservedly modernist in its view of the world. *The Immigrant* is designed so learners do not merely question issues about immigration in the fictional world, but that their understanding and action in the real world will be transformed. We are reminded that violence against migrants is on the rise everywhere in the world. The theatre that is planned here lies within the Brechtian tradition of Lehrstuck theatre and the pedagogical imperatives of Dewey. The purpose is to create citizens who participate in the issues of today.

8

11/09 – the Space in our Hearts

This extract first appeared as '11/09 The Space in Our Hearts' in
Drama Vol 9 No 2 2002: 4-10

A new age?

Until recently it was difficult to try and talk seriously to policy makers about humanising concepts such as the imagination, creativity and the necessity of art. Throughout the post – industrial world policy makers have focussed our attention on the idea of a monolithic, back-to-basics, training, curriculum as being a sufficient education and preparation for our students.

Policy makers have tried to persuade parents, commerce and the powerful constituencies that the greatest challenge we face is not the need to address new cultural, work and career identities, new economies based on communication rather then manufacturing, endemic poverty and the creation of disaffected underclasses. No, the real challenge is falling literacy test scores.

In his analysis of the schooling system and educational policy culture in Queensland, Allan Luke creates resonance with the state of education in the state of England.

These are turbulent times for policy making in public education, which must contend, with claims that it is not meeting the extensive and often conflicting expectations of many stakeholders. Some students, particularly in the middle years, appear disaffected with school routine, disengaged from learning and unchallenged by classroom tasks they regard as irrelevant. Managing student behaviour is a major concern. Many teachers are fatigued by waves of reform that they view as failing to address what really matters in schools – support for classroom teaching and learning. New syllabuses include so many mandated outcomes that many teachers are overwhelmed by the apparent scale of what is required.

Media reports criticise schools and teachers for not producing the educational outcomes most valued by parents, employers and the wider community. More external testing of minimum standards in basic skills is usually advocated as the solution. Taken together, these are complex problems for a state educational system – a state system that has begun to act as a social shock absorber for larger social, economic and cultural change and conflict as early as the mid-1970s.[1]

But of course since 11/09 we are told that we now live in a new age, in a changed world. It seems that we were unprepared for the events of that day – that these events came to me and to others as a shattering surprise. It makes me need to ask what else in this new age I/we may be just as unprepared for.

It makes me wonder about education and whether or not we are busy preparing students for a world that they will in fact be unprepared for. An of course, this feeling that education is preparing students for a world that may no longer exist has been about for some time, certainly before 11/09.

Faced with the challenges of a New World, the idea that improving spelling, handwriting and grammatical awareness will be a sufficient preparation or remedy now seems ridiculous. The idea that technology and the mastery of technologies will resolve political, military and economic problems has been turned on its head by the deadly, low-tech assaults on America.

The human imperatives

In his analysis of the structure of Social Dramas, the anthropologist Victor Turner suggested that there were four phases, shared both by personal and social dramas in our lives and also in the structure of much Euro-American theatre.[2]

These phases are: estrangement the drifting apart or alienation of groups of individuals leading to an inevitable crisis, such as the Twin Towers tragedy, followed by a period of redressive actions to try and put things right which either leads to re-integration or schism.

We can see this pattern very clearly in the events of 11/09. A growing sense of alienation amongst many of the poorer peoples of the world, a genuine sense of anger about the foreign, environmental and economic policies of the world's remaining super power and a sense of impotence and voicelessness created the foul crucible for terrorism that day.

The important point is that these feelings of helplessness and indignation had been festering for some time before September 11th. We did not recognise them, in time, as potentially lethal world-changing energies, nor apparently did we heed enough the warnings of moderate Islamic and other voices that the poor and dispossessed must be given a voice and a place at the table of the richer nations.

Meanwhile, apparently, we believed that raising standards of literacy and numeracy were our prime problem. Basic skills are necessary, but they are not sufficient.

In Turner's model we are now in a period of redressive actions. Trying to make the world safe again. Whether we come out of this period having achieved re-integration between cultures and peoples at war, or whether it results in a deadly and perpetual schism that will make the world unsafe for our lifetimes and destroy the careful fabric of the multicultural, multiracial, multifaith societies we have worked so long to create, has become the most pressing problem of our age.

The human need for art

In times of crisis we turn to art as necessary response. When the events in the world are of such magnitude, such horror, such a challenge to our notions of civilisation and culture we are drawn to the explanations of artists as much as to politicians and 'experts'. For a time our newspapers were full of the words of dramatists and other artists – all trying to offer us some human explanation of these shocking events.

Jeanette Winterson wrote of the human efficacy of art in times of social and cultural crisis in her *Guardian* column:

> Art is part of the answer – not as a panacea but because art has a way of going into the hurt place and cleaning it. Some wounds never heal but they need not remain infected ...[3]

> ... It is not ineffectual game-playing, it is a way of re-energising people who have been hit hard by bewilderment and despair. To understand our lives, and to keep them in context, not unmoored into lonely seas, we need wisdom and truth ... Art can be the creative open space that gives us room to rebuild where there is no steel and glass – the space in our hearts.

Ian McEwan appeared on the front page of the *Guardian* with these words:

> If the hijackers had been able to imagine themselves into the thoughts and feelings of the passengers, they would have been unable to proceed. It is hard

121

to be cruel once you permit yourself to enter the mind of your victim. Imagining what it is like to be someone other than yourself is at the core of our humanity. It is the essence of compassion, and it is the beginning of morality.

The hijackers used fanatical certainty, misplaced religious faith, and de-humanising hatred to purge themselves of the human instinct for empathy. Among their crimes was a failure of the imagination[4].

Of course McEwan was writing in the immediate heat of those events and with the perspective of time he might now wish to add those foreign policy makers over the last two decades whose imagination could not encompass the thoughts and feelings of the poor dispossessed of the world. The same foreign policy makers that first stamped 11/09 in the world's memory when they supported Pinochet's act of terrorism against an elected government, which caused 12,000 mostly innocent deaths, on that day in 1973.

He might also wish to include the negative consequences of curriculum re-forms which have purged and 'dumbed down' the curriculum of its humanis-ing potential and debased our capacity to imagine. Reforms which are not intended to produce a 'thought provoking' curriculum, let alone a curriculum that addresses our humanity. The exorcising of 'empathy' from the History National Curriculum for instance, no longer seems too smart.

And of course the events of 11/09 were not a failure of the imagination at all. They were brilliantly, if terribly, imaginative. For the imagination is, as Edward Bond reminds us, morally neutral; it can imagine for good, it can imagine for evil. Nor does education give a child its imagination – the imagination is natural. The cultural choice is whether schooling is designed to feed, nurture, guide and fulfil the humanising and compassionate potential of the imagina-tion.

The human importance of acting

It is at times like this that an apparently soft and marginal subject like drama takes on a more central and urgent place in the curriculum, for a number of vital reasons.

At the heart of all drama and theatre is the opportunity for role-taking – to imagine oneself as the other. To try and find oneself in the other and in so do-ing to recognise the other in oneself. This is the crucial and irreducible bridge between all forms of drama and theatre work. It is at the core of the legacy of Dorothy Heathcote and it is also the principle aim of actor training at drama schools, for instance:

> A growing ability to analyse text and character and to inhabit it, and to transform into a being other than the self.
>
> There is also a commonality of understanding in DiE and professional training about the personal and social benefits to students of 'acting' – imagining and behaving as the 'other'.
>
> A growth of physical and mental confidence and freedom, enabling the student to embrace the extremes of character and convention that may be encountered in the course of training, and in a professional career.[5]

Many of our students can have an impoverished and limited sense of 'self' and 'other'. Their range of possible selfs is often limited to who they have been told they are by others. Their range of possible 'others' is often similarly based on what they have been told, or shown, of others which in turn may contain prejudicial, stereotyped, distorted images of the other. Through role taking students may discover a more complex sense of other, they may also discover a more complex range of selfs or multiple subjectivities that now includes, as the result of their role taking, a confident self, a powerful self, a risk taking self, a compassionate self.

Students can learn and un-learn through the processes of constructing 'others'. Acting provides the space for students to re-imagine and extend their 'multiple subjectivities' – their possible and potential public and private 'selfs'. The process of acting requires the 'actor' to re-frame himself or herself as the 'other'.

Creating a 'character' includes finding oneself in the 'other' – what if? – finding the 'other' in oneself – behaving 'as-if'. The space of possible 'others' extends to include oneself. The boundaries between 'self' and 'other' meet and merge – the core of our humanity, the essence of compassion, the beginnings of morality are to be found in our capacity to merge 'self' with 'other'.

Communities in times such as these also need performance as a means of collectively grieving, remembering, reaffirming, celebrating, hoping. The scale of the human drama we face requires some representation and, as so many others have done in my culture and others, we turn to drama and to dramatists, asking them for new ways of seeing the new world in which we live.

The problem of individual and collective identities

We are born, of course, with an innate and infinite sense of empathy for the 'other'.

Anyone who has had more than one baby in the house will know the truth of this. When one cries they all cry. The baby has not separated itself from others – it believes that it feels, sees and thinks the same as all others. It is only over time that the child begins to see itself as an individual self, which is differentiated from others – to discover that the image in the mirror is an independent being.

Later the child will discover that others may be experiencing quite different emotions and thoughts – the perfectly happy child who sees an adult who is angry and/or sad realises that the adult's emotion are not hers – they are different. And from that point we grow individually whilst learning to try and see things from other points of view and perspectives. We try to 'read' other people's minds, but of course we can only do this culturally.

In a recent experiment into children's developing capacity to 'read minds', psychologists presented young children with a piggy bank full of coins. Then they changed the coins for marbles. The children were asked what a child coming into the room following the coins/marbles switch would think was in the piggy bank. Less 'developed' kids said marbles because they still assumed the 'other' child would know what they knew; more 'developed' kids said coins because as one of them said: 'Everyone knows that piggy banks are supposed to have money in them'.

To me this is not about reading minds – it's about cultural literacy. The child is acknowledging a shared cultural expectation. In my culture we recognise that people hoard money in plastic pigs! As we grow, we never quite lose that sense of a collective as well as an individual identity. We grow as individuals but we still have a sense of belonging to those who are most like us – those who share and use the same collective cultural and linguistic resources, those whose stories we know and belong to.

We become aware that others are different not just in terms of their individual differences but also in terms of their collective cultural identities and the problem that we have faced and now face with dramatic urgency is the problem of building societies that are inclusive of and representative of different collective identities, different cultural, linguistic and narrative resources.

And for our students, this issue is very complex – they are often between collective identities of one sort of another – of community, kinship, peer, school, mother and adopted cultures. We cannot continue to essentialise them by gender, class, race or creed identities alone. They come with raw and complex

strips of cultural DNA, which demand and seldom receive classroom attention, let alone mediation through the creative processes of the imagination.

The new paradigm

In most theories of change, a crisis such as that precipitated by the Twin
Towers massacre demands a shift of paradigm – new ways of thinking, new
ways of doing things. In his classical analysis of progress and change in the
natural sciences, Thomas Kuhn talked of 'crisis' in terms of the failure of
orthodox or normal science to address new problems and ideas emerging in
the field.[6]

The response of science is to enter into a new period of experimental science
in which people seek new means of addressing the complexities of the new
problems or the failure of orthodox methods to properly account for pheno-
mena in the natural world. Eventually this period of experimentation will
produce new, innovative methods and results, which become the basis of the
new paradigm – the next more or less stable period of normal science.

Clearly our 'unpreparedness' for the crisis of 11/09 and the failure of orthodox
means of detection, diplomacy and military response suggest the need for a
new paradigm.

And that will include a radical rethink of what we mean by 'basics' in education. The parameters of this new paradigm must now include the need for us
to forge a humanising curriculum in which more attention is given to
developing compassion, empathy, tolerance, highly developed interpersonal
skills and respect for difference.

Of course the 'basics' of literacy and numeracy will continue to have a place
in the new paradigm. Literacy is the most important weapon in the arsenal
that the poor, the dispossessed, the underprivileged can use to transform
themselves and the societies that marginalise them. Witness this boy of 14
who has recently been freed from bonded labour in a carpet factory in
Pakistan. He sits alone under a tree with a tattered reader and a scrap of paper
copying with a pencil end.

If you are illiterate everyone can cheat you, if you are literate no-one can.

And this emancipatory theme echoes through the testimonies and struggles
of the dispossessed. In African-American literature and in the writings of
others who have languished under various forms of oppression there is the
same fierce demand for an emancipatory education based on a demand for
access to the linguistic and literary tools and weapons of the oppressors.

It has been my privilege to spend some time this year in so-called developing societies.

In Pakistan for instance, there is a real awareness that emancipation can only be achieved through universal literacy. But these literacy programmes are not narrowly defined in terms of technical competencies and measurable but limited outcomes. No, they are from the outset tied to a vision of a fairer, progressive society. This diagram for instance has been produced by an NGO named INSAN.

It clearly places literacy as a first goal for education not as its end result. Literacy is seen as the foundation for building a 'pro-human' society in which all citizens can participate regardless of gender, caste and difference through virtue of their universal education.

In this new curriculum, concepts such as imagination and creativity will not be seen as 'soft' concepts but as core concepts. Core concepts that may lead to more creative and imaginative responses to the way in which we organise ourselves socially, economically, environmentally and militarily.

What 11/09 has taught us all is that the old methods, the old beliefs, the old paths are no longer sufficient to the day.

The new basics

As well as foregrounding the centrality of empathetic imagination, creativity and art, these events also suggest a radical re-think of what we mean by the basics in education generally. Remember Allan Luke wrote these words some time before 11/09:

> The new work order involves not only skills in high-tech and print literacy, but also skills in verbal face-to-face social relations and public self-presentation, problem identification and solution, collaborative and group capacity and so forth. These are the New Basics, and they extend considerably beyond traditional versions of the '3Rs'.

In this regard, the curriculum challenge is not just preparing people to learn with and learn through new technologies. It is also about preparing people to deal with the cultural and community changes that flow from their use. New technologies, globalised economies and communications media will require:

- new skills and knowledges for dealing constructively with rapid community change
- new forms of cultural and social identity

- the blending and reshaping of cultural traditions
- exercising new rights and responsibilities of citizenship and civic participation
- communication across diversity and difference of culture, gender and background

At the heart of Luke's project is a focus on improving the quality of pedagogy rather than the quantity of outcomes and assessment points. He is implementing in Queensland, a future orientated, humanising curriculum which focuses on four clusters of productive pedagogic practices:

- Intellectual quality: are students thinking, talking meaningfully and responding to their learning?
- Relevance: is learning made relevant to the world and its problems and to the students' lived and imagined experience of the world?
- Student support: are students personally and socially supported and supportive?
- Recognition of Difference: are different ideas about the world and who and why we are given sufficient attention?

Following Basil Bernstein, Luke seeks to reclaim pedagogy as one of the three principle message systems of schooling, which includes curriculum and assessment. In England, of course, we remain obsessed with curriculum and assessment at the expense of pedagogy. There is virtually no discussion of pedagogy beyond the 'official' advocations of single method literacy teaching for all children regardless of their difference.

What does this all mean for us as a community of drama educators? The recent history of drama in education in England at least, now seems to me particularly sad. A decade ago drama was a strong, unique and powerful pedagogy in need of a curriculum and assessment framework. It was a vital and cross-curricular process or method of learning and teaching. Just what is needed now for the future.

Over the last decade, a desperate and uncritical urge to find consensus and to normalise drama so that it appears to have become as arid as any other official subject has led us to ignore, and not continue to debate and develop, the essential pedagogic principles underpinning the best DiE work.

We now tend to use the term Drama Education, rather than Drama in Education to describe our work in recognition that most of us are more eclectic and inclusive in our choices of genres, styles and methods of drama work.

That is a good thing, but the removal of that small word 'in' has, I think, distracted us into debating curriculum content and assessment at the expense of focusing on core pedagogic principles and practices – to focus on what drama is rather than what drama does for students.

The events of 11/09 show us that there is still life left in the old contest between subject and method, process and product. The difference between the way we teach may no longer be transparent in curriculum and assessment documents. The difference now is in the way we teach. The way students learn. What the content of their learning is. What the human purposes of our teaching are. Whether we teach a subject or whether we teach the subjects – our students. Whether drama is our priority or whether understanding and contributing to the world is.

In closing, I would like to offer a vision of a pedagogic contract for drama teaching and learning. It draws on Luke's work and on Dewey, Vygotsky, Bruner and Friere. We are used to the idea of behavioural contracts, which establish the enabling and safe culture of the drama class, but a pedagogic contract, such as this, may serve as a vital re-affirmation of the basic principles of drama IN education. As with so much of my work I'm grateful to the influences of others in preparing this contract and hope that it serves as a confirmation and re-statement of your own values and practices – now in a changed world.

A pedagogic contract for human learning

The deepest impulse was the desire to make learning part of the process of social change. (Raymond Williams)

The pedagogic context is expressed as the living dynamic generated by locating teaching and learning practices and the lived experience of schooling within a set of dialectics.

Notes

1 Luke, A *et alia* (2000) *The New Basics Technical Paper* http://education.qld.gov.au/corporate/newbasics/html/library.html

2 Luke, A et alia (2000) *The New Basics Technical Paper* http://education.qld.gov.au/corporate/new basics/html/library.html

3 Turner, V. (1982) *From Ritual to Theatre*, PAJ Publications; New York

4 *Guardian* page 9-13/11/01

5 *Guardian* page 1-15/9 01

6 2001 – Guildford School of Acting BA Hons Coursebook

Betwixt and between:

Mindfulness ←————————→ *Playfulness*

- We think about what we do

- We take the human content and context of our work seriously

- We consider how what we learn might change us and who we are becoming

- We are mindful of self, others and the world

- We feel safe to experiment, risk, fail, bend and stretch the rules

- We play with language and other sign-systems to find the new, the unspoken, the fresh voice

- We are creative in the world

- Nothing is 'sacred'

Planned ←————————→ *Lived*

- Our local communities have a clear plan or map of where we are going, what we need to learn, how we will be valued

- We are entitled to the knowledge that will give us power

- We are human, with human needs, emotions, fears and dreams

- Our experiences shape our worlds, our learning and our 'becoming'

- Our differences are our strength

Necessary constraint ←————————→ *Necessary freedom*

- We work within a community and live within its traditions, codes and rules

- We access and work with culturally powerful genres of communication

- We have structure and structures to grow with

- We are individuals

- We must have choices in our learning

- We are free to change our worlds

- Knowing the 'rules', gives us more choices, greater freedom to be

Imagination ←————————→ *Knowledge*

- We imagine what we cannot yet know

- We imagine and re-imagine ourselves and others

- We are free from ideologies that replace the imagination

- Imagining reminds us that we are human

- What we imagine is anchored to what we know

- We realise that what we think we know is often 'imaginary' (cultural)

- We create our own 'map of the world'

- We are changeable and so is the world

9

The Art of Togetherness

This extract originally appeared as 'The Art of Togetherness' in
Drama Australia, Vol.33 2009

I write this contribution to the special themed edition of the NJ on Curriculum as an outsider. I am an England based practitioner and academic with some experience of working with Australian drama educators and with great respect for the successes of the Australian drama community in establishing recognised drama curricula at all ages and stages in their various State education systems. Respect also for that sense of community, which has so often refused to be drawn into the kinds of sectarian wars that have characterised the growth of drama in the English education system. I say English rather than British, because even within the UK there are big differences in how drama is positioned, valued and practiced in the four nations that include Scotland, Wales and Northern Ireland[1]. However, I also maintain that the struggles in England to define what drama is, what it is for, who it is for and how it is positioned in the curriculum are central and necessary to the life and vitality of what is increasingly now referred to as Drama and Theatre Education in England. This hybrid term is itself an attempt to capture and animate rather than stifle the tensions between what have historically been seen as different poles of a continuum.

It is not my intention here to rehearse again the history and arguments that have shaped the drama and theatre curriculum in England, but they do inform this article. Nor do I intend to offer a technical model of what a drama curriculum might look like in terms of objectives, teaching approaches and assessment. Australia leads the world in the design of these models and doesn't need my advice! Rather, I would like to outline some of the shaping principles and values of a drama curriculum. To focus on the essential pedagogic and artistic perspectives that are in my view immutable. But I also want to put these local drama essentials into a bigger contemporary and historical field of reference, so that the idea of a drama curriculum connects to a broader struggle in education to sustain important pro-social and critical pedagogic and artistic opportunities for the young, in the face of increasingly narrow and technical approaches to curriculum design and outcomes. Maxine Greene dubs this approach which must be resisted as curriculum 'positivism'.

> Positivism, or a separating off of fact from value, dominates much of our thinking. Systems are posited that they are to be regulated, not by what an articulate public may conceive to be worthwhile, but by calculable results, by tests of efficiency and effectiveness. (1988:54)

From a bigger picture view, of course, the shaping of the drama curriculum will inevitably reflect the dominant values and desired outcomes of the field of power at the level of state or national legislature. These normalising influences will determine first how drama is articulated as a curriculum entity and how the selection of content and valuing of outcomes will be done in state or national systems of education which desire some conformity and control over what is taught and how it is organised into subjects or areas of knowledge or learning. Bernstein's classic axiom still holds true:

> How a society selects, classifies, distributes, transmits and evaluates the educational knowledge it considers to be public reflects both the distribution of power and the principles of social control. (1973:227)

This ideological and social shaping of curriculum at a national level to reflect the current dominant ideology of the government of the time is particularly relevant to a cultural subject like drama. In the UK at least the consumption and distribution of culture also reflects the distribution of power and is highly socially stratified. As Bourdieu (1984) concluded:

> Cultural needs are the product of upbringing and education ...To the socially recognised hierarchy of the arts...there corresponds a social hierarchy of the consumers. (p1)

Drama is a teeny subject of course and must be seen to serve the wider interests of the particular and dominant ideology in the field of power if it to be given any legitimate space at all. Over time, shifts in the field of power itself lead to shifts in the field of educational policy, which in turn will impact on how drama manifests itself in school and beyond. This shifting and its resonances are being felt in Australia as the Howard years become history and in the UK we are beginning to sense the ground moving under our feet as New Labour loses its dominance in the field of power. If in any national system, drama ends up as part of English or as part of an Arts Education grouping, as skills centred or as focussed on knowledge and understanding, this is often due to political circumstances beyond the control of either a community of drama educators or a local school and its communities of learners and teachers. We take what we are given and use it as a germ to develop as many opportunities as we can for young people to engage with the art of drama and theatre; often despite the skin we are in. That's what we do. As Juliana Saxton reminds us in the preface to *Drama and Curriculum* (2009) the excellent and comprehensive new publication from John O'Toole, Madonna Stinson and Tina Moore:

> The discussion of how drama has flexed and shaped itself to fit the latest curriculum fashion offers readers further evidence that ...drama has found ways – honest, inventive, and appropriate – to demonstrate how that fashion can be served ... But in our desire to get in the door, we can be distracted. In our anxiety to be heard, we learn others' language and sometimes forget the power of our own. In our efforts to make things clear for other people, we forget that the art we practice is, of itself, deeply complex. (pviii).

In what follows I want to try to reflect on the 'power of our own' and to re-member the deep complexities and simplicities of the art we practice. I will do this through the lens of two texts that refer to examples of drama and theatre education practice which appear at first to represent quite different paradigms. Both examples are shaped by bigger picture national influences and broader pedagogic and historical traditions, whilst in my view also strongly asserting the common pedagogic and artistic 'power' and 'complexi-ties' and 'simplicities' of 'the art we practice'. My argument is that the evi-dence of a common pedagogy is more important a distinction than dif-ferences in the genre, style of drama and theatre work being done. Drama, of course, by itself does nothing. It is only what teachers do with drama that makes the difference. The work of drama teachers in very different corners of the field – process and performance for instance – can share in this common pedagogy. In my experience 'difference' in drama is more usually at the level of what is in the hearts and minds of teachers using drama rather than in technical differences of content and traditions.

Riding the mobius strip[2]

I will start by presenting both texts. The first is from an article in the *Times Education Supplement* (12/06) on a school web-site in England1[3]:

At first Anna Jones is anxious. She realises creative thinkers and risk-taking problem-solvers will do better in today's world than those who just passively accumulate knowledge.

But asking her to teach history, geography and PSHE through drama three years into a career as an RE specialist – to help her students develop these skills? That is another matter.

Elsewhere on the web site for this 'school of creativity with arts for all' in the North of England, the context for Anna's challenge is outlined:

Cultural Studies is a ground breaking subject introduced at Kingstone for all Year 7 (age 11-12) pupils, which encourages students to innovate and take responsibility for the quality and direction of their own work. Instead of a traditional diet of history, geography, PSHE and RE, staff teach topics which include all these curriculum areas. Students use drama techniques to help them learn while studying themes such as child labour and global poverty, British culture and identity, plots and protests.

The second text comes from the centrefold of the programme for the Royal Shakespeare Company's *The Winter Tale* (Summer 2009 season) performed by an ensemble of actors on three year contracts with the RSC:

Six actors from the ensemble performing *The Winter's Tale* are training to become skilled young people's workshop leaders ... by the time tonight's ensemble open the new Royal Shakespeare Theatre in 2011, a quarter of them will have completed this training and be actively involved in leading Shakespeare workshops with young people...

The first day of training for this *Winter's Tale* ensemble brought the actors together with a group of young people from a girls school in London with a rich and diverse cultural mix. The day focused on a journey of discovery into the characters of Hamlet and Ophelia stressing those themes of love, betrayal, identity and parental pressure which were alive for the young people taking part. By the end of the day the differences between pupils and actors blurred as the group began to take on the qualities of an ensemble committed to exploring the play through action and reflection. For the actors and the young people the journey was beginning.

In the same week, I visited Anna Jones school in Barnsley and watched a session on child labour introduced by a young humanities teacher in role as a father in debt and poverty discussing his options with the class and also, later in the week, watched Joe Arkley, one of the six actors from the RSC, in role as *Antigonus* from *The Winter's Tale* ordered by *King Laertes* to abandon the baby Perdita to the wolves discussing his options with a class in role as fellow courtiers and advisors. Joe Arkley trained to be a classical actor, but realised that in order to share the pleasures and rewards of Shakespeare he also needed to become a workshop leader working with young people as 'participants' in a journey into the text rather than as a passive and unknowing, often reluctant, audience. Anna Jones trained to teach Religious Education, but realised that in order to fully develop the life long and life wide learning needs of her students she would need to become an 'actor' working with young people as participants and co-creators in their learning rather than as passive and unknowing, often reluctant, audience to her instruction.

On the surface, these texts and examples seem to speak of different traditions. Anna Jones has been influenced by the recent renaissance of Dorothy Heathcote's ideas in England and in particular the *Mantle of the Expert* strategy which she has developed and which is now promoted by government agencies as an approved learning strategy for developing an integrated approach to curriculum design and delivery[3]. Anna Jones's school is one of many who have adopted this drama approach as a means of meaningfully integrating the curriculum for 11-14 year old students in particular[4]. Joe Arkley is influenced by the RSC Education Department's ensemble and rehearsal room based approach to teaching Shakespeare, summarised on the RSC web site as:

> The best classroom experience we can offer is one which allows young people to approach a Shakespeare play as actors do – as an ensemble, using active, exploratory, problem-solving methods to develop a greater understanding and enjoyment of the plays. Young people are up on their feet, moving around, saying the text aloud, exploring the feelings and ideas that emerge. There is a focus on physical and emotional responses, as well as intellectual, responses to the text. Active approaches are used to inform and test critical analysis. Pupils investigate a range of interpretive choices in the text and negotiate these with their teacher. Drama techniques are used to explore language, meaning, character and motivation.[5]

The drama work that Anna and Joe are developing has a recognisable and common pedagogic core that transcends the 'differences' between the professional and school models of drama and theatre work. Anna is using drama in the context of the humanities to make the curriculum breathe and to engage her students in journeys of discovery towards personalised and socially constructed 'truths'. Joe is using the same drama techniques to engage young people in a journey of discovery and interpretive choices in a canonical play text, which is also a great text to play with – to socially construct personalised 'truths' in their own playing of the text.

Joe comes from the theatre through an actor training route, but he does not lead voice and movement workshops for young people, or mimic an ersatz actor training course for them. He understands, in common with Anna, that subject-specific, or disciplinary, skills are more successfully developed in the pursuit of knowledge and understanding of the human condition. Anna does not isolate the humanities from the arts; Joe does not isolate the arts of theatre from the humanities. Both recognise that there must always be rich and relevant human content at the heart of theatre and drama. Rehearsals for the RSC include voice and movement training of course but also the kinds of socio-historical, political and literary research and inquiry associated with the humanities. As the late John McGrath (2002) reminded us, theatre teaches through its *paedia* which he identified as having three aspects:

1. Its **accuracy**: the audience must recognise and accept the emotional and social veracity of what is happening on stage, must identify with the core situation, whatever style may be used to present it.

2. Its **relevance**: the core situation must reflect the central, most profound realities of its time, must speak to its audiences about a truth that matters in their lives, whether social, moral, political, emotional, or individual

3. Needless to say, the theatre must use all possible means to **reach** every citizen in the demos, and not itself act as an excluding agency, whether by the price of its tickets, the manner of its box-office staff, its location or its impenetrability.

In both examples, the teacher and the actor are in a historical line of pedagogic theory that embraces contemporary Heathcotian drama education practices and cutting edge rehearsal practices in the professional theatre. They both recognise what Dewey called 'the organic connection between education and personal experience' (1997:25). Following in this line that includes Dewey, but also Bruner, Vygotsky, Donaldson and Freire[6], both are working to make the curriculum – Child Labour, Shakespeare study – personal, relevant and connected for students. Both offer learning as an active experience that is cognitive and affective. Both use their expertise and artistry to give students choices and power over the direction of their learning.

Joe, in particular, recognises that every drama 'lesson' should be an artistic as well as an educational journey – his playing of Antigonus in a darkened candle lit studio, clutching a baby in a basket, is intended to create an authentic and felt theatre experience for the students. They are motivated to engage with

Shakespeare's language through their existential engagement with the dilemma of the cruelly abandoned child. In the Cultural Studies class, 'coming to know' the father who is preparing to 'abandon' his child to cruel labour motivates them to identify with and explore the wider issue of child labour. Again we are in the line of an ancient tradition of drama and theatre with its origins in 5th Century BCE Athens. The philosopher, Cornelius Castoriadis (in Curtis, 1997) explains that the political mindset of the Athenian Tragedy was universality and impartiality (p284). Tragedies such as *The Persians* and the *Trojan Women* made heroes out of the Athenians' enemies even when they were at war. Through theatre and drama, in this sense, we come to recognise and feel for those who are different from us and in so doing we recognise our common humanity and their struggles become ours.

The pedagogic line underpinning the pedagogy of drama and theatre education has other contemporary echoes. *Mantle of the Expert* for instance is seen by the UK government as being a means of addressing an influential and substantial criticism from economists and employers about the irrelevance of narrow subject based curricula. In *The Creative Age* Kim Seltzer and Tom Bentley[7] (2000), for instance, argued that:

> Learners and workers must draw on their entire spectrum of learning experiences and apply what they have learned in new and creative ways. A central challenge for the education system is ... to find ways of embedding learning in a range of meaningful contexts, where students can use their knowledge and skills creatively to make an impact on the world around them.

Here we find congruence between the economic necessity for workers who can embed learning in meaningful contexts and make an impact with the pedagogic claims of *Mantle of the Expert*. There are other similarities in the argument of the *Authentic Achievement* project which was a key influence on the development of the New Basics curriculum in Queensland. Newmann (1996) defines *authentic achievement* as:

> The kind of achievement required for students to earn school credits, grades and high scores on tests is often considered trivial, contrived, and meaningless by both students and adults, and the absence of meaning breeds low student engagement in school work. Meaningless schoolwork is a consequence of a number of factors but especially curriculum that emphasises superficial exposure to hundreds of isolated pieces of knowledge. The term authentic achievement thus stands for intellectual accomplishments that are worthwhile, significant and meaningful, such as those undertaken by successful adults: scientists, musicians, entrepreneurs, politicians

Again, it is easy to see how this idea connects with the work that Anna's colleague is doing, where students become 'experts' supporting the needs of children freed from labour. But Joe's work is also authentic in the sense that his students work as actors whose interpretive choices represent worthwhile, significant and meaningful intellectual accomplishments. It is interesting in any case to consider what the work of 'successful adults' in drama and theatre might look like and what kinds of intellectual accomplishments young people might be engaged in drama and theatre education. Maxine Greene (1987) offers a perspective which combines a pedagogic as well as artistic purpose:

> Artists are for disclosing the extraordinary in the ordinary ... they are for affirming the work of the imagination – the cognitive capacity that summons up the 'as-if', the possible, the what is not and yet might be ... They are for doing all this in such a way as to enable those who open themselves to what they create to see more, to hear more, to feel more, to attend to more facets of the experienced world.

A Pedagogy of Hope, Change and Choice

In both our examples, there is hope in the power of collective human agency to make a difference to the world. Both classes are offered a problem which can only be resolved through their own actions. In both cases knowledge is considered provisional, unfixed, waiting to be discovered anew. Action and acting are at the heart of the process drama tradition as well as the processes of professional rehearsal. In process drama nothing can happen unless young people take action, initially through their social participation in making decisions, taking on roles and interacting with each other, and subsequently by carrying through the choices that they make in relation to the developing 'plot' or 'situation' they co-author with the teacher/leader. In Joe's class, the students can act to influence the action of the Perdita sub-plot but they are also being encouraged through practical discovery and skilful questioning to make their own 'interpretive choices' as actors about how to play Shakespeare's language. They learn that his play texts are open to interpretation and that they can 'change' the playing of the play through their choices. There is here the hope that they may also learn that they can make interpretive choices in the wider world as well, including choices about who they might become or how the world might be re-imagined.

A pedagogy of hope-based-in-action that offers young people the possibility of 'futuring' (as Greene (1978:173) describes it) and actioning a better world for themselves and others is essential to the work of Anna and Joe. Again this commonality is stronger than the technical surfaces of difference between using drama to teach Shakespeare and using drama to teach a social issue. It has resonances in the broader pro-social pedagogic tradition to which it belongs. With John Dewey for instance and his ideas about the necessity of a certain kind of liberal and social education for the progress towards participatory democracy (1997, 2007). And Paulo Freire (1992) who first named the 'pedagogy of hope':

> I am hopeful, not out of mere stubbornness, but out of an existential concrete imperative. I do not mean that because I'm hopeful, I attribute to this hope of mine the power to transform reality all by itself ... No, my hope is necessary, but it is not enough...But without it, my struggle will be weak and wobbly. We need critical hope the way a fish needs unpolluted water. (p2)

Within Western modernist aesthetics there is also a long tradition of ascribing personal and social transformations to drama and other kinds of 'artistic' experiences. From Ibsen to Brecht to Boal, Brook and Bond one can trace a faith in the idea that through artistic transformations of the stage, society itself can be changed. Within this modernist perspective we have become used, as Raymond Williams put it, to: '... the general idea that some relation must exist between social and artistic change' (Williams, 1961:246).

In both classrooms, students are encouraged in imagining 'what is not and yet might be' and in deliberating on what kinds of actions will realise, or express in some material form, the 'yet might be'. They are doing this in social circumstances. Drama and Theatre is the quintessential social art form and this quality is also essential to its educational uses. People must come together in order to make and to share in its makings. It is the art of togetherness even if much of its content and form is about representing un-togetherness. Another common and essential feature of Anna's and Joe's work is the focus on creating high quality relationships for learning and being together.

The common term to describe this is 'ensemble-based' learning and this has been described recently by Neelands (2009), based on participation in RSC rehearsals and teacher led drama classes, as having these key common characteristics; the uncrowning of the power of the director/teacher; a mutual respect amongst the players; a shared commitment to truth; a sense of the intrinsic value of theatre making, a shared absorption in the artistic process of dialogic and social meaning making (p183). Neelands argues that 'ensemble-based learning' is a bridging concept between those pedagogies of the rehearsal and class rooms, that centre on democratisation of learning and artistic processes through high quality relationships for learning and living together.

In terms of the bigger picture of education, the idea of 'ensemble based learning' connects with the influential English cultural and educational thinker Charles Leadbeater's (2008) ideas about education in the 21st Century:

> The route to a more socially just, inclusive education system, one which engages, motivates and rewards all, is through a more personalised approach to learning. Learning with, rather than learning from, should be the motto of the system going forward: learning through relationships not systems. (p72)

The quality of relationships and the necessity of risk and trust are common to an ensemble based theatre company like the RSC. Geoffrey Streatfeild, who was in the previous Histories ensemble at the RSC, described the ensemble in terms which are very similar to the claims made for other forms of drama and theatre education:

> Our ever growing trust enables us to experiment, improvise and rework on the floor with an astonishing freedom and confidence. This ensemble is a secure environment without ever being a comfort zone. All of us are continually challenging ourselves and being inspired by those around us to reach new levels in all aspects of our work.

The making of relationships in drama and in the professional ensemble often requires the taking of extraordinary risks for all involved. The teacher/leader is taking risks in seeking a shift in the normative power relations within the class and between the class and the teacher and by even moving back the desks in some cases. Young people must make themselves vulnerable and visible in order to participate and must know that there is protection and mutual respect for difference from within the group to match the personal and social challenges of taking a part in the action.

In the face of the two realities which are constant for teachers of drama, that is that drama will never be top of the curriculum pile and nor can young people be forced or coerced to do it, they have developed a pedagogy of choice. In every drama class students have to make a positive choice to join in or not, without this willingness bred of interest and engagement there can be no active drama. Both the world of professional theatre and the world of classroom drama share this common feature that theatre has to be by choice. For this reason, drama has often been associated with a rich and engaging pedagogy. A pedagogy which turns the pedagogic and artistic traditions and lines it draws on into a contemporary praxis. In a very real sense what makes drama teachers like Anna and Joe important is that they are learning how to teach as if the students had the choice of whether to be there or not. And it matters to both of them that students would want to make this positive choice. Imagine if every lesson in every subject in the curriculum were taught as if the students had the choice to be there, or not.

Notes

1 Scotland and Northern Ireland have their own distinctive National Curriculum and in both cases the Arts including drama are a core component of the curriculum. In England drama is subsumed into English even though it is taught in every Secondary school, more usually either as a subject in its own right or as part of an Arts grouping.

2 The Möbius strip has several curious properties. A model of a Möbius strip can be constructed by joining the ends of a strip of paper with a single half-twist. A line drawn starting from the seam down the middle will meet back at the seam but at the 'other side'. If continued the line will meet the starting point and will be double the length of the original strip of paper. This single continuous curve demonstrates that the Möbius strip has only one boundary.

3 http://www.kingstoneschool.co.uk/culturalstudies/tes.htm

4 http://www.mantleoftheexpert.com/

5 See for instance: http://www.queensbridge.bham.sch.uk/index.php/home/yr7enterprise/pupil.html

6 http://www.rsc.org.uk/standupforshakespeare/content/manifesto_online.aspx

7 My argument here is that the pedagogy associated with process drama in particular has not developed in a theoretical vacuum. The important characteristics of this pedagogy grow out of this line of social constructivist thought which further validate its efficacy. See for instance: Bruner 1975, 1996; Vygotski 1978; Donaldson 1987, 1993; Freire 1998, 2000, 2004

8 Bentley is currently Executive Director for Policy and Cabinet for the Premier of Victoria, Australia, advisor to Australian Deputy Prime Minister Julia Gillard and part-time director of the Australia and New Zealand School of Government.

References

Bernstein, B. (1973) *Class, Codes and Control.* London, Paladin

Bruner, J. (1975) *Towards a Theory of Instruction.* Cambridge, MA, Harvard University Press

Bruner, J. (1976) *The Culture of Education.* Cambridge, MA, Harvard University Press

Curtis, D. (1997) The Castoriadis Reader Oxford, Blackwell

Dewey, J. (1997) *Experience and Education.* New York, Touchstone

Dewey, J. (2007) *Democracy and Education.* Teddington, Echo Library

Donaldson, M. (1987) *Children's Minds.* Harmondsworth, Penguin

Donaldson, M. (1993) *Human Minds.* Harmondsworth, Penguin

Freire, P. (1998) *Pedagogy of freedom: ethics, democracy and civic courage.* London, Continuum

Freire, P. (2000) *The Pedagogy of the Oppressed.* London, Continuum

Freire, P. (2004) *Pedagogy of Hope.* London, Continuum

Greene, M. (1978) *Landscapes of Learning.* New York, Teachers College Press

Greene, M. (1987) 'Creating, Experiencing, Sense Making: Art Wolds in Schools' *The Journal of Aesthetic Education* Vol.21, No. 4, Winter Issue, pp11-23

Greene, M. (1988) *The Dialectic of Freedom.* New York, teachers College Press

Leadbeater, C. (2008) *WHAT'S NEXT? 21 Ideas for 21st Century Learning.* London, The Innovation Unit

McGrath, J. (2002) Theatre and Democracy. *New Theatre Quarterly* No 18 May 2002

Neelands, J. (2009)'Acting together: ensemble as a democratic process in art and life' Research in Drama Education: *The Journal of Applied Theatre and Performance*,14:2, pp173-189

Newmann, F. and associates (1996) *Authentic Achievement; restructuring schools for intellectual quality.* San Francisco, Jossey-Bass

Seltzer, K. and Bentley, T. (2000) *The Creative Age; Knowledge and Skills for the New Economy.* London, DEMOS

Vygotski, L. (1978) *Mind in society: the development of higher psychological processes.* London, Harvard University Press

Williams, R. (1961) *The Long Revolution.* London, Chatto and Windus.

10

Mirror, Dynamo or Lens?

This extract was originally presented as the Seamus Heaney
Address in Limerick, Eire in 2006

I n this talk I will outline a collection of metaphors in search of an idea that
can express theatre's potential as a form of social pedagogy and socialisa-
tion both for young people of school age and also for its other audiences
and makers. In talking of a pedagogy of theatre I will borrow from the late
John McGrath's use of the term a 'learning paedia' which he succinctly distils
into two main features:

> Accuracy – the audience must recognise and accept the emotional and social
> veracity of what is happening on stage, must identify with the core situation,
> whatever style may be used to present it.

> Relevance – the core situation must reflect the central, most profound realities
> of its time, must speak to its audiences about a truth that matters in their lives,
> whether social, moral, political, emotional or individual I (McGrath, 2002:138)

To these features of truthfulness and relevance he adds the core principle that
theatre should use all possible means to reach every citizen and not act as 'an
excluding agency, whether by the price of its tickets, the manner of its box
office staff, its location or its impenetrability' (*ibid*:139).

To this idea of an inclusive 'paedia' in theatre I want to add at the outset a
further pre-condition for a pro-social theatre which is captured most fully by
the idea of 'ensemble' which is given fuller treatment at the close of this discussion on metaphors. For now, Mihail Stronin, dramaturge of the Maly St
Petersburg Theatre, provides us with a succinct description of the ensemble
as 'one body with many heads, but many heads working in the same direction'. This desire to create pro-social theatre through collaboration, co-artistry

and sophisticated uses of social intelligence forms the matrix for the discussion of metaphors.

Theatre as mirror: using God's scissors

This search for a meaningful metaphor for a pedagogic theatre is of course prompted by the use of the most well known – *Mirror up to Nature* – as title for this lecture series which is also subtitled as Drama in the Modern World. The metaphor of theatre as mirror offers a particular take on the ideas of accuracy and relevance, which is that theatre 'merely' reflects ourselves to ourselves. There is a suggestion that the life likeness of a mirrored reflection is a guarantee of its accuracy, authenticity and 'naturalness'.

> Speak the speech, I pray you as I pronounced it to you – trippingly on the tongue ... Suit the action to the word, the word to the action, with this special observation: that you o'erstep not the modesty of nature. For anything so overdone is from the purpose of playing, whose end, both at the first and now, was and is to hold as 'twere the mirror up to nature, to show virtue her own feature, scorn her own age, and the very body of the time his form and pressure. (Hamlet 111/ii 1-45)

What Hamlet asks of the players is to tell his story as if it was the only story in town. It is a monologic, representative and authored account of the 'truth' of his father's death. He demands that the players adopt what would become known as a 'naturalistic' style of performance without any exaggerated or 'unreal' gestures. In Hamlet's mind the 'truth' of events will be confirmed by the 'realism' of the playing. The more life-like the actions, the more convincing the argument of his story. Hamlet imagines that by stripping away all that is artificial in the players' performance, they will appear to be more authentic; more true to life. And this criterion of authenticity and 'life-likeness' is still key to our aesthetic judgments of theatre.

In encouraging his actors, Hamlet makes a qualitative distinction between a 'realistic' performance for the educated courtiers and the 'dumb shows and noise' associated with the 'unskilful' and the 'groundlings'. We have here the beginnings of a tradition of a serious literary theatre, exclusive to certain classes, which distances itself both from the profane tastes and preferences of the lower orders and also from their world view. To the idea that theatrical naturalism is closer to the truth than other forms of representation is now added the political idea that the 'mirror' belongs to an educated elite with the sensibility to discern the 'accuracy' and 'relevance' in a performance of scientific verisimilitude.

The play within a play here is no mere entertainment. It is not planned as an evening's escape from the cares of office for Claudius and Gertrude – it is intended to be effective as a means of exposing their betrayal of the murdered king and so to directly bring about their downfall. So Hamlet introduces another theme associated with the 'educated' theatre which is that is can illuminate and reveal the world and bring about a result or change in those who attend it.

This speech, with its iconic metaphor of the 'mirror unto nature', is often seen as presaging what has become the dominant genre of theatrical and dramatic representation in the West. The tradition of 'realism', which has its origins in a specific interpretation of Aristotle's concept of 'mimesis' and the close relationship between politics, philosophy and tragedy in 5th century Athens, conflates reality with realism and realism as a style with truth. It is based in a belief that external appearances can mirror the soul. That only that which can be directly apprehended through the senses exists. There is no room in this educated sensibility for a theatre of dream worlds, ghosts, demons and other spirits. This positivist and pragmatic world view bridges the Early Modernism of Shakespeare's age with the scientific rationalism and fatalism that would shape the Modernist aesthetics and theatres of the 19th and early 20th centuries with their obsessions with forensic accuracies of setting and acting.

The Western tradition of 'realism' underpins both the canonical 'serious' theatre associated with the subsidised sector and also the daily entertainments offered on TV and film. In the case of the subsidised theatre, this realism is associated with a literary tradition of authored plays offering an authoritative and authorised interpretation of an individual world view – just as Hamlet authors the play within a play in his own likeness. In both cases the conflation of realism with reality serves to naturalise the specifically cultural and self-interested imaginaries of certain social and cultural groups. The tradition of a subsidised theatre serving the interests of a few goes back to the Athenian tragedies which, as Arnold Hauser (1999) and Augusto Boal (1998) argue, were little more than apologies and propaganda for aristocratic rule. The tragedies tell the stories of princes and kings, not slaves and women. The gods are to be served. The more popular but crude and distinctly un-realistic mimes and satyr plays of Athens required no subsidy; they were popular enough with the masses to be afforded. And Hamlet is of course speaking as an aristocrat planning a performance for his own class. He seeks to naturalise his own aristocratic world view and to present his perspective of the world as the only legitimate one. As if it was scientifically proven.

In popular forms of realism, the naturalising of specifically cultural and social perspectives can feed any number of phobic injustices from racism to misogyny and homophobia. To what extent are *Ballykissangel* or *Father Ted* true mirrors of the nature of the Irish, for instance? Both sacred and profane forms of drama contain the same trick, which is to reassure ourselves that the order of things is as we imagine it. In both forms we continuously naturalise the politics and world view of a powerful few.

The cultural power of the 'mirror' and the naturalistic fallacy it contains – that behavioural realism is more accurate and truthful than other styles of theatre representation – spreads into the education domain as well. Drama in Education for instance, also holds to the idea that by 'living through' human experiences in a 'realistic' and 'life like' way in real time young people will discover the 'truth' of human existences which they can only imagine and never in reality know. Living through the experiences of peoples who are temporally, spatially, culturally, and socio-economically different 'as if' these experience were actually happening here and now for the participants in a process drama is seen as being more truthful and 'life like' a learning experience than other more stylised and self-reflexive forms of theatre. In truth, whatever the appearance may be, we can only ever learn more about our own personal and collective self through imagining ourselves differently. We may develop empathy and understanding from our experiences of 'playing' others but we cannot in actuality walk in shoes other than our own. Spending four hours or more in the classroom 'building investment' and 'belief' in an imagined character and situation prior to an 'authentic' role play is, in fact, a mythologised dilution of the working practices of Stanislavski, Michael Chekhov and their followers who constitute the historical and contemporary face of behavioural realism in acting.

But at least Hamlet seeks a form of theatrical representation that has social agency. This is the idea that the world is changeable, not determined, and that through the agency of theatre we may come to understand the power of human action in shaping destiny. As Raymond Williams (1954) commented, whilst the genre of action drama would become increasingly the domain of commercial film, the trajectory in serious theatre since Shakespeare has been towards a theatre of social inaction and passivity. A theatre which suggests that there is nothing that can be done. That human agency is impotent in the face of a world claimed and owned by the powerful whether they be aristocrats or the educated middle classes. That the world if not determined is at least determining of human existence. This tendency towards the passive inaction of social and artistic actors already suggested by Hamlet's inability to act to right the wrongs done to his father, finds its apogee in *Waiting for Godot* where nothing at all happens ever.

If there is nothing that can be shown to be done, the mirror becomes a place for narcissistic gazes into the individual rather than the social psyche. A theatre of introspection, fixity and stasis rather than of action. A psychological theatre of the individual trapped in an unchangeable world, suffering an inevitable destiny beyond self control. The social self of collective public action in the *agora* that characterised the early Athenian *polis*, of renaissance England, of the other great social and revolutionary movements of the 19th century becomes in the mid/late 20th century the privatised and psychologised self-haunting empty and closed rooms, literally blinded, and searching for the truth within rather than seeking it without. Until Sarah Kane so exquisitely collides the intimate with the public, the epically tragic with the banally domestic in *Blasted*, in which the unavoidable ugliness of the world beyond crashes at last through the fourth wall of self-protecting and privileged illusion.

In any case the origins of the 'naturalistic' theatre lie in the origins of a representative democracy in Athens. It is not the theatre of a direct or participatory democracy. Hamlet does not design a theatrical meeting between his story and Claudius's or his mother's or any of the other multiple voices entangled in his plot. He speaks for all. Just as in our own politics we still rely in theatre on our 'representatives' to tell the theatrical truth and make our decisions for us. We are shown the world 'as it is' rather than forging the world as we see it could be from our diverse perspectives. The technical term for the 'realist' style of acting which would become codified as a method by Stanislavski and his followers is 'representational'. Actors create a world for a distant audience as if the fictive world exists independently from the actual world of the spectator. There is no communication or communion between actors and audiences. There is no dialogue; it is monologic and monolithic. There is no interaction of ideas or posing of alternatives.

The alternative mode of performance, which is closely associated with Bertolt Brecht, is named 'presentational' and does make direct contact between performers and audience and may well include interaction and banter. There is a direct correspondence between the fictive world of the stage and the actual world of the audience. This tradition belongs to the history of popular forms of entertainment and despite Hamlet's disparagements is often cited as an example of Shakespeare's plays being popular with the 'groundlings' who were seldom quiet in their gaze on the 'mirror' of theatre. It is part of my argument here that the theatre of direct democracy must be a participatory theatre which is made by all who engage with it. A theatre in which the roles of social and artistic actor are fluid and transposable. A theatre which negotiates different perspectives of the world and different possibilities for changing it. A theatre which is more like a hologram or a kaleidoscope than a finely focussed and well lit mirror.

In a recent survey final year English students at my own University were asked whether they preferred an active approach to their core Shakespeare course rather than lectures and seminars. Eighty seven per cent of respondents preferred lectures to a more active exploration of the plays as actors. Of these 67 per cent disclosed a fear and in some cases 'hatred' of acting. In a theatre of mirrors we cease to see ourselves as actors in either the social and artistic spheres. Both require public action in a public engagement and for these students at least this idea of public action, acting up to make things happen, is terrifying.

And of course we also need to trouble the metaphor of the mirror even further. Whose mirror is it? Who holds it up and what is their relationship to the viewer/subject? Is it a kind mirror? Does it flatter or demean the viewer? Does it tell the truth – whose truth? Does it dare to 'o'erstep the modesty of nature'? Does it offer a mirror of reality or a comfortable escape in which 'temperance may give it smoothness'? These were not innocent questions for Shakespeare and the 'Kings Men' writing and performing during a period of emergent republicanism in England. The festivals of Athens, much like our own subsidised theatre, depended on producers and paymasters who were more likely to patronise work which confirmed their power and naturalised their influence within a 'democratic society'. There is always a *Maecenas* – the one who pays the piper.

These questions around the ownership of the means and processes of theatrical representation and whose world view is naturalised are of course critical for our young people. We live now in a world of mirrors seemingly held up to nature. Much of what young people know about the world beyond their own immediate experience is through the representations of the mass media and the prejudices of their own communities. They need to be helped towards a more critical and challenging response to the truth of the Murdoch News and other mediated pictures of the world beyond.

In his poem *On Leaving the Theatre* Edward Bond (1978) captures these questions in these words:

To make the play the writer used god's scissors
Whose was the pattern?
The actors rehearsed with care
Have they moulded you to their shape?
Has the lighting man blinded you?
The designer dressed your ego?

You cannot live on our wax fruit
Leave the theatre hungry
For change.

What I have described here is the politics of the 'naturalistic fallacy' in theatre; the politics behind the idea that the more realistic a piece of theatre is, the more truthful it is. Despite Hamlet's tutoring, the play that follows will of course be artificial – it cannot be real in the sense that daily living is real because it is a conscious and selective human reworking of reality. It is necessarily false to nature in this sense, however life-like it might appear to be. It is 'artifice' rather than 'reality' that gives theatre its power. Theatre gives human shape and form to experience in order to hold it for a while as if it was reflected in a mirror but as an abominable imitation of humanity not as lived experience itself. This power is contained in the gap between how we experience the world and how it is mirrored to us; in the differences as much as in the similarities. The truth is neither in our own subjective experience nor in the play – it emerges through the dialectic and dialogue between.

Theatre as dynamo; man is a helper to man

I am a playwright. I show
What I have seen. At the markets of men
I have seen how men are bought and sold. This
I, the playwright, show.
How they step into each other's room with plans
Or with rubber truncheons or with money
How they stand and wait on the streets
How they prepare snares for each other
Full of hope
How they make appointments
How they string each other up
How they love each other
How they defend the spoils
How they eat
That is what I show. (from The *Playwright's Song,* Bertolt Brecht)

This second metaphor is borrowed from Darko Suvin's paper on Brecht's aesthetics titled *The Mirror and the Dynamo* (1968). Suvin argues that the mirror metaphor is more appropriately applied to what he calls the aesthetics of 'illusionism' – taking for granted that an artistic representation in some mystic ways reproduces or 'gives' man and the world'. In its place he offers a new scientific metaphor for Brecht's theatre with its origins in the idea of the promethean human potential to create and use transformative energy and action to better the world. In Brecht's take on Modernism, there is the belief that theatre and the arts can be catalytic to the wider human struggle to determine the world rather than be determined by it. Brecht assumes this action will be associated with the creation of egalitarian democracies to re-place the aristocratic and totalitarian systems of governance which dominated his age and place. Indeed Brecht referred to his work as symbolic action rather than as representation. Suvin explains the metaphor thus:

> Art is not a mirror which reflects the truth existing outside the artist: art is not a static representation of a given Nature in order to gain the audience's empathy: Brecht sees art as a dynamo, an artistic and scenic vision which penetrates Nature's possibilities, which finds out the 'co-variant' laws of its processes and makes it possible for critical understanding to intervene into them. (Suvin, 1968:59)

Brecht's idea of truthfulness is quite different to that of the search for 'authentic' appearances that characterises the theatre of mirrors. Brecht seeks illumination rather than illusion. To show how things work, to whom they belong, whose interests are served and how this might be changed. Brecht's aim was to reveal the world, to look behind the mirror, to ask questions of it, not merely to reflect a particular and naturalised illusion of it. It is a reflection *on*, not *of* nature. Suvin argues that Brecht's dramaturgy presupposed that the audience were seeing the work from the perspective of a utopian future 'an imaginary just and friendly future, where man is a helper to man'.

Brecht reclaims a theatre of action that is more concerned with the sociology of human behaviour and the dynamics of history than with the inner psycho-logical workings of alienated individuals. One of his models was Shake-speare's Histories with their emphasis on human action and the forging of futures through human agency rather than through fate or destiny. He was drawn to the epic scale of the Histories, which moved rapidly from place to place without the fussiness of 'naturalistic' sets, and to the idea that seventy or more years of history could be distilled into three hours of playing.

In terms of the aesthetics of the theatre as dynamo, it is well known that Brecht insisted that the means of production were made as visible as possible to the audience and that the work was inclusive of a wide range of performance traditions associated both with the popular theatre and other entertainments associated with the working classes and also from other great 'non-realist' performance traditions including the Chinese Opera.

> We shall make lively use of all means, old and new, tried and untried, deriving from art and deriving from other sources, in order to put living reality in the hands of living people in such a way that it can be mastered. (Brecht, 1938: 189)

Rather than creating an illusion for an audience of 'peeping toms' (as Artaud (1938) once described the naturalistic theatre's patrons), Brecht kept reminding his audience that they were engaging with an 'artifice' a conscious and transparent construction of the world according to his own Marxist principles. He showed that we can bring the world closer by moving it further away – by de-familiarising it and making it strange so that it has to be consciously and cognitively re-recognised by a critical and conscious audience hungry for change. Brecht turned events on their head, shattering the comfortable illusion of cause and effect which characterises the 'realist' narrative. Making his audience think about the story rather than merely hear it. If accuracy of 'realistic' detail marks the metaphor of the mirror, it is the accuracy and cognitive adequacy of the account of human history which characterises the metaphor of the dynamo. Brecht's actors were still 'representatives' but they combined the social within the artistic in their acting – the stage actor as social actor acting the part of a social actor on stage. In Brecht's world we are all social actors making our destiny as living people.

If one puts aside for a moment Brecht's unwavering faith in the scientific 'truth' of Marxism and allows for a less certain but still critical attitude both to theatre making and to the changeable world theatre represents, there are some attractions in the metaphor of the dynamo when we consider what kind of theatre young people deserve.

There is for me a welcome honesty in the dynamo metaphor – there is no attempt to create a seductive and partial 'mirror' of the world. There is the hope, at least, that through our own individual and collective social acting we can change the world and ourselves. There is a commitment to justice and to social responsibility and to a theatre that shows us how and why the world is often an unfair place. In its gaze from the synoptic vantage point of a utopian future it promises a glimpse of justice and authentic democracy to the young who are becoming the future. It is a theatre which demonstrates both through its treatment of the world and through its means of production that the social, educational and political structures we work within are capable of being re-imagined and transformed by creative human action. The Canadian literary theorist Northrop Frye (1963) wrote that: 'The fundamental job of the imagination in ordinary life, then, is to produce, out of the society we have to live in, a vision of the society we want to live in'.

There is here a belief in our individual and collective capacity to act in and on the world in ways that are original and significant. This belief that we are individually and collectively able to re-make ourselves, our technologies, our cultures and common life offers young people a doctrine of hope in the hard times ahead.

At the heart of a pro-social, action based dynamo metaphor of theatre is the vibrant tension between structure (constraints) and agency (freedom to act). Being creative means acting to shape the structures that shape us; controlling and shaping nature as well as cultural institutions. Prometheus stole fire from the gods artfully, and with that fire man created warmth, shelter, technology and culture. The primal shaping structure is nature, and throughout history mankind has shown that through human action, nature can be overcome and transformed rather than merely mirrored or copied.

Theatre as lens; acting to learn, learning to act

I want to now add a third metaphor of my own crafting which is that of theatre as a lens – as a window for looking into 'nature', rather than as a surface that reflects it or copies it. This metaphor has its origins in a book I wrote in the 80s as a young teacher about my own first experiences in using drama in the classroom (Neelands 1984). I wanted to try and capture the relationship between drama, the curriculum and the teacher and learners. I suggested that in a conventional transmission model, what is being learnt about is only really seen by the teacher. The teacher stands between the learners and what they are learning about and decides what they should know and when and how it should be interpreted. This model is described by Basil Bernstein (1973) as a 'collection code', a rigid and insulated subject based curriculum which isolates the 'legitimised' knowledge to be acquired in the classroom from the everyday knowledges beyond the school and which is supported by the authority of the teacher as the one who knows. Bernstein described the effects thus:

> Knowledge under collection is private property with its own power structure and market situation ... children and pupils are early socialised into this concept of knowledge as private property. They are encouraged to work as isolated individuals with their arms around their work. (p240)

and

> The frames of the collection code, very early in the child's life, socialise him into knowledge frames which discourage connections with everyday realities. (p242)

Here is an example which captures the difference between a theatre-as-lens approach to learning and a normative curriculum approach. A class of urban eight year olds in role as 'landscape gardeners' are asked by the teacher in role as the Head Teacher of a Special School, to create a garden for her pupils, some of whom are visually impaired and some of whom use wheelchairs. The pupils are asked to use their 'expert' knowledge to design a suitable landscape for the garden and suggest appropriate planting so that all of the pupils can get enjoyment and access the garden. The Head Teacher also wants her pupils to be involved in looking after the garden.

In order for the landscape gardeners to present their plan to the Head Teacher, they must research the needs of visually impaired and wheelchair bound children; which flowers and plants might offer textures and smells for visually impaired people; how to design the garden so that it is interesting and accessible for wheelchair users; how sounds and textures might be used; how to design and build paths and beds so that wheelchair users can do some gardening themselves.

In addition to this work, pupils will also have to consider the maths of the project – how big the space is, how big beds and other features will be, how many plants will be needed etc. They may also look in science at why plants have scents and which insects, like butterflies, might be attracted by certain plants. From a technology perspective they might also consider how to install a watering system on a timer so that the garden users don't have to struggle with hosepipes and watering cans, or they might invent their own self-watering system using collected rain water.

In fact the lens offered here is 'imagined experience' rather than an optical object or tool; learning through being in a dramatised situation and a role that requires researched and responsible action. Learning through imagined experience allows us to engage with learning, directly, physically, contextually, with real life purposes and motives. Theatre in all its forms has this capacity to engage our emotions very directly in the lives of others and in situations which are beyond our own daily experience. To feel for them and want to do something positive. Freud reminds us that 'Art is a conventionally accepted reality in which, thanks to artistic illusion, symbols and substitutes are able to provoke real emotions' (cited in Petocz (1999) p93).

This enactive and inquiry based model of learning fits well with Margaret Donaldson's argument in a chapter with the beautiful title of *The Shape of Minds to Come*:

> By the time they come to school, all normal children can show skill as thinkers and language users which must compel our respect, so long as they are deal-ing with 'real-life' meaningful situations in which they can recognise and res-pond to similar purposes and intentions in others. These human intentions are the matrix in which the child's thinking is embedded. They sustain and direct his thought and speech, just as they sustain and direct the thought and speech of adults – even intellectually sophisticated adults – most of the time.

The lens metaphor of theatre is commonly associated with those forms of im-provised and participatory drama which make up the 'process drama' tradi-tion in schools. One of its leading exponents, John O'Toole, and his co-author Julie Dunn, describe it in these words:

> In the classroom there is no outside audience. Most of the time we are im-provising with the children, exploring fictional situations through various kinds of role-play, mixed with theatrical and dramatic conventions, games and exer-cises. We call this working in 'process drama', which is like children's play, with all the players actively involved. (O'Toole and Dunn, 2002:2)

This process approach to theatre making presupposes a radical shift in the relationship between theatre and its audiences. In the popular imagination, theatre is often thought of as the performance of plays by professional or amateur actors to a paying audience. It is a picture of theatre that is based on an economic agreement between the producers and the audience. The pro-ducers rehearse and develop a theatre product to the best of their abilities and when the time comes, they perform their work in exchange for the price of a ticket.

More often than not, in Western forms of theatre, the product that is ex-changed is based on the work of a playwright. There is an assumption in this model of theatre that the majority of us will see rather than be in such plays. Acting, producing theatre, is seen as something only a few can achieve. There is also the assumption that the audience in this literary theatre will be silent and attentive to the work of the actors – audience responses are private rather than publicly shared as they might be in more popular forms of entertainment.

If this popular image of theatre is the dominant one in most Western societies it should be remembered that there are alternative models of community theatre and performance which may bring us closer to recognising drama-making in schools as theatre.

In local communities in my society and in many traditional societies, the arts still serve the important civic and community functions that ritual and art making once provided for us all. In the so-called golden ages of Athenian and Elizabethan drama, going to the theatre was an important and integral part of the public life of the citizen. The theatre still offers communities a public forum for debating, affirming and challenging culture and community ties. In this community model, the arts are seen as important 'means' of representing and commenting on the cultural life and beliefs of the community, in turn the communal participation of the whole community in art-making strengthens their cultural bonds. Every member of the group is seen as a potential producer – a potential artist. In this model, theatre is produced on the basis of a social agreement between members of a group who come together to make something that will be of importance to them; something that will signify their lives.

This alternative social and community model of theatre shares some of the characteristics of drama in schools. A school is a community and drama is a living practice within it. The drama that young people make is often based in the concerns, needs and aspirations shared within the school community or the community of a particular teaching group. It is often based on a social agreement that all who are present are potential producers – everyone can have a go at being actors and/or audience as the drama progresses. The coming together to make drama is also often seen as an important means of making the teaching group more conscious of themselves as a living community.

Theatre can offer young people a mirror of who we are and who we are becoming. Theatre can be a dynamo for social change by providing the space to imagine ourselves and how we live differently. Theatre can be a lens through which young people can discover the embodied relevance of the real in the curriculum. But beyond these optic metaphors is the most important – the social metaphor of the ensemble as a model for living together in the world. Through acting together in the making of ensemble based theatre, young people are provided with what Trevor Nunn calls 'an ideal of a world I want to live in'. The ensemble provides the basis for young people to develop the complex levels of social intelligence (Gardner, 1988) needed to embrace the challenges of the future, whilst also developing the social imagination required to produce collaborative social art which reflects, energises and focuses the world for young people. The social knowing which comes from acting in an ensemble mirrors Friere's concept of 'indispensable' knowledge:

> The kind of knowledge that becomes solidarity, becomes a 'being with'. In that context, the future is seen, not as inexorable but as something that is constructed by people engaged together in life, in history. It's the knowledge that sees history as possibility and not as already determined – the world is not finished. It is always in the process of becoming. (Friere, 1998:72)

Working together in the social and egalitarian conditions of the ensemble, young people have the opportunity to struggle with the demands of becoming a self-managing, self-governing, self-regulating social group who co-create artistically and socially. It's better to be in an ensemble than a gang. The ensemble is a bridging metaphor between the social and the artistic; between the informal uses of classroom drama and professional theatre. Michael Boyd, Artistic Director of the RSC, captures this duality in his support for ensemble based theatre:

> We've never had more cause to realise the grave importance of our interdependence as humans and yet we seem ever more incapable of acting on that realisation with the same urgency that we all still give to the pursuit of self interest. Theatre does have a very important role because it is such a quintessentially collaborative art form.

The principles of the ensemble require the uncrowning of the power of the director/teacher, a mutual respect amongst the players, a shared commitment to truth, a sense of the intrinsic value of theatre making, a shared absorption in the artistic process of dialogic and social meaning making. The social experience of acting as an ensemble, making theatre that reflects and suggests how the world might become, in the hope that it is not finished, is of course of paramount importance to our young. We pass them the burden of the world that we have made in the hope that they will in turn have a world to pass on to their children. In this task socially made theatre will be their mirror, dynamo and lens – their tool for change.

References

Artaud, A (1938) *Theatre and its Double.* Grove Press Books: New York

Bernstein, B (1973) *Class, Codes and Control Vol 1.* Paladin: St Albans

Boal, A (1998) *Theatre of the Oppressed.* Pluto Press: London

Bond, E (1978) *Theatre Poems and Songs.* Eyre Methuen: London

Brecht, (1938) *The Popular and the Realistic. Twentieth-century theatre: a sourcebook* ed. Richard Drain (1995) pages 188-191. Routledge: London and New York

Friere, P (1998) *Pedagogy of Freedom.* Rowman and Littlefield: Oxford

Petocz, (1999) *Freud, Psychoanalysis and Symbolism.* CUP: Cambridge

Hauser, (1999) *The Social History of Art: from prehistoric times to the Middle Ages Vol 1.* Routledge: London and New York

McGrath, J (2002) Theatre and Democracy. *New Theatre Quarterly.* No 18 May 2002

Neelands, J (1984) *Making Sense of Drama.* Heinemann: London

O'Toole, J and Dunn, J (2002) *Pretending to Learn.* Longman: Frenchs Forest NSW

Suvin, D. (1967) The Mirror and the Dynamo; on Brecht's aesthetic point of view. *TDR* Vol 12 No 1 pages 56-67

Williams, R (1954) *Drama in Performance.* Penguin: Harmondsworth.

11

The Arrival

Rich Task 1

Class devise a docudrama for live performance based on the stories and other writings of migrants of today and from history. The class will need to research their own families and communities to generate the material for performance and script the piece using as much original material (oral history) as possible. The docudrama should reflect the personal family experiences of the class as well as the broader experience of those migrants who have been the engine of Brum's history. The docudrama should also reflect the different performance traditions associated with the diverse cultures represented in the stories told. In addition to the performance, the class also organise a major foyer display of photos, memories, maps and other artefacts related to the theme.

(key subject areas: expressive arts, English, history)

Rich Task 2

Class devise and make a short documentary film that presents a more or less factual account of migration today and historically. The purpose of the film is to illustrate the title of this enterprise and focus on the positive contributions of different migrant groups both in B'ham and more widely if possible/manageable. The film should also highlight some of the difficulties and dangers that migrants experience and the attitudes and legislation towards migrants in UK and other EU countries. The class should research quantitative and qualitative data for the film. (key subject areas: history, geography, social studies, IT, maths, media studies)

Key Resources

The Arrival by Shaun Tan (Lothian Books ISBN 0-7344-0694-0)
Ghosts a film by Nick Broomfield (Tartan DVD)
The Namesake a film by Mira Nair (available soon on DVD)

Introduction Workshop based on The Arrival (3 hours)

1 The Walk

Learners find a space in the room and begin walking as if they were in a busy city – careful not to bang into other people but moving quickly about their business. Instructions are given as to how they should alter their 'walk':

- as if they feel like they 'belong'
- don't belong

Ask learners to look around them as they walk and see for themselves who belongs/doesn't belong – how can they tell the difference? Encourage learners to exaggerate the signs as they walk.

On a hand clap, find and greet someone

a) who is an opposite
b) someone who is the same

As they walk those who belong and those who don't begin to form their own groups so that there are now a group of those who belong and group of those who don't – how do the groups look at each other?

Discuss how it feels to belong/not belong and what the visual clues were for identifying who is who. Compare to experience of 'new arrivals' who may pass from a place where they felt they belonged to a place where they don't feel they belong.

2 Talking Pictures

Show the class slideshow presentation of selected images from *The Arrival* with soundtrack of *Somewhere over the Rainbow/Wonderful World* by Israel Kamakawiwo'ole (from the album *Facing the Future* track and album available from iTunes).

Share initial responses with partners.

Divide the class into groups of approximately five and give each group a set of laminated images from the slideshow presentation. Using the collection of images in front of them the group must agree upon a narrative order, considering which illustration might begin the story and which should end it. As they do this they should consider reasons for their choices and be prepared to articulate these if/when asked.

During this exercise produce the factual handout from Migrant Rights International – allow reading time before asking the group to consider if and how this changes the narrative order.

On completion of this task ask each group to elect a 'host' and then one group joins up with another, and to take it in turns to share their ordering of the images and their theories behind these choices whilst also responding to questions that the other group may have. Hosts are responsible for welcoming and managing each meeting.

3 Hand in hand

Learners find a partner and stand in a formal circle. Teacher draws attention to the image of the mother and father clasping hands on the closed suitcase. Teacher asks learners to imagine how the hands came together – was it accidental/deliberate, slow/quick/certain/clumsy. What are the 'hands' a sign or symbol of?

At game speed, partners are asked to find five different ways of getting their hands to meet just like the photo (or nearly meet if class can't hold each others' hands for whatever reason!). Teacher goes 1, 2, 3 five times to cue the work. Then partners decide which one worked best for them. Then each pair around the circle performs the 'hands' in silence. Discuss effects of this small piece of ritual theatre.

Divide the class into groups of three. Each group is given the image, depicting the mother and father, their hands meeting, an old suitcase and a stage block (or piece of brown sugar paper) to represent the suitcase to work with.

Label the group A, B, C. A and B will play the mother and father and C will for the first part of the exercise work as the 'outside eye' or 'director'.

Each group invents a 30 second mime showing what the mother and father were doing immediately before their hands meet on the suitcase. These are shown around the class.

Ask the learners to consider what the mother and father have been talking about prior to that image being made? They must then write this idea down on a piece of paper, eg, packing, the children, don't go, angry about going.

The slips of paper are passed on to the next group to work on. Each group, with the aid of their director, is now expected to improvise the conversation outlined by the other group (up to and including the point of the still image produced earlier).

Once they feel confident with their work the director must now position him or herself in the scene as 'the son/daughter' of the parents and where s/he is observing them talk from, eg, at her mother's side/at a distance from both of them/staring up at the father from between the two of them, etc.

Groups will then present their improvisations with the child in place, freezing their work as it was in the image from the picture.

4 Back to back

In pairs, sitting back-to-back, the learners label themselves A and B. A is to play the role of the young girl who has overheard this conversation between the mother and father and B to play her younger brother and or sister. A's task is to explain what she has heard. The younger child can ask questions to support and encourage further explanation. Discuss how each partner felt about this conversation – what is the role of the older sibling.

5 Sympathy circle

Teacher asks one of the family groups to make their image again of the mother, father and child around the suitcase. Teacher asks the class to decide which of these characters they have the most sympathy for? Who has the hardest future to face? Each learner must then decide and go and stand behind one of the characters and talk together with other learners who have made the same choice. Each sympathy group gives feedback to the whole class.

6 Reasons for leaving

Class is organised into groups of five or six and look at the image from *The Arrival* of the woman and child returning home along an empty street, with the menacing serpent's tail image in the background, after saying goodbye to father. They discuss what it must be like for the mother and child still to live in a society which for some reason the father has already left to try and find a better future.

Teacher places six pieces of paper on the floor with marker pens. The class are invited to quickly think of reasons why the father has to leave and write one idea only on one of the sheets of paper. If someone else gets the idea down first they must think of a new one.

Reasons for leaving might include:

- lack of work and therefore money to feed their families
- war
- ethnic conflicts
- politics
- religion
- in search of adventure

When there are six sheets with six different ideas the teacher invites the groups to 'bid' for an idea to work on. As well as putting their hands up first to get an idea, each group must also give a convincing reason why their group will do a good and interesting job with that idea.

7 Street of Shame

Once groups have their ideas, teacher introduces the next task. Class look at image of the street again. Teacher names the street the Street of Shame and asks class to imagine that as the woman and child walk home they are confronted on the street by the reality of their chosen reason for leaving. If poverty, perhaps they meet a rent collector, or a beggar, or someone asking the mother to do something illegal for money. If religion, perhaps they see graffiti or meet with mocking crowds. The class prepare their work, which can be placed anywhere on the Street of Shame. When ready the teacher in-role as the woman, with a puppet to represent her daughter, walks through the Street of Shame responding and reacting to whatever she encounters along the way!

Alternative

In groups, class make two images – one represents the reason for leaving from the list above and the other represents what they hope they will find 'over the rainbow'. Class work on moving from one picture to the other in a choreographed and stylish way!

What they expect to find in the new country:

- employment
- education
- a place of safety to bring their family to
- a clean start where nobody knows their history / business
- peace

8 Ghosts

Class watch the scenes from Ghosts which deal with the woman leaving her baby and her journey to the UK, and discuss and compare with their own work so far.

9 The Farewell

Family groups from the Hands exercise reform and decide on their own story as to why father leaves and how this will affect the family. Then each family member is given a piece of paper and a pencil. Mother/child find a quiet spot to write a letter to father for him to read on his journey. Fathers write, on their own, a letter for mother/child to read after they have gone.

The teacher reminds the class of the image of the ship of migrants from *The Arrival* and tells class they will now work on the farewell, as the ship leaves dock and sails off to a new future.

Two parallel lines are then created, one side made up of the 'fathers' and opposite them, the mothers and their daughters. They are asked to imagine that the space between the two lines is the space between the deck of the ship and the quayside. One by one fathers carefully fold up their letter and cross over and exchange letters with the mother and return to their line. With the letters still pressed in their hand (and as yet, unread) each learner is asked to consider what 'gesture' and 'face' they would make to either the father or mother/daughter facing them as they prepare to leave. What would the fathers see when they looked out at the mother and child? What would the mother and child see when they looked back at all the fathers gathered on deck to say farewell?

These 'gestures' are then performed to the rhythm of a 'Mexican wave', beginning at one end of the line, moving across the line and back, until the last person presents theirs.

Each group (fathers and mothers/children) is asked to consider how the figures before them look. Then, in turn, they are asked to call out 'across the water' these descriptions, for example: 'lost, alone, determined, heartbroken, confused' etc.

Explain that the ship is beginning to move slowly away from the quayside and with it the images of the fathers begin to fade into the distance. Each person, on the teacher's count, is to take a pace back to create the impression of the ship pulling away from the dock and setting out to sea. They are to take five paces each, signaled by a soft tap on a drum. Ask the learners to consider:

- how does their face/gesture alter as they move away from the figure in front of them?
- at what point do they turn away? For example on the first pace backwards – or do they wait until the very last moment on the fifth pace, when the figure moves out of sight?

Once everyone is still and facing outwards, ask individuals to imagine where they might go to read the note and when they might read it, and then to find a space by themselves and open the note they have been clutching in their hand throughout this exercise. One by one, learners read out their letter and then find a space to begin making a new family picture of reunion in the new land. As the other family members finish reading their letter, they join these images so that the exercise finishes with a room full of family images.

10 Suitcase Theatre
Teacher asks class to look again at the image of the father looking in his suitcase and seeing his family from *The Arrival*. The learners are gathered in a circle on the floor. In the middle of the circle is an old suitcase and around it enough small squares of plain paper and pens for the learners to have one each. On their piece of paper they must draw an object which they think the father might have carried from home in his suitcase. The object must be like a special and precious memory.

All the objects are placed in the suitcase. The teacher in role sits on a chair and opens the suitcase and touches the objects, and responds with sounds rather than words – 'ahhh'.

Class, in groups, choose objects from suitcase (not their own) and devise a scene showing the memory associated with the object. The scenes are shared. Each group begins by one actor sitting in the chair as the father and looking at the object then taking it into scene and finishes by the father returning the object to the suitcase as cue for the next group to begin.

Alternative (intro to Rich Task 1)
In groups, learners look at how the various migrants that the 'hero' of *The Arrival* meets and the stories they tell him. Class imagine that the 'father' in their own drama makes friends with other migrants and together they form the Suitcase Theatre and present a play based on their memories of home and reasons for leaving. The audience will be other migrants so the play may have a nostalgic feel, or an angry voice, or be political theatre about freedom and rights, etc etc.

Migrants Rights International: www.migrantwatch.org/.webloc

Around our globe today, millions of people are on the move – living or trying to live in countries not their own. In some cases, this movement is voluntary. People move across borders for work, education or family reasons. In many more cases, the migration is forced, as people flee civil unrest and war, or search for adequate agricultural land or employment simply for survival.

Currently, one out of every 35 persons worldwide is an international migrant. According to UN estimates, some 175 million people are now living permanently or temporarily outside their country of origin. This vast number includes migrant workers and their families, refugees and permanent immigrants.

Migrants, because of their status as non-nationals, are automatically excluded from certain rights and privileges accorded to nationals of the state. Moreover, in the case of undocumented migrants, the situation is worse, because they are highly vulnerable to exploitation, oppressive conditions at work and without any social security.

Meanwhile, reports continue to come in daily of migrants dying at land borders or drowning at sea. But instead of understanding the causes of these deaths, States, particularly the rich developed countries in the north, are responding with more strict immigration policies and border control measures that can only lead to more deaths and dangers to migrants.

Migration, globalisation and human rights have emerged as central social, economic and political challenges reshaping the world at the turn of the century. The most immediate challenge facing societies and governments worldwide is the frightening rise in violence against migrants, and restrictive government measures directly undermine the fundamental basic human rights of millions of families.

Afterword

Juliana Saxton

'... all the misery of manila folders ...' From *Dolor* by Theodore Roethke (1943)

The other day, I was reading a talk Cecily O'Neill gave at the first International Drama in Education Research Institute (1995) in which she used a few lines from Roethke to highlight the struggles with and of becoming a researcher. It occurred to me as I read about the 'misery' that one of the delights of having Jonothan Neelands' papers between covers means that the ever-deepening pile of folders of 'V. IMP' papers under which I am (and have been for a long time) buried, would now be lighter because Peter O'Connor saw that this was the right time – about time – for this collection.

But that happy, glancing thought is in stark contrast to the sense of despair and *ennui* about which Roethke was writing. The poet spent his career in education and this short poem that speaks of the dust sifting 'from the walls of institutions ... through the long afternoons of tedium' could be a description of many of the schools and colleges in which my own educational career took place and with which, no doubt, most readers are familiar. The 'sadness of pencils', the 'duplicate gray standard faces' of course, gives more than a picture of place, however delicately rendered; it is a powerful metaphor for what can happen in and to the minds and brains of those who occupy those teaching spaces-students and teachers alike-when learning is framed within a curriculum of 'meaningless schoolwork' made up of 'isolated pieces of knowledge' (Newmann, 1996).

Reading these papers, I remember the sheer pleasure of those early days when Jonothan first visited Canada. With what joy I saw awful little conference rooms or vast and dreary teaching spaces become landscapes of imagination: the road on which Ann Graham's body was left; the market place where we all gossiped with the stranger who was so interested in our little world; the raging sea from which we rescued the body of the merman, so like and yet so different from us. (We all *knew* there would be trouble; in Jonothan's class, no deed, however good, was without its implications!) And the warm, safe kitchen of the mother, which grew colder and emptier as she listened to a letter from her son, fighting as a member of the Union Army, a visceral memory that surges up when black hearses bring home the bodies of our dead from Afghanistan.

Jonothan has the gift of creating 'setting' that both frees us from the strictures of our daily lives while at the same time taking us to places that entice, and hold within their expanses, possibilities of 'rich and relevant content.' In the intuitive way that all students sense, we knew this was a teacher who 'delivered.' He did it by having

> the discipline never to pass a book shop, never to pass a junk shop, to read the newspaper with a particular eye, to look around at local resources, artefacts, objects, traditions ... photographs, images, and anything which crystallizes or suggests an experience we can recreate ... anything that speaks of being young in ways that allow students to explore difference, what relates them to other people ... and to keep running them through the filter in your head, picking out that which is dramatic. You have to be a collector; that's what you have to commit yourself to [if you are] doing theatre. (1998:148)

Like our Victoria crows, Jonothan not only sourced out the glittery bits but his teaching made it possible for us to consider the whole effect with a sense of 'real-life motive and purpose'. This was teaching of head and heart, full of 'social, critical, pedagogic and artistic opportunities to consider the world' and weigh up our responses to it.

I remember, too, in the beginning as Norah Morgan and I had begun to unwrap the intricacies of Dorothy Heathcote's and Gavin Bolton's use of theatre in the classroom, how Neelands' teaching provided us with our first opportunity to test out our analyses; how helpful and generous he was with his time and answers to our questions. Thinking back, it was probably the first time I was able to talk to a master teacher on somewhat equal terms – not that I considered myself an equal in imaginative practice (nor do I still) – and all of it eased, perhaps, by the fact that Jonothan was so proud of his Canadian connections.

Teaching can only be considered an art when it can be performed, as Eisner (1985) suggests, with 'such skill and grace that, for the student as well as the teacher, the experience can justifiably be called aesthetic'. Jonothan's ability to 'quicken' (Sendak's term for creating an inner life that 'draws breath' from deep perceptions) his learners can, perhaps, from reading the lessons included here, give readers some idea of that artistry in action, actions founded on a deep consideration of, and knowledge in theatre form and substance.

It is wonderful to trace how, with the help of Peter O'Connor's elegant introductions, Neelands' theoretical foundations have broadened and deepened. In his 1997 keynote at IDIERI 2, he wrote, ' I speak as a Romantic because I believe ... that we should strive towards higher ideals in our work. I speak as a Modernist because I have hope that there can be a better tomorrow and because I believe that our work in drama should be socially committed' (1998:148). These stances combine ever more strongly in the following years, as theatre/drama becomes a place where metaphors enable us to examine 'who we are and who we are becoming', how we might 'live differently' and how we might live *ensemble* which is, after all, the nature of the human condition but so difficult to manage. '[By] becoming a collective of artistic actors,' he writes in 2007, 'there is the possibility of discovering the process of becoming social actors freely engaging in civic dialogic democracy' (p315). As a philosopher, Neelands continues to consider carefully the implications and perturbations in the field as it develops; as a practitioner, he remains a collector, inviting children, young people, pre-service teacher educators and the rest of us to join him at play in this delectable, demanding and complex art form.

Neelands' theatre provides both place *and* space where, after doing and reflecting and reflecting and re-doing until we are filled up, we can begin to see ourselves as actors and agents; where questions wait for us to find them; where, in 'acting to learn', we 'learn to act'. Through these writings he has armed us with arguments that can help us to overturn the deadly inertia of 'the Curriculum Plan.' And he has given us a range of brushes with which to paint a curriculum of 'compassionate potential' and return colour to those 'duplicate grey standard faces' that make Roethke (and so many of us) so sad.

Emeritus Professor Juliana Saxton
University of Victoria
January 2010

References
Note: The unassigned words and phrases in quotation marks, I have taken directly from Neelands' writings in this collection.

Neelands, J. (2007) Taming the political: The struggle over recognition in the politics of applied theatre. *Research in Drama Education* 12(3), 305-317.

Neelands, J. (1998). Three theatres waiting: Architectural space and performance traditions. In J. Saxton and C. Miller (Eds.) *Drama and Theatre in education: The research of practice/the practice of research* (pp.147-164). Victoria, BC: IDEA Publications.

Newmann, F. (1996) *Authentic achievement: Restructuring schools for intellectual quality.* San Francisco, CA: Jossey-Bass.

Miller, C. and Saxton, J. (1997) Jonothan Neelands: Traveler in possible worlds. *Stage of the Art* 9(7), 22-26.

O'Neill, C. (1995) Into the labyrinth: Theory and research in drama. Keynote paper given at the first International Drama in Education Research Institute, Griffith University, Mt. Gravatt Campus.

Roethke, T. (1948). Dolor. *The lost son and other poems.* Garden City: NY: Doubleday. Retrieved from http://www.facebook.com/note.php?note_id=150790785522